FIC
BLA

Black, Saul.

The killing lessons.

$25.99

THE KILLING
LESSONS

THE KILLING LESSONS

SAUL BLACK

ST. MARTIN'S PRESS ❦ NEW YORK

THE KILLING LESSONS. Copyright © 2015 by Glen Duncan. All rights reserved. Printed in the United States of America. For information, address St. Martin's Press, 175 Fifth Avenue, New York, N.Y. 10010.

www.stmartins.com

Designed by Omar Chapa

Black, Saul.
   The killing lessons / Saul Black.
        pages cm
   ISBN 978-1-250-05734-1 (hardcover)
   ISBN 978-1-4668-6109-1 (e-book)
 1. Women detectives—Fiction.   2. Women—Violence against—
Fiction.   3. Children of murder victims—Fiction.   4. Psychopaths—
Fiction.   5. Colorado—Fiction.   6. San Francisco (Calif.)—Fiction.
 I. Title.
   PR6102.L33345K55 2015
   823'.92—dc23

                                                    2015017805

Originally published in Great Britain by Orion, an imprint of the Orion Publishing Group, Ltd.

Our books may be purchased in bulk for promotional, educational, or business use. Please contact your local bookseller or the Macmillan Corporate and Premium Sales Department at (800) 221-7945, extension 5442, or by e-mail at MacmillanSpecial Markets@macmillan.com.

First U.S. Edition: September 2015

10 9 8 7 6 5 4 3 2 1

ACKNOWLEDGMENTS

A *very* big thank-you to my superhumanly brilliant agents, Jonny Geller in London and Jane Gelfman in New York, for doing all that they do with a combination of tact, humor, infallible intuition, and precision-strike professionalism. For a novelist, representation simply doesn't get any better.

It has been a great pleasure to work with my astute and patient editors, Bill Massey at Orion in the UK and Charles Spicer at St. Martin's Press in the US. They both understood immediately where *The Killing Lessons* was going, and put a lot of time, effort—and diplomacy—into getting it there. I am much in their debt.

Two books proved invaluable to my research: *Police Procedure & Investigation*, by Lee Lofland (2007), and *Forensics: A Guide for Writers*, by D. P. Lyle, M.D. (2008), both published by Writers Digest Books, an imprint of F+W Publications Inc., Cincinnati, Ohio. Any deviation from the expertise contained in these works is entirely my own, for the purposes of fiction.

In addition, for reasons too numerous and varied to list, I'm grateful to: Kate Cooper, Eva Papastratis, Kirsten Foster, Laura Gerrard, Liz Hatherell, Stephen Coates, Nicola Stewart, Jonathan Field, Vicky Hutchinson, Peter Sollett, Eva Vives, Mike Loteryman, Alice Naylor, Lydia Hardiman, Emma Jane Unsworth, Ben Ball, and Susanna Moore.

THE KILLING LESSONS

1

The instant Rowena Cooper stepped out of her warm, cookie-scented kitchen and saw the two men standing in her back hallway, snow melting from the rims of their boots, she knew exactly what this was: her own fault. Years of not locking doors and windows, of leaving the keys in the ignition, of not thinking anything like this was ever going to happen, years of feeling safe—it had all been a lie she'd been dumb enough to tell herself. Worse, a lie she'd been dumb enough to believe. Your whole life could turn out to be nothing but you waiting to meet your own giant stupidity. Because here she was, a mile from the nearest neighbor and three miles from town (Ellinson, Colorado; pop. 697), with a thirteen-year-old son upstairs and a ten-year-old daughter on the front porch and two men standing in her back hallway, one of them holding a shotgun, the other a long blade that even in the sheer drop of this moment made her think *machete,* though this was the first time she'd ever seen one outside the movies. The open door behind them showed heavy snow still hurrying down in the late afternoon, pretty against the dark curve of the forest. Christmas was five days away.

She had an overwhelming sense of the reality of her children. Josh lying on his unmade bed with his headphones on. Nell in her red North Face jacket standing, watching the snow, dreamily working her way through the Reese's Peanut Butter Cup she'd negotiated not ten minutes ago. It was as if there were an invisible nerve running from each of them to her, to her navel, her womb, her soul. This morning Nell had said: That guy Steven Tyler looks like a baboon. She came out with these pronouncements, apropos of nothing. Later, after breakfast, Rowena had overheard Josh say to Nell: Hey, see that? That's your brain. "That," Rowena had known, would be something like a cornflake or a booger. It was an ongoing competition between the two of them, to find small or unpleasant things and claim they were each other's brains. She thought what a great gift to her it was that her children not only loved but also cagily liked each other. She thought how full of great gifts her life was—while her body emptied and the space around her rushed her skin like a swarm of flies and she felt her dry mouth open, the scream coming . . .

don't scream . . .

if Josh keeps quiet and Nell stays . . .

maybe just rape oh God . . .

whatever they . . .

the rifle . . .

The rifle was locked in the cupboard under the stairs and the key was on the bunch in her purse and her purse was on the bedroom floor and the bedroom floor was a long, long way away.

All you have to do is get through this. Whatever it takes to—

But the larger of the men took three paces forward and in what felt to Rowena like slow-motion (she had time to smell stale sweat and wet leather and unwashed hair, to see the small dark eyes and big head, the pores around his nose) raised the butt of the shotgun and smashed it into her face.

Josh Cooper wasn't lying on his bed, but he did have his headphones on. He was sitting at his desk with the Squier Strat (used, eBay, $225, he'd had to put in the $50 his grandma sent for his birthday three months back to swing it with his mom) plugged into its practice amp, laboring through a YouTube tutorial—*How to Play Led Zeppelin's "The Rain Song"*—while trying not to think about the porno clip he'd seen at Mike Wainwright's house three days ago, in which two women—an older redhead with green eyeshadow and a young blond girl who looked like Sarah Michelle Gellar—

mechanically licked each other's private parts. Girl-girl sixty-nine, Mike had said crisply. In a minute, they go ass-to-ass. Josh hadn't a clue what "ass-to-ass" could possibly mean, but he knew, with thudding shame, that whatever it was, he wanted to see it. Mike Wainwright was a year older and knew everything about sex, and his parents were so vague and flaky, they hadn't gotten around to putting a parental control on his PC. Unlike Josh's own mom, who'd set one up as a condition of him even *having* a PC.

The memory of the two women had made him hard. Which was exactly what the guitar tutorial had been supposed to avoid. He didn't want to have to jerk off. The feeling he got afterwards depressed him. A heaviness and boredom in his hands and face that put him in a lousy mood and made him snap at Nell and his mom.

He forced himself back to "The Rain Song." The track had baffled him, until the Internet told him it wasn't played in standard tuning. Once he retuned (D-G-C-G-C-D), the whole thing had opened out to him. There were a couple of tricky bastard reaches between chords in the intro, but that was just practice. In another week, he'd have it nailed.

Nell Cooper wasn't on the porch. She was at the edge of the forest in deep snow, watching a mule deer not twenty feet away. An adult female. Those big black eyes and the long lashes that looked fake. Twenty feet was about as close as you could get. Nell had been feeding this one for a couple of weeks, tossing it saved apple cores and handfuls of nuts and raisins sneaked from her mom's baking cupboard. It knew her. She hadn't named it. She didn't talk to it. She preferred these quiet intense encounters.

She took her gloves off and went into her pocket for a half-eaten apple. Snow light winked on the bracelet her mother had given her when she turned ten in May. A silver chain with a thin golden hare, running, in profile. It had been her great-grandmother's, then her grandmother's, then her mother's, now hers. Rowena's distant family on her maternal side had come out of Romania. Ancestral lore said there had been a whiff of witchcraft, far back, and that the hare was a charm for safe travel. Nell had always loved it. One of her earliest memories was of turning it on her mother's wrist, sunlight glinting. The hare had a faraway life of its own, though its eye was nothing more than an almond-shaped hole in the gold. Nell wasn't expecting it, but on the evening of her birthday, long after the other gifts had been unwrapped, her mom came into her room and fastened it around her left wrist. You're old enough now, she'd said. I've had the chain shortened. Wear it on your left so it won't get in the way when you're drawing. And not for school, OK? I don't want you to lose it. Keep it for weekends and holidays. It had surprised Nell with a stab of love and sadness, her mother saying "you're old enough." It had made her *mother* seem old. And alone. It had, for both of them, brought Nell's father's absence back sharply. The moment had filled Nell with tenderness for her mother, who she realized with a terrible understanding had to do all the ordinary things—drive her and Josh to school, shop, cook dinner—with a sort of lonely bravery, because Nell's father was gone.

It made her sad now, to think of it. She resolved to be more help around the house. She would try her best to do things without being asked.

The doe took a few dainty steps, nosed the spot where Nell's apple core had landed—then lifted its head, suddenly alert, the too-big ears (they were *called* mule deer because of the ears) twitching with a whir like a bird's wing. Whatever the animal had heard, Nell hadn't. To her, the forest remained a big, soft, silent presence. (A neutral presence. Some things were on your side, some things were against you, some things were neither. The word is *neutral,* Josh had told her. And in any case, you're wrong: things are just things. They don't have feelings. They don't even know you exist. Josh had started coming out with this stuff lately, though Nell didn't for one minute believe he really meant it. Part of him was going away from her. Or rather he was forcing a part of himself to go away from her. Her mom had said: Just be patient with him, honey. It's a puberty thing. Another few years, you'll probably be worse than him.) The doe was tense, listening for something. Nell wondered if it was Old Mystery Guy from the cabin across the ravine.

Old Mystery Guy's name, town gossip had revealed, was Angelo

Greer. He'd shown up a week ago and moved into the derelict place over the bridge, a mile east of the Coopers'. There had been an argument with Sheriff Hurley, who said he didn't care if the cabin *was* legally Mr. Greer's (he'd inherited it years ago when his father died), there was no way he was taking a vehicle over the bridge. The bridge wasn't safe. The bridge had been closed, in fact, for more than two years. Not a priority repair, since the cabin was the only residence for twenty miles on that side of the ravine and had been deserted for so long. Traffic crossing the Loop River used the highway bridge farther south, to connect with US-40. In the end, Mr. Greer had driven his car to the west side of the bridge and lugged his supplies across from there on foot. He shouldn't be doing *that,* either, Sheriff Hurley had said, but it went no further. Nell hadn't seen Mr. Greer. She and Josh were at school when he'd driven out past their house, but it couldn't be much longer before he'd have to go back into town. According to her mom, there wasn't even a phone at the cabin. When Sadie Pinker had stopped by last week, Nell had overheard her say: What the hell is he *doing* out there? To which Rowena had replied: Christ knows. He walks with a stick. I don't know how he's going to manage. Maybe he's out there looking for God.

Nell checked her pockets, but all the nuts and raisins were gone. The doe sprang away.

A gunshot exploded in the house.

2

Nell ran.

Telling herself it wasn't a gunshot.

Knowing it was.

The ground was a cracked ice floe in a fast current moving against her. Her face was overfull, her hands crammed with blood. There was a busyness to the air, as if it were filled with whispering particles. Details were fresh and urgent: the soft crunch of the snow; the kitchen's smell of just-baked cookies; a complicated knot in the oak floor's grain; the deep maroon of Josh's Converse sneakers by the living room door, light coming through the lace holes.

Her mother lay on her side at the bottom of the stairs. Blood pooled around her, jewelly dark, with a soft sheen. Her skirt was off and her panties were looped around her left ankle. Her hair was wrong. Her eyes were open.

Nell felt herself swollen and floating. This was a dream she could will herself out of. Kicking up from underwater, you held your breath through the heaviness until you hit the thin promise of the surface, then sweet air. But she was kicking and kicking and there was no surface, nothing to wake to. Just the understanding that the world had been planning this her whole life, and everything else had been a trick to distract her. The house, which had always been her friend, was helpless. The house couldn't do anything but watch, in aching shock.

Her mother's bare legs bicycled slowly in the blood. Nell wanted to cover them. It was terrible, the pale flesh of her mother's buttocks and the little scribble of varicose veins on her left thigh uncovered like that, in the front hall. Her mouth went *Mommy . . . Mommy . . . Mommy . . . ,* but no sound came, just rough breath, a solid thing too big for her throat. Her mother blinked. Moved her hand through the blood and raised her finger to her lips. *Shshsh.* The gesture left a vertical red daub, like a geisha's lipstick. Nell staggered to her and dropped to her knees.

"Mommy!"

"Run," her mother whispered. "They're still here."

Her mother's eyes fluttered closed again. It reminded Nell of all the times they'd given each other butterfly kisses, eyelashes against cheek.

"Mommy!"

Her mother's eyes opened. "Run to Sadie's. I'm going to be all right, but you have to run."

There was a sound of furniture moving upstairs.

"Now!" her mother gasped. She sounded furious. "Go now! Quick!"

Something moved much closer. In the living room.

Her mother gripped her by the wrist and spat: "You run right now, Nell. I'm not kidding. Do it or I'm going to be angry. Go. Now!"

To Nell, backing away from her mother, it was as if a skin that joined the two of them was tearing. She kept stopping. There was a fierce emptiness in her ankles and knees and wrists. She couldn't swallow. But the farther away she got, the more vigorously her mother nodded, *Yes, yes, keep going, baby, keep going.*

She made it all the way to the open back door before the man stepped out of the living room.

3

He had coppery hair in greasy curls that hung all the way down to his thinly bearded jaw. Pale blue eyes that made Nell think of archery targets. His face was moist and his dirty-fingernailed hands looked as if they'd thawed too fast. Dark oily jeans and a black Puffa jacket with a rip in the breast through which the soft gray lining showed. His feet would stink, Nell thought. He looked tense and thrilled.

"Hey, cunt," he said to Rowena, smiling. "How're you holding up?"

Then he turned and saw Nell.

The moment lasted a long time.

When Nell moved, she thought of the way the doe had sprung away into the forest. Its head had jerked to the right as if it had been yanked on an invisible rein; then it had twisted and flung itself as if the rest of its body was a fraction slower and had to catch up. It was the way she felt, turning and running, as if her will were a little maddening distance ahead of her, straining to haul her body into sync.

The space around her was heavy, something she had to wade through. At the beach once on vacation in Delaware, she'd been standing on tiptoe in the ocean, the bottle green water up to her chin, and Josh said, Oh my God, Nell, shark! Right behind you! Hurry! And though she'd been certain—or almost certain—he was kidding, there was the agony of the water's weight, soft and sly and fighting her, slowing her, in cahoots with the shark.

Josh.

Mom.

I'm going to be all right, but you have to run.

I'm going to be.

All right.

"All right" meant later, tomorrow, Christmas, days and weeks and years, breakfast in the untidy kitchen, the smell of toast and coffee, TV in the evening, drives into town, Sadie coming over, the scent of her mother's hand cream, conversations like the ones they'd been having lately when they talked woman-to-woman, somehow—

Something crashed behind her. She looked back into the house.

The red-haired man was picking himself up from the hallway floor, laughing, saying: "What the fuck, bitch?" Then shaking his left leg to dislodge Rowena's hand from his ankle. Something in Nell knew it was the last of her mother's strength. It was the last of *her* strength. And yet out of her exhaustion an impulse pushed her and her legs moved, barely touching the packed snow she and Josh had beaten down on their walks to the forest.

She was running.

It seemed impossible, she was so empty. The lightest breeze would lift her into the air like a fall leaf.

But she was running. She had twenty yards on him.

Cunt.

The word was dark and thick with dirt. She'd heard it maybe twice before in her life; she couldn't remember where.

How're you holding up? His smile when he'd asked that meant nothing you could say would stop him doing what he was doing. It would just make him do it more.

She wanted to go back to her mother. She could stop, turn, say to the man: I don't care what happens, just let me cover my mom's legs and put my arms around her. That's all I want. Then you can kill me. The longing to stop was so powerful. The way her mother's eyelids had closed and opened, as if it were a difficult thing she had to concentrate on, very carefully. It meant . . . It meant . . .

The swish of his arms against the Puffa jacket, the thud and squeak of his boots in the snow. He was very close behind her. The twenty yards had been eaten up. How stupid to think she could out-run him. The long legs and grown-up strength. For the first time she thought: *You'll never see your mother again. Or Josh.* Her own voice repeated this in her head, *You'll never see your mother again,* mixed with the man's *Hey, cunt,* and her mother saying, *Yes but how* much *do you love me . . . ?*

She knew she shouldn't look back, but she couldn't help it.

He was almost within touching distance, red hands reaching for her. In the glimpse she saw his mouth open in the coppery beard, small teeth tobacco stained, the pale blue eyes like a goat's, his sharp nose with long, raw nostrils. He looked as if he were thinking about something else. Not her. He looked worried.

The glance back cost her. She stumbled, felt the ground snag the toe of her left boot, threw her hands out in front of her for the fall.

His fingertips swiped the hood of her jacket.

But he'd overreached.

She stayed—just—on her empty legs, and he went down hard behind her with a grunt and a barked *"Fuck."*

Her mother's eyes saying, *Go on, baby, go on.*

Never again. The golden hare's faraway life suddenly close to her own.

Things are just things. They don't have feelings. They don't even know you exist.

Nell could hear herself sobbing. There was a bloom of warmth in her pants and she realized she'd wet herself.

But she was at the tree line, and the afternoon light was almost gone.

4

He was still coming. She could hear the pines' soft crash as he went past them. The forest wasn't in shock, as the house had been. It had mattered to the house, but in here, it barely registered. The smell of old wood and undisturbed snow had always made her think of Narnia, and the wardrobe that led to the magical winter kingdom. It made her think of it now, in spite of everything. Her mind was all these useless thoughts, flitting around the image of her mother's face and the way she'd blinked so slowly, and there was a look in her eyes Nell had never seen before, an admission that there was something she couldn't do, that there was something she couldn't fix.

Your jacket's red, fig brain, she imagined Josh saying. *Red. Don't make it easy for him.*

She crouched behind a Douglas fir and took it off. Black woolen sweater underneath. The cold grabbed her with vicious delight. The jacket lining was navy blue. The smart thing—the Josh thing—would be to turn it inside out and wear it that way. She started—but her hands were faint, distant things to which she'd lost her connection. The hare's heart was hers now, beating into her pulse.

She heard him say, "Jesus fucking Christ."

Too close. Get farther away, then put it back on.

She ran again. It had gotten darker. Somewhere under the snow was the off-road trail, but she had no idea if she was on it. The self-absorbed trees gave no clue. And there were her footprints. No matter where she ran, he'd know. At least until the last of the light went. How much longer? Minutes. She told herself she had to keep going for only a few minutes.

"Come here, you little shit," his voice said. She couldn't tell where he was. The firs and the snow packed all the sounds close, like in Megan's dad's recording studio. Should she climb up? (She could climb anything. Nell, honey, I wish you'd stop climbing things, her mother had said. Nell had said: I won't fall. To which her mother replied: I'm not worried you'll fall. I'm worried you've got monkey genes.) *Should* she climb up? No, the footprints would stop and he'd know: *Here I am! Up here!* She stumbled forward. Found firmer snow. Her legs buckled. Her palms stung when she hit the ground. She got up again. Ran.

The land sloped suddenly. Here and there, black rock broke the snow. She was forced downhill. The drifts went sometimes above her knees. Her muscles burned. It seemed a long time since she'd heard him. She'd lost all sense of direction. Breathing scored her lungs. She struggled back into her jacket. It was dark enough now for the red not to matter.

A branch snapped. She looked up.

It was him.

Thirty feet above her and to her left. He'd seen her.

"Stay there!" he spat. "Stop fucking running. Jesus, you little—"

Something rolled under his foot and he fell. The slope pitched him toward her. He couldn't stop himself.

It seemed to Nell that she'd only turned and taken three pointless steps when she heard him cry out. But this time she didn't look back. All she knew was the tearing of her muscles and the burn of every breath. Stones turned her ankles. Branches stung her exposed hands and face. Something scratched her eye, a mean little detail in the blur. The only certainty was that any second his hands would be on her. Any second. Any second.

5

Upstairs in the house Xander King watched the boy on the bedroom floor die, then sat down at the desk's little swivel chair. The world had come alive, the way it did, but it wasn't right. This had been a mistake, and it was Paulie's fault. Paulie was getting on his nerves. Paulie was going to fuck everything up. It was ridiculous, really, that he'd let Paulie stick around so long. Paulie was going to have to go.

It was a relief to Xander to realize this, to know it for certain, despite the inconvenience, the work involved, the distraction. Anything you knew for certain was a relief.

The cool smell of new paint played around him, from the empty room across the hall. (He'd done a dreamy sweep of the upper floor: the woman's bedroom with its odors of clean linen and cosmetics; another filled with neatly boxed stuff—vinyl records, manila files, a sewing machine; a bathroom with the fading light on its porcelain and tiles—and the half-painted fifth room, small, with a wardrobe and a chest of drawers draped in painters' tarps. A roller and tray, brushes in a jar of turpentine, a stepladder. It had reminded him of Mama Jean, up *her* stepladder in the lounge at the old house, wearing her sour-smelling man's overalls, her face flecked with white emulsion.)

The boy's TV was on, with the sound down. *The Big Bang Theory.* Another show like *Friends,* with too many bright colors. Xander found the remote on the desk and flicked through the channels, hoping to find *Real Housewives of Beverly Hills*. Or *Real Housewives of New York*. Or *Real Housewives of Orange County*. There were a lot of shows he was drawn to. *The Millionaire Matchmaker*. *Keeping Up with the Kardashians*. *America's Next Top Model*. *The Apprentice*. But no luck. His body was rich. He teased himself a little, looking at the dead kid's blown-open guts, then looking away, feeling the richness come and go in his limbs, as if it were a dial in himself he could turn up and down at will.

The kid's guitar had fallen facedown on the rug. The rug was Native American style. Which reminded Xander of a fact he knew: White settlers had given the Indians blankets infected with diseases in the hope that they'd all get sick and die. There were certain facts he was familiar with. Certain facts that made sense in the way that so much else didn't. So much else not only didn't make sense but exhausted him as well. He was constantly struggling with exhaustion.

Remembering the disease blankets made his beard itch. A beard. He hadn't shaved for four days. His routines had been suffering. The battery shaver was dead. The good thing about the battery shaver was that you could do it without a mirror.

He thought about the woman downstairs. He would go down to her soon, but for now it was very good just to sit and enjoy the richness. It was a wonderful thing to know he could go down to her anytime he liked. It was a wonderful thing to know she wasn't going anywhere. He could go anywhere and do anything, but everything and anything she wanted to do depended on him. His face and hands had the plump warmth that was both impatience and all the time in the world.

But still, it wasn't right. Too many things, recently, hadn't been right. There was a way of doing what he needed to do, and lately he'd been losing sight of it. The cunt in Reno, for example. That had been Paulie's fault, too. Paulie definitely had to go.

6

The world stopped and Nell flew through it. A non-silence like when you put your head underwater in the bath, the loud private quiet of the inside of your own body. She ran through the darkness and with every step knew she couldn't take another step. It was as if his hands were on her and yet she was still moving. How could she still be moving if he had her? Perhaps he'd lifted her off her feet and she was just pedaling air. Like her mother's bare legs kicking slowly in the blood. Her mother's blood. Leaving her. Spreading on the floor. So much blood. When blood came out, it didn't go back in. Never again. You'll never see . . .

The trees ended. A deeper cold from the ravine came up, sheer air and the sound of the rushing river far below. The snow was coming down faster now, at a wind-driven angle. The bridge was fifty feet to her left. Which meant she was half a mile from home, going the wrong way. But she couldn't turn back on herself. When she thought of turning back on herself the only image she got was of him stepping out from behind a tree and the warm thud of her running straight into his body, his arms coming quick around her. *Gotcha.* She could hear him saying that.

She ran to the bridge. There was, incredibly, a parked car a few feet away from it.

Whose car? Empty?

She stopped. *His* car? With someone else in it?

She peered through the falling snow.

There was no one in the car. Could she hide under it? No. Stupid. First place he'd look. People nearby?

She scanned the ravine's edge. No one.

There was no time. Move.

She ran to the bridgehead.

A red sign with white lettering: BRIDGE CLOSED DANGER DO NOT CROSS.

Rusted metal struts driven into the walls of the ravine. Wooden sleepers she remembered wobbling the few times her mom had driven them across in the Jeep. A mile to the west, she knew, the ravine narrowed to barely twenty feet before flaring out again. Last year an ice storm had brought a Douglas fir down across the gap. Teenagers proved themselves by crawling over to the other side and back. You had to go there and back. That was the thing. Josh and his friend Mike Wainwright had spent a whole morning working up the courage. Daring each other. Double-daring. In the end, neither of them had done it. Two hundred feet. The ravine's dark air ready. The river waiting.

She edged around the sign. Her wet jeans were icy between her legs. The creases bit her skin. Her feet felt bruised. The snow here was above her knees. How far to the other side? In the Jeep it took seconds. She seemed to be wading forever. There were invisible weights on her thighs.

Halfway across she had to stop and rest. She wanted to lie down. She could barely see an arm's length in the slanting snow. The distance between her and her mother and Josh hurt her insides. She kept imagining it being morning, the gray daylight and the warmth of the kitchen, her mom turning to her as she walked in and saying, Nell where've you *been*? I've been out of my *mind* . . .

She forced herself to move. Three steps. Ten. Twenty. Thirty. The end of the bridge. The back of a metal sign, identical, she supposed, to the one at the other end. A broken spool of barbed wire hung between the railings and dangled into the emptiness of the ravine.

"Goddamn you," the man's voice said. It sounded as if he were inches behind her. She turned. He was at the BRIDGE CLOSED sign, struggling to squeeze past it. It seemed impossible that she'd be able to get her legs to move.

She staggered forward. Two more steps. Three. She was almost there.

Something made her stop.

Apart from the whisper of the racing snow and the intimate din of her own breathing, there was nothing to hear. But it was as if she'd heard something.

The actual sound, when it came, wiped everything from her mind.

And when the world fell from under her, a small part of herself felt a strange relief.

This part of her—her soul, maybe—flew up out of the fall like a spark with the thought that at least it was over, at least wherever her mom had gone, she would go, too. She believed in heaven, vaguely. Where good people went when they died. Some place where you could walk on the clouds and there were white stairways and gardens and God—although she always imagined she'd rather just know he was around than actually meet him. She'd sometimes wondered if she was a good person, but now that it came to it, she wasn't afraid.

Far away was the sound of grinding, metal against rock.

All around her, the gloom and the snow somersaulting slowly.

Then something rushed up at deafening speed to strike her face.

7

It was still dark when Nell opened her eyes, though she had no idea how long she'd been out. Her first confused thought was that she was in bed, and that the comforter was wet and freezing. Then her vision cleared. Not the comforter. Snow. Three or four inches on her. It was still snowing.

As if it had been waiting for her to realize this, cold rushed her, seized every molecule, and said: *You are freezing. You are freezing to death.*

She pushed herself up onto her elbow. Too fast. The world spun. The sky's soft chasm and the looming wall of the ravine churned like clothes in a tumble dryer. She rolled onto her side and vomited, and for what felt like a long time afterwards just lay there, though her body not only shivered but occasionally jerked, too, as if someone were jabbing her with a cattle prod. Through the cold she was aware of two pains: one in her right foot, one in her skull. They throbbed together, in time with her pulse. They were bad, but she knew they weren't so bad as they soon would be. It was as if they were telling her this, with glee, that they were just getting started.

It didn't matter. None of it mattered. *I'll never see my mom again.* It brought back the time she was very small and got separated from her mother in a department store. All the unknown adults and intimidating heights, the panic, the full horror of herself in the world alone. The world had been hiding how terrifying it was. It drew back again half a minute later, when Rowena found her, but there was no forgetting it. And now here it was again.

Nell pushed herself back up onto her elbow and looked down. She was lying on a narrow shelf that stuck out from the ravine about fifteen feet from the top. If she'd rolled another eight inches, she'd have gone, two hundred feet down to the dark green river and its scattered rocks. On the opposite side, struts mangled, the bridge hung, ridiculously, from one of its huge rivets.

The golden hare bracelet had snapped its chain. It lay in the snow next to her, in flecks of blood. *You're old enough now.* The hare marked the edge of her fall. Another few inches and she'd be dead. She imagined it had a certain number of times it could save you. This was one. She wondered how many. Very carefully, she closed her fingers around it. It seemed to take a long time to work it into her jacket pocket. Safe travel.

She got to her knees. The pain in her foot turned up its volume. She clamped her teeth together. Her head went big and solid and hot, then cold and fragile. Her scalp shrank. She couldn't stop the shivering. She could feel the sheer drop behind her like a weight pulling at her back.

I wish you'd stop climbing everything. I'm worried you've got monkey genes. Nell had thought monkey *jeans* (chimps in little Levi's) until Josh, rolling his eyes, explained. She hadn't really grasped it even then.

The ravine wall was frozen black rock, veined white where the snow held. Not quite vertical. Not *quite* vertical, but still.

I'm going to be all right, but you have to run.

She reached up for the nearest handhold. Her fingers were numb. Her face flooded with heat. And when she tried to stand, the pain in her foot screamed.

8

Paulie Stokes was in agony. His fall had brought him with the full force of his body's weight up against what turned out to be a two-foot tree stump half buried in the snow. His bent left knee had hit it hard, and now, back within sight of the house, the pain was so bad he was beginning to think it must be broken.

He'd thought she was dead.

He'd stood there for maybe fifteen minutes. Until her head lifted. He'd watched her body get its bearings. He'd watched the little bitch climb. *Climb,* Jesus.

Xander couldn't know.

Xander could not and must not know.

Which Paulie knew was an insane decision to have made—but he'd made it. There were a lot of decisions he made this way, with the sense that the thing they were intended to avoid couldn't be avoided. He did this with a mix of lightness and terror and fascination. He lived a light, terrified, fascinated life slightly to one side of Xander. But the longer he hung around Xander, the smaller and less reliable that life became. So now in a kind of looped dream he told himself Xander mustn't know about the girl and Xander would find out and Xander mustn't know and it was only a matter of time before Xander found out and he wouldn't tell him and then the dream loop dissolved like a skyrocket's trail in the night sky and he took a few more excruciating steps with no room for anything but the forked lightning of his shattered knee until in spite of that the dream loop started again and Xander mustn't know and Xander was guaranteed to find out and he wouldn't tell him and it would be all right and it wouldn't.

"Where the fuck have you been?" Xander said to him as he limped into the living room. "What's wrong with you?"

The wooden blinds were down and two table lamps were on. They gave a gentle buttery light. The room had a friendliness to it, from the corduroy couches to the scattered kids' DVDs and the thick hearthrug with its pattern of squares and rectangles in different shades of brown. The woman was lying on the floor on her back where Xander had dragged her. Her pale blue panties lay nearby, stained with blood. She was still alive. Her mouth was moving but there was no sound. The thought of what would become of him if Xander left him reared up in Paulie, a feeling like the one he got in the dream of the tidal wave he used to have as a kid, where he was standing on a bright boardwalk eating an ice cream with his back to the ocean, and the sky darkened, and when he turned, there was a thousand-foot wall of black water coming toward him, flecked with sharks and shipwrecks. At the same time, the fact of the woman's helplessness, the look of ebbed strength in her bare limbs, filled him with a kind of nourishment, as if fabulous proteins had been rushed into him.

"I thought I saw someone out there," he said. "But it was a deer. Hurt my goddamned leg. Need to strap it up or something."

"A deer?"

Paulie had actually seen a deer on his stumble back through the trees.

"You shouldn't have left her," Xander said.

"She wasn't going anywhere."

"You don't know that. This is your problem: You don't think. Not going anywhere? Women lift fucking trucks when their kids are trapped underneath. You don't *think*. I've told you."

"OK, OK. Fuck, man, how'd it be if there *had* been someone? You'd be thanking me." Paulie had to turn away as he said this. Xander looked at you and your lies crumbled. His hands were wet. The pain in his knee was a blessing, since it kept short-circuiting everything else.

"Go and strap your leg," Xander said. "Don't come back in here till I tell you. And for Christ's sake, shut the back door, will you?"

When Paulie had hobbled out, Xander moved to stand over the woman on the floor. The feeling of wrongness, of not having what he needed to do this properly, was still with him, but it was made negligible by the pounding richness of his body and the bristling aliveness of the world. Every detail of the room, whether it liked it or not, said that whatever this woman's life had been up until now, he had all of it in his hands. His controlled impatience was a delight to him. It was like holding back a horse he knew would win every time, no matter the competition. There was a sort of hilarity to it, the certainty of power, the certainty of victory. There was a moment of balance, between holding it back and letting it go. You had to wait for that moment and make it last as long as possible, because the surrender to it was the sweetest thing of all, a sweetness that went through your every cell so that all your movements were perfect, every bit of you was perfect, from your fingerprints to your eyelashes, and so much of the exhaustion simply fell away like a rotten harness and you were free.

"What?" he said to the woman, getting down on his knees and putting his ear next to her mouth. "What are you saying?"

9

Rowena Cooper had been in and out of consciousness. She remembered waking at the bottom of the stairs to find herself soaked and heavy. A terrible delayed understanding that she was soaked and heavy with her own blood. The gun's butt had hit her like a meteor. Those last fragments of thought: that they'd find Josh; that if only Nell heard and ran; that Nell *wouldn't* run, that she'd come in, see, scream—and they'd have her, too.

Then blackness.

She hadn't heard the gunshot. She didn't know.

But when she'd surfaced again, there was a frank silence upstairs. A dead intelligence had replaced her son.

Then Nell, close, smelling of snow and the forest, the little face that was like a brand on Rowena's heart. The appalling energy it had cost her to get Nell to run. *Run.* Saying she'd be angry if she didn't and seeing in her daughter's eyes that the child knew the anger was a sham to hide something much worse. It was an understanding between them. Her daughter's strength in that moment had fractured Rowena with love and pride.

The last image, after the red-haired guy had picked himself up off the floor, was of him going after her, toward the dark line of the forest. *Go on, baby, keep going. Hide, hide in the good trees.*

She'd sunk into nothingness again, and when she returned was being dragged by her ankles down the hallway and through the living room doorway. The liverish stink of her blood mixed with the Christmas tree's smell and the waxy odor of gift wrap. She was cold and thirsty. (She thought what a long time it had been since she'd lain on the floor. When you were a kid, the floor was part of your perspective. You forgot the view from down here, the skirting boards and secret spaces under the couch with their lost items and fluff.) She could see the fireplace Josh had set ready for lighting earlier that day. Only ever lit at Christmas. It was one of the rituals he'd taken over a few years back, with shy masculinity. The first time he'd done it without asking, Rowena walked into the empty room and saw it and stood there swallowing back tears. Her husband, Peter, had died in a car accident when Nell was only four years old, Josh seven. All the ways in which she'd worried she wasn't enough for her children. And then her son's quiet act of compensation. She'd felt such an excess of tenderness and loss.

The reality of death came to her through the cold and the thirst. The immense sadness of the fact. Her time going like the last grains of sand sucked through the hourglass's cinched middle. Going. Going. Images from her past detonated: childhood in Denver; the little house's parquet flooring and weedy yard; her father reading *The Hobbit* to her when she was ill; the heady first weeks at college in Austin; the certainty when she'd met Peter, the happy sensual pigs they'd made of themselves that first year, love and pleasure like a ridiculous fortune they'd inherited; the thrill of telling him she was pregnant and the astonishing casual knowledge that he wanted it as much as she did, that this was really their life, shaping itself; Josh being born, Nell, the messy, ordinary, unappreciated gifts of having a family. Then the accident, the shredded life, the incremental acceptance. The dull practicality of the insurance payout and the move back to Colorado. Last house on the road. A peaceful corner to raise the kids and heal your wounds.

She felt the sprawling idea of the future—Josh and Nell growing up, college and love affairs and houses and children, phone calls and the ache of their absence and the peace of putting her arms around them when they came home, the things she still wanted (maybe a man again; her body had been telling her lately, saying enough was enough, she was still only forty-one) and through all of that the imagined relationship with the taken-for-granted physical world, of sunlight and red leaves on a forest floor and the breathtaking first whiff of the ocean—she felt all of this dissolving into blankness, pointlessness, a bereavement she couldn't accommodate. She had an odd, flimsy image of Nell's half-painted bedroom. Nell had been sleeping with her these last nights while the redecoration inched forward. It would never be finished now. It had been sweet being close to her daughter through the nights. She wanted to say good-bye to her children. Above everything else, she wanted to see and smell and hear and hold them one last time. And all the while, the darkness came and went, and very vaguely a confusion of wondering if there was anything on the other side and would she, after all the horror of grief, see Peter again?

"What?" the man said, his face close to hers. "What are you saying?"

But a blood bubble formed and burst between her lips. She saw the ceiling's central light, the gold tinsel sparkling, felt the cold turning to warmth as the image formed of Nell running through the shadows in the snow.

10

Thirty-eight-year-old San Francisco homicide detective Valerie Hart knew she'd made a mistake. The latest in a sequence of mistakes that had started with her smiling at the guy—Callum—in the softly lit cocktail bar less than two hours earlier. He'd smiled back, but with a look of self-congratulatory entitlement she'd known wouldn't go anywhere good.

Things hadn't improved during their brief conversation—he worked "in banking, but let's not talk about that, it's a turnoff"—nor in the cab, when he ignored a call from what they both knew was another woman, nor when he closed the apartment door behind them, watched her take a few paces into the room, then said: "Jesus, your ass is an argument-winner." Valerie knew he'd said it countless times before. And in her case didn't mean it. She knew exactly what she was in his eyes: a one-night downgrade. An older woman who wouldn't object to whatever he wanted to do in the sack, because she was grateful just to *be* in the sack.

The apartment only confirmed the mistake. It was in the Ashton complex by Candlestick Park with a floor-to-ceiling view of the bay. Valerie knew the place. Two bedrooms would cost you the better part of four million dollars. Unsurprisingly, the decor—some hired designer's idea of minimalism (glass and steel) plus fun (cowhide rug)—said: Rich asshole lives here.

And here she was. With only herself to blame.

"Stop," she said when he took his tongue out of her mouth for a breath.

They were on the bed and he was lying on top of her. Her blouse was open, and he'd pulled her bra cups down awkwardly below her breasts. He lowered his head, took her left nipple in his mouth, flicked his tongue over it. Nipped it.

"Stop," Valerie said.

He ignored her.

And this is one of the ways this happens, Valerie thought. *One of the countless ways.*

"Stop," she said a third time, louder.

"Fuck," he said. "What? What is it?" No disguising the impatience. Which would become annoyance. Which would become anger.

His left hand was behind her head, gripping her neck. His right was in the open V of her unzipped pants, fingers exploring her through her panties. Jesus Christ, Your Honor, she was *wet.* I mean, come *on.*

She *was* wet. Residually. There had been enough of her that wanted this when they'd started. Not because she'd had any illusions about him. In fact, precisely because she hadn't had any illusions about him. These days—since Blasko—if she went to bed with a man, it had to be one in whom she had no interest beyond physical desire. These days—since she'd killed love—it had to be someone she didn't like.

But there wasn't enough of her that wanted it now. Now the bulk of her just felt sad. Although she knew very well that sadness wasn't going to be any use here.

She put her hand on his chest and pushed, not hard, just a civilized statement. "You need to get off me," she said.

"Well, you're half right," he said. "I need to get *off.*" His hand pressed harder between her legs. "It's OK if you want to play," he said, tightening his hold on the back of her neck. "Just don't draw blood."

"That's not what this is," she said, pushing a second time. "Get off me."

"That's not what your pussy's telling me," he said.

Guile or force. Those were her options. Certainly not *argument*. He weighed, she guessed, around 170, and vanity sent him to the gym three or four times a week. It was a long, *long* time since academy training, and she'd been slack on the workouts for months, but the thought of trying to trick her way out from under him exhausted her. Hey, I've got some coke in my purse. Let's do a couple of lines. He wouldn't believe her. He was alert to her change of heart. In the academy, every session of Practical Police Skills was conducted to the sound of the instructor's mantra: You will survive. You will survive. You *will* survive.

Leah's eye out fork balloon the mess between Shyla's legs Yun-seo's body flecks of soil he started alone but shallow grave river stop—

Stop. *Stop.*

Her purse was fifteen feet away, where she'd left it on the arm of the bedroom's cream leather couch.

Third option: guile *and* force.

She softened underneath him. She'd had a cold for two weeks. She was aware of her sinuses, throbbing.

"That's better," he said, pushing himself up on his left hand to get a look at her while his right hand sneaked into the top of her panties. "That's a good girl."

She eased her right knee under his, got a purchase with her heel (she still had her shoes on)—then punched him as hard as she could in the side of his throat.

He was so shocked by the pain, she barely needed the full force of her right leg to flip him, but she was past such calculations. She was off the bed and at her purse in three seconds.

Be careful, the drill instructor had told them all. A punch to the throat can *kill* a scumbag.

This scumbag wasn't dead. He was on his knees on the bed, swallowing, swallowing, swallowing, holding his throat.

"What the fuck?" he gasped, looking at the Glock in her hand. "What the *fuck?*"

Valerie was a mix of adrenaline and emptiness. She zipped up her pants and resettled her bra.

"Christ are you—" Swallow. "—are you a *cop*?"

Valerie buttoned her blouse. Her coat was on the floor next to the couch. "Just shut up and stay there," she said quietly. Her face was hot. She could feel the days' and weeks' and months' exhaustion pressing hard on the adrenaline, waiting for it to give, when it would come crashing in like the ocean through a plate glass window.

"Listen," he said, one hand raised, palm outward, his whole body trying to reinvent itself as the personification of innocence, "we were just—" Gulp. "—I mean I wasn't—"

"It's better for you if you don't speak," Valerie said, getting into her coat. The sound of her own voice disgusted her. Proof that this wasn't a dream but a real situation she'd put herself in.

When she was ready, she moved a couple of paces nearer the bed, with the gun pointed directly at him.

"Hey," he said, trembling. "Hey, Jesus, come on." Swallow. "I'm sorry. Don't do anything crazy. I didn't do anything to you. I didn't *do* anything to you!"

"Then what are you sorry for?"

He was shaking his head. Disbelief. How had this happened to him? How could this be happening to him?

There were a lot of things she could say. Laura Flynn, one of her colleagues, had said not long ago: Give every woman a gun and a badge and watch the rape stats fall. What Valerie most wanted to say to the man on the bed was: And this is how *this* happens.

But somehow everything died in her mouth. She just wanted to go home.

Keeping the gun trained on him, she backed out of the bedroom, then turned and walked out of the apartment, closing the door behind her.

11

She woke at 4:30 A.M., after an hour and thirty-five minutes' dream-infested sleep, to the sound of poetry. By design: sometime back, she'd started setting the radio alarm to a digital station that read poetry through the night. Poetry didn't make sense. But it gave you things. That was one of a small number of truths she'd discovered. A pitifully small number. Like a bum's last nickels and dimes in a world that required a thousand dollars a day to make it bearable.

"'He must / Become the whole of boredom,'" the soft male voice on the radio said, "'subject to / Vulgar complaints, like love, among the Just / Be just, among the Filthy, filthy too, / And in his own weak person, if he can, / Must suffer dully all the wrongs of Man.'"

Valerie switched it off. *All the wrongs of Man. In his own weak person. Filthy. Among the Just. Be just.* The words shuffled in her head, gave her a few precious seconds before the Case took over: *Refrigeration RV candy apple stuffs objects guts cut out with fish knife what kind of fish knife limited number maybe fisherman too much traffic enforcement footage fork jammed in vagina he knew Katrina had to had to had to otherwise why'd she go with him them not one guy two guys but it started with one guy I don't know how I know this Kansas the midpoint have to call Cartwright again they're not taking it seriously have to have to . . .*

Unlike the radio, this couldn't be switched off. The Case was there at her sleeping and there at her waking and there with her through the day. X-rated tinnitus. Tinnitus designed by the Devil. When she was a child, her grandfather (the last practicing Roman Catholic of the family) had said to her: First the Devil lets you know there are terrible things. Then he tells you which room they're in. Then he invites you in to look. And before you know it, you can't find the door to get out. Before you know it, you're *one* of the terrible things.

She got up and went to the bathroom.

A positive result is indicated by a blue line. That morning three years ago was with her every morning. As if the bathroom's humble features couldn't forget it. *She* certainly couldn't. That morning she'd sat on the floor wrapped in a soft white bath towel. Waiting.

> A pregnancy test detects the presence of a hormone called human chorionic gonadotropin (hCG) in your blood or in your urine. hCG is produced in the placenta shortly after the embryo attaches to the uterine lining and builds up rapidly in your body in the first few days of pregnancy.

The idiom of impersonal biology. *Chorionic gonadotrophin. Placenta. Uterine lining. Embryo.*

As opposed to the personal idiom: Baby. Child. Mother. Father.

Blasko said to her once, in the heart of their life together, before the Suzie Fallon case had driven her to wreck it: The best and worst thing about being a cop is that it makes it easier to tell the truth. They'd been in bed at the time, subsiding in the warm wake of a small-hours fuck that had started half-asleep, then woken them with dreamily escalating dirty-sweetness. They had these encounters, took them as an entitlement. Afterwards, Valerie liked to drift back into sleep to the sound of his voice. It makes it easier, he'd said, because every day you're surrounded by the pointlessness of lying.

She'd remembered it that morning three years ago, sitting

wrapped in the giant towel on her bathroom floor, waiting for the line on the test to turn blue.

Pregnant. Five to six weeks.

She'd wondered, knees hunched up to her middle, bare shoulders tender, why they didn't make two kinds of home test kit: one for women who were trying to conceive, in which a positive result flashed up: *Congratulations! You're* PREGNANT; and one for women who were dreading it, in which the same result came with: *Fuck. Sorry. You're* PREGNANT.

But of course, she knew the manufacturers had done their research. Neutrality. No expectation. No judgment. Just the facts. *Pregnant. Five to six weeks.*

The impulse had been to phone Deerholt and tell him she was sick. But the thought of spending the day alone in her apartment had terrified her. Because by that time, only weeks after the Suzie Fallon case and the death of love, she *was* alone.

Instead she'd forced herself up off the floor. Got dressed. Gone to work. Spent the day behaving normally while inside she churned loss and panic and all the damage she'd already done.

That night, lying in a foamless bath up to her throat, she'd told herself: You don't have to decide anything yet. You have some time. You can wait.

So she'd waited. Spent days going through the same wretched circles, dropping off into the same unknowns. Multiple futures shuddered in her, fighting each other. And still she'd waited.

Until the decision was taken out of her hands.

She ought to have had a nervous breakdown, but she didn't. Instead, after the Suzie Fallon case, after the death of love, after what had been taken out of her hands, she simply carried on. She wasn't the same. She brought a new seared clarity to her work, a relentless, mechanical energy. She became a better cop. Everyone noticed. No one said anything.

Three years had gone by, granted. But in imaginal time, that morning in the bathroom was only a moment ago. Would always be only a moment ago. Imaginal time had no respect for chronology. Especially the past.

•   •   •

Her cold was worse. Her nostrils were raw and her body ached. The booze had crept up, these weeks, these months, these three years. Her recycling sack yesterday had been half Smirnoff empties. She could do with a drink right now, when the rest of the world was drinking coffee. It was a line of thinking she'd gotten used to ignoring.

When she was a little girl, she'd hated going to school. In the mornings, her mother used to say: I know you feel like killing yourself, honey, but brush your teeth and you'll feel a little better. And she was right. Washed and dressed, Valerie was always forced to admit, grudgingly, sheepishly, that life was, after all, bearable.

She went to the washbasin and reached for her toothbrush. Her hands were shaking.

Blasko's message was still by the medicine cabinet mirror, where he'd tacked it to the wall three years ago, written in black permanent marker on a clean sheet of legal:

NOT TODAY.

As in, you can quit being a cop anytime you like. Just not today. It was the only trace of him still in her apartment. Not even a lone sock or a toothbrush or a department-issue pencil. And whose fault was that—?

Leah's eye was out and she'd swallowed four of her teeth the tires are Goodyear G647 RSS too many too many Lisbeth unicorn crystal lacerations to anus and vagina I can't do this YES TODAY YES TODAY YES TODAY . . .

Brush your teeth, for Christ's sake. You'll feel better.

Halfway through brushing, she threw up in the washbasin.

12

Eighty minutes later (eighty minutes divided between standing under the near-scalding jets of her shower, then staring out her apartment window at the Mission's predawn start-up—delivery trucks, joggers, dog-walkers, and people still drunk from the night's revels), Valerie sat in the incident room at the station, thinking the thought that had been part of her for so long now, she couldn't remember what life had been like without it: that they were no nearer to catching the man, or most likely *men,* who did this than they had been from the discovery of the first body three years ago.

Katrina Mulvaney, thirty-one years old. Educational outreach officer at the San Francisco Zoo. First reported missing June 3, 2010. Her body had been found three weeks later in a shallow grave a mile east of Route 1, halfway between San Francisco and Santa Cruz. She'd lived in a fifth-floor walk-up in the Castro. Without knowing each other, she and Valerie had practically been neighbors.

Among the photographs Katrina's boyfriend had supplied—the "before" photographs—there was one Valerie had gone back to repeatedly. In it, Katrina had obviously not been expecting to be photographed. The boyfriend had probably just gone "Hey," and she'd turned. It was what Valerie thought of as an "outlook" shot. As in, outlook on life. You could see it in people caught like that, unprepared. Katrina's outlook was one of cautious hope. The look said she wasn't stupid; she knew the world could fuck you up without warning. But it also said she knew she'd been loved as a child, and that she was still moved by beauty, and that she knew her faults and weaknesses but knew, too, that she wasn't a bad person. The look said she had not long before realized that she was in love. That was part of the fear still left in her outlook: that the love, somehow, might go wrong.

Love hadn't gone wrong.

What had gone wrong was that someone abducted, raped, mutilated, and murdered her.

Then that person—per*sons*—had abducted, raped, mutilated, and murdered Sarah Keller, twenty-four years old. Then Angélica Martínez, then Shyla Lee-Johnson, then Yun-seo Hahn, then Leah Halberstam, then Lisbeth Cole. Seven women between the ages of twenty-four and forty. And it had taken the better part of three years for the authorities to realize that what all these women had in common was that the same man—or men—had killed them.

Valerie imagined the millions of astonished TV crime show addicts. Three *years*? Are these *retarded* cops?

If she thought of trying to answer that question, she came up against fatigue like a wall of raw earth. The way the shows' crime scenes exploded with evidence. The way the leads always led somewhere. The way the investigative net tightened in a whisk of phone calls and snappy deduction. The way detectives tossed out requests like *"Get me a list of every place that sells roll asphalt and transaction records for the last four years"*—and got what they wanted in a matter of minutes. Crime show TV was an industry devoted to peddling the necessary fairy tale: You can't do terrible things and get away with it. You do a terrible thing, sooner or later *you will have to pay.*

Whereas . . .

She imagined taking the complaint to her grandfather's God, that sinners were supposed to get punished. And God smiling and raising his Santa Claus eyebrows and saying: Whereas . . .

"Cappuccino?" Will asked. "I'm going." There were three other detectives in the low-ceilinged and fluorescent-lighted room. Will Fraser (Valerie's partner), Laura Flynn, and Ed Pérez. Along with Valerie, the insomniacs. The spooked. The obsessed. The burning out. Over the next couple of hours, the rest of the team would assemble and the incident room would fill with the collective vibe of irritation and effort and frustration and exhaustion and boredom. In spite of which, Valerie knew, she'd have to gather herself to brief the new FBI liaison. She thought of Callum last night saying: Your ass is an argument-winner. She thought of the distance she'd traveled from her body since Blasko. Since love. Blasko had said to her, in the first few weeks of their relationship: You're prettier than a seahorse. His compliments were delivered like dispassionate scientific conclusions. They'd filled her with shy pride. Some men, he'd said, will be scanning the room for the icy blondes with pneumatic tits. For other men—a minority, I'll grant you—you'll be the only woman *in* the room. I'm one of those men. Just remember that when you start thinking about dumping me.

"Yeah, thanks," she said to Will without looking up from her desktop screen. There was a time when she would have answered more creatively. Something like: "Two sugars. And stir it counterclockwise, dickhead." She'd lost the impulse to joke. Will still had it. He was the kind of good human being whose goodness derived from knowing the precise degree to which he was a shitty human being but not letting it cancel out the degree to which he wasn't.

"Today's rating?" he asked.

Valerie looked up at him. He was forty-two, tall and leanly built, skin the color of faded mahogany, long eyelashes and an expression of languid mischief.

"Five," Valerie lied. "You?"

The "rating" was on a scale of one to ten. One being certainty that what you were doing was going to solve the Case and be a victory over the Powers of Darkness, ten being a terminal admission of failure, walking out the door and never being a cop again. And possibly *joining* the Powers of Darkness.

NOT TODAY.

"Eight," Will said. "But Marion told me this morning she's not sure she desires me anymore. Also, I've got a huge boil on my ass. It's possible the two facts are connected."

When he'd gone for the coffees, Valerie sat listening to Laura

Flynn's superhumanly fast fingers at work on her laptop. She knew that very soon she'd have to get up, walk across the room, and stand in front of the murder map. She'd have to stand in front of the murder map and try for the ten thousandth time to make it talk. The murder map didn't want to talk. The murder map's line was that it had nothing new to say. But the murder map was a liar. You had to believe the whole Case was a liar. You had to believe the whole Case was trying desperately to keep something from you. You had to believe that eventually you'd catch the Case out. And you had to do it before the Case killed you. Or before it made you break your lover's heart.

13

"As you know," Captain Deerholt said when the task force had gathered, "Special Agent Myskow is on sick leave. So as of today, Special Agent York will be joining us. She'll be meeting with each of you individually later. I know you're up to your necks, but please try to make yourselves available within the next twenty-four hours. Right now I want to give her an overview while you're all here. Detective Hart?"

Valerie stood by the murder map. She didn't need notes. She didn't need to refresh her memory. Most of the time there was nothing else *in* her memory. (Apart from Blasko, and the Suzie Fallon case, and the death of love.) Special Agent Carla York was early thirties. A petite but visibly fit woman with hazel eyes and precise, understated makeup. Mousy hair scraped back into a short ponytail. Navy blue pantsuit. Low-heeled snug-fitting black boots. No wedding ring. No jewelry at all, in fact, as far as Valerie could see. The thought of dealing with her—someone new—had been draining Valerie all morning. A new person was a restatement of the only fact that mattered: You haven't caught him yet.

"OK," Valerie said, indicating the "before" photograph of Katrina on the map. "First victim, Katrina Mulvaney, thirty-one-year-old white female. Educational outreach officer at the San Francisco Zoo. Resident of the Bay Area, body *found* in the Bay Area. Second victim, Sarah Keller, twenty-four-year-old white female, prostitute, resident of St. Louis, Missouri, body found near Richfield, Utah. Third victim, Angélica Martínez, twenty-eight-year-old Hispanic female, schoolteacher, resident of Lubbock, Texas, body found near Laramie, Wyoming. Fourth victim, Shyla Lee-Johnson, thirty-four-year-old white female, prostitute, drug addict, resident of Lincoln, Nebraska, body found near Elk City, Oklahoma. Fifth victim, Yun-seo Hahn, twenty-five-year-old Korean-American female, grad student at Berkeley, resident of the Bay Area, body found in the Bay Area. Sixth victim, Leah Halberstam, forty-year-old white female, housewife, resident of Plano, Texas, body found near Salina, Kansas. Latest victim, Lisbeth Cole, thirty-four-year-old white female, prostitute, resident of Omaha, Nebraska, body found near Algona, Iowa. This is not the order in which the bodies were discovered. It's the best-guess order based on approximate date of death."

Valerie paused. She wished there were windows in here. It would have done a lot for her right then to be able to look out and see the sky, even a mid-December sky in San Francisco. From their long way away, the dead women had turned their attention on her. Not with urgency. Not with expectation. Just with dumb sadness. Because they knew she felt nothing for them.

"All the victims were mutilated, most likely before being killed. Mixture of knives and tools. We know for certain three of them—Katrina, Yun-seo, and Lisbeth—were raped. All of them carry fingerprints and DNA from the same individual, and the last three victims—Yun-seo, Leah, and Lisbeth—carry fingerprints and DNA from a second individual. We don't know if it's been two guys from the start, or if the second guy's been recruited. Neither, in any case, has a match in the databases."

The impatience and boredom in the room were palpable. This meeting was tactically redundant: York was going to get all the information anyway, through the eight investigators working the Case, and Valerie was going to sit down with her in private later this afternoon. The real reason Deerholt had gotten them together was because he was worried about the creeping sense of futility. He was worried about *morale*. This was a reminder: Hey, come on, we're doing this together, we'll get there, don't give up. We're a family.

"Linkage blindness was inevitable," Valerie said. "Given the time line, the geographical spread, and the victim demographic, three years isn't bad. If it weren't for the signature and DNA, we'd probably still be blind, at least beyond the two Bay Area victims."

The two Bay Area victims were Valerie's blessing. And her curse. It was the only site for more than one of the murders. It was assumed (desperation, Valerie admitted privately) that Katrina's killer was either from or had close connections here. Everything else was scattered around Middle America. The Bay Area (desperation insisted) was special. It was Valerie's belief that if the killers had known any of their victims before they *became* their victims, that victim was Katrina Mulvaney. *Start with what you know* was what Valerie's creative writing tutor told her in a class she'd taken when she was a teenager. Now applied to the reasoning of murderers. Life never tired of these perverse connections. On the surface, Yun-seo Hahn didn't help, since serial killers, as Jodie Foster had made big screen gospel, tended to hunt within their own racial and social group. But since they had nothing better than geography to go on, the working principle was to set up the task force in the place where it was believed the unknown subjects either currently lived, had formerly lived, or at the very least had forged some sort of connection to the first—and possibly fifth—victim. That was part of the San Francisco rationale. That and the simple fact that it had a bigger budget and better resources than any of the other states involved.

"As far as the signature goes," Valerie continued, "it's probably the one thing that doesn't need repeating. But for the record, our guys leave objects inside their victims. Random objects or objects with significance, we don't know yet. No rare moths or butterflies, sadly. Nothing, in fact, that helps us narrow it down. They leave them in the vagina, mouth, or anus, except in the Cases of Yun-seo and Leah, when they left them in the opened abdomen. We're assuming because the objects were simply too large for their first-choice orifices."

Valerie had spent hypnotic hours with the body photographs—the "after" shots in the murder makeover. Yun-seo's gaping guts. A heavy-duty clawhammer jammed in between the large and small in-

testines. Surreally worse than this—a hammer was at least a potential instrument of violence, was at least grimly congruent—was the
glazed and depressingly cheery pottery goose her murderers had left
in Leah Halberstam. It wasn't life-sized, but they'd still had to cut
out half her internal organs to make room for it. According to the
forensics report, the evisceration had been done with a serrated fish
knife. In the movies, the goose would have borne a maker's mark,
would have been an antique, would have reduced the number of
people who might own or know where to find one. But this wasn't
the movies. The goose had been mass produced throughout the '70s.
There were tens if not hundreds of thousands of them out there—
or rather, there had been. If you wanted to buy one now, you'd have
to trawl garage sales or junk shops or kitsch vintage boutiques that
depended on people with more money than sense. It was the sort of
object that would feature on an emo-hipster Web site called something like thingsmyparentsownthatfreakmeout.com.

"Katrina Mulvaney had the remains of a candy apple in her
vagina," Valerie said. "Sarah Keller had a deflated balloon shoved
down her throat. Angélica Martínez had a scrunched-up flyer from
the Los Angeles County Natural History Museum's dinosaur exhibit
stuffed into her anus. Shyla Lee-Johnson had a fork in her vagina.
Lisbeth Cole had a two-inch-long piece of clear crystal—the consensus is it's meant to be a unicorn's horn—in her anus. If they're
trying to tell us something"—Valerie looked at Carla York, not with
hope but with reassurance that she didn't expect *her* to confirm this
hypothesis—"we don't know what it is yet."

She could feel the room's deadness to the dead women. And her
own. The homicide wisdom she'd come to late: In order to figure
out who had done these things to a person, you had to get the reality of the person out of the way. The person became a victim. A victim was a conundrum in flesh and blood. Catching the perp was
earning the right to think of the victim as a person again. Trouble
was, by the time you caught the perp (if you did), you were so fucking fried that you didn't give a shit about the person anyway. You just
wanted to get drunk and watch sports. Or go out and fuck a complete
stranger. You wanted to do anything, in fact, to postpone the reality,

which was that tomorrow there would be another dead body, another conundrum in flesh and blood, another testimony in the case against the world as a place of hope, and light, and love. Especially if you'd already killed love yourself. That, for Valerie, had been the trade-off, the lesson she'd learned eventually. Before the Suzie Fallon case three years ago, her weakness as a cop was that she *couldn't* stop thinking of the victims as people. Because she'd had love in her life, she'd been unable to stop thinking of the love the victims had had in theirs. Then, with the help of the Suzie Fallon case, she'd killed love. Now the victims were just ugly puzzles to be solved. She knew it had made her better at her job. But she saw the way people looked at her sometimes, the question their eyes asked: How come you're so cold, so clinical, so fucking *dead*?

"We're also aware of the possible irrelevance of the objects," she continued, for Carla York's benefit. "There are really only two ways to look at them. Either they have meaning—useful meaning, meaning that will help us figure out who these guys are—or they're just them fucking with us, giving us Serial Killer Standard Practice because they've seen the movies, too."

Everyone, Valerie knew, was sick of the objects. Each of the victims' before and after photos on the murder map had a label naming the object found inside her. It was soul-destroying to have to keep seeing the word "balloon" or "goose" attached to the image of a mutilated female body. It was exactly the sort of thing some twisted fuck would get a kick out of.

"Nutshelling it: Our guys abduct the women in one state, do what they do, then dump their bodies in another. Which obviously requires either a traveling job or no job at all. They could be independently solvent, but BSU is telling us that doesn't fit the profile." Valerie felt Carla York not interjecting. Not yet, at any rate. Myskow would no doubt have told York that there was, to put it mildly, *doubt* among the team about the usefulness of profiling. Let me guess, Ed Pérez—*uber*-FBI-skeptic—had said before Myskow even got started, we're looking for a white male between the ages of twenty-five and forty, with delusions of grandeur and a history of abuse. Low affect.

Maybe a harelip or a speech impediment. Am I missing anything? It wasn't fair, Valerie knew. Behavioral science had long since ditched the cookie-cutter psycho. The bureau's 2005 San Antonio symposium on serial murder had devoted a lot of time and energy to exposing "Myths About Serial Killers," many of which, they admitted, had been bred by early behavioral science's own reductive optimism. The problem was, obviously, the more they conceded it wasn't an exact science, the less useful it looked to investigating officers.

"Either way, the high mobility is self-evident," Valerie said. "The good news is Leah Halberstam and Lisbeth Cole were found less than seventy-two hours after their deaths. We have dry casts of tires that put a Class B RV within a mile of each burial site. The pool of compatible makes and models is big, and since more than eight million Americans own RVs, you can do the math. Plus we can't rule out the possibility they're using multiple vehicles. We're working through traffic enforcement footage, but if they kept off the major routes we're blind."

She glanced at Deerholt. That's enough—right? We're wasting time. Deerholt's eyes flicked agreement. Wrap it up. Everyone's still fucking depressed anyway. "With all the usual probability caveats," Valerie said, "we're looking for two white males. One dark-haired and dark-eyed, the other almost certainly a redhead. One at least with ties to the Bay Area. Shoe sizes ten and eight, respectively. Footwear prints lead us straight to Kmart shitkickers, so no help there. We've got everything we could possibly hope to get from Serology, and as I said, they're not shy with their DNA. But all of that's evidence dressed up with nowhere to go if we don't have suspects. We've been working on this for seven months. To date we've conducted more than two hundred and fifty interviews and questioned six suspects, all of whom have been ruled out. We've got good liaison with law enforcement in eight states, not to mention the bureau—and yet here we still are. It feels like we know nothing. But one thing we do know is that they're speeding up. There were approximately eight months between victims one and two. Since then the intervals have been getting shorter. The last two victims are separated by only seven weeks.

Acceleration breeds mistakes. They're going to make one. Let's not forget that."

This was for Deerholt, and he knew it. Lead investigator rallying the troops.

The troops didn't believe it.

Neither did Valerie.

14

"You feeling OK?" Carla York said to Valerie. They were in Valerie's Taurus, en route to Katrina's parents' place out in Union City. It was snowing, the pointless sort that wouldn't stick, tiny flakes whisked by skirls of wind. Will Fraser was on a lead. What *he* called a lead. He'd been scouring vehicular refrigeration suppliers in the Bay Area (and beyond, though only Valerie knew this), convinced that if the killers were transporting corpses hundreds of miles, they'd want to keep them on ice. RV freezers aren't big enough for a body, Will had said. Not unless you cut it up, which our guys aren't doing. What if they broke down? What if they got pulled for a busted taillight? If it were me, I'd have a dummy shelf stocked with frozen steaks and waffles.

Valerie missed him. More acutely in the presence of Carla York, who knew nothing about her. Who'd spent the last hour of Valerie's time giving her what felt like a recap exam. Why don't you just go away and read the fucking reports? Valerie had several times been on the verge of saying. Savvy or paranoia had stopped her: there was a calm to Carla's hazel eyes she didn't trust. She imagined the FBI briefing: We're a little concerned about the lead on this. She's showing signs of stress. Word is there's a no-joke drink problem. Go up there and take a look at her.

And now, on Deerholt's instruction, she was riding with Valerie until further notice.

"I'm fine," Valerie said. "Can't shake this damn cold." Which she regretted immediately. All the investigators had at one time or another been forced to attend the department's stress awareness seminar. "Physical Warning Signs and Symptoms of Stress" was the first component. "Frequent Colds" was one of them. As were inexplicable aches and pains, nausea, dizziness, chest pain, and rapid heartbeat. As was, probably, throwing up in the middle of brushing your teeth.

"Not that it matters much anymore," Valerie said, "but are our guys psychos?"

Take control. Make *her* answer some questions.

"The alpha killer, maybe," Carla said. "But my money's on not both of them. It's more likely the beta's in thrall to him in some way, though it's obvious from the serology that he's at the very least getting his jollies with the corpses. Like a scavenger. It's unlikely the alpha would let him interfere while they're actually alive."

Valerie sneaked a sidelong glance at her. Carla was staring straight out the windshield. Her hair was pulled back so tight, it looked painful. Small face (*squirrellish,* Valerie thought), clean features, and a maddeningly neat little mouth. Attractive? Not to men who were looking for surface glamour. But there wasn't a spare ounce on her, and her skin was flawless. The good thing about getting older as a man, Blasko had said to Valerie once, is that you get better at seeing beauty in women. Well, not beauty, maybe, but sexual wealth, sexual . . . *character.*

"If the alpha's a classic," Carla said, "then the control has to be all his. Which won't stop him blaming the beta for everything, including the murders. It's a good bet that's the dynamic. But the alpha will probably kill him when he's done."

"Done?"

"If he ever gets done. Which he won't, because we're going to stop the motherfucker."

The profanity was a jolt. Until now, Carla might have been speaking to a class of grad students. Valerie's cynic stepped in: *She's just mirroring. She's heard you swear, so she swears. It's what losers are coached into doing on dating shows. It's what psychopaths learn to do.*

•   •   •

Ostensibly Valerie was seeing Katrina's parents because the mother, Adele, had called to say she found something that might be significant. In reality, the visit was just to let them know they hadn't been forgotten. That their daughter hadn't been forgotten. That the hunt for the man or men who'd killed her was still live. There were, of course, victims' liaison officers, who kept all the families updated, but Valerie had spent a lot of time with the Mulvaneys in the early months. Too much, according to Will, who'd warned her about victim surrogacy. It wasn't Valerie he was worried about—Will was one of the people she caught looking at her with a little sadness these days—it was the parents.

"We found this in the basement," Adele Mulvaney said, handing Valerie a plain black shoe box. "It should have been in one of the plastic crates when she moved, I guess, but it was under a pile of Dale's junk. I thought you'd want to take a look at it."

Dale was Katrina's father, and he wasn't home. The victim liaison officer had told Valerie he'd been drinking a lot. No surprise: one murder took more than one life. Adele was trimly dressed and her graying hair was still cut in its nifty bob, but you could see the wreckage in the light brown eyes, the broken world, the loss from which there would be no recovery. The house was cursorily decked for Christmas (they had grandchildren from Katrina's older brother, and the family would huddle to get through the holidays) but you could feel it had nearly killed them to do it. Even the tinseled tree had something strained and plaintive about it.

"It's just oddments," Adele said. "Ticket stubs and pens and some jewelry she'd outgrown. But there are some photos, and I thought . . . I knew how much time you spent going through the photos on her phone and computer. I don't know. I just . . ."

"You did right to call," Valerie said. "Would it be OK if we looked through this at the station? I'll get it back to you as soon as I can."

They stayed for a half hour. Drank the obligatory coffee. Did their best to sound as if investigative energy was high.

Dale Mulvaney staggered onto the porch as they were leaving. Raw bourbon breath. To her own disgust, it made Valerie want a drink. Again.

"How many is it now?" he said.

"Dale, honey—"

"How many?"

"Seven," Valerie said. "Mr. Mulvaney, this is Special Agent York. I know it must seem—"

"Special Agent? What's special about her?"

"Dale, stop it."

"You told us you'd get him," Dale Mulvaney said. "Except now it's two of them. Now it's *them*. You stood right there where you're standing now and told us you'd find him. And now seven girls are dead. What are you doing? What the fuck are you *doing*?"

"You should just go," Adele said. "It's better if you just go. Dale, come on inside."

Dale Mulvaney put his back against one of the porch posts and slid down to his bottom with a bump. "It's a rhetorical question," he said. "I know what the fuck you're doing. You're doing nothing. Absolutely fucking *nothing*."

In the car on the way back to the station, Carla said, "Don't let it get to you."

"What?"

"The father."

Valerie bristled. The assumption that it *was* getting to her. For a moment, she was so annoyed, she couldn't reply. Then she said, very calmly, "I don't let it get to me." She'd almost said: It *doesn't* get to me. Altered it at the last second. Then wondered which version was the truth.

"Well," Carla said. "It's the brutal part of the job."

Again, Valerie found herself unsure what the right rejoinder should be. Everything that came out of Carla's mouth sounded like part of an elaborate mental sting operation, innocent remarks designed to expose the guilt of your responses. It was the woman's self-containment. She had a way of watching you without looking at you. Plus her plain physical neatness made Valerie feel like a slob. Carla smelled of freshly laundered clothes and slightly citric shampoo.

"Brutal is having your daughter raped and butchered," Valerie said. Which also felt like the wrong thing to say.

But Carla just nodded and said, quietly: "Right."

While Carla went to get a sandwich, Valerie sat at her desk and looked through the shoe box. Half a dozen barrettes and scrunchies, a traveling toothbrush, a lunch monitor pin, ticket stubs from concerts—Radiohead, the White Stripes, Nick Cave—a set of ridiculous windup chattering teeth, a clean white handkerchief, a half tube of L'Oréal foundation, some My Little Pony fridge magnets, and fourteen photos, all but one of them featuring friends or family Valerie was sure they'd already interviewed.

The exception was a Polaroid of Katrina that looked to have been taken when she was around ten or eleven years old. She was wearing cut-off jeans (you could just make out the crescent birthmark on her left leg) and a bright yellow T-shirt that said HOPPERCREEK CAMP, and she was standing in front of what Valerie could only think of as a deformed tree—in that it appeared to have two trunks, one upright, the other growing at a thirty-degree angle to join it about five feet from the ground. Katrina had put one hand on her hip, in the mock-sexy way young girls did, and she was smiling, squinting into the sun. The same outlook of cautious optimism, tempered only slightly by juvenile awkwardness.

She put all the items back in the box and made a note to get someone to double-check there was no one in any of the other photos they ought to have spoken to but hadn't. It wasn't likely. Adele had given them a boxful of a mother's desperation.

Valerie's cell phone rang. It was Will.

"No joy," he said. "There's a guy in Santa Cruz had a big freezer unit installed in his Freelander four years ago. Turns out he's a sixty-four-year-old taxidermist with severe macular degeneration and a Seeing Eye dog. Had to give up driving *and* stuffing critters two years back."

"Sorry," Valerie said. "Worth a shot."

"How're the traffic cam numbers?"

"Restricting it to the four days before Leah and Lisbeth were found, we've still got more than a hundred and fifty Class B RVs on the possible relevant interstates unchecked. They're doing it, but it's slow."

"And Miss Quantico?"

"I think we're being evaluated. Or I am. So don't come in drunk."

"But I just opened a bottle of Cuervo."

"Don't even."

The thought of a shot of tequila had made Valerie's salivary glands contract. And it was barely past noon.

"All right," Will said. "I'll be back in an hour."

Valerie dropped her phone. When she bent to retrieve it, pain shot from the base of her spine all the way into her shoulder blades. Enough to make her freeze for a few seconds, eyes shut.

When she opened them and sat back up, slowly, Blasko was standing in front of her desk, with his hands in his pockets.

"Hey, Skirt," he said. "Long time no see. You look terrible."

15

Xander King—who had not always been Xander King, and was reminded of that fact when things like this happened—couldn't believe it. What kind of country place didn't have a milk jug? He'd been through every cupboard in the kitchen. Just a plain fucking milk jug! Or even a gravy jug. Preferably brown. What they called earthenware. It didn't matter what they called it. There wasn't one. If there were one, he could put this mistake—which was Paulie's fault—right. This mistake could be . . . not corrected, exactly, but . . . brought into line. How far *out* of line this was was a terrible irritation to him, like roaches scurrying under his skin. Mama Jean flickered and bloomed on his peripheral vision, smiling at the mess he'd made. It was Paulie's *fault,* goddammit. Let me do one. *I* want to do one. And Xander had said OK. What was he thinking? If Paulie *had* done it, it wouldn't be his problem. But of course, useless shit that Paulie was, when the time came he, Xander, had had to take charge, because Paulie chickened out. Which made the whole thing his. Which meant there should have been a jug.

"I should go in there," Paulie said. He was sitting on the floor in the kitchen gripping his injured knee. His face was wet with sweat. Xander—who, in desperation, was standing on one of the countertops and running his hands along the top of the wall cupboards, just in case for some reason there was a jug up there, maybe chipped or with a missing handle, that they hadn't used for years—ignored him.

"Xander?" Paulie said.

Still no response.

"Hey. I'm saying—"

"Shut up," Xander said. Then, after a pause, "You hear the way I'm saying that?"

Paulie radiated silence. But after a few moments said, "That's not right."

Xander got a splinter in his palm. The small pain made his scalp hot. He got down off the counter. There was no jug. This couldn't be put right. The bit of ease he'd gotten from what he did to the cunt in the living room was all gone. All the knots were as tight as ever. He was trying not to dwell on how all this had cheated him. But it was as if the whole day were laughing at him.

"Go get the RV," he said.

"It's not right."

"Go get the RV. I've said that twice. Do you want me to say it a third time?"

Paulie looked away. Xander examined the splinter. Now he was going to have to look for tweezers. The roaches darted under his skin.

"I can't fucking *walk*," Paulie said.

"It's not far," Xander said. "You'll do fine."

Paulie didn't move. Then, quietly, he said, "When we've got her inside, then."

Xander was wondering if he shouldn't just do Paulie right here and now. But this whole thing was enough of a mess already. And he was bone tired.

"Yeah," he said. "When we get her in there."

Paulie struggled to his feet, wincing.

No point telling him yet that she wasn't going in the RV, Xander thought. No point telling him that this couldn't—since there was no milk jug—be fixed. No point telling him that they were leaving her and her son where they were and driving away. No point telling him until he'd fetched the vehicle. No point telling him much of anything anymore, because soon he'd be dead.

16

Nell didn't know if she was awake or dreaming, alive or dead. Nothing was certain. Something dragged her through the snow. When she was small, Josh had terrorized her with talk of the Abominable Snowman. A monster—Nell had pictured a huge creature covered in long white hair with eyes like ragged black holes and a mouth filled with blood—who loomed up, suddenly, in the midst of a blizzard and just . . . *took* you. (Nell had had mixed feelings. To her it seemed the sort of creature so ugly and alone, you could feel sorry for it—if only it weren't *taking* you. To its cave. To lift you in its pure white hands and bite your head off and crunch your skull between its teeth.) Something dragged her through the snow and she thought: *Oh, it's the monster.* It was a light thought. It came and went, not bothering her much. Many things came and went, snapshots that flashed in and out of complete blackness. Snow falling out of a dark sky. An old-fashioned iron stove like a dwarf with a potbelly. Someone's hands touching her face. An old man crawling toward her on all fours, his face twisted. She hadn't gone to heaven after all. But it didn't feel like hell. Or she was having a fever. Her mother would be somewhere near: Poor Nellie, you're burning up. Josh whispering: Is she going to be OK? Abominable Snowman got confused with Abdominal Cramps. Her mother had had those.

Hands undressed her.

This was in the complete blackness.

Vague shame when she felt her jeans being unzipped.

She tried to come out of the blackness to make sure it was her mom, but the blackness wouldn't let her. It was a soft weight, like warm dark water.

The hands—no, it wasn't her mother; the smell and touch were wrong—pulled her panties down over her legs and there was the sound of wood popping in a fire. Maybe the Devil undressed you when you arrived in hell? In a picture of hell Josh had shown her, all the people were naked, stuck on skewers or big wheels or being stabbed and burned by little demons with pitchforks. The weird thing was all the naked people looked unconcerned, as if they weren't even aware of what was happening to them. She was only mildly concerned herself. The hands undressing her were a sort of annoying distraction, stopping her from falling properly asleep. She was very tired, and the warm blackness promised deep, restful sleep. She tried to speak: *Hey, stop that. Leave me alone.* But her mouth made no sound. The words went around under the skin of her face instead of out into the world.

She came back again and saw the same old man, still on his hands and knees, still with his face twisted (by crying, she thought; there were tears) crawling away from her on a wooden floor she didn't recognize.

Then the warm dark water closed over her head. Her last thought was that she didn't want to dream. Because the last dream she'd had was a nightmare, in which her mother had been lying at the bottom of the stairs in a pool of her own blood, telling her to run.

17

Irony, thought Angelo Greer, waking in breathtaking pain from a dream of an earthquake to discover he'd passed out on the cabin's moldy floor, was immortal. Or if not immortal, then a guaranteed last survivor. When the world ended, the final vestige of the human presence on earth would be a whiff—like the odor of spent gunpowder after a firework—of irony.

The two and a half years since his wife Sylvia's death had been an incrementally expanding demonstration of the fallacy of grief. The fallacy of grief was that it passed. The fallacy of grief was that when someone you loved died, you suffered, you went to the underworld, you found the measure of yourself in the small hours' darkness, and eventually (because the commitment to life overrode all else) you found that the measure of yourself was enough. Slowly, you raised your head. You began to look about you. You saw that the world—via cloud formations and product labels—was re-insinuating itself. You understood that the world was still enough. You understood that the will to live was a thing of benign slyness. You began to *get over it*. You were changed—enlarged and deepened by your loss—but you accepted the renewed contract. You knew you were going on. You discovered that this thing had not, as it had threatened to, killed you.

That was the fallacy, and he was the living proof.

He'd stopped writing, of course. Of course, because a novelist had to be amorally in love with life, all of life, even death—and he was not. Not anymore. He'd believed it was art's job to imaginatively accommodate the world, to find room for everything. But after Sylvia's death, he had room only for her absence and his own stubborn presence.

They had been married for thirty years when the diagnosis arrived: grade 4 astrocytoma. Inoperable. Radio- and chemotherapies until she'd said: Enough. She died in the late afternoon in their bed at the apartment on Twenty-third Street. Angelo had been lying with her, spoons fashion, in the bed's oblong of sunlight, his arm wrapped around her. He'd fallen asleep for perhaps twenty minutes and when he woke up she was gone. Eyes closed, facing away from him. Facing away from him. Toward elsewhere. Toward wherever the dead went. Which was maybe nowhere. She'd been fifty-six years old. A year younger than him.

Since then his orientation had gone. *Things fall apart,* as the poem said. He couldn't think. He had no view of himself. He found himself doing various things: lying on the floor staring at the ceiling; fucking a twenty-four-year-old Latina prostitute; walking the width of Manhattan in concussive heat, heavy with his own sweat. He was aware of the people in his life (he had no living family, but there were friends, there were professionals) at first tiptoeing around him, then willing him to pull himself together, then getting annoyed, then gradually conceding that perhaps he'd lost his mind. A very remote part of himself knew how it must seem to them: his life ought to have furnished him with the resources to survive losing his wife. He was a successful literary writer. He had won awards. His work had been translated into twenty-five languages. He had long lunches with editors in restaurants of winking glass and fat white napkins. He went on international tours. But they didn't know, the friends, the professionals, that the thing at the center was Sylvia. They didn't know that what made it bearable was that she didn't take him seriously. They didn't know that the only time he was peacefully himself was when he was with her. They didn't know it had been the kind of love the world thought it had outgrown.

And without her the paltry dimensions of everything else had been revealed with a violent molecular vividness. He could connect nothing with nothing. As another poem said.

He had come to the cabin with no clear purpose but with the vague intuition that he might never leave it. That was as far as the thinking had gone. The place had belonged to his father. Unused for more than two decades. Angelo had been there as a child. Somewhere in the midst of his grief he'd found himself remembering it. The ravine like a Halloween pumpkin grin. The dense evergreens. There was something in the land he wanted. He didn't know what. He got in the car and drove west from New York for two days. Snow fell, eventually, which soothed him, somewhere at the edge of himself. He picked up supplies in Ellinson. He didn't know what he was doing, but there was a quietness and solidity to the place that was a kind of spartan endorsement.

Six days had passed. He had brought no books to read. Reading had gone the way of writing. Reading and writing were proof that you were still interested in the world, still intrigued, still *bothered*. Instead he watched the snow. He lay on the couch. He let himself be reduced to simple actions. He chopped a stack of wood. He ate tinned food. He kept the fire in the stove going. His mind operated with a sleepy skeleton crew.

Then, last night, irony had arrived. In the shape of something as medically unspectacular as sciatica.

Sciatica! He'd been introduced to the condition four years ago. Had one operation to trim the herniated disc in his spine that was pressing on the nerve (L5 compromising S1, as he came to know them), done his Pilates exercises with a kind of numb fascination, accepted the slight limp and the use of a cane and led a physically pain-free life since then.

Until last night, when, without preamble or warning, the sciatica had come back.

He'd forgotten what it was like. He'd forgotten what excruciating and completely debilitating pain was like. Before passing out, he'd spent two hours on all fours on the floor, comprehensively incapable of moving. The pain had made him cry. He hadn't cried for months. Grief had given up on tears. Grief had worn out their mechanism and moved on to other things. The universe had granted him one random mercy: He'd hit the deck within reach of a bottle of single malt, a gift from his publisher, with whom he'd had a pointless lunch more than a year ago, back in the days when people were still expecting him to get over things. The whisky—a twenty-five-year-old Macallan—had been on the passenger seat of Angelo's car ever since, and he'd added it to the box of unthought-out supplies he brought from Ellinson when he'd arrived. In the absence of pills (the thought for *physical* pain had long since stopped being part of his scheme of things) the Scotch had presented itself as the only pain-relief available, and he'd drunk the better part of the bottle. Now, therefore, on top of the screaming crisis in his legs, he had a brain-bashing hangover. He needed water. He was dying of thirst.

The woodstove's fire had gone out, but there was a little radiant heat still left in its iron. His feet hadn't, quite, frozen, but the rest of him was shivering ludicrously. (Sylvia would have taken care of him had she been here, but not without humor. Once, having suffered a sudden onset of diarrhea at a friend's book launch and raced home in a cab, he shat his pants before he'd quite made it to the bathroom. Sylvia, in a black evening dress and globular gold necklace, had stood in the bathroom doorway, quoting from his press reviews—". . . unflinching honesty and a richly ambiguous imagination . . . ," ". . . one of our finest writers . . . ," ". . . while lesser novelists are satisfied with cute entertainments, Greer is still going after the big stuff . . ."—while he'd flailed on the floor, trying to divest himself of his soiled clothes, the two of them laughing like children. They had seen each other at their best and worst. It was a continuum. There was nothing of either of them love hadn't found room for.)

The question was: Could he make it to the sink? He had to move. He had to have water. No matter what the pain said. And after that, somehow, he was going to have to make it to the car. To a phone. To a doctor. Which the pain was already telling him would be impossible. The pain was already telling him it would be a miracle if he made it to the sink.

It nearly killed him. He had to crawl and pull himself up by the edge of the stove. The nerves in his right leg shrieked. He took as much of his weight on his arms as he could and stuck his parched mouth under the faucet's icy stream (spring water, allegedly, it tasted fresh and stony), feeling goodness ease back into his cells with every gulp. He couldn't tell how long he drank. It seemed like hours.

But he still couldn't walk more than three steps, even doubled over, even with the cane. On his hands and knees, working in increments that jammed his teeth together and brought tears back to his eyes, he loaded the woodstove and got a fire going. It was another half hour before he managed to struggle into his thermal jacket and hat, in the stubborn hope that by the time he got them on, he'd be able to walk.

Which he could not.

It was a joke. The car was on the other side of the bridge across the ravine, and the bridge was a ten-minute walk away even for an able-bodied person. But the only other pain relief available was the last fifth of Scotch, and with the best will in the world, he knew that in his current state he wouldn't keep a mouthful down. He wondered if he could knock himself out *manually*. Whack his chin on the edge of the stove. Wallop his own head with a skillet. It was a measure of how much pain he was in that the comedy of the idea was lost on him. All he could think was that he'd fuck it up and break his jaw and knock his teeth out. Sylvia, of course, would have laughed. It had brought the spirit of her very close to him, this absurd predicament. He could sense her smiling at the contrast, his soul's drama reduced by his body to farce. She appreciated it. Irony had been her element.

He decided to crawl to the door and look outside to see how deep the snow was.

And though, when he'd gotten the door open, he saw what he saw straightaway, it took his understanding a moment to catch up with what his brain had already unpacked.

He was looking at the body of a little girl.

18

She was lying on her front on the edge of the porch, where the snow was thinner, one leg bent, arms limp, face turned toward him, eyes closed, the hood of her red jacket loose around her tangle of dark hair. There was a little puddle of blood by her mouth. Beyond her, the land was sculpted white. Snow still fell heavily through the darkness. The ravine was twenty yards away. Across it, the forest climbed the western slope, confected evergreens, like an overdose of Christmas. The light from his open door showed her footprints—or rather leg-prints, since every step had taken her at least shin-deep—trailing away north toward the bridge.

Dead.

The blood by her mouth.

The body's posture of indifference, as if she'd lain down to take a snooze on a sunny beach.

A dead child. Here. Now.

For perhaps three seconds, adrenaline blocked Angelo's pain when he moved—but he could feel it pushing to get back through to him by the time he'd staggered to where she lay and dropped to his knees beside her. Thoughts smashed and dead-ended:

Check for pulse . . .

Don't move her . . .

This is because . . .

Too late for . . .

No phone, nothing to . . .
This is because . . .
From Ellinson, one of the houses . . .
Be breathing, be breathing . . .
They'll think I've . . .

Blank of all but instinct, Angelo put his ear as close to her open mouth as he could.

And seemed to wait forever.

Then it came. Faint. But warmer than the air on his skin. She was breathing.

If she had broken bones, then moving her would be risky. But if he didn't get her out of the snow, she might be dead in seconds. No contest.

Except he could still barely move himself. If he tried—and succeeded—in picking her up, there was no guarantee he wouldn't fall, or drop her. Plus he still needed one hand for his stick. It was awful but he was going to have to—very gently—*drag* her inside.

Angelo knew even as he was bracing himself what that was going to cost him. But there was no alternative. Still on his knees, he loosened the girl's jacket zipper around her neck, then carefully turned her onto her back. The snow helped. He took hold of the back of the hood with his left hand, got his stick ready in his right, then pushed himself, by degrees, to his feet.

And almost collapsed immediately, the pain was so bad. In the first instant of getting his spine unbent by more than ninety degrees he felt his body's reflex to go back down onto its hands and knees. He cried out involuntarily—and cried out with every step until he had her in front of the stove. Then he collapsed, weeping, and though the cabin's front door was still open on its perfect winter wonderland, there was nothing he could do for a while.

The girl didn't stir. Angelo wondered if she was in a coma. Her jacket was waterproof but her jeans were soaked and half frozen. He wasn't the man for these situations, but he knew you weren't supposed to leave someone in wet clothes. The evaporating water lowered the body temperature. He had a vision of the girl coming to and finding him undressing her. The terror that would overwhelm her instantly. But there was nothing else for it. For all he knew, she was in the last stage of hypothermia. He remembered reading somewhere that in cases of *extreme* hypothermia, the most obvious symptom—shivering—stopped. And this little girl wasn't shivering.

Do it now, Sylvia's ghost said. She was very close to him just now, very engaged. (He would never, since childhood, have said he believed in ghosts. His rational self still didn't. But since Sylvia's death, his rational self had been left far behind on the beach of his time, along with much of the clutter of who he was. He was a stranger to himself now, and his life was a dream he no longer questioned. Vaguely, since he'd begun sensing her presence—in his head if not in the air around him—he was well aware of what his rational self would have had to say about it: that her ghost was nothing more than the generative power of his own obsessed memory. But it made no difference to him. She came when she came. It was what he still lived for. It was the only thing that felt real in the dream.) *Don't waste time,* Sylvia said. *Door first. Crawl. Then sleeping bag. Something under her head. How long was she out there?*

He did all of it on his hands and knees, wretched with pain. He got the wet things off the child (but knew as soon as he removed her right boot and saw the dark swelling that her ankle was probably broken) and draped them on the stove so she'd see them as soon as she woke up. He opened the sleeping bag out completely on the Karrimor mat, very gently rolled her into it, then zipped it up around her. He eased his pillow under her head and put more wood in the stove. By the time he was finished, he was drenched in sweat.

19

How old? Nine? Ten? There were pine needles in her dark hair. Her face was covered in scratches.

Scratches because she was running through the woods.

Who was she running from?

Where were they now?

And what use was a cripple going to be if they showed up?

Sylvia, very focused, sent clipped, practical bulletins: *Keep her warm. Get fluids into her.*

No landline. No cell reception. He had to get to the car. He couldn't get to the car. It had nearly done for him just getting to the front porch and back. He had an image of himself crawling on all fours through the snow to the bridge. Impossible. It didn't matter how many times he approached the problem, the facts remained: He was stuck here with her until L5 decided it had had enough of torturing him and released the pressure on S1, or until whoever she belonged to showed up to claim her. Someone *would* show up, obviously, sooner or later. She couldn't be anything other than missing. But what had happened to her? And what if she died in the meantime?

Who was she running from? He consulted Sylvia. Could feel her shaking her head, see her dark eyes bright with the mystery.

When he'd had to undress the girl, he wanted to do it briskly, out of a panicky care for her dignity. But the swollen ankle meant he'd had to be careful and slow (who knew what else was broken?), and he was ambushed by an awkward piercing sadness at the sight of her pale legs and hairless vulva. The forlornness of her bare chest. As soon as her panties were dry, he'd slipped them back on for her.

The world was full of awful things happening to kids. He and Sylvia had been childless. Sylvia had had scarring from a miscarriage when she was eighteen and he had sperm with such low motility they might as well have been dead. They'd tried in the early years of their marriage, five attempts at IVF without success. They'd felt it start to consume them, the cycle of hope and disappointment. They'd had the wisdom to know when to stop. It had made a little sadness between them. But it had also asked the necessary question: In the absence of a child to love, will this be enough? Will the two of you, for each other, be enough? And the answer, they'd both known, was yes. It had brought them closer, gently. It had confirmed them.

Looking at this child now, Angelo was appalled by her vulnerability, the small wrists and tender throat, the eyes like shut buds. When her jeans were dry, he decided, he'd put those back on for her, too.

He felt her forehead. The chill had gone, but she didn't stir. Her stillness was awful. If she were shivering or raving, it would be something, a sign that she was still here. As it was, he imagined her spirit wandering somewhere between here and the afterlife, lost, confused, alone. *No, I can't help with that,* Sylvia said. *She's still with you.*

There were more difficulties. Even with the woodstove he was going to be pretty cold without his sleeping bag. There was one moth-eaten blanket in the chest in the bedroom (no bed) and two bath towels he'd dried yesterday, but that would be the limit of his insulation. He'd been sleeping on the Karrimor on the floor by the stove, but she needed that, so he'd have to take his chances on the busted couch, which would almost certainly make his back worse, if it *could* get worse. He'd have to put on extra clothes. Which meant moving again. Which meant ringing the L5 to S1 doorbell.

Who was she running from?

In a minute, he decided, when he'd gathered his strength, he'd go through every drawer in the place for anything he might— however pointlessly—use as a weapon.

20

Shock had addled his brain. He spent an agonizing, indeterminate time crawling around the cabin—he found a rusted file, a broken saw, a broom with half its bristles gone—before being forced to conclude that all he really had at his disposal was the woodstove's brass-handled poker, which was barely a foot long.

Then, astonished at his own dimness, he remembered the axe.

Which was, of course, in the woodshed that adjoined the cabin.

Forget it. The search indoors had exhausted him. He had nothing left.

But the image of the girl running in terror through the woods wouldn't go away. Nor the poignancy of her bare legs and the state of utter helplessness to which she'd been reduced.

I can't do this.

Try.

He tried to argue Sylvia out of it. Even if he got the axe, what, exactly, was he going to do with it? In his state, did she seriously think he was going to be any kind of match for an attacker? He might as well hurl insults. And why were they getting so obsessed with the idea of an attacker? The kid could have been . . . The kid could have been what? Playing hide-and-seek? Fallen out of a tree she'd climbed? Escaped from an asylum?

It was terrible, the clarity with which he felt the need to protect her. It was a new measure of his own weakness, as if he needed one.

Sylvia's energy bristled near him: *It's fifteen paces to the shed. Or a short crawl in the snow. Come on. Put the gloves on.*

Shock had also, apparently, erased his hangover. The last of the Scotch winked its promise.

No. Don't dull yourself.

OK.

Come on. Do it.

By the time he got back—he'd managed five paces bent double with the cane, then been forced down onto his hands and knees in the snow by grinning L5—he was certain of one thing: that if an attacker kicked in the door right now, there would be no resistance he could offer.

He shoved the axe under the stove, out of sight. Not the sort of thing he wanted to have on him when she opened her eyes.

She was shivering now. Not in a good way. She was covered in sweat. Her forehead, when he put his hand on it, was burning. Fever. He should get water into her. Somehow.

Shaking, and in a sweat of his own, Angelo wrestled himself to the sink and filled a tin mug with water. Repeated the wrestle in reverse to get back down on the floor next to her.

"Come on," he said, lifting her head and cradling it in his left arm. "Drink. It's good for you. Please. Come on. Take a sip. You can do it."

But she couldn't do it. He'd been hoping for some rehydration reflex deep within her to kick in. He'd been hoping that wherever her soul was wandering, her body would know it needed water, would feel the cup at its lips, would open her mouth, sip, swallow.

That didn't happen. The water just ran down her chin.

You've done what you can for now. Rest for a while.

Gently, he laid her head back down on the pillow.

21

"Actually, I've been back a few weeks," Nick Blaskov-itch said. "My dad died. My mom's in no shape to be out here on her own. Serena can't move home. She's got a life."

Whereas I haven't. Not since you broke my heart.

Valerie's hands were shaking. She'd forced them flat on the desk for disguise.

Three years.

Three years that disappeared into nothing the minute the two of you were in the same room again. In this case, a room humming with the cramped energy of police, working. Love didn't care which room it was. Love wasn't criminal. Love was breezily amoral.

"I'm sorry," she said. *Sorry.* The air went dense with the history of that word between them. Quickly, she added: "I'm so sorry about your dad. What happened?"

"Cancer. Ugly, but quick."

"Oh God, Blasko, I'm so sorry."

Three "sorrys" in five seconds. There would never be enough.

"I know."

They looked at each other. What was there to do except look at each other? What was there to see except that it was all still there? Everything they'd had. Everything she'd wrecked.

He was seeing it, too. They'd always been mutually transparent, fundamentally in cahoots. When they'd been together, the world revealed itself as a beautiful-ugly horror-joke they were both in on. Sometimes you laughed your ass off and sometimes you despaired, but once you'd discovered each other, you never had to do either alone.

Except there's something I never told you, Nick. You thought you hated me before? Just wait.

"You're back at work here?" she said.

"'Fraid so."

Seeing him every day. The calm, dark-featured face with its look of tired but restless intelligence. The familiar smell of him. His voice. She had a quick, compressed vision of herself moving away to a hot poor country where no one knew anything about her. An adobe hut. Red dust. Bare feet in the sun. Liquor. Loneliness.

"Still Vice?"

"Computer Forensics. A lot of desk. I retrained. High-tech. Do you know what a hardware write blocker is? You don't, do you. *I* do."

"Seriously?"

"Seriously. So if your TiVo crashes, call me."

Call me.

No wedding ring, but that proved nothing. She was looking for the presence of another woman in his eyes. She couldn't help it. It shocked her, the reflex. He knew. His look said there wasn't anyone. It also said take nothing for granted. You nearly killed me. You could nearly kill me again.

"You're on the serial duo," he said, glancing down at the shoe box. "You getting there?"

She shook her head, looked away. Let's not talk about that. Too close to history. Too close to home, to the Suzie Fallon case, to love, and her protracted murdering of it.

You've done this because you don't feel entitled to happiness, he'd said three years ago, weeks before the bathroom, the test, the language of impersonal biology. *You think shitting on love is going to bring Suzie Fallon back? It won't bring any of them back.* And he'd been right.

"Holy Christ on a cracker," Laura Flynn said. "You?"

She'd been walking past, Starbucks in one hand, half-eaten sub in the other, three bulging files under her arm.

Blasko smiled at her. Two of the files slipped from under her arm, spat their contents out in a slew on the floor. She nearly lost the coffee, too.

"Easy," Blasko said, laughing. "Easy there, tiger."

"Fucking great," Laura Flynn said. "This is your fault." But she set the rest of her burdens down and put her arms around him. She was a small, fiery woman with very dark hair and very blue eyes, and could beat at least half the guys in the station in an arm-wrestle. "What are you doing here?" she said, looking over his shoulder at Valerie while he hugged her. A look that said: Holy shit. You OK? What does this mean? Is it all going to start again?

Valerie's look back at her said: No. I don't know. I can't. I don't know. He won't. *I don't know.*

And now I'm going to have to tell him. Everything.

22

At her apartment in the small hours, Valerie sat in front of her desktop going through the new San Francisco Zoo CCTV footage. Or rather, she sat with the footage running without being able to focus on any of it. She was halfway through a bottle of Smirnoff, and there were too many Marlboro butts in the ashtray. Someone had said to her a long time back: Once you've agreed to let them kill you, cigarettes will stick with you through thick and thin. Cigarettes will *be* there for you. The apathetic snow had given up. Now rain purred against the windows. Her eyes itched and her body ached.

Blasko.

Nick.

She'd only ever called him Nick in bed. In bed they'd belonged only to each other. Everywhere else they were Police. Everywhere else they belonged to the City, the raped, the beaten, the abducted, the abused, the dead. Bed had been their refuge, the one bit of reality that made the rest of reality bearable.

Until the rest of reality had gotten greedy and decided to drive Valerie mad, by murdering Suzie Fallon.

Watch out for the One Case, her grandfather told her, when she'd joined Homicide. There's always one that gets to you. There's no explanation for it, but every cop gets one eventually. Every homicide cop. You won't see it coming. All you can do is recognize it when it hits and hold on. Listen to me. I know. By the time he'd told her this,

he had an upstanding thatch of white hair and fractured green eyes
and deep lines in the thin dough of his face. He'd been Homicide
himself, for twenty years. Valerie had asked, of course, what *his* One
Case had been. I don't talk about it, he'd said. And it wouldn't help
you if I did. Valerie knew it was the Case that had changed his Ca-
tholicism: it did away with belief in God, but left his belief in the
Devil stronger than ever.

You won't see it coming. She hadn't. She knew Suzie Fallon's dead
body was the worst thing she'd ever seen, but initially she took it the
way she took every other corpse, as another conundrum in flesh and
blood, another challenge. If you were Homicide, the world presented
you with horror after horror and asked the same two questions:

1. Can you deal with this?
2. Can you catch the person who did it?

Valerie's answers were always the same:

1. Yes.
2. I can try.

Seventeen-year-old Suzie Fallon had been abducted on her way
home from a Saturday-night party in Presidio. Or rather not on her
way home. She and two friends, Nina Madden and Aiden Delaney,
a couple, had taken LSD, and at some point in the evening wandered
out into the streets. According to Nina and Aiden, the plan was to
go into the park, but Suzie had become paranoid and run back to
the party. Aside from her murderer, Nina and Aiden were the last
people to see her alive. Her body was discovered two weeks later,
dumped between 580 and the Brushy Peak Reserve. It was barely
recognizable as a body. The autopsy revealed that she couldn't have
been dead for more than four days. She'd spent ten days captive,
during which time she was repeatedly raped and tortured, with
everything from an acetylene torch to sulfuric acid. They needed
dental records to confirm her identity.

The investigation lasted six months. Valerie couldn't say at what point it shifted for her from professional rigor to personal obsession. She couldn't say at what point she stopped being able to shut out the images from Suzie's last ten days. She couldn't say at what point she was *living* in the room of terrible things. She couldn't say at what point she started hating herself. She couldn't say at what point she started trying to ruin love. Only that she did, and that she knew she was doing it, and that she couldn't stop.

The more she screamed at Blasko, the more he absorbed it. It became her mission, to see how far he would stretch. She began to hate him for loving her. Love became an obscenity. An obscenity next to the obscene things that had been done to Suzie Fallon. It was the only thing that gave Valerie ease, the knowledge that she was, day by day, torturing and murdering what was between them. It seemed the most natural and inevitable thing in the world.

In the end, in despair at his tolerance, she took the FBI agent working with them—Carter, a complete asshole—home to her apartment and fucked him over and over, until, as she'd known he would, Blasko came home and walked in on them.

Two days later, as if the world had agreed that she was finally entitled to a release, she arrested the man who'd murdered Suzie Fallon.

But by that time the world had exacted its price. Nick Blaskovitch transferred out of San Francisco, and she didn't see him again.

Until today.

Just in time for it to all happen again.

He'd gone before she realized she was pregnant.

You don't have to decide anything right now. You've got time. You can wait.

But she'd woken in pain bleeding heavily one night in her eighth week. Put a towel on the car seat and driven herself, in agony (you deserve this), to the ER, where, midway through her explanation of what was wrong, the pain had doubled her and she'd dropped to her knees. She'd spent what had seemed a long time on a gurney in a brightly lit room, waiting to be seen. The attending doctor was a young woman with a tired face and a long froth of dark curly hair pulled back into a ponytail. There was a large round lamp above Valerie from which she could feel soft heat on her exposed belly and legs and which reminded her of the time she and Nick had gone on vacation to Brazil and sunbathed nude on an utterly isolated beach, the feeling of shocking license, the sense that Adam and Eve would've felt like this, before the Fall. After a little while, the doctor said: Yes, it's come away. That's the whole thing. I'm sorry. Do you want to see it? Valerie had wondered what there could possibly be to see at eight weeks, but she looked anyway. And added what she saw to the many things she had already seen. The tiny head webbed in blood vessels. The putative eye like a precise blot of ink. The snub beginning of a nose.

They'd kept her in overnight. In the morning she'd driven home. A bright, blue-skied day. Traffic. People. Life.

There was a baby, Nick. But I didn't know if it was yours. I lost it, anyway.

Valerie finished the half glass of vodka in a gulp, lit another Marlboro, and forced herself to look at the new footage. *You will have to think about him. You will have to tell him. But not yet. Not yet.*

The zoo's CCTV material had only ever been a long shot: the hope the cameras would've caught Katrina talking to someone they hadn't interviewed, something odd in the interaction, something slightly off that police eyes would spot. Myskow, Carla York's predecessor, had put the killer into the "organized" category, which would mean prep, planning, stalking, familiarizing himself with the victim's routine (although along with all the other profile points, it was best-guess stuff; and there was no saying an organized predator wouldn't start losing his shit as the victims piled up) but how much footage could you look at? The week before the incident? The month? The year? Only Valerie *was* still looking. And right now she was looking mainly to take her mind off Nick Blaskovitch.

Valerie thought of any case as a series of concentric circles, like an archery target. You started from the center, the bull's-eye. Finding what you needed in the bull's-eye—via hard evidence, interviews, detection while the whole thing was *fresh*—meant the Case took hours, days, maybe two or three weeks to solve. But if you didn't find what you needed there, you moved out to the next circle—less-likely suspects, broader interviews, circumstantial evidence. Weeks turned into months. Each circle you moved out into was less likely to give you what you needed. But there was nothing to do but move through them. And the circles went on forever.

The circle she was now operating in—the new zoo footage—was a long way from the bull's-eye. The new material was six months' worth from *the whole zoo,* not just, as the previous stuff had been, camera angles featuring Katrina. Nor was it really new. Valerie had had it for four weeks now, and every night she spent hours trawling through it. It had become a ritual. It was what she did to maintain the sense—in the wretched time between getting home and falling asleep—that she was doing *some*thing, however desperate.

She'd restricted herself to the zoo's entrance footage, excluding (in the first instance) women, family groups, the elderly. She was looking for a man on his own, or two men together. (*Two men together?* her inner skeptic had scoffed. *This is San Francisco, for Christ's sake.*) It wasn't (the gay-male-couples problem excepted) such a crazy idea. It didn't take much footage to establish that lone male visitors to a zoo were a minority. Of course, there was the possibility such men were meeting someone inside, but short of going through all the extant footage from the entire zoo, there was no way of checking that. That would be, she thought, the *next* fucking circle of desperation. It wasn't a *crazy* idea, no. But it was pitifully remote. Her method was simple: Each time a single male in the age range entered the zoo, she froze the frame, screen-grabbed a time-coded still of the guy, and filed it. Which left her with a growing gallery of—the phrase was laughable—"potential suspects." All this based on the optimistic assumption that if someone wanted to stalk Katrina, the zoo was the place to do it.

She worked through the images. Two hours went by. She lost focus. Told herself she was wasting her time. Got so sick of the process that she went back to the Katrina footage, dipping in at random. But there was nothing there. She'd seen it all before. Too many times before, the crowds milling around the concession stands, families deep in their own lives, kids laughing in the monkey house, the visible collective thrill in front of the big cats.

But the dead women throbbed, silently around her.

She forced herself back to the CCTV from the zoo's entrance. Spent another hour zooming and pulling back, rewinding, pausing, screen-grabbing, filing, her mind a surrealist mess of moments with Blasko and yawning lions and *among the Filthy, filthy too* and the exhausting catalog of Katrina's wounds and another drink and another cigarette and the Case *Kansas midpoint goose fork balloon acceleration we don't even know job or maybe none Dale won't make it time code 15.36.14 . . . 15 . . . 16 . . . 17 . . .*

She leaned forward in her chair, rested her head on her arms on the desk. *Don't fall asleep here. If you're ready for sleep, go to bed.* Not sleeping in your bed when you could was like not drinking from a water hole when you were lost in a desert.

Her eyes closed. It was sweet, the surrender, the yielding of the wiser part of herself. It was like childhood.

She woke with a start from a dream of falling.

Goddammit.

The timecode now said *37.11.06 . . . 07 . . . 08 . . .*

She'd lost twenty-two minutes.

Her intention, stretching, feeling her vertebrae tick, was to just rewind to the point at which she'd fallen asleep, shut down, then pick it up again tomorrow.

But for no reason she could identify—beyond guilt for having fallen asleep in the first place, a perverse or superstitious feeling of having been cheated of twenty-two minutes—she went back to where she'd nodded off, hit play, let the tape run.

15.36.14 . . . 15 . . . 16 . . . 17 . . . 18 . . . 19 . . .

She stopped the tape.

Had she seen this guy before?

The hundreds of faces shuffled in her head.

These were the intervals in which the God who wasn't there operated. The two seconds after your eyes closed.

Her scalp tingled. The dead women gathered their sad energy around her.

White male, approximately six foot and 180, dark brown hair, dark eyes, possibly early thirties. Khaki combat pants, navy blue Raiders T-shirt, no wristwatch, no visible jewelry.

Her head was a station crowd of lone men. It was like straining to find a familiar face in the throng. It was like looking for a loved one. The fear you'd miss them in the confusion . . .

The Raiders shirt tantalized her.

She'd seen him before. *Surely* she'd seen him before? A different day. A different time code. A different visit to the zoo. The same clothes. The fact of the same clothes was that kind of fact.

Calm down.

She pulled up the filed stills as thumbnails. There were more than three hundred, but her mind burned through its mess of dream and booze into unnatural awakeness.

Faces. Faces. Faces.

Half an hour in, she stopped.

Same guy. Same clothes.

Three days earlier.

Alone. Definitely alone at the entrance on both occasions. The dark eyes simultaneously intense and remote.

Valerie stubbed out her cigarette. Kept the two stills open, then raced back into the footage of Katrina that corresponded to the two dates of the guy's visits. If she had to, she'd go frame by frame. But right now she went at double speed. The Raiders shirt would jump out at her, she believed. Her eyes itched. The pixels had a fizzing life of their own. She was balanced between certainty and hopelessness. Everyone else had given up on the zoo footage. She'd given up on it herself, except as a form of self-help, a form of hypnosis, a sop to her inexhaustibly dissatisfied conscience.

All the while she scanned, she told herself not to get excited. There was no law against a lone white male visiting a zoo—every day of the week if he wanted to.

But it wasn't nothing. She'd been doing the job long enough.

Five minutes. Ten. Twenty.

Stop.

Jesus.

Raiders.

She replayed what she'd just been watching. Katrina was with a mixed group (adults and children) by the Sumatran tiger enclosure. It was a day of flaring and subsiding sunlight. She was wearing one of the zoo's black, yellow-logoed T-shirts, canvas hiking shorts (she'd outgrown hating the crescent birthmark, Adele had said), white ankle socks, and white Nike sneakers. She was, as always, talking with bright animation, the ordinary happiness of a person who liked her job. Every member of the group was transfixed by the tigers.

Except the dark-haired guy in the Raiders shirt on the very edge of it.

He didn't take his eyes off Katrina.

Calm down, she repeated. All right, this isn't nothing, but it's not much.

Cop sense said otherwise. The stillness of the guy. The obliviousness of everything but Katrina. The fact that he was alone at the zoo. Twice. At least twice. Tomorrow she would get one of the team to go back through more of the footage. She knew they'd find him again. She had no right to know, but she did.

It was just after five in the morning. She called the office. Ed Pérez answered.

"Write this down," Valerie said, and gave him the description.

"Got it," Ed said. He sounded strung out. Valerie wondered if this case was the one that was going to fuck up Ed's life. She knew exactly the state he'd be in, slumped at his desk, in need of a shave, one white shirttail hanging out, paunch at full liberty.

"I'm sending stills and footage," she said. "Get it out to all the other agencies."

"Press?"

"If I get my way. Have video go back to the preedits and get everything you can from the ticket booth at the zoo entrance. He's probably not dumb enough to have paid with a credit card, but you never know. Ditto parking lot footage. If he drove there, we'll get a plate. I'll be there in an hour."

Excitement pushed through the exhaustion. The booze lay in not quite shreds in her system. Christ, why had she drunk so much? (*Because that's how much we drink these days, my love . . .*) She would take

a shower and force down a pint of black coffee and eat whatever carbohydrates were in the refrigerator.

Twenty minutes later she was showered, dressed, and brutally
caffeined into a kind of shocked brightness. Her eyes were raw and
her sinuses pounded. She felt tender but sharp.

She was walking out the door when her phone rang. It was Carla
York.

"We may have another one," Carla said.

Valerie's cells gathered, tight.

"Nevada. About fifteen miles south of Reno. It's in dry decay,
so it could have been there for anything between two months and a
year. Or more. Can you be at the station in an hour?"

"I'm on my way now."

"There's a chopper. We should go."

How many? Dale Mulvaney had said. Seven. Jesus Christ, don't
let it be eight. But Valerie already knew it would be. The killer's magical revenge for the zoo footage. You couldn't help but make these
disturbing equations. But if that were true, it meant at least the guy
caught on camera was him.

"What makes them think it's ours?" she said.

Carla's phone rustled slightly, as if she had it cradled against her
shoulder while her hands were doing something else. Valerie didn't
catch her answer.

"Say again?"

"I said there's a traveling windup alarm clock wedged in the
corpse's mouth."

23

Xander King wasn't sleeping. He was back at Mama Jean's house. Somewhere on the edge of himself he could feel the flicker of the RV's interior light and hear Paulie talking, asking him why they'd stopped, but it was a thin outer reality he couldn't reach. He knew this was happening because the woman and the kid yesterday had been out of the scheme of things. If there'd been a milk jug, he could've made it right, could have brought it in. But there wasn't a goddamned jug, and now because of that, here he was back at Mama Jean's. This was what happened when you didn't do it right. *And we're going to keep doing this until you get it right,* Mama Jean said. Always. He never got it right. He could feel the dry ache of his eyes having been open too long, but in Mama Jean's house, he was blinking normally.

He was in the living room. The alive things in the living room were the sunburst wall clock and the black fireplace and the green couch and the drinks cabinet with its crowd of bottles like winking jewels, and each of them was alive, too. They were pretty things, but they were more Mama Jean's than anything else in the house, except maybe the television. None of the alive things talked to him. They just watched everything that happened.

The television was on. Different-colored people in bright vests and shorts doing sports. An orange running track with peaceful white lines. A deep green field.

Leon wanted to go there.

He was Leon in Mama Jean's house. Long before he became Xander King. Long before the money came.

He wanted to be sitting at the very edge of the orange running track with all the people watching from the seats behind him and feel the thrilling *whoosh* of the runners going by. Just before the ads came on, five linked circles appeared on the screen, a row of three and two. Leon had learned the colors: blue, black, red, yellow, green. The circles gave him a strange feeling of a world a long way away.

"How about some ice cream?" Mama Jean said.

Leon looked up. Just looking up at Mama Jean was like lifting a big weight with his neck.

"You can have a scoop of chocolate and a scoop of vanilla. How's that sound?"

Leon felt his face go hot and his hands thicken and he needed to pee. But they'd already been up to the room today, just a little while ago. Surely it was just a little while ago? It hadn't worked. The brain demon was still in his head, Mama Jean had told him afterwards. Like a hand made of black smoke. If it was still there when he had to start school, every girl would laugh at him. Did he want that?

Without speaking, Leon got to his feet and followed Mama Jean into the kitchen. The countertops were scrubbed and bright, the windows full of sunshine. Outside, the leaves on the trees shivered.

He got halfway through his ice cream before he felt Mama Jean go the way she went.

When Mama Jean went the way she went, a kind of stillness and heat and quietness came off her. Leon could always feel it. When it happened, all the objects in the house went kind of hard and tight, because they knew, too. He wanted to spit out the spoonful of ice cream he'd just put in his mouth. The smell of Mama Jean's big pale blue jeans and hair spray and tobacco swelled in the kitchen.

Leon took a few paces toward the back door, holding the red plastic bowl of ice cream very carefully in both hands.

He got all the way to the threshold before Mama Jean said, "Where the fuck do you think you're going?"

24

For Paulie, the long drive with his bad knee had been no kind of fun, but it was no kind of fun to be stopped here in the middle of nowhere with Xander looking like a fucking hypnotized person, either. They'd only just crossed the border into Utah and were heading east down to Interstate 15 when he'd been woken by the RV's swerve and Xander apparently asleep at the wheel. He'd nearly shit himself in the struggle to get Xander's foot off the gas and the RV safely halted at the side of the road. It was still early, not much after ten.

"Hey," he said, shaking Xander's shoulder for the umpteenth time. *"Hey."*

It wasn't the first time this had happened. And it had been happening more often recently. It terrified Paulie, Xander's absence. It measured how alone he would be in the world without him.

And he still couldn't believe he hadn't got his time with the woman. It had filled him with a hot weakness and desperation, as if his anger were a cripple in a wheelchair. It had made him think, for just a moment, that *he* should leave *Xander*. But the thought—even for its moment—had made the open land's darkness yawn with a kind of gravity that made him feel sick.

Xander turned his head, slowly, and looked at him.

"Jesus," Paulie said. "You OK? What the fuck?"

Xander blinked. Moved the muscles of his face around. "I'm real thirsty," he said. "Get me some water."

"Christ, man, you—"

"How long've we been stopped?"

"I don't know. Half an hour maybe."

"Get me some water."

Paulie went to the back of the RV and took a plastic bottle of deVine from the cooler. Xander drank all of it. Paulie was mesmerized by the movement of his Adam's apple. He had a vivid memory of the little girl running ahead of him in the forest. He should've told Xander. Why hadn't he told him? It had been crazy not to tell him. *A little kid got away from me.* Shame had stopped him. Shame and fear. *Don't think about it. We can't go back now. Fuck.*

"Tomorrow we have to get a jug," Xander said.

"What?"

"A milk jug. One of those little jugs with a lip. For milk. And batteries."

"Batteries?"

"I want to shave."

"OK. But now we need to get going. We need to get going now, right?"

Xander sat still, staring out the windshield at the road's pale meander through the empty land. Paulie felt desperate, suspended. It was agony when Xander's will, which was normally like a warm searchlight on him, moved away somewhere else.

And when Xander turned to him this time, it was with a blank look that could have meant anything. Paulie couldn't bear it. He almost blurted out the whole story of the little girl right there and then.

"Go on in the back now," Xander said. "Make some coffee."

Paulie forced a laugh. "Man, when you nod out like that . . . Sheesh. I don't know whether to . . . I mean, you know?"

"Go on in the back," Xander repeated, shifting the RV into drive.

Paulie, still forcing laughter, went to put his hand on Xander's shoulder to give it a friendly shake. Somehow couldn't. Xander gunned the engine. Holding his wrecked knee, Paulie clambered between the seats into the back of the vehicle. Praying that they weren't—as he suspected they were—out of fucking coffee.

25

The body—it felt wrong calling it "a body" when there was so little of it left—had been found by night hikers en route to Carson City from Reno through the state parks bordering Washoe Lake. It's a new thing, apparently, Carla had said in the chopper, people walking in the dark. She said it without surprise. No one in law enforcement was surprised at anything. *He must / Become the whole of boredom,* Valerie thought. Poetry, like dreams, had delayed detonation. The scene was barely a quarter mile from shore, in a thicket of bare trees.

The corpse had been buried, but dug at and worked to the surface by wildlife. All the organs and soft tissue were gone. Scraps of leathery cartilage clung to the bone. The bottom jaw was off, either through natural collapse or because it had been broken to get the alarm clock in. The clock itself was about three inches in diameter, black-faced with white numerals marked with luminous dots, surrounded by a brass-effect plastic rim. You could buy one for less than ten bucks. It was the sort of thing saved from obsolescence by nostalgia.

Three Nevada CSI were still here, taking photographs. All the measurements were done. A taped perimeter had been set up and the grave site was tented. Two Reno Homicide detectives, the medical officer, a half-dozen uniformed RPD officers on guard. Everyone in the protective gear that would look ridiculous if you didn't know why they were wearing it. It was a dull morning, gloomy under the trees. The land smelled damp and loamy.

"At least they read the memos," Will said to Valerie. He looked like shit. They'd landed at Reno and been driven down in a squad car. Of the three of them, only Carla appeared to have slept. Either that or she'd evolved past the need for sleep altogether.

"Yeah," Valerie said, again feeling the gap where a quip would have been, long ago. They read the memos. Objects in the mouth? Vagina? Anus? Call the San Francisco team. They're collecting them. Instead of catching the guys who are putting them there.

"Detective Hart?"

Valerie turned.

"Sam Derne," the man approaching said. "Reno Homicide."

"Hey," Valerie said. Derne was late forties, a short, compact guy with pale skin, a gray crew cut and glittery blue eyes. He was holding a large-format digital camera.

"According to the medical officer, there's no telling how old the remains are until we get forensic entomology," he said. "And maybe not even then. But months, for sure. Possibly more than a year. We left the clock where it was for you to see, but we did remove this."

He handed Valerie the camera. "It's on-screen," he said. "It's been bagged. Found it next to her right hand."

The shot on-screen was of a torn piece of dark blue fabric, canvas or denim, Valerie guessed, embroidered with what might have been letters, maybe the bottom part of an *R* with the curve of a *U* or a *J* overlapping it. The color of the thread was impossible to make out, since it was heavily soiled.

"Looks like part of a bowling shirt pocket," Valerie said, handing it on to Will. "Except it's too heavy. Blue-collar uniform?" Mentally she raced through *bus truck train driver auto-shop utilities car plant delivery maintenance* . . .

Derne nodded. "Anyway, we have it."

"It is a woman, right?" Valerie asked.

"We'll have to wait for the pathologist's report," Derne said. "But at first glance, yeah. Hair, bone size, jaw, pelvic inlet. Medical officer seems pretty sure."

How many? Seven. No. Eight.

"You think this is deliberate?" Will said, indicating the image of the torn pocket.

"God knows," Valerie said. "Maybe it came off in the struggle. But if it's our guys, the primary scene's elsewhere. She'd have to have had it in her hand all the way here."

"But if they froze her, they might have missed it."

"What's the nearest freeway?" Valerie asked Derne. "Interstate 580—right?"

"Yeah. But I don't know how long they keep the cam footage, and we're not exactly short of RV traffic here. There's Lake Tahoe right over there. If this was done in summer . . ."

Valerie called Ed Pérez and told him to get the zoo suspect images to the Reno office.

"What is it?" she said to Will when she'd hung up. He was studying the photo of the torn pocket.

"Nothing," he said. "Too much crap blowing around in my head."

They'd been at the scene for two hours when Valerie started to feel faint.

"I'm taking five minutes," she said to Will. She ducked under the tape and walked deeper into the trees. Her head was hot. Her bones hurt. She was very conscious of her skeleton. Of the fact that underneath, she was exactly the same as the woman they'd found. She imagined speeded-up film of herself going through the stages of decomposition, flies arriving, maggots heaving in an ecstatic mass, her flesh disappearing, her bones starting to flash white.

She stopped and leaned against a tree. She was trembling. She went down onto her hands and knees.

The five minutes passed. Then another five. She lost track of how long she'd been gone.

She got to her feet, shivering.

She'd taken maybe ten paces before she heard a twig snap under someone's foot up ahead of her. She stopped. Convinced she'd been observed.

By Carla York.

26

Pain woke Nell. She opened her eyes. She was looking at a low wooden ceiling with cobwebbed beams. She was lying on her back in a soft dark blue sleeping bag on the floor. She was desperately thirsty. She recognized nothing.

Instinct told her not to make a sound. She lay there, blinking. Her right foot was a lump of fire. Her face felt like a cold skin mask someone had put on her. There was a whispery sound and throbbing heat to her left.

Very carefully, she turned her head.

A stove.

Old-fashioned. Squat. Iron.

The stove she'd seen. Her boots were next to it, laces undone.

She lifted her head and looked about her.

A small wooden room. Yellowy light came from two oil lamps, one on a table by the window (snow was still falling, the sky not quite dark), the other on a small shelf above a big white sink. A thin front door with a half-rotten backpack hanging from a hook.

She pushed herself up onto her elbows.

Opposite her a pale green wing-backed armchair, like old people had. A few feet past the sink another doorway, with no door. She could see a third doorway beyond it, showing the edge of a brown-stained bathtub.

She twisted—*very* carefully—to see what was behind her. A battered couch, also green, but not matching the chair, with bits of its foam showing through rips in the fabric. Above it on the wall a crookedly hanging picture of three white horses drinking at a stream, with a forest behind them.

Hey, cunt.

The words. The dream.

It was a dream.

It wasn't a dream.

Everything stopped. Like the split second on the roller coaster just before the drop.

Then she was falling. Then everything fell back in on her.

It fell back in on her and inside her and filled her with emptiness that swelled and in a moment would break out of her like a fruit bursting through its skin. And there would be nothing after that. Nothing.

Mom.

Run.

I'm going to be all right, but you have to run. Now!

Mom.

Oh God please please please—

The front door banged open.

An old man on his hands and knees. Longish gray hair and a beard. Bright green watery eyes in a lined face. He was dragging something behind him.

He collapsed on the threshold, breathing heavily. Cold snow-flavored air rushed in.

Nell had started, shoved herself backwards. She'd hit her head on the base of the couch. Moving had made the pain in her legs blare.

For what felt like a long time she remained frozen, watching the man on the floor. Something in the stove popped. The couch smelled sour. Beyond him she could see a wooden porch, big flakes of falling snow, the dark forest across the ravine. Mom. Josh. She had to get back. She—

He raised his head. "Oh," he gasped. "You're . . ." But he couldn't catch his breath. He bent his forehead to the floor. Wheezed. Raised his hand, as if telling her to wait . . . wait.

Nell pictured herself jumping over him, out onto the porch, running into the drifting snow. She tried to get up. The pain in her legs stopped her again immediately. There was no arguing with it. There was nothing she could do.

The old man lifted his head a second time. "You're awake," he said.

Nell imagined him undressing her. The hands in the dream.

But she was wearing all her clothes. They felt stiff and hot.

"Don't be afraid," he said. "You're safe. I found you outside. What happened? Where do you live?"

Nell was aware of her mouth open, nothing coming out.

"Listen," the old man said. "Just give me a second. You're safe, I promise. Just . . . I'm not going to hurt you. Are you OK? How are you feeling?"

Nell didn't answer.

"This looks weird," he said. "I know. I'm . . . I have a problem with my legs. Can't really walk at the moment. You shouldn't try to move. I think your ankle's broken. Let me get this door."

She watched him push himself back up onto his hands and knees—wrists trembling—and drag the sack of logs inside. He turned around and pushed the door shut. It all seemed to take a long time.

"Can you tell me what happened?" he asked her. He'd crawled to one of the foldout chairs and was propping himself up on it in an awkward position. His face was moist.

The blood coming out of her mother. All that time. How long? *They're still here.* They. More than one. Was he one of them? Josh would be looking for her. Was Josh . . . ? But when she thought of Josh, she got dark silence from the place where God was. The feeling of how much she'd wanted to put her arms around her mother came back, hurt her chest. Her mother slowly opening and closing her eyes. The blood on her mouth like crooked lipstick.

Mom is—

No she's not.

"It's OK," the old man said. "You don't have to say anything. It's OK. Everything's going to be all right."

The room's loud quiet was like water boiling away.

"How about I ask you and you just nod your head for yes and shake it for no?" the old man said. "I know you're scared, but I promise you don't need to be. All I want is to help you and get you home to your mom and dad."

Your mom and dad. Nell remembered her dad making scrambled eggs and waffles in the morning, saying: I hope you appreciate the consummate skill going into this, missy. *Consummate.* He purposely used big words he knew she didn't know the meaning of, so she'd have to ask him. She remembered finding her mom curled up in the shower with the water crashing down on her and her face like she'd never seen it before and her mom not being able to speak, then recovering and saying, Shshsh, baby, it's OK, I'm sorry, it's OK.

"Can you tell me if you live nearby?" the old man said. "Just nod your head."

Should she tell him? What if he was one of them?

But the thought popped into her head: He was the man from the cabin. Mystery Guy. This was the cabin. There was nothing else on this side of the bridge. She started trying to work out if that made him safe, but the words were out before she could stop them.

"My mom's hurt."

The sound of her voice shocked her. It made everything more real: the cabin; the old man; everything. It was as if everything had been waiting to catch up with her. And now it had.

He seemed surprised that she'd spoken. His eyebrows went up. "OK. You're mom's hurt. Did she have an accident? Can you tell me where she is?"

Her throat tightened. "At home," she said. "Ellinson. You have to call an ambulance."

An ambulance. Doctors. Medicine. But she kept seeing the red-haired man standing in the hallway, the calm excitement in his face. *Hey, cunt. How're you holding up?*

Tears welled and fell, hot and intimate on her cheeks. Something had gone out of the world when she saw her mother lying there. Something had gone and now the world was huge tilting spaces.

"Hey," the old man said, raising his hand. "It's OK, don't cry. It's OK. We'll figure this out. Don't cry."

"You have to call an ambulance," Nell said again, her voice small and ugly to herself. Stupid thoughts like the old man looked like the guy on one of her mom's CDs. Kris Kristofferson. In the mornings sometimes her mom put on "Me and Bobby McGee." Nell liked it.

"There's no phone here," the old man said. He looked around the room as if there might be a phone in spite of what he'd just said. "I don't . . . Is your mom . . . Is anyone else with her?"

Stupid useless thoughts. Bobby McGee. Her mom's skirt pushed up all wrong. The pale light still coming through the front door's little frosted window, falling on her bare legs.

"Josh," she said. "My brother."

"Was Josh hurt, too?"

"I don't know."

There's no phone here. And the blood coming out. Bits from TV hospital dramas flashed. The word "hemorrhage." How could there be no phone? He was lying. She'd made a mistake.

"You have to call an ambulance," she repeated.

"There's no phone here," he said. "I'm sorry. There's no electricity. I'm not lying to you, I promise. You don't have a cell phone, do you? You know? Like one your mom maybe has?"

She shook her head. The home screen on her mother's iPhone was a picture of her and Josh, grinning into the camera. Josh had kept changing it for pictures of rock bands until her mother had put a security code in.

"Me neither," he said. He kept looking around the room. There was a tremor of panic in him. The room's stillness and the stove's soft breath were terrible, because of the blood coming out of her mother and all the time passing and the world just going on, not caring, not even knowing.

"You have to *do* something," she wailed, trying again to get up, crying out when the pain in her legs jammed her.

"Hey, easy, take it easy. You'll hurt yourself if you try'n put weight on it. Come on now, calm down. We're going to figure something out, I promise."

But hopelessness crushed Nell, and she sobbed, her hands over her face. She thought of her grandmother, who lived in a retirement complex with a bright turquoise pool like a big mosaic tile. In Florida.

"I'll tell you what," the old man said. "How about I start? You must be wondering. First, my name's Angelo. My dad used to own this place, and now it's mine. I came out here to . . . Well, for a sort of vacation. Yesterday—no, the day before—I found you lying in the snow outside. You were unconscious. I could see you were hurt, so I brought you inside and built up the fire to keep you warm. You've had a fever. In fact, hold on, you must be thirsty."

Nell lowered her hands and pressed herself back against the couch. Angelo struggled across the floor and hauled himself up on the sink. His body shuddered with the effort.

"I have this thing wrong with me," he said, filling a tin mug with water from the tap. "Something in my back's gone wrong, and it means my legs don't work properly. Which is why—" He lowered himself, carefully, wincing, back onto his knees. "—which is why I'm crawling around like this. Here. Go ahead. It's just regular water. Don't drink it too fast."

But she couldn't drink it at all. She watched her hands taking the cup from him, but her throat was twisted shut and she couldn't stop the tears. She wanted to be sick, but the sickness stuck inside her. It just kept rising and knotting and not coming out.

"Well, have a sip when you're ready," Angelo said, moving away from her, back to the chair, propping himself up again. "But you should try, because you'll feel better."

Nell stared into the cup. The smell of the tin and the stony water reminded her of when they went camping. She couldn't control her thoughts. More and more useless thoughts.

"What's your name?" Angelo said.

Nell forced herself to swallow. Not speaking was worse. Not speaking left her raw to the new way the world was, giant and ugly and empty. She had a brief image of cities full of dark traffic and millions of strangers.

"Nell Cooper," she said.

"Nell Cooper. OK, that's a start. And you live across the ravine, in Ellinson, right?"

She nodded. She didn't know if she should be telling him, but she didn't know what else to do.

"With your mom and dad and your brother, Josh?"

Swallowing the tears hurt. Brought all the times she'd cried before, then her mother close, saying, Shshsh, Nellie, it's all right, it's all right . . .

"Just my mom and Josh."

Angelo paused. "Got it," he said. "And your mom's hurt, and maybe Josh, too, so we have to try to figure out how to get help." Another pause. "Can you tell me what happened?" he said.

"There was a man," Nell said. "He . . . There was a man in our house and he hurt my mom. She said they were still there when I came in and she told me to run. I didn't want to run. I didn't want to run, I should've stayed with her but she told me to run." More tears she couldn't swallow. Couldn't. But she did. Forced herself. The way her mother had pretended to be angry. She'd pretended to be angry because . . .

"Well, I know one thing," Angelo said. "If your mom told you to run, she meant it, and you did the right thing to listen to her. You did *exactly* the right thing. Now, let's look at what else. Do you think Josh might have run, too? To a neighbor maybe?"

Nell tried to see it. Josh running to Sadie's. Sadie calling the police, an ambulance screaming through Ellinson, pulling up outside their house.

But she couldn't.

She shook her head.

Angelo opened his mouth to say something—then changed his mind. He looked around the room again. His hands were shaking, Nell could see. Then he seemed to come to a decision.

"All right," he said. "Here's what I think. I think . . . I'm going to put on every piece of clothing I've got and I'm going to try to get across the bridge. My car's on the other side, so I can get to your house. To a phone, at least. I don't know if I'm going to be able to make it like this, but I'll try. You can't move on that leg, so you're going to have to stay here. But I'll build up the fire and—"

"You can't," Nell said.

He looked at her. "What?"

The words felt dead in her mouth. Her whole body seemed to collapse into a new hopelessness. "You can't go over the bridge," she said. "It's gone. You have to go over the tree."

27

Keep your friends close, but keep your enemies closer. Something like that. Valerie had read it or heard it. Back at the station she waited until Carla was gathering up her things. It was just after nine in the evening.

"I haven't eaten all day," Valerie said to her. "Want to grab a bite?"

There was only the slightest hesitation, but she clocked Carla having to stop, calculate, recalibrate. There was, Valerie decided, a Carla scheme of things. A Carla *agenda*. Balanced on a wire. The woman's physical composure was in fact a pitch of tension so extreme, it manifested itself as calm. It satisfied Valerie, with a kind of thrilled dread.

"Sure," Carla said, as with pleasant surprise. She opened her mouth to add something, stopped, started again. "What did you have in mind?"

They went to a tapas bar a few blocks away. Valerie's strategy: she wasn't hungry. Tapas you could pick at. The restaurant was low-lit, less than a dozen mosaic tables and a compact, tempting bar at one end, its liquid treasures glimmering. To drink or not to drink? That was the question. But Carla ordered a glass of Shiraz, apparently without conflict. Which would make me *not* drinking look suspicious, Valerie thought. Bluffs and double-bluffs. Fuck it. "Vodka tonic," she said to the waiter.

Valerie didn't, she now realized, have a plan for how this should go. Having made the decision to play along, Carla appeared relaxed. Tired, even, which made Valerie doubt herself. Maybe Carla was just an irritatingly efficient person who didn't wear her traumas on her sleeve?

"Sacramento, mainly," Carla said, in answer to Valerie's question of where she grew up. "My parents moved down to Phoenix in '02, but I was already at Quantico by then. My dad was bureau. He retired a few years back."

"You were always going to do it?"

"Pretty much. He was against it, actually. As was my mom. Although my mom never got over me giving up ballet when I was nine."

A sense of humor. OK. Not *entirely* the clipped machine her professional self suggested. Valerie took an injudiciously large gulp of her drink.

"I don't know what it was like for you," Carla said, "but I wanted it more or less as soon as I understood what it was."

"Catching bad guys," Valerie said.

"Yeah. You either have the disease or you don't."

"I know." And the disease either kills you or it doesn't. Goddammit.

Carla untied her ponytail—to redo it, tighter—and when her hair fell into its soft bob it changed her face, showed the nervily focused young girl she'd once been. Now filled with grown-up losses and regrets. Then she refastened the hair-tie, and the hard, locked-up adult was back.

"Too bad it doesn't leave much room for anything else," Valerie said.

The waiter, a very small old Hispanic guy with a mustache that looked too big for his face, brought their plates.

"You don't have anyone?" Carla asked, not really looking at her, when the waiter had gone.

For a vertiginous moment Valerie wondered if Carla was a lesbian. If she was, she might be reading this entirely differently. Shit. She really hadn't thought this through.

"No," Valerie said. "You?"

Carla took a green pitted olive from the bowl, scrutinized it briefly, then said, "No. Not for a long time," before popping it into her mouth.

Which brought them, all but palpably, to an impasse. Valerie's next words were out before she had a chance to rehearse them in her head.

"Listen," she said. "Are you here to evaluate me?"

Carla stopped chewing. Looked down at the table. Chewed again. Swallowed. Looked back at Valerie. "What?" she said.

"Does the bureau think I'm not doing my job?"

Carla looked genuinely baffled. "Why would you say that?" she said. She said it with such manifest perplexity, Valerie felt foolish.

She backed up slightly. "I don't know," she said. "Because those fuckers are still out there. On my watch. If you're here to put me under the microscope, I'd rather know, that's all."

Carla was still for a few moments, as if unpacking it all slowly. Then she said, "No way." And after a pause, "Everyone knows how hard you've been busting your ass on this."

Which stalled Valerie. Jesus, *was* she just being paranoid?

"You're worrying needlessly," Carla said.

"Am I?"

"Yes. I know how it feels. No matter how much you do, it's not enough if they're still out there. There's nothing to do but keep doing as much as we can until we get them."

"We don't get them all. Maybe we won't get these."

"No point thinking that way. You focus on the ones you got. You got Suzie Fallon's killer when no one else could."

The name still detonated something in Valerie, three years on. Still detonated everything. Everything the Suzie Fallon case had cost her. Everything it had made her become.

"You know about that?" she said.

"I was following it. It's why I jumped at the chance to work with you."

Flattery? Carla hadn't delivered it that way. Rather as if merely reporting a fact. It embarrassed Valerie. She felt her face warming. She also felt herself wanting to like Carla. And somehow not being able to. Her animal self couldn't. When she and Blasko met, their animal selves had recognized each other immediately. They'd joked about it, later, the pheromonal doom humans still lived under. This, with Carla, was the exact opposite: a recoil without reason.

Somehow she made it through the rest of the brief meal. Having been asked, the direct question—which had of course revealed *Valerie*'s agenda, *Valerie*'s scheme of things—left both women awkward again. Forced the conversation back into small talk: real estate prices; Myskow's sick leave (a duodenal ulcer); *Mad Men;* the world's current obsession with not eating carbohydrates. Valerie couldn't say why, but it still seemed to her that there was something Carla was holding back. Every time their eyes met, it was as if Carla were watching her through a two-way mirror.

When they'd paid their check and were gathering up their things, Valerie's phone rang. It was Laura Flynn. As per Valerie's instruction, she'd been back through more of the Katrina footage from the zoo. Raiders had shown up three times. Always on the edge of the crowd, always watching Katrina.

Carla made no pretense of not waiting for the outcome of the call.

"Don't get excited," Valerie said to her. "But it looks like we've actually got a suspect."

28

"The truth is," Claudia Grey's older sister had said to her during their last phone conversation a week ago, "you don't know *what* you're doing. You're too old for this rubbish. It's not as if you're bloody eighteen."

Claudia, who was twenty-six, with dark hair cut in a long bob and a promiscuous intelligence that in the wrong mood could do damage you wouldn't walk away from, had been sitting in the window of the shared two-room apartment (a sublet on the least crummy edge of Beach Flats), enjoying in spite of her sister's admonishment the thin Santa Cruz sunlight on her bare feet, the nails of which she'd just painted Cleopatra Gold. She'd pictured Alison in London, six thousand miles away and eight hours ahead, gathering up the supper dishes with the phone wedged under her chin while rain slithered down the dark windows. Years ago, when they *had* both been teenagers, Alison said to her: You know what you are? With all your brains and opinions? You're *unlikable*. Claudia had been hurt and vindicated. She'd clamped her jaws together for a few seconds, then answered: Yes, well, I'd rather be right than popular. And that dress, Alison, is *fucking execrable*.

"I mean how much longer is all this going to go on?" Alison said transatlantically, with crockery clattering. Claudia thought of how different it would feel over there, three days before Christmas: dark at four in the afternoon; the crisp mornings; maybe snow.

"How much longer is all what going to go on?"

"All this. Ms. Kerouac. Traipsing around stupid America."

"I'm not traipsing around. I've got a waitressing career. And an apartment. And a *boyfriend*. I'm a paragon of static legitimacy. I might as well be in Bournemouth, in fact."

"Do you have any idea how worried everyone is about you?"

"They're not worried," Claudia had said. "They're jealous."

The stubborn bit of her believed it. But there were other bits that didn't. If most of the people in her old life weren't worried about her, it was only because they'd written her off as mad. Three years ago, having realized that not only did she not want a career in academia, but that it would also probably make her kill herself, she'd dropped out of her Ph.D. ("Negative Capability and the Egotistical Sublime: A Comparative Study of George Eliot and Charles Dickens") at Oxford and entered a phase of uninspiring and unremunerative jobs in London—waitressing, bar work, admin that was glorified tea-making—living chaotically beyond her means, going out too much, getting wasted, sleeping with arty but going-nowhere men, and generally continuing the war inside herself between the conviction of her own potential greatness and the terror that she was just another too-smart girl who'd terminally lost the plot.

Then her grandmother died and left her (and Alison) some money. Not, as the game show hosts said, *life-changing* money, but enough to finance a temporary escape. Claudia had spent a year globe-trotting on a shoestring. Quick friendships, sunsets, exotic odors, dirt, surprising conversations, exhaustion. There were prosaic hours on asthmatic trains, of course, dismal hotels, the perpetual migraine of not being able to speak the language; but compensated for by the feeling of liberty and flux, of not knowing what tomorrow would bring, of seeing her reflection in the mirrors of unfamiliar rooms. She'd discovered the bliss of drinking a cup of coffee alone at an outside table while the French or Spanish or Italian or Greek Monday morning bustle surged around her. An expat cliché, yes, but still, the coffee was good, and the warm air around her bare ankles, and the frank lust of frequently stupid Mediterranean men with whom she nonetheless slept and sometimes enjoyed.

At times, she thought herself ridiculous. She thought herself ridiculous because she truly believed it was her duty to have an ex-
traordinarily rich, adventurous life filled with love and lust and ideas
and achievement and sensation, that expanded her mind and refined
her soul and freed her libido and deepened her understanding and
in the long run prepared her (subtextually, as it were) for a graceful
death. She knew how ridiculous this sounded. But she also knew it
sounded ridiculous because people were too shit and weak and damaged and scared and embarrassed to accept that that was what life
was for, if it was for anything. Better to laugh at your intensity than
weep at your mediocrity.

She'd saved California for her last stop. In San Francisco, with
less than a thousand dollars left in her fund, she'd decided—in an
occult rush of certainty—that she wasn't going home. Which pitched
her back into on-the-breadline—not to mention illegal—life. Since
then she'd got by working under the immigration radar for anyone
(bars, restaurants, parents in need of a cheap babysitter) willing to
bend the rules and pay her in cash. Most recently, thanks to an incredible stroke of luck, for Carlos Díaz, owner of the Whole Food
Feast in Santa Cruz. Carlos was himself the child of illegal immi-
grants. He had an avuncular soft spot for Claudia (harmless, she'd
decided), was tickled by her accent and IQ and sympathetic to putting one over on those sonsofbitches at the INS. She'd started the
job four months ago without any understanding other than that she
needed a place to rest up for a while and earn a minimal crust.

But Santa Cruz was seducing her. She liked her flatmate,
Stephanie, also a waitress, who was three years younger and happy
and uneducated and unreliable and untidy and unashamed of not
wanting much more from life right now than beach days and HBO
and white wine in the fridge and to be dating someone cute. She
liked Carlos and didn't mind the job. She'd made friends with a local misanthropic sculptress with whom she could talk books and
art and misanthropy. Most thrillingly disturbing: she'd met a very
not stupid guy, Ryan Wells, who owned a small digital editing company downtown, and with whom she'd been on a couple of dates

and whom she'd enjoyed kissing and with whom, barring some disaster, she was ready to have sex.

More than ready. There'd been six celibate months since her last fling, back in San Francisco, and a feeling of frustrated entitlement had crept in. "Boyfriend" was overstating the Case for Alison's benefit, but Ryan Wells definitely had potential. Probably for ultimate wreckage, but more than likely, since he was almost as well read as Claudia, with a healthy sense of the absurd and a quietly thudding quota of Eros, for something intense and rousing and usefully messy in the meantime. The first time they kissed, he'd put his hands on her hips and her body had said *Yes, yes, Jesus, yes.*

She was going to a barbecue party at his house this evening. The idea of a barbecue three days before Christmas made her internal clock queasy, but nonetheless.

"Look at you, all glamorized," Carlos said to her.

Claudia had finished her shift at the Feast and spent twenty minutes getting ready in the washroom. Light makeup, clean Levi's, a blue halter top, thrift store suede jacket, and sandals it was still warm enough (sixty-two degrees, for all that it was December) to wear. Overnight essentials (shameless!) in a silver sequined bag. Ryan's place was across the river up off Graham Hill Road, and since her shift didn't finish till eight, there wasn't really time to trawl back to Beach Flats. He'd offered to come and pick her up, but she'd resisted. Told herself she wanted to be able to change her mind (fat chance, you *wanton*) right up until she got to his front door; but there was prickly independence in it, too: Ryan had money. Not a fortune, but enough to make her not want to feel like a needy British pauper female, Oxford genius or not. There was a city bus that would drop her less than ten minutes from his house.

"This is just for the public transport," Claudia said to Carlos. "I've got stillies and a cocktail dress to slip into when I get there."

"You got *what* and a cocktail dress?"

"Stillies. Stilettos. *High heels.* God, it's a drag dealing with the developing world."

"Never mind that, you behave yourself. I heard what British

women are like. It's an illness with you people because you don't get enough vitamin D."

"See you Monday," Claudia said.

"Buenas noches, chiquita. Have fun."

The bus dropped Claudia at Graham Hill Road and Tanner Heights. Walking up the incline (good call on the sandals) she was—for the umpteenth time, and deeply at odds with her wider politics—calmed by the cleanliness of American suburbia. Languid cedars and pristine asphalt. Silence. No litter. The spirit of Updike hovering over the crisp lawns and dozing autos. This was her entire psychology in microcosm, she knew: charmed by the things it most mistrusted. She opened her nostrils and inhaled the perfume of affluent domesticity. She'd stopped smoking when she moved to Santa Cruz, and she was grateful for it at moments like this. Not that her head wasn't a mess. A perpetually fizzing cocktail of abstract thought and concrete impulses. She was still married to Literature, to Ideas, to the Life of the Mind—still married, yes, but in the raw beginning of a trial separation. When she thought of her room at Oxford, the walls of books with spines cracked in testimony to dogged engagement, when she thought of how clearly she'd sensed the scale of the imaginative relationship—what the reading life *demanded* (which was, in the end, to keep finding room for everything human, no matter how ugly or beautiful or strange)—it was as if she'd turned her back on her child. Out of fear. That she simply wasn't up to it. That Literature would keep reminding her that she wasn't big enough for Literature. And if she wasn't big enough for Literature, how could she be big enough for Life? There was a flashier explanation for what she'd done—that she'd grasped the truth that for someone like her, there was a danger reading would become a *substitute* for living, that her wiser self had rebelled against it, righteously—but she mistrusted that, too. It was, she thought, the Devil's explanation. Meanwhile God waited, sad and patient, for her to come back to him.

Christ, Claudia thought, having gone through the familiar mental loop, *if that isn't an argument for getting my brains fucked out, I don't know what is.*

Twenty paces ahead of her, just before the tree-lined bend that would, according to the Waze app on her twitchy phone, take her within a hundred meters of Ryan's house, a dark-haired, unshaven guy was tightening the wheel nuts on the rear offside of his RV.

She thought: *Weird spot for an RV.*

But she'd been in this country long enough to know not to be surprised by anything.

29

"Fuck," Xander said. "We got a flat."

"I'll do it," Paulie said.

They had been driving for two days. The wrongness of events in Colorado had set Xander in motion. The road soothed him, though the signs were like barbed wire if he tried to decipher them. The RV had a talking GPS. A guy with a classy robotic voice. It was a weird thing to have with you, a sort of friend that could see everything though it was calm and blind.

Xander sat with his hands on the steering wheel, eyes closed. Then he opened them. "You?" he said. "You'll take forever."

Paulie opened his mouth—then closed it again. They'd entered a phase now in which he had to choose very carefully when to speak and what to say. Xander's will, which had been for so long like a supportive suit snug around him, had started to feel different. It still fit snugly, but there was heat and mass and pressure now in its embrace. Paulie had an image of a picture he'd seen once as a child: a torture device from olden days, a big metal mummy case lined with spikes. You put the person inside it and when you closed it around them the spikes went into the flesh. Incredibly, he remembered what it was called: the iron maiden. Which—these connections your brain could make shocked him, disturbed him—was where the rock band must've got their name from: Iron Maiden. How weird that there were these connections you made. Was the whole world like that? Was everything somehow connected to everything else? He imagined it: the whole planet and everything in it just a massive web, things like cigarette butts and ants eventually joined up with things like presidents and the space shuttle. It made him feel sick, as if he'd just looked down and realized he was standing right on the edge of a sheer drop into nothingness.

Xander hadn't moved. Now he turned in his seat and looked at Paulie. It had always been occasionally pleasurable to make Paulie suffer, but of late it had become a necessity. The warm feeling of contempt he could summon—watching Paulie's face become a big vivid thing full of easily hateful details—was a cheap but satisfying drug. And the longer he went without doing what he needed to do, the more he relied on it. It had been too long. Not doing what he needed to do started a sound, whispers you could barely hear at first, like the fever when he was in Mama Jean's house, that grew steadily, moment by moment, day by day, until it was deafening, as if his head—as if his whole body—were filled with a furious mass of bees. Only doing what he needed to do made them disappear. For a while. Colorado, two days ago? That didn't count. He hadn't done it right (the image of the little brown milk jug tormented him), and not doing it right, it turned out, was almost worse than not doing it at all.

"You got any idea how fucking useless you are?" he said to Paulie now.

Paulie looked away, down into his lap first, then out the side window of the RV. The vehicle was filled with evening sunlight. Xander let the words swell in the silence between them. Even doing just that eased some of the muscles in his neck. He could feel how badly Paulie wanted to get out, how the air outside would very slightly thin the pressure he was putting on him.

"You think you're doing something?" he asked Paulie. "You're not doing something. *I'm* doing something. What you do? That's nothing. They don't even feel it. They're not even *there*."

"When we pass a store, we need to get some water," Paulie said, unbuckling his seat belt.

"You know what I'm telling you is the truth, don't you?" Xander said, smiling.

Paulie didn't answer. His face was hot.

"You know you're scared of them, don't you? How do you live with that? Being scared of them. What do you think they're going to do to you?"

Paulie didn't answer. Looked everywhere but at Xander. It was as if Xander had him in an invisible net.

"It's like carrying you on my goddamned back," Xander said, unbuckling his own seat belt.

Paulie bowed his head. His smell wafted to Xander. Damp canvas and sour socks and stale sweat. Paulie, Xander thought, not for the first time, didn't wash often enough.

"I'm just saying," Paulie said, staring hard at the dashboard. "We need water. I'm fucking starving, too. There was a McDonald's back there on 17."

"Like carrying you on my goddamned *back,*" Xander repeated. "Do you hear me?"

"Fine," Paulie said.

"Do you hear me?"

Paulie made a quick movement with his head, as if suddenly realizing *his* neck muscles were seizing up. "I said *fine,*" he said.

Xander kept the invisible net tight for a few seconds, watching Paulie breathing hard through his long, narrow nostrils. Then he opened the driver's door and jumped down out of the RV.

30

It took Claudia half a dozen more paces to start thinking it would be a good idea to be talking to someone on her cell phone as she passed this guy. Not because she thought he was dangerous, but because there was enough in his aura—and enough on her radar—for her to feel sure he was going to try to engage her in an exchange she didn't want to have. (It wasn't strictly true that she didn't think he was dangerous—she was a woman, alone, approaching a man on a stretch of road screened by trees from residential view—but it was strictly true that she was suppressing the thought that he might be dangerous. She was thinking, too, of all the times she'd had the maddening argument in the wake of some woman's assault or rape or murder in a lonely spot, the argument made—with insidious, shoulder-shrugging reasonableness—that surely it wasn't very smart of the woman to be walking alone in such a place? Surely the woman was making herself fair game? Surely the woman was, when you got right down to it, *asking for it?* Half the time it was women who made this argument. Women who didn't seem to understand that what they were defending wasn't a woman's right to move through the world as freely as a man, but rapists' and murderers' right to do their thing so long as there weren't likely to be witnesses.) She'd started scrolling through her contacts for Ryan's number (*Hi, it's me. I'm two minutes away. Mix me a gin and tonic!*) when the RV guy—less than fifteen paces now—yanked the wheel brace from the final tightened nut, straightened up, stretched, arching his back, and said: "Miss, you wouldn't happen to know if I'm going the right way for Paradise Park, would you?"

Adrenaline, in spite of herself. Her knees sent the delirious message that they were ready to sprint. But the stubborn social protocols kicked in, too: *You don't just turn and run away from a guy because he asks you directions.* To which another inner voice responded: *How many women have ended up dead because they didn't?* She had an image of Alison watching all this on a screen on the other side of the world. Thought how much, in spite of all the wounds they'd inflicted on each other, she loved her sister. The habit Alison had of blowing her fringe out of her eyes.

How far back down the hill was the nearest house? Another three paces. She speeded up. Walk with a purpose. Show no fear. Show brisk entitlement. Show *consequences if you try to fuck with me, dickhead.*

"I really don't," she said, smiling. "Sorry."

Keep walking. Cheery, yes, but with undeflectable purpose. Paradise Park was, she knew, just slightly northwest of where they were. But that would mean stopping to give him directions. That would mean him saying: You got a map on your phone? Do you mind if I take a look?

"I know it's around here somewhere," he said, opening the RV's driver door and slinging the wheel brace inside. "I've got a map in here, too, but I'm damned if I can find it."

In five paces, she'd be level with him. It was all right. He'd turned his back on her. He was searching for his map. And he'd ditched the tool. It wasn't *that* situation after all. Forgivable paranoia. But keep walking. The clothes don't match what that camper would've cost. Rental. Stop fretting.

But he turned back to face her too quickly. Exactly as she drew level.

And he was holding a tire iron in his right hand.

31

Time cracked.

One half—Claudia's past—gathered on one side of a line of white light. The other half—her future—rushed up in a mass of blackness. She was caught, while all her reason devoted itself to the simple imperative—RUN!—in a neural snarl-up, because despite the imperative, the tire iron was already coming and the reflex to shield her head was jamming the one in her legs.

The world pitched and swung its details: the glittering asphalt; the cedars' deep green; his smell of rubber and burnt oil and sweat; the tire iron's flecks of rust; the surprised, greasy face of a second guy who appeared, leaning out of the driver's door, long reddish hair swinging bright sickles around his bearded jaw.

Then her arms were up to protect her head and the iron hit her in her gut and the air flew out of her lungs and all she knew was that she was never going to breathe again. Something hard hit her knees and she realized she'd collapsed and his hands were on her. A second of intense pressure on her throat. Her weight lifting and her sandaled feet touch-typing the air. Impact. Her back slammed against the RV's white flank and a voice saying Jesus fucking Christ, Xander, Jesus fucking Christ, with the soundtrack of suburban birdsong still audible around it. She had an image of Alison's face distended in horror. She realized as if for the first time that this had happened to women from the beginning, got a glimpse of the billions, living and dead, the scorched sorority who could only watch, who could offer her nothing except that this would be her unique instance of the historical constant, *her* rape, *her* death. All her childhood and adolescence and womanhood, everything she'd done, so many conversations and kisses and laughs and thoughts, so many things taken for granted because they were part of a world she never imagined would be changed like this. Like this. By something coming into it and blasting a divide between what she had once been and what she would be forced to become hereafter. If she lived.

If she lived.

In the blur of him lifting her and her left elbow hitting the door and her heels cracking against something and the overwhelming sickening reality of strong hands and the smell of a cramped space of vinyl and gasoline and stale sweat and the panic that swelled her every cell, Claudia thought: *I want to live. I want to live. I want to live.* All her life's schemes and nuances reduced in these seconds to a singularity: Survive. Whatever happens, you must survive. You *must* survive.

She couldn't see properly. The struggle to breathe kept dumping darkness on her, blacking her out. She was aware of the uselessness of her limbs. The windscreen loomed up, the dash choked with litter, Styrofoam cups and crushed doughnut boxes. The dark-haired guy's voice saying: Get the ties, get the fucking *ties*. Her immediate understanding that "ties" meant tying her up. Which released fresh screaming urgent weakness in her wrists and elbows and ankles and knees. She still, it seemed, hadn't breathed since he hit her. She still, it seemed, hadn't made a sound. Her arms and legs were light and adrift, though she was vaguely aware they were trying to fight him. *Him.* The reality sickened her, that he was a person, with a voice and a face and a smell and a history and a will that had brought him here, that had closed the distance between him and her, that had introduced them to each other. The little girl having her breakfast in the bright kitchen in Bournemouth, her bare legs swinging—and him, here, now. All those moments leading to this one. All those moments leading to her death.

A motorcycle went past.

Please see this. Please see this.

But it was gone. No change in the receding engine sound. No sign. No hope. And what could its rider have seen anyway? The driver's door was closed. Nothing to see but a parked RV. Nothing to see.

"Fuck," the red-haired guy said. "It's her."

"What?"

"It's the girl from the café."

"What?"

"From the goddamned café. This afternoon. Jesus."

"What the fuck are you talking about?" His hand around her throat tightened.

"When I got the coffee. This afternoon. Jesus, Xander, when we stopped to get coffee. Fucking Whole Food whatever. She's one of the waitresses."

Claudia had gotten barely a glimpse of the second guy. Hadn't recognized him. If he'd been in the Feast, she hadn't noticed him.

But the world was full of women not noticing the men who were noticing them.

The dark-haired guy had her pressed across the two front seats with the bulk of his weight on her. The gearstick's knob was digging into her spine. Her left wrist was wedged under the handbrake. Consciousness was dark-edged. There would be full darkness, an eclipse, if she didn't get oxygen soon. He still had his hand around her throat. His other hand pinned her right wrist under her bottom.

"Will you just get the motherfucking ties?" the dark-haired guy said, looking up and through the windscreen. To check the motorcyclist wasn't coming back, Claudia thought. To make sure absolutely no one was seeing this. And she knew absolutely no one was. No one and nothing. She was alone. The clean curve of road that at other times kids would be riding their bikes down. The stately cedars and plump pines. The birds singing and the soft golden Californian evening. None of it cared. None of it was any use. None of it was even aware. All her life she'd indulged a playful anthropomorphism. Gone. You were nothing to the world. The world was nothing to itself.

The hand on her throat opened. She still couldn't inhale properly. Swallowed one lump of air like a hard-boiled egg. It made her want to vomit.

Which she might have done, had he not yanked her up and slammed her head into the dashboard.

32

"Wait up, Skirt," Blasko called to Valerie. She was on her way out of the station. It was just after eight in the evening. The sound of his voice behind her shifted her body's gear. She'd been craving it. Expecting it. Dreading it. She had no right to anything from him, but here it all was. The wrecked but indestructible entitlement. It was hopeless. She waited for him. Excitement and sadness and fear.

"Let's not have the pointless conversation," he said.

"Which one?"

"The one that ignores the way this is."

"What way is this?"

He didn't need to answer, since they were looking at each other. Valerie felt all the objections gathering. In a moment the objections would be a crowd with one voice and one demand: *Leave him alone. Either tell him everything or leave him alone.* And if she told him everything, what difference would it make?

"Let's get a drink," she said, and felt as soon as the words were out the deep thrill of releasing herself into doing the wrong thing. She hadn't known what she was going to say until the words were out of her mouth. Then within seconds she was walking with him. She was going somewhere with him. She was *with* him.

They went in his car, left hers at the station. I'll pick it up later, she said. Which alone was an admission of the night's possibilities.

He just nodded. Understood. There was no not understanding each other. That had always been their joy. And, naturally, their curse.

Their after-work spot, formerly, had been Juanita's, a tequila bar on Divisadero, so they didn't go there. Instead, to a new-looking place—Pelican Bar—on Folsom, with a dark interior and a red neon strip running the length of the black vinyl bar, which was tokenly decked with a strip of gold tinsel and sprinkled glitter. Less than a dozen patrons, small tables, subdued music courtesy of the bartender's iPhone and Bose. Tom Waits, by the time they were sitting with their drinks, though Valerie recognized nothing that followed it. When she was a teenager, life without music had been unthinkable. Now she never listened to it.

"This thing's taking its toll," Blasko said. The Case, obviously. It wasn't a question. Their corner table had a little candle in a dark red shot glass. Valerie had an image of herself slumped at the desk alone in the incident room, the huge photos of the dead women above her and around her, like objects of worship.

"It's OK to just say I look like shit," Valerie said. "I know I do."

He glanced at her. You never look like shit to me. Then he looked down into his drink. The damage had damaged him. He was sure he was doing the wrong thing too. But sadness was this moment's enemy. Whatever this moment was. Sadness or madness, Valerie thought. Take your pick.

"It's been going on a long time," she said.

"What'd you get from Reno?"

"It's our guys. I'm sure of it. Coroner's report's a formality. Victim had an alarm clock wedged in her mouth." The ugliness of the words shut both of them up. Talking about the Case wasn't an alternative to talking about them. It *was* talking about them. A Case had ruined them. A Case had left her with a miscarriage and him with his heart shredded. What had changed since then? Nothing. Except that thanks to it, she was a better cop. A cop who didn't believe in anything and had no trouble not seeing the victims as people. A cop empty of everything bar the fascinating mathematics of solving the flesh-and-blood riddles. Until now. Suddenly Valerie regretted the impulse that had brought her here. She almost—*almost*—got up and left.

"Last time I was at my sister's," Blasko said, sensing it, changing tack, pulling them—just—out of danger, "we were sitting at the dining table after lunch, and the kids were arguing in the next room. You know, Jenny's nine now. Walt's going on six."

This was a gift of his. To remind her of the absurd jewels still in the world, in spite of the horrors. She didn't know what he was going to tell her. Only that with the shift in his voice, her body relaxed. Love. Still love. Or the remains of it. Embers not out. Just a couple of tender breaths would be enough. (Until she told him everything. Then a different blaze. She shut the thought down.) Just a couple of tender breaths and she could go back to being a worse cop than she was now. Wouldn't that be what love cost her? Wasn't it the same transaction, in reverse?

"So, the kids are going at it," Blasko said, "and we can hear things are getting pretty heated in there and Serena's rolling her eyes, getting ready to deal with it—then Walt storms in looking outraged and wounded and says Jenny called him an ass-burger."

Valerie smiled. Felt how alien the sensation had become. Walt was still in diapers the last time she'd seen him. Jenny an imperious little thing, inseparable from her soft toy, a monkey named, inexplicably, Earl. (*If we have a kid,* Blasko had said one day from the shower, while Valerie was brushing her teeth, it'll be a girl and we should name her Daisy. It was how they had talked about it. They'd known they had a little allowance of talking about it not-seriously before they'd have to have a real conversation. Until Nick, Valerie had never imagined herself having a child. Then love. And the shocking intuition that there was a whole other gear of herself she could shift into: motherhood. Make a baby with Nick. It had terrified and thrilled her.)

"He's followed by Jenny," Blasko said, "who's looking guilty as hell, but sort of delighted with herself too."

"I don't blame her," Valerie said. "'Ass-burger' is pretty good."

"It's better than that," Blasko said. "Serena turns to Jen and says very seriously, 'Did you call Walt an ass-burger?' Jenny cracks up. She's really, genuinely laughing, in spite of obviously being in deep shit. Serena's like: This isn't funny, young lady, that's not a very nice thing to say to your brother. But Jen can't stop laughing. Even Walt by this time is sort of fascinated by her reaction. Then Jen goes: '*Asperger's*. I told him he had *Asperger's*. Jesus. *Ass-burger!* Walt is such a dummy!'"

Valerie was laughing quietly. Blasko smiled, took a sip of his Scotch. "Poor Walt," he said. "He was the only one who wasn't laughing. He's standing there completely baffled. Eventually, though, seeing he was outnumbered, he joined in."

It was too easy. Too good. *I've missed you. I miss you.* Present tense.

But the damage she'd done was there too, in all the spaces the laughter didn't cover. And when she stopped laughing, here they were again. Sitting looking at each other, with the incontestable facts of their history like a grinning genie between them. Three years. And now, again, the certainty of not being alone in the world. It was lovely. It was awful. And it was missing the central fact. The untold tale.

"Are you seeing anyone?" he said.

Oh. OK. We're going straight there. Valerie felt the bar open onto a void. Her view of the universe was that it was Godless and meaningless, but threaded with random forces whose accidental job it was to make you think there was a twisted plot to the whole thing.

She shook her head, no. "You?"

"What do you think?"

She knew the answer. Otherwise, what were they doing here?

"What do you want?" he said.

Ask me something easier, Valerie thought. She was remembering the way he looked at her when he'd walked in on her with Carter. Not anger. Capitulation. A complete understanding that she'd done the thing there would be no coming back from. In that instant she'd seen his whole life gather in his dark features, as if all its details had rushed together to receive this giant betrayal. A disinterested part of herself had been merely fascinated by the change in his face, the fracture. Now there was always a disinterested part of her fascinated by things: hearts she'd broken; murderers she'd caught; corpses mutilated beyond recognition; a fetus the size of a shrimp in a doctor's rubber-gloved hand. Years ago, when she was just out of the academy, a seasoned detective had said to her: You want to work Homicide? Get rid of your heart. Your heart won't help you. Rip your heart out and put a big, lidless eyeball in its place. Feel nothing. See everything. Well, now she did.

"I want not to do anyone any harm," Valerie said, at last.

Blasko sat back in his chair and looked at her.

"Especially you. I just—"

"I'll consider myself warned."

Which silenced both of them again. It was impossible, Valerie thought. He might think he wasn't still angry with her—he might think a part of him didn't still *fucking hate her*—but he was kidding himself. For all the breeziness, he was still enough of the mess she'd made of him. *This is wrong,* she told herself. *This is so wrong. You might as well tell him now and get it over with.*

But even thinking it stirred her excitement. Life coming back into her life.

"You haven't told me what you're working on," she said. Stalling.

He dipped his finger into his glass, stirred the ice cubes. Weighing up, Valerie knew, whether to accept that they'd veered away from the question of what they were going to do. She realized, too, that he'd come here not entirely knowing what he wanted. Aside from wanting to go to bed with her. *That* didn't change. In spite of everything, being near each other was enough to establish sexual necessity. Even now (as soon as she let her mind go that way) the thought of his hands on her, the image of straddling him and easing herself down onto his cock—started the familiar sweet ache between her legs. It was a delight, the irreverent reliability of their lust. She remembered lying with him in bed after the fourth or tenth or twentieth time they'd made love, thinking: *This is wealth. We're millionaires with this.* At which the stubborn cosmic dramatist in her had whispered: *Yeah, but it will all have to paid for, someday.*

And it had been.

"Nothing that wouldn't spoil the ass-burger story," he said.

She understood. Tech forensics was, broadly, either financial crime or child pornography. She'd seen some of the images. Used to be you needed to be physically present at a murder scene to see the worst of the dark side. Now you could see it on your laptop, while drinking a beer or talking to your mom on the phone. She wondered what it had done to him. What it was doing. The disinterested lidless eyeball was intrigued. *I shouldn't have been a cop,* she thought. *I should've been a fucking scientist.*

"Do you know how it felt when I knew I'd be coming back here?" he said.

"How did it feel?"

"Inevitable." He paused. "Like a guilty verdict."

His phone rang.

"Goddammit," he said when he hung up.

"You have to go."

"Yeah."

Saved by the bell. Temporarily.

Valerie would rather have stayed where she was and let him go back without her, but she needed her car. And in any case, stay where she was and do what? End up with another Callum? The Case had taken her to the place where any conscious activity not devoted to the Case was immoral. She thought of all the hours she'd spent with the files and photographs. The risible phrase "off duty." There were more off-duty hours waiting for her, an army of them, drumming their fingers.

They drove back in silence, the city's lights sliding over them, the car's interior rich with the impasse of desire and fear. Valerie knew the only way she'd find out how she'd react to him kissing her was if he kissed her. Part of her wanted it, to be forced into letting her body decide.

Bullshit. She knew what her body would decide. She just didn't know what decisions the rest of her would make, afterwards.

When they pulled up at the station lot, he killed the engine and the two of them sat there, staring out the windshield. Somewhere along the way, he'd switched his phone to silent. She could hear it vibrating in his jacket pocket.

"So?" he said.

"I don't know."

"But you know what I was thinking about back there in the bar."

"Yes."

Pause.

"It's what I was thinking about too."

But not only that.

"I'll come by and see you later," he said—then when he saw her about to reply: "Don't say anything. Just don't answer the door if you don't want to."

Oh God.

She was shaking her head. But she didn't say anything. It was terrible how the flash of desire had brought the three years of loneliness upon her. It was terrible the way the naturalness of being with him just *declared* itself, beyond argument. The human *heart* was a room of terrible things.

He didn't kiss her. The vibrating phone, amongst other things, said *not yet.* Instead they got out. He took her hand briefly. Their mutual visibility was shocking. Then he turned and hurried away into the station. Valerie, thrilled and appalled at herself, headed to her car.

She'd got in and fastened her seat belt when she noticed, four cars down in the opposite row, Carla York's black Jeep Cherokee. With Carla in it. She was sitting in the driver's seat with her head leaning against the window, staring straight ahead. Her posture said she either didn't know she was being observed—or didn't care. Her mouth looked slack. Her whole face's tightness was weirdly compromised.

Valerie sat and watched. It seemed odd to her that Carla hadn't seen her. She would have heard the car door, surely. Didn't you automatically look up?

Carla lifted a crumpled tissue and blew her nose. Sniffed.

Crying? Jesus.

On the one hand, so what? Carla was law enforcement. No less likely to have the odd private meltdown than anyone else in the game. On the other, it shocked Valerie to see the prim package unraveled. It was poignant and obscene.

More out of curiosity than sympathy (*let's be honest with ourselves, Valerie*) she got out of her car and walked down to Carla's. Halfway there, Carla looked up and saw her. Valerie expected her to be startled, to be embarrassed, to attempt the hasty facial reboot. But Carla just watched her approach without expression, then rolled down the driver's window. Her nose was red. It was that sort of face, Valerie now realized, ravaged by the shedding of even two or three tears.

"Hey," Valerie said. "You OK?"

Carla smiled. As at the minor nature of whatever had upset her. "Yeah," she said. "I'm fine. Just one of those days."

"What's the matter?"

"Really, it's nothing. I'm just . . ." She didn't finish. Instead shook her head and forced a laugh. She shifted her purse from her lap to the passenger seat, where her overcoat was slung over a slew of papers, a *Chronicle,* a couple of envelopes. The rest of the Cherokee's interior was immaculate. "I'm fine." Then, as a shorthand token dismissal Valerie knew she wasn't meant to take seriously: "Time of the month."

As in, whatever it is, I'm not discussing it.

"OK," Valerie said.

Carla sniffed, shook herself, sat up straight, and put her left hand on the wheel. "Hey," she said, "that was a great job with the zoo footage. I meant to say so earlier. I know everyone else had given up on it."

"I'd given up on it myself. It was just an alternative to counting sheep."

Carla nodded. "I get it," she said. "But still."

A few moments of neither of them knowing what to say. Long enough for Valerie to be slightly fascinated by the part of herself that still couldn't quite like Carla. Even now, having seen her vulnerable, something in her refused.

"Well, if you're sure you're OK," she said.

Carla reached for her seat belt. "I'm fine. And thanks. I'll see you tomorrow."

Back in her car, Valerie made an effort not to look toward Carla's. But Carla was still parked when she drove out of the lot. She was on her cell phone. She raised her hand to Valerie without a pause in her conversation.

33

Xander wasn't feeling well. The truth was he'd been feeling rough since they crossed into California. There was the need to correct the fuckup in Colorado (the dead woman without the jug pressed on his brain like a tumor; why, why, *why* in God's name had he let Paulie talk him into that?) but now it was as if his *body* were rebelling against the mistake as well, in spite of the little bitch he'd just grabbed. She'd just been *there*. A gift. The seconds it had taken him had been clean and quick and full of certainty. Sometimes it came together like that, in a kind of sweet rush, as if he weren't doing something new but recognizing something he'd done before, in a previous life or vivid dream. The empty road and the trees and her bare throat with the sunlight on it. It all gathered in his hands and face and then he was doing it and every movement was perfect and everything happened exactly as he knew it would. The exact opposite, in fact, of the mess in Colorado. He lay on the RV's bed-couch, shivering a little. His head was warm. His limbs were starting to ache. He'd heard if you crossed too many time zones or changed climates too often you got sick, but he'd never really believed it. Maybe there was something to it after all. Snow in Colorado. Sun in California. All the weather he'd passed through over the days and weeks and months was busy in his body, trying to sort itself out. He knew Paulie wanted to trade places with him because of his busted knee. Tough shit. Paulie would just have to grin and fucking bear it.

He should sleep. How long since he'd slept? He didn't know. Too long. There were the other times, when it didn't feel like sleep, but he never felt rested afterwards anyway, those times when he went back to being Leon and Mama Jean's house formed dense and electric around him. Those times were more exhausting than being awake in the regular world. When he'd finished doing what he had to do, all of that would stop. Imagine that! A time when the world just stayed the world, and Mama Jean's house never crammed up around him and Mama Jean herself would have nothing left to say. He'd be able to do anything, uninterrupted: watch TV, lie around drinking beer, swim in the ocean, eat his dinner.

Shivering, he turned onto his side and drew his knees up.

34

Back at the computer forensics lab, Nick Blaskovitch worked for an hour on the latest material from the Lawson case, but he knew he wasn't concentrating.

Valerie.

He hadn't lied. It *had* felt inevitable. When it became obvious that his father wasn't going to recover and the future's options had begun vaguely stacking up, he'd lived a double inner life. On the surface a range of schemes and alternatives. Underneath, the certainty that he would go back to San Francisco and Valerie would still be there and there would be no stopping himself. There was barely even a concession to the possibility that she would have found someone else. And when he did make the concession, his response to it was simple: He would take her away from whoever she'd found. Because whoever the poor bastard was and whatever she had with him, it wouldn't be what *they* had had.

What they had had. Recognition. Instant and ridiculous. Attraction, sure—he had the rare gift among men of knowing some women found him very attractive (he wasn't personally vain, but he had an ease in his own skin he was wise enough to know was a kind of power), and Valerie had the subsurface sexuality the right guys would know was worth seeking out—but the feeling of inevitability had caught both of them by delicious surprise. Half a dozen conversations. A drink after work. The heat of her standing next to him at the bar. They hadn't even discussed where the evening was going. Just got into a cab and within twenty minutes were in her apartment, kissing. The first touch—his hands on her waist—was a simple homecoming. After sex they lay on her bed like starfish. The impulse was to laugh. It was hilarious how good it had been. They didn't even congratulate themselves. Just accepted that they had come into their vast, unearned inheritance.

If some other guy were telling him all this about someone— some (dear God) Love of His Life Story in a bar—Nick knew he'd dismiss it. He'd feel sorry for him, this hypothetical loser. He knew he was, on the face of it, being ridiculous. Nor had quite all the damage she'd done healed. When he'd walked in on her and Carter at the apartment, she'd been sitting astride the guy, his hands on her ass, the groove of her lovely back wet with sweat from the dirty work she'd put in. Nick had stood there and stared for what felt like a long time, feeling the world changing. When you imagined these moments, you saw yourself exploding into action—violence, rage, grief, madness. But in fact, you just stood there, a spectator at your own crucifixion. The perverse part of you was relieved that the world had been once and for all proved to be a place of emptiness and betrayal and shit. It absolved you of having to hope.

It ought to have finished her for him.

But it hadn't.

The trouble was he'd understood why she'd done it. She'd turned and looked at him over her bare shoulder, and her face had been like a calm scream. Even in that moment, he'd known the understanding would eventually let him forgive her. Understanding was a twisted gift love gave you. Understanding had said, even as he was turning and walking out the door: *You'll find room for this. The hatred will burn out. It'll still be her.*

And three years later, it was still her.

The events and decisions that brought him back to San Francisco had been a gentle, irresistible choreography. He'd made the arrangements with a feeling of surrender, but with quietly building excitement too. Now that he'd done it, now that he was here, there was both deflation (the scale of the imaginative lead-up guaranteed it) and a deep vindication: because it hadn't changed for her, either. He'd seen the recognition in her face the first moment she looked up at him from her desk.

He got up now from his own cluttered desk, and stretched. It was ten after ten. Another hour's work, then he'd go back to his place, shower, change, drive around to Valerie's, and ring the buzzer for her apartment. If she answered, she answered. If she didn't . . .

Fuck that. She'd answer. It was foregone. It was in her when they'd said good-bye in the parking garage. In her hand. In her eyes. In the space between them where the current of life flowed.

He took a bathroom break and returned to his office to find a sealed manila envelope on his desk.

It was addressed in plain marker in small, neat capitals: NICHO-LAS BLASKOVITCH.

He opened it.

A filled-in form. Photocopied. He registered the word "clinic."

But that wasn't what first caught his eye. What caught his eye was a bright yellow Post-it stuck to the top right corner of the single sheet. The same tidy caps, smaller.

BABY KILLER, it said. NOTE THE DATE.

Cop reflexes were, mutedly, firing. A part of him was thinking: *latex gloves, prints, wait.* Someone had just been in here and left this. Who? But by now he'd noticed the content of one of the filled-in boxes:

PATIENT DETAILS
Surname:	Hart
First Name:	Valerie
Appointment Date:	06-23-10
Surgeon:	Dr. Paige
Procedure:	MVA

The "appointment date" and "procedure" entries had been high-lighted in pink. MVA. What the fuck was MVA? Nick groped, men-tally, while his eyes scanned, and the phrase "baby killer" carried on detonating.

THE BRYTE CLINIC. 2303 FELL STREET, SAN FRANCISCO, CA 94118.

He didn't recognize it.

He Googled "MVA procedure," though the wiser part of him turned what he read into déjà vu.

Up to 15 weeks' gestation, suction-aspiration or vacuum aspiration are the most common surgical methods of induced abortion. Manual vacuum aspiration (MVA) consists of removing the fetus or embryo, placenta, and membranes by suction using a manual syringe, while electric vacuum aspiration (EVA) uses an electric pump. These techniques differ in the mechanism used to apply suction, in how early in pregnancy they can be used, and in whether cervical dilation is necessary. MVA, also known as "mini-suction" and "menstrual extraction," can be used in very early pregnancy, and does not require cervical dilation.

Note the date.

06-23-10.

Three years ago. Less than two months after he'd left her.

35

Claudia woke an indeterminate time later lying on her back in what felt like complete blackness.

The first sensation was the desperate need to pee.

Three or four slight movements revealed her situation.

The worst situation.

She'd been bound and gagged.

And put in a box.

And buried alive.

Three, four, five seconds of blank denial. Not even the sound of her own breath, since shock held it.

Then an explosion of panic, her bound limbs trying to flail, knees and elbows and head thumping the flanks of the casket and her bladder emptying and *no no God no please no* and the reality like a demon in there with her saying *yes yes yes, this is it, this is what's happening, this is what's happening.*

Her mind was nothing, just a scream. Her actual scream was a hot rasp in her throat, since the gag in her mouth locked it in.

Buried alive. Buried alive. Buried—

A jolt.

And what the shock and panic had hidden: the hum of an engine.

She was moving.

She was in a vehicle. The RV.

Which meant she wasn't underground. Which lifted the mass of dead earth off her. Thank God. Thank—

The relief died. She wasn't underground *yet*.

Another explosion of panic, another timeless chaos of thrashing, her heart pounding in her throat, her head swollen with blood. She was suffocating. *Suffocation* was a corpse jammed on top of her, covering her, eyes, nose, ears, mouth. No matter what, she had to get out. No matter what "out" would mean. No matter what. She screamed again.

The vehicle slowed. Stopped.

Oh God oh God oh God—

A dozen pencils of light by her feet.

Air holes.

They didn't want her dead.

Yet.

Someone was moving. His shifting weight registered through the floor. Sound of latches snapping. The coffin lid yawned and the light cut her eyes.

"You woke me up," the dark-haired man ("Xander," she remembered) said to her quietly.

"I can't drive anymore," the other guy's voice said from up front. "Seriously, my fucking leg is killing me."

Claudia hadn't been aware that she was sobbing, until now. Snot rattled in her nose. The warmth from where she'd wet herself made itself felt, an absurd little flower of detail.

"You pissed yourself," Xander said. "Guess that means we're too late for a toilet stop."

Claudia screamed. The gag made it nothing. Her throat burned.

"OK," Xander said. "You better listen to me very carefully. Are you listening?"

The gag was sour. Somewhere far under the terror, her body was pounding with dehydration. The ties on her wrists and ankles might as well have been cheese wire. Frantic calculations: How long? Ryan would have called. Hours? Days? Missing. They wait twenty-four hours. Forty-eight. The police wait—don't they? Carlos. Not till

Monday. Stephanie. Would assume she'd stayed over. Her phone. Dropped in the struggle? Someone finds it. Someone—

"You need to do anything else?" Xander said, indicating the wet patch in her jeans. "Nod your head if you need to do anything else. I don't want you making a mess and stinking up the place."

You get out and somehow get them to untie your legs and then no matter what you run. You fucking *run*.

She nodded her head.

"Well, that may or may not be true," Xander said. "But if you've got any ideas about getting away, forget it." He reached around into the back of his jeans and pulled out an automatic handgun. Let her see it. Let her eyes track it as he lowered it slowly to her crotch and pressed it against her. Involuntarily her knees came up. She tried to twist away—but of course, she couldn't. He leaned in and held her legs under his forearm. Wedged the gun in harder.

"Be still," he said. "Hey. Be still."

She couldn't swallow. The gun hurt. She forced herself to stop struggling. Forcing herself to stop was like breaking her own heart.

"That's better. Wriggling like that isn't going to help you. It just *isn't going to help you*. Understand?"

She was sobbing again, though she was aware of it only as if she were spectating on someone else's distress. Beyond his head she could see the RV's snug domestic fittings. An electric kettle. A microwave. The last things you see. There was room in her for precise griefs: that she would never have tea and hot buttered toast with Alison in the family kitchen again. Nor hear her father's distinctive rattlecrash of the newspaper, as if he were trying to shake the truth out of it.

"All right," Xander said, withdrawing the gun and tucking it back into his jeans. "Let's get you up."

The manhandling forced intimacy. Every touch—his lifting her, helping her stand, his hands on her hips then transferred to her neck and the waistband of her jeans—stamped him on her body like a brand. The box she'd been in was the base of one of the vehicle's bed-seats. The bright orange cushions were on the floor behind him.

"Stand up straight," he said.

The blood unpacking itself in her legs made her unsteady. Her limbs were too full of sensation. All the sensation she didn't want. Death bulged and beat against her. Every second of life now testified to death.

He reached over to one of the kitchen drawers and brought out a large knife. Viciously serrated. Handgrip-molded black heavy-duty rubber handle. It looked military. Over his shoulder Claudia could see the red-haired guy turned around in the driver's seat, watching everything. His mouth was open, his thin face damp and tense. Beyond him the windscreen showed a headlit patch of scrub dissolving into darkness. No visible road. No sound of traffic, either. The middle of nowhere. She died in the middle of nowhere. She remembered Alison saying once: I don't mind how I die as long as it's not a *lonely* death.

Xander bent and cut the ankle ties. They were the cheap plastic ones the police sometimes used instead of steel cuffs. The blood pushed back into her numb feet.

"Walk," he said.

Four steps to what turned out to be the vehicle's bathroom. No windows. A round fluorescent light, flickering slightly. In spite of everything it reminded Claudia of the way your eyelid twitched when you were short of sleep. He grabbed her wrists and slashed through the ties.

She had her arms and legs free.

And they were no help.

"You've got two minutes," he said. "Don't bother trying to make a racket. There's no one out there to hear you. You touch that gag and I'll cut your tongue out."

It surprised her that he closed the door. There was no lock on it. Of course. She stood in the tiny space, shaking, choked by her own tears. The joy of having her limbs free. The uselessness of it. Her body was crammed with impulses with nowhere to go. Though she scanned every inch, the bathroom offered her nothing. White molded plastic, the sleep-deprived fluorescent, a chemical toilet, a showerhead, a sink barely big enough for both hands. No escape. No weapon. Nothing. She just stood there, feeling the moments hemorrhaging away. The need to remove the gag was overwhelming—but she didn't. I'll cut your tongue out. He expected her to use the toilet. At the thought of unzipping and pulling down her jeans, the touch of his hands came back on her flesh. There was a little mirror over the sink. When she looked in it, the sight hurt her. Her face wet with sweat and snot. Her left eye bruised. Blood crusted under each nostril. And the central horror of the gag. Her face—*her*—gagged. The love of her family—her mother and father, Alison—thousands of miles away and her, here, now, with this happening. She thought of them seeing her like this. Her father broken, her mother's gentle face made ugly by grief, Alison curled up on her bed, groaning like a wounded animal. Never see them again. Never—

The door opened. She realized a part of her had been thinking about breaking the mirror, a shard of glass . . . But it was reflective plastic, not glass, and he would have heard her do it and by the time those calculations were made she was out of time and there he was.

"Done or not," Xander said. "Out. We got a ways to go yet."

36

It was still dark when they stopped and took her out of the box.

"Go open up," Xander said to the other guy.

More manhandling to get her out of the RV. His hands under her arms, her heels whacking the steps down, scoring the dust when he dragged her toward the house.

She saw open dark land, an overgrown field, a sky full of stars. A dirt yard. Three low buildings and two old cars, one with its wheels missing, standing on cinder blocks. Silence. The emptiness said no neighbors. A farm? It didn't smell like California. The air was cold and dry and mineral. The sweat began to cool on her skin. The outside space was precious and brought the reality of her dying here big and close. She felt the thousands of miles between her and home, the warp of the time difference, her family's lives going on with no idea of what was happening to her.

Xander dragged her over the open doorway's threshold. Derelict. But still, apparently, with power. In the low-wattage light from a bare ceiling bulb Claudia saw a big kitchen of dirty tiles and archaic fittings. A cupboard door open: canned goods and bottled water. A big, stained Belfast sink with a chunk cracked out of it and a dripping tap. Damp patches on the walls. Two doors off the kitchen, one open on a dark corridor.

"Home sweet home," the other guy said.

From the corridor, a door, wooden stairs, down.

They were taking her down. Belowground. Panic rushed her again.

"Paulie, get her feet, for Christ's sake."

The reflex to struggle was unstoppable.

Xander let go of her and her head whacked the sharp edge of a step. The knife was at her throat.

"Keep that up," he said, "if you want this in you. Do you want this in you?"

Claudia felt the skin on her neck open. A fine line of fire. Wetness. Blood. Her blood. She had an image of the laminated poster from biology lessons at school, showing a man reduced to his circulatory system. Capillaries, veins, arteries. They used to call him Skinless Jim. She stopped struggling. The knife was the only reality. The knife was the only thing that meant anything. If it went into her, all the blood would come out. Nothing—*nothing* superseded that fact.

"That's better," Xander said. "But that's your last warning. You make another move and I'll open you up. Understand?"

They carried her down the stairs. The basement was big and low-ceilinged, lit by three more bare bulbs. Through the warm blur of the wound on her neck Claudia registered broken crates, a furnace, a busted armchair with half its stuffing out like ectoplasm, empty beer bottles. In several places floorboards were missing. No windows. The walls showed patches of baizy mold. Her heart cried out for the open space she'd been given a few cruel seconds of between the RV and the house. Open space she'd never appreciated. Open space her body screamed to be running through right now. Running fast, away from them, into the concealing darkness and the clean night air. But the basement was a neutral intelligence that simply stated: *That was the last clean air you'll ever breathe. This place, these bare walls, this low ceiling, is the only place you'll know from now on. For the minutes or hours or days you have left until they kill you.*

Between them they carried her to an alcove by the furnace and, to her astonishment, cut the ties on her hands and feet and yanked the gag down out of her mouth. She couldn't speak. She put her hand up to her throat, felt it wet with blood—but the cut wasn't deep.

Paulie went to the other side of the room, then came back with a bucket in one hand and a two-liter bottle of water in the other. He set them down next to her. Then both men stepped back, staring at her.

"Please," she gasped. "Let me go. If you let me go, I won't say anything. I swear I won't say anything. Just let me go." The sound of her own voice was terrible to her. It confirmed that all this was real. She was really here. It was really her.

Paulie smiled. Lit a cigarette with a copper Zippo. Xander reached up above his head, where the end of a steel cable dangled. He grabbed it and pulled.

A flexible metal security grille—like the ones stores used—descended with a loud rattle. A padlock that went through a corresponding metal hoop bolted to the floor.

She was sealed off from the rest of the room.

In a cage.

37

I'll come by and see you later. Don't say anything. Just don't answer the door if you don't want to.

Back at her apartment, Valerie tried to imagine not answering the door. She tried to imagine hearing the doorbell and ignoring it, the seconds and minutes that would have to pass before she'd know he'd given up and gone away. She tried to imagine the strength required for waiting that out, all the while knowing that if she hit the buzzer, let him into the building, unlocked her apartment door, and stood in her living room, it would be a matter of moments before he was with her, his arms around her, the warm fit of their bodies, the blur and surrender that would take them from kissing to hurrying each other's clothes off (the priceless friction of fabric leaving skin, the little ticks of static, the first tender shock of flesh on flesh) to the bedroom, the bed, the giving in, the certainty, the homecoming of fucking and the knowledge that there was nothing, nothing, nothing better than love. She tried to imagine what it would feel like to know all that was there, that life was ready to burn brightly again—and refusing it. She tried to imagine all this and failed. The failure itself was a kind of sweetness.

But in the shower (her body, for so long nothing to her, now reasserting its sexual self through her breasts and midriff and neck and thighs, through the livening between her legs) other truths jabbed at and cut into the fantasy. That she would have to tell him.

Everything. Before anything else happened. And if she did tell him, it was almost certain that nothing else *would* happen.

I was pregnant, Nick. But I didn't know if it was yours. And I never told you.

I want not to do anyone any harm.

Too late for that. She'd already done him harm. Was doing him harm now, with these erotic preparations.

It didn't stop her. There was a momentum at work in her whether she liked it or not. She shaved her legs and underarms, washed and conditioned her hair, brushed her teeth. Put on a skirt for the first time in years. No perfume. He never wanted her to wear perfume. He wanted, he'd said, just the smell of her skin. It had been a shocking introduction to what love could do that she'd believed him. If they were going out, he'd watch her getting ready. She'd be half naked at the dressing table putting on her makeup and catch him observing her in the mirror. Haven't you got anything better to do? she'd said, the first time this happened. He'd said: Nothing better than this, no. And because she'd known he wasn't lying, her flush of narcissistic pleasure had been innocent. It was the first time in her life she'd known she was desired and loved for exactly who and what she was.

Dressed, she looked at the clock. It was after eleven. She mixed herself a vodka and tonic. Just one. A large one—but just one. Sip, slowly. For courage.

An hour passed.

Her apartment's tension started to tell her he wasn't coming.

The downed vodka added: *Because he's thought better of it. Because he knows there's something you're not telling him. Because he'll never love you the way he did. And if he does, what do you think you'll do with the love? What did you do the last time?*

She poured herself another.

By 1 A.M. she wasn't drunk, but the vodka had grown in candor. *Nothing's changed. He's not coming, because you were right the first time: You don't deserve it. Eight dead women (and one dead baby) and here you are with a fucking skirt on waiting for love. By what right? By what right?*

She drank another.

You had love and you shat on it. That's what you did. That's what you'll do. He knows that. He's not stupid.

With bitter satisfaction, she went back to her desk.

That's right. Work, not love. There's only work for you, now, so do it.

She went through every case file, over and over again, until the uncooperative facts were a snowstorm in her head, with a backdrop that was a mishmash of human remains and the obstinately unrelated objects. The objects. There had been a phase early in the investigation when she went down the psych route of their symbolic meanings—if they had any. It had gotten her nowhere. Not least because there was no consensus on what any given object symbolized. The Internet had taken her into a labyrinth of contradictions. The hammer was everything from a destroyer to a defender, from an inverted cross to a cycle of death and rebirth. Apples were sin and death, but also beauty (when he'd stood behind her and wrapped his arms around her and said You're beautiful, she'd believed him) immortality, the cosmos, breasts, knowledge . . . It was pointless. Asking the Internet was like asking God; how could the answer not contradict itself and go on forever? And this was to say nothing of the crackpot stuff. One source apparently obsessed with rescuing the symbol of the goose from its associations with silliness. The goose was bravery, loyalty, navigation, teamwork, protection . . . She'd given up. Wild fucking goose chase. Like love. (*Hey? What? I love you.*)

She unrolled the murder map (a copy of the one from the incident room) looking for something—anything—that would narrow the geography down or reduce it to any kind of logic. She found nothing. The red lines were an impenetrable cat's cradle. For a little while she revisited the theory that it was a group, a homicidal cabal of killers working together. It wasn't impossible. It wasn't impossible—but it only made the situation worse. To make the connections between suspects, you needed suspects—and there weren't any. The half dozen they'd had in the frame at one time or another were—as far as their confiscated communications technology revealed—utterly unconnected to each other; and the alibis that had eventually ruled them out remained. The investigation had scrutinized correspondence from serial killers already incarcerated, the Hollywoodish conceit of someone locked up directing an acolyte or fan club from behind bars. It had yielded nothing plausible. (A depressing amount of convicted wackos' letters were to and from women who were infatuated with them, wanted to marry them, get fucked by them, save them, have their children. *If we have a kid, we'll let it stay up late sometimes for no good reason. Once or twice a year we'll go into its school and say there's an emergency and take it out of class and just blow off the day at the park.*)

She spent an hour calling around the enforcement agencies in the states the zoo footage had gone out to. Nothing. Or rather a dozen alleged sightings that had so far come to nothing. She called Reno for progress on ID'ing the alarm clock victim, but of course, the process had only just begun. It would mean every Nevada missing person case in the last . . . what, two? three? four years? Contacting the families. Dental records. And that was assuming the victim had even been reported missing. That was assuming she had people to whom she was missing. Low-rent hooker? Drug addict? A lot of the women in either category (and sometimes both) simply didn't have anyone who'd give a shit whether they disappeared or not. They didn't have anyone who'd *notice*. Add to that that if this was the serial duo, chances were the victim wasn't from Nevada anyway. Valerie looked at the map and felt the entire country like a swirling liquid, particles drifting from one state into another, untrackable, untraceable, defying procedure. (The road trip to Mexico in their first year together, the hours of warm windshield sunlight on her bare legs, his hand there, the shared truancy, the way delighted calm female ownership of him pierced her when she'd come out of a gas station toilet and seen him talking with the pump attendant. Love ambushed you with these humble revelations, stamped itself on you through the oblique and the mundane.)

Out of sheer desperation she spent another hour dipping into and out of the traffic enforcement footage. RVs. RVs. More RVs. What was she even looking for? A driver wearing a T-shirt that said MURDERER? Time and again she returned to the zoo footage. The dark-haired guy in the Raiders shirt watching Katrina. She was sure it was him. But she couldn't stand her own intuitive certainty. It meant she was looking at the man who might even now be doing what he did—again, for the ninth or tenth or for all she knew fiftieth time. It made her powerlessness collusive, as if by looking at his image and knowing it was him she were giving him permission—encouragement, even—to carry on doing what he was doing.

It was 4:30 A.M. when she laid her head down on her desk and closed her eyes. Her skull was throbbing—from the hours of fruitless concentration, yes, but also from the vodka and cigarettes that had kept her company through the night. Her cold, which the excitement had occluded, revved up its symptoms. Her head pounded. Her skin was sore.

Blasko had changed his mind. He'd seen sense. He'd remembered who she was, what she was capable of, what she'd done. Of course he had. He'd done the right thing.

Experimentally, Valerie sat up and raised her hands in front of her face. They were shaking. They shook all the time now. Have to watch that. Make an effort. Keep them busy. Especially in front of Carla Fucking York.

Two hours after she'd crawled into bed (alone, alone, alone; shedding the skirt was like an act of self-ridicule) and fallen into fraught sleep, she was woken by the sound of her cell phone.

And the information that would change everything.

38

Angelo had known, struggling into extra layers, that he wasn't going to make the fallen tree. I don't know how far, Nell had said. A mile, I guess. *A mile.* It had practically killed him just putting on the additional clothes. But what else was there to do? If there was a way, he had to try, if only for her sanity.

He'd managed ten paces with the walking stick—then collapsed. The day was bright blue and glaring white around him. Indifferent beauty. He'd got up again. A mile would take him, what, three hours?

Keep going, Sylvia had said. *Come on. It's like that film,* Touching the Void. They'd watched the movie together. The climber who'd walked all the way down the mountain on a broken leg. The guy had managed it by picking out landmarks—a particular rock or snowy hummock—a few paces ahead, then setting himself the challenge of just getting to that. Then he'd select another spot a few feet away and aim for that, and so on, until, having done this countless times (in agony), he made it all the way back to base camp.

Angelo had tried. Just five more steps. Just six more. Just *three* more.

But less than thirty paces from the cabin, he'd been reduced to crawling through snow that came up to his elbows.

He didn't have the requisite psychology. The *Touching the Void* climber, while astonishing, had always struck both him and Sylvia as a psychopath or suffering from a version of autism—or at the very least devoid of human warmth and realism. Sylvia conceded as much now.

You would be so much better at this than me, he'd said to her through his pain. Sylvia had always had more strength and courage than him. Sylvia had always had more of all the good stuff than him. Integrity. Honesty. Empathy. Depth. *She* should have been the novelist. Except what she *didn't* have was the desire for public affirmation, for peer acknowledgment, for glowing endorsements, for fame. Unlike him. Unlike him, what she had was quiet sufficiency and the ability to take pleasure in a life without shallow social backslaps or professional flattery. What she had was the ability to love, and be loved— and for that to be enough. She conceded that, too, when he'd given up, collapsed on his side in the snow. She conceded it as she conceded all her merits: not with self-satisfaction, just with a smile and a shrug. The truth was the truth, and there was no point denying it.

All right, my love, she'd said as he began the return struggle to the cabin. *All right, you tried.*

The worst thing had been seeing Nell unsurprised by his return. I'm sorry, he'd gasped, his face wet with pain. I'm so sorry.

Now, no matter how many ways he looked at it, the situation didn't change. They were stuck here. Her, courtesy of the broken ankle (fractured hip, too, he suspected; and the pain when she breathed in said a rib had cracked as well); him, at the mercy of L5 and S1. Two cripples, no meds, no phone, no transport. *He hurt my mom.* Every minute that passed testified that no one had found her yet.

"Yet" felt irrelevant. The more Angelo gleaned, the more certain he was that Nell's mother was dead. Murdered. He'd had to ask the questions delicately. Detail brought the whole thing up in the kid, huge, unassimilable. Blood. She kept saying her mom was bleeding. Every time the word left her mouth, it was as if another bone in her broke. Her face lost its bearings. Shock renewed itself. He'd had to keep easing back. Eventually he'd stopped trying to build the picture of what had happened. And in any case, since no amount of narrative changed their predicament, what was the point in getting it? Whether the woman was dead or not, there was still nothing to do but wait. If Nell's brother had escaped or survived, he would have gotten help. The house had a landline and cellular reception. There were neighbors a mile away. And given that no help had come, there was only one conclusion to draw.

He'd splinted her ankle as best he could. Two bits of flat wood he'd found amongst the chopped logs and kindling bound with shreds torn from one of the towels. He hadn't known what he was doing, but he held to the idea that anything that helped keep it still couldn't make matters worse.

He was perpetually exhausted. The sciatica wouldn't let up. He kept testing it. Kept getting the same blinding result: *Stop trying to move.* Filling a cup with water was a grueling ordeal. Replenishing the woodstove, an odyssey that left him drenched in sweat, shaking, sick. The only favor his condition did him was that the grotesque spectacle of it absorbed the girl's attention for a little while. He could see that a remote part of her registered his suffering, her distant sympathy circuits were still trying to fire. But all the circuits were dimmed, blotted out by the giant thing that had happened to her, that would not go away, that had taken up colossal and tyrannical residency in her changed world. The grim mathematics were plain. A mother didn't tell her child to run away from her protection unless she knew she had no protection left to give.

Sylvia came and went. When she was there, it was bearable.

I can't be here all the time.

Angelo believed there was a finite allowance granted to the dead. Precious currency, to be spent wisely.

"I know you don't want to," he said to Nell, "but you should really try to eat something. You must be starving."

It was late evening. She was lying on her right side in the sleeping bag with her back to the stove. She had a choice between pains, he knew. Lying on her side eased the pain of breathing but increased the pain in her ankle. Lying on her back turned down the pain in her ankle, but made every breath a precise, mean stab.

"Nell?"

She shook her head. He could see what an effort even the most minimal interaction was for her. He could see that what had happened devoured every gram of consciousness. She was condemned to replay what she had seen, over and over. Some part of her, for the rest of her life, would always be replaying it. If she lived to be a hundred, the reel would still be running. It was her legacy now.

"I need to go to the bathroom," she said.

This had occurred to him. He'd been dreading it.

"OK," he said. "No problem. I'll carry you on my back."

She thought about that.

"Can I use your stick?" she said.

If she fell . . . If she fell . . . Oh God.

"Sure you can," he said. "Just be very, very careful."

She had to think it through. It would require getting her one good leg under her and pulling herself up with her arms via the sink. In other words—

Her scream told both of them everything they needed to know. It was impossible. She could get upright, but even with the stick taking the weight of the bad leg, moving forward under her own power was unbearable. The ribs made every jolting step agony. She'd never make it.

She lay back down, sweating, in tears, sobbing.

"Hey," he said. "Hey, come on now, don't cry. We'll work something out. Hold on. Just give me a minute to think. They used to say I was a smart guy. I'm sure I can figure something."

After a few moments, he said: "If I get you to the bathroom, will you be able to sit on the toilet?"

But for a little while she was inconsolable. The shame and the weakness on top of everything else. He was worried she would wet herself. (At *least* wet herself. He didn't have it in him to ask her if peeing was all she needed to do.)

"OK," he said. "Here's what I think we should try: We unzip the sleeping bag and get that out of the way. Then I'll pull you on the mat. We'll deal with the rest when we get there. How's that sound?"

It took a long time, but eventually they made it to the bathroom. It cost him a lot. He was in tears himself, silently, by the time they got there. He lay on his side for a moment, gasping, the nerve in his leg jangling.

"I can do it," she said through her misery. "I can do it myself."

"You sure?"

"I can do it. You have to go away."

"OK," he said. "But I'll be right outside the door. You shout if you need me, OK?"

He did not look, though he was terrified she'd fall. She sobbed continuously, a misery like that thin rain that could last all day. He could picture her small shut face suppressing the pain, the contortions pulling her pants down and getting onto the toilet seat would require. It was a great relief to him to hear the flush. He wondered how long she'd been lying there by the stove, plucking up courage to tell him she needed to go. The courage children needed for these things.

By the time they made it back to the stove, both of them were spent. They lay a few feet apart. Her embarrassment was still coming off her, an aura of distressed energy.

"Well, it's probably going to make me faint," he said, "but I'm going to try to heat something up. Let's see what we've got in here."

Before his abrupt incapacitation, he'd lugged a few boxes of supplies over the bridge on foot, in defiance of the sheriff. (The sheriff. What he wouldn't give to see that guy right now.) The cabin's two tiny cupboards had enough in them, he guessed, for maybe ten days, if they ate sparingly. Apart from a dozen eggs and a stale white loaf, nothing fresh—but there was canned stuff that would stop them starving for a while. It was a mercy that the faucets still yielded apparently drinkable water, although he supposed they could melt snow in a pan on the stove if they had to. How many days could you go without food? He stopped himself wondering.

"OK," he said, shuddering from what crawling to the cupboard had taken out of him. "We've got soup. We've got dried pasta. We've got canned tomatoes, canned peaches, canned ham, canned beans, canned sweet corn. We've got Fig Newtons. No idea why we have those. I don't even like them. We've got olive oil. We've got rice. Dried chilies. Two bulbs of garlic . . . I have to say, none of this is exactly making my mouth water." He reached farther back into the cupboard. "Although, wait a second. What's this? Coq au vin. In a *can*? OK, I'm going to heat this up. I'll make some pasta, too. Do you know what coq au vin is?"

When she didn't answer, he looked over at her. Tears were streaming. She hadn't made a sound.

He remembered her pale legs and narrow sternum when he'd undressed her. It had made him picture her mother drying her after a bath, with a huge towel that would have felt good, that would have smelled to the child of home and safety and love. He knew, by contrast, how he must seem to her: a crazy old cripple living in a hut. He'd spent half his life finding what he believed were the right words. Getting it right at the level of the sentence, he'd said, countless times, in interviews. There was no getting it right here. He couldn't think of a single thing to say that wouldn't make it worse.

He stood for a moment, bent over his stick, watching her, the can a dead joke in his hand.

What do I do? What the fuck do I do?

There's nothing you can do, Sylvia said. *Except keep her alive. There's nothing you can do except take care of her.*

Saying nothing, he turned to the stove. He had no idea where the can opener was.

39

There was no time in the basement. Time didn't pass. Claudia was confined to an endlessly burgeoning present of the bare bulbs and the furnace's exhalation. That was something, that there was warmth. She sat with her back to its radiant heat. Its comfort was a betrayal. It testified to her body, to her incarceration in her skin, to the reality of her flesh and blood and the impossibility of escaping the things that would happen to it. Care for her body wedded her to fear for its suffering. She'd read somewhere: *You don't believe in the soul until you feel it struggling to escape the body.* She would have settled for that, to have her spirit or essence let loose. She'd go like a wisp across the Atlantic Ocean to her parents' house in Bournemouth, spend her disembodied days moving around the solid lives of her family like a cat around its owners' legs.

It had been, she supposed, hours. After they pulled down the security grille, they'd left her and gone upstairs. At first, after she'd forced herself to stop crying (she could always, throughout her childhood, throughout her *life,* force herself to stop crying; it was one of the reasons, she'd assumed, she was unlikable) there was only fear. Maximal fear. That every sound was the sound of them coming back. Her entire being devoted itself to listening. There was no room for anything else.

But she was human. After a while, portions of consciousness were hived off for other business: seeing if she could lift the grille;

searching her pockets for something to work the padlock (though her inner realist told her it was only in movies that locks were ever picked); scouring the cage for something—anything—of use, for defense, for escape. Not that the search turned anything up. She had a couple of quarters and a dime in her jeans pocket. Useless. Her cell phone and bag were gone. They must have taken them before they put her in the box. Her bag, anyway. She held on to the golden straw of possibility that she'd dropped her phone in the struggle and they'd missed it. Had a repeated vision of someone finding it, of Ryan calling, of the wretched dots of her disappearance beginning to join up. But even if she had dropped it (the realist again) who would be walking that stretch of road at this hour, whatever hour this was? She'd been there on a mild early evening and not seen a soul on foot. This was America: roads were for driving, not walking. Walking was Third World, unless you were doing it in the wilderness, with a backpack and a baseball cap, to burn carbs.

Only rape.

Just rape.

It was obscene to be able to think that, to hope for that. It was also (there was nothing wrong with her brain, there was no stopping it) a measure of what there was beyond rape, in *addition* to rape. What there was when rape was merely the starting point. There was death, yes. But there was everything between rape and death. Between rape and death was torture. An indefinite landscape. A journey that could be made to seem endless. A journey—she had a confusion of unbearable images—so ugly and exhausting, it could make you want death, crave death, beg for death. Which they wouldn't give you. Not giving you death was the whole point of torture.

These were her thoughts. Her mind was her enemy.

She ran her fingertips around the grouting in the wall at her back. Crumbling mortar. A loose brick. The start of many loose bricks. A hole. Escape. Freedom.

But the mortar didn't give. Her fingertips came away sore.

Floorboards then. Nails. A protruding rusty nail she could jab into the smaller one's eye.

But there were no protruding nails, rusty or otherwise.

"You're lucky," Paulie said, appearing halfway down the basement stairs.

Claudia started. Involuntarily flattened her back against the wall, elbows tight to her ribs, fists clenched. Her own movements had distracted her, blocked out the sound of the door up there opening. Suddenly he was *there*—and all her powers of reason fell apart.

"You're so lucky. He's sick."

The space in the basement came alive, a bristling guarantee of his ability to move through it. To her. He was holding an iPad in his right hand. It made her imagine him in an Apple store, talking to a sales assistant. Stores. Malls. People. Life. Everything you'll never see again.

He came down the remaining stairs.

"It's the flu," he said.

Claudia didn't want to look at him. She didn't want to look at him for fear of what else she'd see. The knife. The gun. Any of the innocent objects that would do what they did, what they were designed to do. To her.

Paulie was at the grille. She couldn't press herself any harder against the wall. The furnace purred.

"I did these," he said, touching the screen into life and beginning to finger-swipe through its files. "He forgets that. He doesn't understand. How would he get these if it wasn't for me?"

The screen lit his face. A fond smile had formed on his mouth. He might have been looking over photos of a favorite vacation. He stopped. The smile expanded into a grin. Small, nicotine-stained teeth. "Oh yeah," he said, "I remember this one. This one was the best."

He touched the screen.

Ugly sound bloomed. A woman's half-strangled screams.

He turned the screen toward Claudia.

Claudia couldn't move. The world drained away. There was nothing except her trying and failing not to look.

The footage was shaky. Of course it was. His compressed excitement. The naked dark-haired woman's gagged face a wreck of tears and blood, her arms spread, ropes around her wrists. The men's shadows over her bare flesh. Xander's shoulder. His hands. The serrated knife. Their silence louder than her screams.

Claudia wasn't aware of closing her eyes. Only of moments of blackness. When her entire being collapsed into nothingness.

But was forced back. Saw. Believed and disbelieved. Knew and refused the knowledge.

The screaming came tinnily from the iPad. Reached a crescendo.

Then silence. Xander on his knees over her, working something with dense concentration. Paulie's voice off-camera saying, quietly, "That ain't gonna fit, man."

Xander sitting back on his heels, breathing through his nose.

The flesh of the woman's midriff gone.

Something inside her, instead of her insides.

Something big, white, hard, shiny.

"See that?" Paulie asked Claudia. "See what that is? Can you make it out?"

He turned the screen back to himself, briefly, to double-check she was seeing what she needed to see.

"It's a goose!" Paulie said, then laughed. "A goddamned . . . I mean where does he *get* this stuff?"

The camera pulled back.

Claudia recognized the room in the film.

It was the room she was in.

She found herself on her hands and knees. The world crowded back, put its whole weight on her.

"I got all of them on here," Paulie said, finger-swiping again. "Here, take a look. Come on, look."

Claudia remained where she was. She wanted to wrap her arms around her abdomen but she had no strength to move. Her mother and father and Alison and her utter aloneness and her whole life a beautiful mass of detail leading only to this. She wanted to die now, this instant go forever into the blackness. She'd accept death if only it were immediate, if only it would spare her what would happen, what they'd do.

But the moments came and went—innocently, like children filing past—and here she still was, alive, and the facts of where she was and what had just happened and what *would* happen did not change. Could not change. The facts were innocent, too. If they tied you down and pushed the knife, your body opened. The knife had no choice and your body had no choice. It was part of a universe of cause and effect. Morality was irrelevant.

"And this one?" Paulie continued, as if to himself. "Jesus. Wriggliest bitch I've ever seen. She was like a goddamned bag of *snakes*. Come on, you're not looking."

Shaking, Claudia crawled to the furnace. She put her back to its heat, drew up her knees, turned her face away from him, at last managed to wrap her arms around herself. It brought her childhood back, small traumas, the intimate warmth of tears on her cheeks, pity for herself.

"Not playing, huh?" Paulie said.

She didn't answer. A remote part of herself wondered about the woman in the video. Who she'd been. Her life. Her family. The sadness and horror and disgust of what she'd been reduced to. In the churning sickness of her state, Claudia imagined meeting her in a neutral afterlife, something like an infinite dull waiting room. They would know each other. What they'd shared.

"It doesn't matter," Paulie said. "We got plenty of time." He chuckled to himself again. "We got all the time in the world."

40

Xander hadn't been ill for a long time. The odd cough or cold. That ingrown toenail that had gone septic, so it was like having a little volcano in his shoe. Diarrhea from lousy takeout now and then. But nothing like this since he was Leon, at Mama Jean's house.

He lay on the bed in the big damp room upstairs, shivering. His face ached. His head was warm. It was getting light outside.

The objects revolved and overlapped in his mind's eye: balloon, goose, apple, hammer, clock, fork . . . jug. The goddamned jug. In Colorado, Paulie had said to him: I'm gonna do one. Let me do one. And he, Xander—fucking *idiot*—had let him. Except of course when it had come to it, Paulie *couldn't* do it, chickenshit that he was. He couldn't do it, so Xander had to. Why in God's name had Xander agreed to even let him try? What had he been thinking? It was no wonder he was sick. That could never happen again. You started letting things like that happen and the whole . . . You just . . . Things started drifting away from each other.

A wave of heat went over him, made him feel like the way the air buckled in the desert, that shimmer on the road. The jacket normally hanging over the wardrobe's long mirror had fallen to the floor. His reflection, even though he wasn't looking at it, was another ache. He'd never liked mirrors. A part of him didn't believe it *was* a reflection. A part of him always thought the movements of the

person in the mirror never quite matched his own. Like it was someone else who looked just like him, watching him from the world on
the other side.

His mother had always covered mirrors up.

He was very small when she went away, but he remembered her.
He remembered her not being there. Long dreamlike stretches of
time when he wandered around the two-room apartment in the hot
afternoons. It smelled of drains and garbage. He was too small even
to reach the light switches. Daylight leaked away. At night monsters
had the run of the place and he'd shove himself into the cupboard
under the sink until he heard her come back (with someone, different
men, but always a man), by which time he would've pissed or shit
himself and would know she was going to punish him for it. It was
like a car crash in his head, seeing her when she came back, because
she was glitteringly beautiful. Her green eyes were like Christmas,
her hair a fascinating gold tinselly mess. It was the beauty and the
rage coming off her that crashed the cars in his head. It seemed impossible that they went together, but they did. If she and the man
had already injected themselves, he might get away with being locked
in his room. If not, there was no telling. If not, even the monsters
would draw back to watch.

The last clear memory he had of his mother was the day at the
fairground. It had been a strange time when one man—Jimmy—
was around a lot. He barely spoke to Leon and Leon kept out of his
way—but somehow the three of them were at a fairground and Leon
was sensitized by the lights and the rides and the smells of cotton
candy and hot dogs. It was evening, the sky beyond the neons dark
silver blue with thin feathers of black cloud. Leon wanted to go on
the carousel. Up and down horses with bulging eyes and saddles in
thrilling colors. Some of their faces were frightening, but all the kids
on them were laughing and waving and sometimes letting go of
the reins and just gripping with their legs. It was a world to him, the
horses and the riders. It seemed like an astonishing magic, that he
could get up there and be one of them. If he got up there, he *would*
be one of them. They wouldn't talk or anything, but they would look
at each other and know that they were all riders together.

She said: You're too small for that. I'll have to go on with you. Jesus Christ—wait till it stops, will you?

She and Jimmy were drinking beer from plastic cups. She had her hair tied back and her face looked small and hard.

When it *stops*, for Christ's sake. Get *off* me.

But when it stopped, she and Jimmy had moved away to a stall where Jimmy was firing a gun at playing cards pinned to a board.

Leon went through agony. The kids got off and other kids got on. There was one horse he wanted, white with a golden mane and a green saddle. In a minute someone else would get on it and the carousel would start again and again he wouldn't be in the magical world. He went back to her and pulled at her hand. Not hard, but she was wobbly on her high heels and she lurched and nearly fell. She spilled some of her drink and bumped Jimmy and he missed his shot.

Leon didn't fall when Jimmy hit him on the side of the head, but the blow felt huge and hot.

His mother was shaking beer from her fingertips, her bracelets clattering, saying Jesus Christ, Jesus fucking *Christ*.

Leon went back to the ride. It had started again. His horse didn't have anyone on it. It was unbearable, his need to be on the white horse with the green saddle, to be in the world of the laughing riders.

He crawled under the guardrail. The speed and the rise and fall of the horses. But every time the white one came around, its eyes invited him to grab hold and jump on.

Leon stepped closer. Two more steps. One more would take him up onto the carousel's round wooden floor.

Someone's voice shouted, Jesus, kid, hey—stop!

But Leon felt as if he were being moved forward by invisible hands. The sounds of the fairground dropped away. The white horse passed him again. Said: *Next time. Next time around.* Leon could feel the joy waiting.

He took another step. He could do this. He knew he could do this.

The girl was wearing white knee socks and buckled leather sandals, and her outstretched leg hit Leon—harder than the blow from Jimmy—on the softly throbbing side of his head.

He didn't remember much more after that. Just the fairground noises falling back onto him like an ocean wave and a few screams and the smell of the floor's flaking paint and undersides of the horses' hooves dropping down to within a couple of inches of his face, hundreds of them, it seemed, over and over, for hours or days—until someone's hands grabbed his ankles and pulled him so that his shirt rode up and the boards scraped his bare back and he had a vivid image of a fat woman in a pink dress holding an ice cream, gawping at him from the guardrail, her mouth open, her face lit by the neons.

There were other, confused memories after that, but glimpsed through a warm daze: the dirty vinyl smell of Jimmy's car; road lights; his mother forcing him to eat potato chips; Mama Jean standing in her doorway, smoking a cigarette, shaking her head.

It was at Mama Jean's house that the lessons began.

Shuddering, he rolled to the edge of the bed and reached under it.

For the only possession he'd kept from his days at Mama Jean's.

41

Valerie gathered enough consciousness to read the incoming on her phone's screen: *Liza Terrill calling.*

"Liza?" she croaked. "What's up?"

"Hey, Val," Liza said. "You still sleeping?"

Valerie looked at her watch. Six thirty. She should've been up half an hour ago. She'd forgotten to set the radio alarm. No poetry.

"No, I'm good," she lied. "Anything wrong?"

Liza worked Homicide in Santa Cruz. She and Valerie had been friends since the academy. These days they were lucky if they saw each other three times in a year, but whenever they did, it was just picking up the conversation wherever they'd left off.

"I'm fine. I might have something for you. Since you said you're happy to clutch at straws."

"Tell me."

"Missing girl. Well, a *probably* missing girl. It's only been twenty-four hours, and the guy who called it in is barely even a boyfriend. You told me you wanted anything like this as soon as it came in, so here I am, doing as I'm told."

"You think it's more than a straw or you wouldn't be calling," Valerie said.

There was a pause. "Yeah," Liza said. "I know. I wish I didn't. But the fucking Machine's been working since I picked it up."

Valerie understood. The Machine. Cop sense. The inexplicable certainty. It was both a dread and a thrill. And it was coming from Liza even down the phone.

"Let me grab a pen," she said. She was already halfway to the desk, her circuits rushing into life. "OK," she said when she was seated, legal pad open in front of her. "Give me everything you've got."

Claudia Grey. British national. Twenty-six years old. Living and working illegally in Santa Cruz.

Two photographs. The first from her passport, taken when she was just eighteen. The second run off her roommate's phone, taken only a couple of weeks ago: Claudia holding a glass of wine and looking straight into camera with a slightly exasperated expression. Dark hair cut in a soft, jaw-length bob. A look of warmth, humor, and potentially cruel intelligence.

Valerie's own Machine moved up a gear as soon as she saw it.

The afternoon in Santa Cruz was spent in four straightforward interviews. Carlos Díaz (the employer), Wayne Bauer (the bus driver), Ryan Wells (the boyfriend), and Stephanie Argyle (the roommate). Carlos confirmed that Claudia had left the Whole Food Feast at 8 P.M. Wayne Bauer (plus the city bus CCTV) confirmed that she'd boarded at 8:17 P.M. and gotten off at the Graham Hill Road stop at 8:38 P.M. Ryan confirmed that she hadn't made it to the party. Stephanie confirmed that she hadn't come home. Somewhere between the bus stop and Ryan Wells's, she'd disappeared.

Valerie showed all four interviewees, plus the staff at the restaurant, the image of the zoo footage suspect. No recognition. If the killer or killers had been shadowing Claudia, they'd done it without being noticed by any of the victim's people. She sent the Whole Food Feast's CCTV material to Liza at the SCPD, who would pass it on to Valerie's team in San Francisco. Valerie had hoped, too, for a camera angle on the parking lot, but the shot was only partial; at least a third of the bays were out of frame. None of the Feast's staff recalled seeing an RV, but that didn't mean there hadn't been an RV there.

She worked her way through the guests who'd been at the barbecue, all of whom had driven there, with the exception of Ryan

Wells's brother and sister-in-law, who were staying with him on vacation. On the phone with guest number eight of fourteen, she caught a break.

Damien Court had arrived at the party on his Harley.

"Yeah," he said when she asked if he'd seen an RV en route. "Actually, there was one parked on the hill. In a bad spot, too, just before the bend."

"I need you to show me where it was," Valerie said. "How soon can we meet?"

"I just ordered short ribs," Damien said. "Like . . . in a couple of hours?"

"No," Valerie said. "Like right now. Give me the name of the restaurant. I'll come get you."

Damien Court, Ryan Wells's chief digital editor, was early thirties, tall, with soft brown eyes, a short dark ponytail, and a goatee. He was also, by the time Valerie picked him up, in the heightened state people entered when they found themselves witnesses, when "crime" stopped being something on a crime show and started being something in their lives. Valerie could feel the thrill coming off him in the car. The dark eyes a little wider than they'd normally be. The current of fear that ran through the innocent when dealing with the police, because the world was crazy and innocence was no guarantee against anything and after all they weren't so innocent as they wanted to be. One of the first and most quickly wearying things you discovered if you were a cop was that everyone—*everyone* reacted to you as if they had something to hide. Because everyone *does* have something to hide, her grandfather had told her. It might only be a sugar habit or kinky fantasy—but a cop shows up and it's like the eye of God turned on them. It's depressing.

"I'd say about a hundred yards from here," Damien told her. They were slightly more than halfway up Graham Hill Road. "But that's a rough guess."

"It'll do," Valerie said. She didn't want to drive over the site and fuck up any tracks. She'd called Liza and told her she might need a CSI team.

"Are you even going to be able to see anything?" Damien Court asked. It was almost dusk, and under the cedars almost dark. Valerie didn't answer. Just pulled over and took the flashlight from the Taurus's trunk. Gloves, evidence packets, tweezers, two sets of over-shoe plastics. "Put these on," she told him. "Walk behind me."

She was excited. There was no other honest way to describe it. Racing up through her body's exhaustion was the knowledge that this was—please, God—a live case. Not a corpse. Not a too-late. Not another reiteration that they'd *got away with it*. Claudia Grey was—please, please, *please,* God—still alive. Which meant her life was in Valerie's hands. A beating heart and a ticking clock. Valerie felt the Case stirring, the mountain of details and reports, the interview transcripts, the forensics data, the murder map, the wretched gallery of signature objects, and most of all, the dead women. And under the excitement her own nearness to collapse. The dregs of her fuel that would somehow have to be enough. That would have to be *made* to be enough.

"I'd say about another twenty paces," Damien said.

"OK. Stop. Stay there."

She needed the flashlight. She went slowly, moved the beam back and forth across the asphalt and grass shoulder section by section. No substitute for CSI micro-scrupulousness, but the rhythm of the beating heart and the ticking clock were already embedded in her pulse. Every second was a second that moved Claudia Grey closer to death. It was as if she could hear the girl breathing.

She halted in the middle of the flashlight's arc.

Tracks.

Clear in even the battery light. The finest film of dirt between the grass and the road, maybe only six inches in width—but a vehicle had definitely stopped here. Goodyear G647 RSS. The dry-cast had become one of Valerie's neural pathways. She'd let SCPD forensics confirm it, but her own mind was already made up. Besides the gap between front and rear wheels fitting RV length, it was as if the dark air here were still raw from where Claudia Grey had been torn into her nightmare, as if the atmosphere were still in shock from what it had seen.

Valerie mentally taped off the scene and moved through it me-thodically. On her second pass (she was peripherally aware of Damien Court standing, tense and still exactly where she'd told him to stand; the casually exercised power of police authority—if she'd told him to stand on his head, he would have tried), something glinted in the flashlight's beam.

She bent to the ground. Steadied the light.

A sequin.

Two more lying within a few inches.

Silver sequins.

From Claudia's purse.

42

"How do you want to handle it?" Liza Terrill asked Valerie. They were back at the Santa Cruz station, drinking too-strong coffee. Calling Claudia Grey's family couldn't be put off any longer. Technically to idiot-check that Claudia hadn't upped sticks and flown back to England on a whim. But neither Valerie nor Liza regarded that as remotely likely.

"It's a missing person," Valerie said. "That's nightmare enough. Who've you got on it?"

"Larson. He's fine. He gets it."

"OK. Plug it into NCIS and get a rush on forensics. Hit everyone you can with Zoo Guy. Looks like they're still using the RV, but we can't rule out vehicle swaps unless they're complete morons."

Valerie's phone rang. It was Carla.

"I gather you're down in Santa Cruz?" she said.

"I'm heading back shortly. We've got another one."

Pause. Loud with Carla controlling what Valerie imagined was irritation.

"I got the call early this morning," Valerie said, caught between guilt and annoyance herself. "Had to leave at short notice."

"I'm supposed to be with you on this," Carla said. She sounded wounded. Or rather, she sounded as if she'd spent the pause crafting a tone of woundedness.

"Together as in surgically attached?" Valerie said. Regretted saying it.

Another pause.

"I just want to be as useful as I can be," Carla said. "I don't know why you wouldn't call me."

"It was four in the morning," Valerie lied. "It didn't need both of us." It was as if she could *hear* Carla architecting her responses in the silences. The next was preceded by an audible sigh.

"OK," Carla said. "What've we got?"

It took Valerie a few minutes to bring her up to speed, and a tremendous effort not to tell her to back off and let her get on with doing her job. Liza observed Valerie's facial expression with obvious understanding.

"It's not going to help that our girl's illegal," Liza said when Valerie had hung up the call.

"I know," Valerie said. "We'll just have to push. This is the first live one in three years. And if we don't get this right, she's going to end up dead regardless of when her visa ran out."

"No joy on the press release?"

"Too much. Reports from a dozen states. The agencies are doing what they're supposed to, but we don't have a name or a licence plate, and the one thing we know for sure about these guys is they're supermobile. See me in Nebraska? Good for you. Next day I'm in fucking Texas."

"You don't think they're still here?"

"They could be. If there's no HQ, they're driving around in an abattoir on wheels. And this is the third California victim, so there's an argument for assuming an in-state base. But the spread so far makes it look like the victim's displacement is part of the process. They grab her, then break the geographical connection. Makes whatever they leave behind go cold fast. I don't know. Gut says they're on the road, far from here already. But there's *some* West Coast factor. I think the alpha grew up here. Lived here. He keeps coming back."

.   .   .

Driving back to San Francisco in heavy rain, Valerie had to fight the absurd temptation to just start cruising the off-freeway roads, *looking for them.* It was what the families of the missing often did. To fight the impotence. To fight the guilt that quickly attached to doing anything that *wasn't* driving around, looking for them. In the early stages of a loved one's disappearance, the families (their minds naturally assuming the worst) lost any claim on their own lives. The simple act of making a cup of coffee or taking out the trash—anything that testified to normal life going on—had the power to fill them with shame and disgust.

The families, she reminded herself. *Not you. Not the police.*

You've done this because you don't feel entitled to happiness, Blasko had said three years ago, when Suzie Fallon had been missing and missing and missing, and the ticking clock and the beating heart and the unknown life in her hands had driven Valerie mad. *You think shitting on love is going to bring her back? It won't bring any of them back.* And of course, he'd been right. It hadn't brought her back. Not until there was nothing left of her anyone would recognize.

Now it was as if Blasko were in the passenger seat next to her, silent, looking at her, calmly and sadly seeing the same madness ready to blossom again. She wouldn't let it.

But it was hard. She liked the Claudia in the picture. The humor around the mouth and in the warm dark eyes, the look of being able to laugh at herself, the hint of not suffering fools. She's like, really smart, the blond roommate had said with nervy amazement. I mean . . . I mean, like, you need a *dictionary.*

It hit her: You like her because you're seeing her as a person. And why are you doing that?

Because of Nick. Because in spite of everything that's happened and everything you've become, when love comes back, it has the power to reverse everything. You think you've changed? You haven't changed. You've just been *waiting.*

Valerie wondered if Claudia had been following the story of the murders in the press, if she'd recognized Zoo Guy from the pictures they released to the media, if she'd been left in no doubt about what was going to happen to her. But the fact was it didn't make any difference: a man had abducted her. Whether she recognized him or not, she'd assume he was going to do all of it to her, all the terrible things, all the worst things, all the final things. They'd probably already started. Claudia had probably already been changed, forever.

The moral impulse, thinking this, was to fire up, make an inner vow built of rage: *I'll find her. I swear by all the . . . If it takes . . . by God, I will not let this one die. . . .*

But the impulse failed. If you were anything other than a rookie, it had to. Oaths didn't catch murderers, nor promises save the lives of their victims. Only the Machine did. The endless work, the stubborn instincts, the refusal to stop.

I can promise you that, Valerie thought. *I can promise you I won't fucking stop.*

But even as she thought it, she had an image of a heavy pair of household scissors closing around Claudia's breast, razor wire tugged between her legs, a fish knife hammer fork machete axe—

Stop. Stop that.

The Taurus had crept up to ninety-five. The rain was coming down harder. Wipers on what looked like self-destructive speed, and she still had to lean forward and peer through the windshield. Her head ached. She hadn't seen her mother for a while, but she knew that when she did, her mother would ask what she always asked: Are you taking care of yourself, sweetheart?

She pulled it back down to eighty. Lit a Marlboro and took a swallow of the station's now cold coffee. She couldn't remember the last time she'd eaten hot food off a plate, with cutlery. She could barely remember the last time she'd eaten. It mattered. Not because she was hungry (her appetite was dead) but because she understood that she had to put food in her stomach to avoid collapse. She had to eat to carry on working.

Eat when you get home. (And there's a bottle of Smirnoff in the freezer.)

You're becoming an alcoholic.

(I know.) No, I'm not.

No, that's right, you're not. You are an alcoholic. You've got that to offer him, along with all the other things that should make you leave him alone.

She switched lanes to pass a pickup truck loaded with rubble.

Picturing, as she did so, the dead women traveling with her, hovering just above the roof of the Taurus in a sad, trailing constellation.

Then everything went black.

Or rather, something happened that ended in total blackness. Her peripheral vision went rainbow-edged, as if light were passing through a prism, then collapsed in on her like the walls of a beveled glass tunnel.

She thought, quite calmly: *I'm dying.* The colors darkened. Blackness around a narrowing aperture, her view of the windshield, the road, the world reduced to a shrinking dot. Then blackness.

Light.

Brake light, singular.

BRAKE!

The light exploded the world back fully into view. She was aware of her foot down hard on the brake, calf muscle straining. She thought, calmly: *There's not enough time. I'm going to hit it.*

She didn't hit it.

Nor, courtesy of ABS, did she go into a skid.

But there was a yawning, suspended moment in which the single red brake light of the van that had stopped in front of her rushed through the windshield's skin of rain toward her like an unblinking demonic eye, thrilled at the prospect of introducing her to her death.

Horns blared. The pickup rushed past her. Her back, neck, shoulders screamed their reflex preparation for impact from behind.

But nothing hit her. Nothing hit her because the driver behind was going under the speed limit, at a rain-safe distance. Unlike her.

If ignored, extreme stress can cause severe reactions, including blackouts.

She imagined describing what had just happened to her doctor, Rachel Miller. Rachel, a calm, competent woman only five years older than Valerie, would listen in nonjudgmental silence, making notes in her illegible freehand, then tell Valerie that she'd need to take at least two weeks off work.

People always know what the right thing to do is, her grandfather had told her. *They just pretend they don't.* The right thing to do. Accept that she was falling apart. Accept that her efficiency was compromised. Stop working the Case. Stop.

The reasoning terrified her. Because it was sound. Underneath it was her trying and failing to convince herself that what had just happened hadn't happened. Like trying to stop yourself from shivering in the cold just by telling yourself you were warm.

All right, it had happened.

It had happened but it was a one-off. Not enough food, not enough sleep. It wouldn't happen again. Because she wouldn't let it.

And if it did?

If it did . . . If it did, she'd do something about it.

She pictured Blasko shaking his head, smiling, sadly, knowing her.

She pictured Carla York sitting next to her, saying: OK. Enough. That's all I need to see.

Valerie sat with her hands on the wheel, letting the rush subside. The cigarette, incredibly, was still between her fingers. She rolled down the window and tossed it out. The damp air refreshed her hot face. She ought, she knew, to hit the siren and pull the van with the busted taillight over.

But as the snarl-up ahead unpacked and the lane started to flow, she also knew (driving too fast, too close, and with a bloodstream still presided over by last night's vodka) that she wasn't going to.

And she was supposed to be Claudia Grey's best hope.

43

Will Fraser couldn't sleep. He'd been in bed three hours and now the clock said 4:48 A.M. The red digits throbbed, as with gremlin glee. His wife, Marion, was snoring softly. By rights, given they'd had miraculous sex when he came home at midnight, he ought to be snoring softly himself. But the Case was an insomniac brain infestation that didn't give a fuck whether he'd just had sex with the entire Raiders' cheerleading squad. "Miraculous" sex was no joke. First time in maybe six months. *A Christmas miracle,* he'd been tempted to whisper when he came. (He resisted. He wasn't an idiot.) He and Marion loved each other. In which "loved" meant knew each other inside out, drove each other to daily, weary domestic distraction, frequently didn't *bother* to have the next available argument because they were too tired and knew deep down it wouldn't go anywhere apocalyptic, that they were in for the duration (they had prosaic mutual tenderness exactly equal to their irritation), were welded together through their exhausting kids (Deborah, seventeen; Logan, fourteen), and when they were apart for more than a couple of days were ambushed by how much they missed the small things in each other. In Will's case, the sound of Marion's laugh, which was as honest and good as anything from Eden before the Fall. But they'd been married twenty-three years. Sex was more often than not half-hearted or functional. Still, lust, when it did put in a rare appearance, was a rich rejuvenation. Hey, Marion had said when he'd finished brushing his teeth earlier, I'm feeling dirty. She'd been lying on her front in a long pink T-shirt and nothing else, and suddenly the soles of her bare feet and the little tangle of varicoses on her thigh had driven him crazy, had, in a few seconds, reminded him of the wealth of her flesh—the half dozen beauty spots on her back, the creases behind her knees, the softness of her mouth—and they'd fucked with intense, entitled, languorous greed. Afterwards, he'd lain with his face in her bare underarm and thought, *Jesus Christ. Jesus* Christ. He'd kissed the length of her flank. Then she'd said, Fuck, I needed that— turned over, and fallen asleep.

Since then, despite his body's razed bliss, Will had been wide awake.

It was the pocket (if it was a pocket) from the body in Reno. The embroidered letters (if they were letters) wouldn't leave him alone. And he'd been a cop long enough to know when to listen to whatever it was that wouldn't leave him alone.

Will eased himself out of bed, dressed, and went, via the kids' rooms (Deborah had fallen asleep with her iPod headphones on, lying in exactly the position Marion had been in when he finished brushing his teeth; it sent him an anxious bulletin of his daughter's burgeoning womanhood—while Logan slept openmouthed on his back, one leg outside the comforter, lit by his screen saver's still of Liv Tyler on horseback from *The Lord of the Rings*) downstairs to the kitchen.

He made coffee and sat at the scrubbed oak table, going through his notes. The Case was kicking Valerie's ass, he knew, but his own wasn't exactly getting off lightly. Each body that turned up was an indictment of his share in the task force's failure. They'd been on it so long, it was his brain's permanent depressing weather. *Torn-off pocket,* he'd written in his notebook. *Possibly overalls? Maybe edge of a J, def R and poss S. Check back—familiar.*

It was no good. He needed all the files and to see the pocket again. He knew it was something, rang some maddeningly vague bell, was (he laughed, mentally, at the phrase) "a clue." He pictured Marion waking to get up to pee and finding him gone, saw her face's annoyance and disappointment and resignation. Married to a cop?

she'd said, drunk, at a party, years ago. Might as well be married to a crackhead. Get used to coming second in the scheme of things. Get used to *crumbs*. The thought of her, the way she'd been with him earlier—focused and impersonal and selfish for her own pleasure—stirred the blood in his cock again, tempted him to go back upstairs and wrap his arms around her and bury his nose in the soft warmth of her nape and *gloat*. Maybe, if the universe had gone truly, wonderfully insane, she'd be in the mood again when she woke up?

But Valerie's call from Santa Cruz only hours ago was still an abrasion in his head: We've got a live one, Will. Whatever we've been doing, we need to do it faster. Starting right now.

With regret, and some realism (the chances of Marion wanting more sex *first thing in the morning* were laughably slim), he wrote his wife a note and left it on the table. It was 5:17 A.M. The evidence room didn't open until eight, but the off-hours supervisor would be there. The pocket itself hadn't come back from the lab, but there was a print of the photograph the Reno guy had taken. He swallowed the last mouthful of his coffee—*possibly J, R, maybe S* revolving in his head—grabbed his car keys, and headed out into the predawn light.

44

"Here," Angelo said. "I made you this." It was a packet chicken noodle soup. "It's hot. Be careful."

They hadn't spoken again about her mother and Josh. He understood. Trauma had given her a small allowance of language to report what she'd been through. Now it was spent. It couldn't be spoken again. She had a child's ability to recognize the facts of her situation. Childhood was rich in imagination, yes, but it provided an underappreciated gift for the real, too. Children were brutal realists. The only alternative was outright suppression. They had no knack for kidding themselves. It took adulthood to bring that dubious talent.

In spite of this, he'd thought, under Sylvia's occasional guidance, that he was getting better at talking to her. He had two safe subjects: himself, and the immediate concerns of their shared present. Neither took her back to her past nor forward into her future. Neither reinforced the passage of time. The passage of time was verboten. The passage of time meant nothing except all the time her mother had been bleeding. He hoped she didn't have an understanding of how long it would take a person to bleed to death. A forlorn hope: he saw the look that came into her face at moments; the failed effort not to know; the will to hope running smack into the stone wall of knowledge. It was terrible to him that he had nothing to give her in answer to that. He fought his own impulse to lie, to concoct fabulous contingencies by virtue of which her mother and brother would somehow be saved. She wasn't young or stupid enough for any of that. He was watching her hour by hour being force-delivered into a new, brutal existence. Every breath she drew was heartbreaking evidence that she was trying to survive it, though its only purpose seemed to be to destroy her through violence and grief. She was, in fact, only dimly aware of him. It wouldn't have been much more strange to her if she'd found herself in the care of a talking animal or a benign extraterrestrial. A remote practical part of her had, at some point in their time together, decided that he was not dangerous to her. It was a great relief to him that at least that had been established, that his every word or movement didn't trip the switch of her fear.

Now that the first shocks of the situation had subsided, a little of Angelo's deeper self had woken up. A little, in fact (this was the first thought in a long time that came close to making him laugh), of the novelist. He could see how he'd write it. He could see the obvious architecture: the dead-hearted old man given a chance to come back to life through the innocence of a child. Sylvia's response to this thought had been her distinctive smile—of recognition and mischief. He had come out here, he now knew, to decide whether he wanted to live or die. To stay or to go. To carry on without his love—or to follow her into the mystery. He had imagined, coming to this admission, that Sylvia would have something to say about it. But again, all he got was the smile. The look of quiet, delighted conspiracy. It was the look that had always defined her for him. It was the look she gave him across the room at parties they were bored by. It was the look she gave him at moments of unexpected happiness. It was the look she gave him in her favorite sexual position, sitting astride him, when she knew he was just about to come. It was the look of knowing him as well as he knew himself, and it had made his life worth living. He had come out here to determine whether he could live without it.

Well? Can you?

Nell was drinking the soup. Angelo bit back the encouragements: *That's right, honey, good girl.* Such encouragements were unaffordable: any one of them might bring her out of the animal trance, might remind her what she was doing, eating, even though her mother and Josh, even though . . . No. He must be quiet. He must let her body mesmerize her mind with its need. If he interrupted her now, she might never eat again.

But after only a few sips, she stopped. Turned her head and stared out the window. Tears welled and fell.

"Hey," he said, resisting the urge to go to her. "What's wrong?"

She didn't answer. His powerlessness to alleviate her suffering brought the worst of the time with Sylvia back. The otherness of the other person. The privacy of her pain. The number of times he'd asked the universe to take the tumor from her and give it to him instead. *I'll accept any deal you like,* he'd said inwardly. *Just take it away from her. Just let her be all right again.*

I know, Sylvia's spirit sent him. *It made leaving bearable, knowing I'd had that kind of love in my life. Knowing I'd had the best thing.*

Nell's tears stopped as suddenly as they'd started.

"No one's going to come," she said.

45

Valerie had been at her desk a couple of hours when Nick Blaskovitch walked up just after 9:30 A.M. and handed her a manila envelope. She hadn't spoken to him since the parking garage. Since *I'll come by later*. Since the sudden bloom of mad hope. (Followed by its not-so-sudden withering.) The shower, the shampoo, the skirt. He'd called her "Skirt" from the start. A satire on police chauvinism. And because it was him, because she knew it meant the opposite of what it would have meant coming from a sexist prick, she'd liked it. She'd only ever worn skirts for him. To feel the pleasure of his hand sliding up inside. The enjoyable shamelessness of it bunched up around her waist, her panties halfway down her legs, him inside her.

"Not your handwriting, unless you disguised it," he said.

Valerie looked at the envelope. It was addressed to NICHOLAS BLASKOVITCH.

Not her handwriting.

"What is this?" she said. He wasn't looking at her. He was averted. Palpably angry. And sad.

"Just let me know when you're ready to talk about it."

"Nick?"

But he'd turned and walked away.

She opened the envelope.

The Bryte Clinic.

Oh God.

For a few moments, after she'd read the appointment form, Valerie just sat still. Then she slid the single sheet back into the envelope, folded it, and put it in her purse.

How?

It didn't matter how. Only *that*. Only that he knew the truth. Or rather half the truth.

Her intention, when she got to her feet, was to go straight to Blasko's lab. But her phone rang en route. It was Liza.

"Tire dry-cast is a match," Liza said. "Looks like it's your guys."

"Fuck."

"Yeah, I know."

"DNA from the sequins?"

"Couple of hours."

"Call me as soon as you have it."

"I will. You OK? You sound weird."

"I'm fine," Valerie said. "Just call me as soon as it's confirmed."

Blasko was alone in a room filled with baffling equipment, working on a desktop. Valerie saw him kill the screen when she entered. A back room of her mind thought it knew why.

"It's not what you think," she said.

"You weren't pregnant?"

"Yes, I was pregnant. But I didn't have an abortion."

He shook his head. As in, what's the point of lying *now*?

"I had a miscarriage."

Which checked him. Yanked the anger choke chain. It hurt her heart that she could see him thinking, immediately, of her pain. Of what that would have been like for her. Never mind what it was like for him. It pierced her that his reflex was still there, to care for her more than for himself.

"I made an appointment with the clinic," she said, the nakedness of the words shocking to her. "To buy myself time. I didn't know what to do."

His shoulders—his whole body—relaxed a few degrees. Into sadness.

"But I lost it anyway," she said, bowing her head. "A week before I was supposed to go."

They were silent for a moment. Then he said, very quietly: "Was it mine?"

Options shuffled in her head. Her abdomen ached. She remembered the young doctor's tired face, her outstretched latexed hand. What it held. The fetus curled like a question mark. There was only the truth to offer him.

"I don't know. I'm sorry."

Sorry. Sorry. Sorry. The word was their disease. Along with "love."

The lab was windowless, fluorescent-lit. In a corner, a piece of equipment the size of a washing machine emitted a soft sound.

Valerie sat on the edge of his desk. She didn't trust her legs to hold her up. Her face was heavy with heat. She kept her hands pressed in her lap.

"I did everything wrong," she said. "Don't think I don't know that."

She was aware of him trying to make room in himself for all of it. Because that was how much he loved her.

Eventually he said, "Someone put the appointment letter here for me to find."

Aside from the horror and intensity and exhaustion, this fact had been quietly working at both of them. Cops.

"I realize that," she said.

"Someone here got it in for you?"

"Looks that way."

"How'd they get access?"

I just want to be as useful as I can be, Carla had said. The FBI could get access. If they put their minds to it. Allowing full paranoia in, Valerie pictured Carla going through her garbage and counting the empties, watching her via hidden cameras in her apartment, clocking her near miss on 280, compiling a get-her-off-the-case file.

Then she remembered the envelopes on the passenger seat of the Cherokee. Manila envelopes.

"I don't know," Valerie said, not quite knowing why she didn't mention York. "I really don't."

"Well, it's not a small thing," Blasko said. "We need to find out."

We. Collusion. Was there ever a time since they'd met when she stopped thinking of them as allies? We. Us. You and me. Thinking of a future without him was like thinking of never being warm enough for the rest of her life, the big world a place of edged drafts and icy currents, the daily building fatigue of restless cold. Which wouldn't kill you, but which wear you down. Which would leech the joy. Which would leave you empty and functional. Since she'd lost him, that was how Valerie imagined herself growing old. Empty and functional. A dead-hearted, stunted woman you could count on.

"Don't worry," she said. "I'll find out."

"You should have told me."

"I know."

"Why didn't you?"

"Because I didn't want to drag you back in. What if it hadn't been yours?"

"Would you have gone ahead and gotten rid of it if it had been?"

Well? Would she? She'd barely admitted to herself making the appointment. Just as she'd barely admitted to herself what would be involved in determining paternity. Could they even test for that while the child was a tiny thing inside her? Wouldn't she have had to *have* it, first? There were so many questions she'd just shoved to the back of her mind, telling herself: *You don't have to decide anything right now. You have time. You've bought yourself some time.*

"I had no right to ask you to come back," she said.

"I had a right to know if I had a kid."

"I know. I *know*."

The machine in the corner exhaled its soft sound. Valerie thought it would be claustrophobic to work in here, no windows. At least from her desk there was a view, uninspiring rooftops, but an occasionally cheering slab of San Francisco sky.

"Was it a boy or a girl?" he said.

"I don't know. I didn't want to know."

His effort to accommodate all this was almost audible. It was as if she could hear his mind or soul trying to expand, to grow around it. *And in his own weak person, if he can, / Must suffer dully all the wrongs of Man.* All the wrongs. This wrong. Her wrong. Was there any situation in her life this fucking poem didn't apply to?

"Did you want me to come see you last night?" he said.

Every ounce of her decency gathered and told her to lie.

But the one indecent weakness was stronger.

"You know I did," she said. Then, after a pause: "But I understand now why you didn't."

She wanted to touch him. Bypass the razor wire of words. Instead, she reached for the desktop's mouse.

"Hey," he said. "Don't."

She ignored him. The screen saver's vortex of colored dots disappeared and was replaced by rows of thumbnail photos. Their content half evident, even at reduced size.

"You don't want to see those," he said.

She didn't know why she did. Except that she wanted so badly to put her arms around him that if she didn't distract herself, that was exactly what she'd do. And even the indecent weakness knew that wouldn't be fair to him. She clicked on a thumbnail at random.

She'd prepared herself, she thought. But she wasn't prepared. She'd been expecting pornography, the gross disproportions of pedophilia. What she saw was a child's scarred torso, latticed with cuts, some healed into silver threads, some rawer, infected. The child was too young for Valerie to tell whether it was a boy or a girl. She felt Blasko's body go slack with defeat.

"Christ," she said, though the word felt dead in her mouth.

She clicked on another image. And another, and another.

They were all children, all maimed by abuse. By torture, since there was no more honest a word for it. Backs, chests, legs, arms, genitals. Systematic mutilation. Mutilation with thinking behind it. It was wearying, that she could see the delight doing this would have given the people who'd done it.

"These are . . . This is . . ."

"Yeah," Blasko said. "It's an emerging market. You want the icing on the cake? Some of this stuff is coming out of CPS."

Child Protective Services. The work goes into you. The work sows its seeds.

"We've got fifteen different agencies under investigation," he said. "America's not going to want to swallow this. Not that it's peculiar to America."

Valerie couldn't stop. There was an appalling rhythm of disbelief and recognition. It was always the same, whatever the horror. You thought: Surely we couldn't be doing this? Then immediately felt nauseous déjà vu: Of course we were doing this. We'd always been doing this. This was just another of the things we did. The human story was the story of the things we did. And this, like it or not, was one of them. Along with poetry and the Sistine Chapel and jokes and forgiveness and compassion and love. *Among the Just, / Be just, among the Filthy, filthy too . . .*

"Do you need to see all of them?" Blasko asked quietly. Valerie knew he'd understood the question her actions were asking: *What room will any of this leave for us? What room will it leave for love?*

"Please stop," Blasko said, putting his hand over hers.

Valerie looked away from the screen. *Could* they remain uninfected by this? It was just their particular version of the standard cop question: Can you see what you have to see every day and yet live whole, with tenderness and humor and hope?

With the last of her perverseness or selflessness or sheer confusion, she turned back to the screen and clicked on one more image, his hand still lightly on hers.

It wasn't the worst she'd seen, but it was the most bizarre. A child's bare back covered in cuts and burns—dozens, scores, more than a hundred—that at first glance looked random. That still looked random, even after she'd noticed what looked like a letter *A* on the left shoulder, formed of cigarette burns. A fluke, an accidental initial.

Then she looked more closely.

There was an *F* just above the sacrum. A *B* halfway down the spine. A deep, barely healed *R* below the right scapula. Letters. Whoever had done this had carved or scorched or slashed or gouged the alphabet into this young flesh. Sometimes the same letter appeared more than once.

"Hey," Blasko said. "Come on. Stop. Enough."

He lifted her hand from the mouse. Clicked. Killed the screen. They sat, not looking at each other. Sadness and damage and loss. Yes. But in spite of all of it, the sweet, flickering insistence of the connection between them.

"I'll say this one last time," she said. "Because if I keep saying it, it'll start to poison both of us: I'm sorry."

He reached out and put his hand on her knee. The weight and warmth of it there. How starved of intimacy she'd been. How starved of affection. Three years of telling herself that part of her life was over. Three years of not believing what she told herself. Three years (it was obvious to her now) of waiting for their story to start again.

"OK," Blasko said. "There's no—"

But the door opened and a technician entered, talking on his cell phone. Blasko dropped his hand, not quite in time. Valerie stood up straight. She and Blasko exchanged a look. Later? Yes, later.

Halfway back to her office, Valerie ran into Carla York in the corridor.

"Oh, hey," Carla said. "There you are. Listen, I don't want to—"

Valerie went to move past her. Carla blocked her.

"Valerie, Jesus. I'm talking to—"

Valerie pushed her aside. "Stay the fuck out of my way," she said.

"What the hell is *wrong* with you?" Carla said.

"You think I don't know what's going on?" Valerie said.

"What?"

"You think I don't know what you're doing here?"

"I don't know what you're talking about."

"Listen to me," Valerie said. "You're not going to—"

Valerie froze.

Carla was looking at her as if she *didn't* know what she was talking about. Or rather Carla was *trying* to look at her as if she didn't know what she was talking about. And not quite succeeding.

But all of that had become, in an instant, secondary to Valerie.

Oh my God. Holy fuck.

"Look," Carla began, "I don't know what you think is—Hey! Valerie?"

Valerie had turned and was hurrying down the corridor.

A blurred half minute later, she was back at Blasko's office. The technician had finished his call and was now at his desk, spectacles on, lit by the computer screen's light. Blasko was over by the quiet machine in the corner. He turned when she entered.

"Get the last image I was looking at back up," she said.

"What?"

Valerie was at his desk, reaching for the mouse. "The pictures I was just looking at. The last one. Jesus . . ." She'd clicked the screen open, but it was now on a page of online dialogue exchanges. One of which said: *Vanilla, of course! What's yours?*

"The pictures, Nick. Fuck."

"Hold on, hold on," Blasko said. "Let me . . . Wait."

He closed the page and returned to the desktop. Answered the security prompt with a password Valerie didn't catch. Opened a folder. The thumbnails reappeared.

"What's going on?"

Valerie grabbed the mouse and began opening and closing the images, searching.

"Wait," Blasko said. "Here. This one."

The image of the kid's body reopened. Valerie scrutinized it. Blasko didn't ask. Didn't need to. He knew the shift in her aura. What it meant. His own went the same way, when the work took over. The work took over and everything else—*everything* else—dropped away. It excited him to feel it in her again. It was the other big force that bound them, the disease they'd signed up for, years ago.

"Where's enlarge?" Valerie said. The software was unfamiliar. The drop-downs didn't mean anything.

"Here. Double size?"

"Do it."

The image expanded.

Valerie stared.

Felt all the exhaustion burned away in a second.

The child's body with the tortured flesh. The brutally carved letters. The scars. *A . . . R . . . Q . . .*

But it wasn't the written-on body she needed to decode. It was the environment in which the body had been photographed. It was the *background.*

A child's room. The corner of an unmade bed. A window looking down onto a lawn with an out-of-focus solitary tree. A wall with the corner of an alphabet chart, each letter illustrated with a brightly colored image.

A is for APPLE
B is for BALLOON
C is for CLOCK
D is for DINOSAUR
E is for ELEPHANT
F is for FORK
G is for GOOSE
H is for HAMMER

All her sane instincts said: *Calm down. Wait. Let it settle. Hundreds of thousands of homes and kindergartens probably have the exact same chart.*

"Reduce it again," she said. "Get the window view in focus."

Blasko moved the mouse again. Clicked. The image returned to its original size.

Valerie bent closer to the screen.

But she didn't need to. She already knew.

The tree on the lawn outside had a double trunk. An inverted *Y.*

The tree in front of which Katrina Mulvaney, a little more than half her short lifetime ago, had been photographed.

46

"Get me everything you have on this image," Valerie said over her shoulder. She was half out of Blasko's office. "Where it came from. Who uploaded it. When it was taken."

"There's only—," Blasko began, but Valerie was already racing down the corridor.

Back at her own desk, she Googled "weird shaped trees." Five million results. She typed in: "weird shaped tree Hoppercreek Camp." Hit Images.

It was the first result.

Our resident freak-tree, the caption said. *Redding, CA.*

Redding. Maybe two hundred miles north of San Francisco.

Her internal phone rang.

"Valerie, listen to me," Blasko said. "We already have the distributors. They're serving time. This case was one of—"

"It's not the distributors I'm interested in. It's the kid in the picture."

Silence. Cop computation.

"Jesus Christ," Blasko said. "It's your guy?"

"Do you know who took it?"

"No. It's a Polaroid. Scanned five years ago. No original. But I can talk to someone who might be able to give you a best-guess circa."

"Do it. Call me. I have to go."

Her body was livened. The dead women bristled around her.

When it happened, it was always like this: the kaleidoscope confusion of case details at a single twist starting to rearrange themselves into a picture. You couldn't see it fast enough. You had to force yourself not to let the thrill blur your focus, not to miss the *one* detail that could still cost you the seconds or minutes or hours that would leave someone dead.

Valerie collected herself and called Katrina's parents. *Please don't let it be Dale who answers.*

"Hello?" Dale Mulvaney said.

"Mr. Mulvaney, it's Valerie Hart." They'd been on first name terms through the investigation, but the memory of their last encounter made her formal. There was a pause before Dale replied. Valerie could feel what was happening in him, the atomized despair regathering in an instant.

"What is it?" Dale said. He didn't sound drunk. Just hoarse. Just fraught. Just a step away from blowing his brains out.

"I need to know exactly when Katrina attended summer camp at Hoppercreek."

"When she . . . What?"

"When Katrina was around eleven or twelve, she went to summer camp at a place called Hoppercreek, upstate in Redding. I'm just trying to pin down a date."

Another pause.

"Someone from . . . You think . . ."

Adele's voice in the background. "Dale? Is it something? What is it?"

"When did Kat go to this place Hoppercreek?" Dale said.

Valerie pictured Adele's confusion, the groping through grief for facts. Dale's brewing impatience.

"I don't . . . It was . . . She was eleven, I guess. She was eleven."

Valerie did the math: 1990.

"What is it?" Dale said to Valerie. "You got something?"

Valerie knew what would happen: She would tell them, and their anger and loss would refocus. They'd been drifting through bereavement. This would wake them up again, give them something to hold on to. But it would be a betrayal, even if Valerie caught the killers. Beyond the token resolution, their daughter would still have been raped and murdered. Their daughter would still be dead. Victims' loved ones said they wanted justice. And they did. But all justice proved was that justice wasn't enough. How could it be? The only thing that could possibly be enough was the victim brought back, whole and alive. The only thing that could possibly be enough was for none of it to have happened.

"It's very remote," Valerie lied. "You know we've felt all along that Katrina must have known the person responsible for her death. It's hard to abduct someone in broad daylight in a city like San Francisco. But none of the interviews we conducted gave us a viable suspect. It's just possible that Katrina knew her killer from a *long* time ago. And it's possible that he was the person who took the photograph of her Adele gave me at our last meeting. Please don't raise your hopes too high. It really is very remote."

It took her desperate minutes to get off the phone (Claudia Grey minutes; all time now was Claudia-time). Dale and Adele wanted to go through it, the reasoning, the probability, the wretched chain of cause and effect. Tough for Valerie to do while leaving out the alphabet chart and the mutilated child's body. But she wasn't going into that. It would bring back the objects. Katrina's object. The candy apple forced into her vagina. Valerie wanted to spare Dale and Adele hearing about that again. A is for APPLE.

"I'll call you as soon as I have more," she said. "But right now, I have to get going. I don't want to lose a moment."

That worked. Guilt. Tell them they're slowing the process down. Make them understand that the longer they kept her talking, the longer their daughter's killers were out there enjoying their lives.

And the nearer Claudia Grey got to death.

"Right, right, OK," Dale said. "Understood. You'll let us know as soon as—"

"You'll be the first," Valerie said. "I promise."

The best-case scenario was that the kid in the picture was now a grown man (and serial killer) still living in the house he'd been tortured in as a child. Valerie barely admitted it as even a theoretical possibility. Because the best-case scenario made it its business never to be the *actual* case scenario.

The novelty tree was hardly a secret. On the contrary. It was a quirky attraction people with too much time on their hands drove out to see. A call to Redding's Visitors' Bureau got her the address. Current residents since 2008 were listed as Warren and Corrine Talbot. A second call to the County Recorder's Office at the local city hall got her—eventually—the name of the owner in 1990: Jean Ghast. According to the records, Jean bought the place in 1974.

On the surface it didn't fit: a woman. But there would have been a lover, Valerie supposed, a man to whom she was in thrall. There would have been someone. It was a refinement of male cruelty: to manipulate women into surrendering their own children to abuse.

Valerie hit keys and opened windows, scrolled, selected, entered. That pause waiting for information to load that made you acutely conscious of your existence. She thought of her grandfather's time on the force. Manila files, indexes, carbon sheets, paper clips. The fragility of physical records, the smell of ink and the heavy insect natter of typewriters. How much harder the job would have been then. How much easier for killers to go uncaught. And here she was without the excuse of antiquated equipment, with all the help technology could give—and eight women were still dead.

With a ninth woman waiting on her.

She forced herself to slow down, repeat what she knew. What she knew was that in the summer of 1990, someone had photographed Katrina in front of the two-legged tree. The house to which the tree belonged contained an alphabet chart depicting objects that corresponded to the ones found in the bodies of the victims. A brutalized child—a male child—had been photographed in that house. There was no logical necessity that the juvenile in the photograph had grown up to be Katrina's killer. There was no *logical* necessity. (Valerie wondered, briefly, if the photographer of *both* kids—the abused boy and Katrina—was the person she was looking for.) But there was something about the figure in the photograph.

A hopelessness spreading from his scarred shoulders like invisible wings. Cop sense insisted. The Machine insisted.

In the midst of her rush was a small deflation: that grotesque mistreatment had produced a grotesque person. That there was mitigation. That there was partial cause, partial explanation. The world didn't want it that way, of course. The tabloids liked their monsters simple: *pure evil*. No excuses. No history. No comprehension.

And in his own weak person, if he can,
Must suffer dully all the wrongs of Man.

The poem, she realized, might have been about a cop. In his own weak person. In *her* own weak person. Christ. Weakness she had in spades.

None of which altered the facts. That the child had grown up. That he had killed at least eight women. That he could be killing Claudia this very minute. That there were eighteen letters of the alphabet still to go.

47

It took longer than it should have.

It took more Claudia-time than it should have.

But mid-trawl through Vital Records, she got a call back from the Redding local newspaper.

"Valerie Hart," she said.

"Detective Hart," a woman's voice replied. "This is Joy Wallace at the Redding *Record Searchlight*. You were inquiring about the death of Jean Ghast?"

"Yes?"

"Oh, boy." Pause. "This is the serial case, right?"

Valerie tensed. Journalism's quid pro quo reflex. Not many in the world knew she was the Lead on the Case. But everyone in the media did. The cop who couldn't stop those women getting butchered. Famous National Failure.

"It's off the record," she said.

"Relax, Detective," Joy Wallace said. "I'm not angling. Listen, I'll send you a link to the story, but I can give you the basics right now."

"Go ahead," Valerie said, pen poised over her legal pad.

She knew. She knew the information was *the* information. The information like a single string sticking out of an impossibly knotted ball that, when pulled, unraveled the whole mess. The moment just before you got the information fired up your certainty, as if you weren't discovering something new, but remembering something you'd always, deep down, known. The moment before the information was a moment of recognition.

In the early summer of 1992, Joy Wallace told her, fifty-eight-year-old Jean Ghast was found dead at the bottom of the stairs in her Redding home. The coroner's verdict was an equivocal combo of natural causes and accidental death: Jean, with a known coronary condition, had had a heart attack. Either she'd had the attack at the top of the stairs and fallen, or she'd fallen first and the shock had precipitated the attack. There was no sign of a break-in. Nothing was missing from the house. She'd had a reputation as a woman who kept herself to herself, but no known enemies. She'd lived alone ever since her troubled daughter, Amy, moved away (*ran* away, gossip said) in 1979, at the age of sixteen. There was no Mr. Ghast. Jean had raised Amy on her own.

Some six years after leaving home, Amy had reappeared for a few days, with a man and a five-year-old son. They didn't stick around, but thereafter the boy sometimes spent weekends with his grandmother. He never went beyond the house's front or rear yard, and Jean Ghast rarely brought him into town. The kid was, gossip also insisted, "not all there." He barely spoke, in fact.

Two days after Jean's body was discovered, hikers in the Lassen Volcanic Natural Park found a twelve-year-old boy, wandering, "disoriented," all alone. When they could get sense out of him, he gave his name as Leon Ghast.

It took another two days (twenty-four hours with the Redding PD, twenty-four hours with CPS) to establish that the kid was the grandson of Jean Ghast. Five years earlier, Amy (now a heroin-addicted prostitute of fluid abode) had gotten pregnant by Lewis Crowe, a bipolar Las Vegas pimp and drug peddler who'd been killed in a narcotics deal gone wrong a month before his son was born.

"But that wasn't the half of it," Joy Wallace told Valerie.

Leon Ghast had not been "visiting" his grandmother on the weekends. He'd been living with her for seven years.

"The house is on the edge of town," Joy said. "Bordered by Hoppercreek Camp on one side and the woods on the other. It was only when it all came out that people conceded that they'd never actually seen Amy dropping the kid off there or picking him up."

"It all," when it did come out, was still a talking point in Redding.

"The kid had been *ravaged*," Joy said with the twenty-first century mixture of horror and boredom. "She'd kept the signs of damage off his arms and legs, but the rest of him was a mess."

Amy Ghast had died of an overdose in 1989. There were no living relatives either willing or in a position to take care of Leon.

"So he went back through CPS," Joy said. "You can imagine the story. Four years of foster homes, bounced in and out of care . . . To say he had behavioral and learning difficulties is an understatement. Acute word-blindness plus seven years of brutal alphabet aversion therapy. He hadn't been to school in years. Seriously? It was a miracle the kid could *talk*."

Then, in 1997, Leon caught a break. He was fostered by Lloyd and Teresa Conway, wealthy, childless born-again Christians, residents of Fresno. Lloyd had built a highly successful thermal engineering company—CoolServ—and started training Leon at the nuts-and-bolts end of the business, which specialized in custom freezers.

"For all I know," Joy said, "he still works out of the plant there."

Valerie's palms were hot. Around her, the office was vivified. Claudia-time passed in a deafening hiss. "Do you have contact details for the foster parents?" she said.

"Yeah, but they're from way back. Don't know if they're still good. We did a follow-up story a year after they took him in."

Valerie took down the information. "You did a follow-up story. Photograph of Leon?"

Pause. Joy giving her room to appreciate the points she was racking up.

"Fax or email?"

"Both."

"Give me five minutes to dig it out."

"Will the Conways remember you?" Valerie said. "Was it you who did the follow-up story?"

"Yes."

"Then call them. I need a current workplace and address for Leon. Do it right now."

Pause.

"Please," Valerie added.

"OK, Detective."

"I have to repeat," Valerie said. "This is off the record."

"Is it him?" Joy said.

"I don't know," Valerie lied. "But we can't afford for any of this to get out prematurely. I mean it. Office gossip lockdown."

"I'll do what I can," Joy replied. "But you should've pretended to be someone else when you called. I'm safe, but this is a newspaper. I guess the clock's ticking."

The clock's ticking.

The email came first. Valerie opened the attached image.

It was a sunny outdoor shot of Lloyd and Teresa Conway on a green lawn, a sprightly couple in pastel casuals, smiling shyly into the camera. Between them was a dark-haired boy of (the caption said) sixteen years, broad-boned and taller than both his foster parents, with a smile that didn't quite disguise its reluctance.

Valerie brought the zoo suspect image up alongside it.

Two pictures separated by thirteen years.

But unless her system of resemblances was completely awry, it was the same person.

Leon Ghast.

48

Earlier that morning Will Fraser had prepared himself for a long and dismal trawl through the case files. He sat at his desk just after 6 A.M. with a large Starbucks latte (he refused to use the word "grande" when ordering; the imported terminology for coffee sizes was close to making him quit *going* to fucking Starbucks) and the photograph of the torn pocket propped between his desktop's keyboard and screen.

Even a first glance through the amassed material was enough to bring down the feeling of hopelessness. All that information that led nowhere. Individuals fleetingly in the suspect spotlight. Addresses, phone numbers, interview transcripts. Leads that dead-ended. The appalling weight of detail gathered around the dead women, yielding nothing, a pent thunderstorm that wouldn't break.

He went through the victim photographs, accepted the occasional images from last night's ornate sex with Marion they set off: a bare leg; breasts; the sole of a foot. He was used to these neural necessities, juxtapositions, connections. It was years since they'd had any power to surprise or worry him. You were a cop. The job made death and violence and ugliness part of your mental continuum, part of your frame of reference. You had to learn not to be alarmed. You had to learn how to accommodate yourself. It wasn't the end of the world. Most things, if you were a cop, weren't the end of the world.

If you were a cop, you made room for the new version of yourself the job forced you to become—or you quit.

He took another sip of his latte (he had misgivings about the word "latte," too), thought about going out—already—for a cigarette, resisted the temptation—then, since it was the most recently added folder on his desktop, clicked open FREEZER IN RV.

He'd been disappointed that his theory hadn't provided results. But even in the absence of results, he hadn't been quite able to leave it alone. He had a recurring vision of two guys in a top-of-the-line RV easing a garbage-bagged body into its coffin-sized deep freeze, then refitting the dummy shelf of frozen burgers, pizzas, and ice cream. Birds Eye. DiGiorno. Ben & Jerry's. Comforting brands concealing a monstrous secret. Valerie hadn't been enthusiastic when he'd pitched it to her. He was worried about Valerie. She was less and less herself. Never the same since the Suzie Fallon case. And now Blasko had returned. It was all still there between the two of them, though half the department knew what had happened three years ago. But he'd come back—for more, presumably, poor bastard. Not that Will could blame him. Valerie was worth coming back for. Will had had a dangerous crush on her himself when they started working together (it had taken Marion a long time to like her, not surprisingly); but he loved his wife. The truth of that was what made everything bearable. That and the kids they'd—

Jesus Christ.

He froze.

URS.

Universal Refrigeration Services.

Oakland, California.

It was the third place he'd visited.

URS.

Motherfucker *worked* there. They had no record of a custom RV job, because he did it himself.

A thrill went through Will's tiredness like an arm sweeping all the objects off a cluttered desk.

He Googled URS.

We specialize in creative solutions for multiple industries, including food and beverage distributors, food processing, supermarkets and grocery stores, liquor and convenience stores, restaurants, wineries, breweries, florists, biotechs and laboratories, as well as other specialty projects like ripening rooms and beer caves.

And freezers to transport corpses in your RV.

Fuckin' A.

But the logo didn't match. The pocket scrap was white on blue, in caps. The Web site showed lowercase black with a yellow border on a red background. It was on the vans, the trucks, the letterhead, the warehouse.

He broadened his search. Maybe there were two outfits with similar names? He'd checked several first time around, maybe half a dozen. All he had on the pocket was a definite *R*. The other two letters were only partial. The *U* could be a *J,* or possibly a *W.* The *S* could be . . . Well, it couldn't much be anything other than an *S.*

He tried "JRS San Francisco." Got a bunch of stuff, none of which was anything to do with freezers. Ditto "WRS San Francisco." A religious group . . . A digital radio station . . . A dance company . . .

Fuck. Was he crazy?

But he knew he'd seen it.

He called URS.

No answer. Too early.

He snatched the photo from the desktop and grabbed his jacket.

Driving to Oakland, Will mentally reran his first visit to the plant. Two industrial units at right angles to each other, an asphalt yard, and a fleet of trucks. He'd gone through the warehouse, up two flights of stairs, down at least three corridors, into the manager's office. The logo had been the same everywhere. *Not* the one on the pocket. The manager was Tony Dawson, a paunchy guy in a plaid flannel shirt and chinos. Hair the color of wet sand and meaty, freckled hands. A little thrilled (and suspicious) to be suddenly dealing with True Crime—not that Will had given anything away. (The press knew Valerie—the *public* knew Valerie—but the rest of the team was faceless, thank God.) Dawson had taken him into his office (feebly tinselled, here and there,

with a bedraggled artificial tree in one corner) and spent thirty minutes going through job histories for the date range. The office wasn't
exactly a mess, but it needed sorting out. One of the filing cabinet's
drawers was broken. Dawson's golf bag was on the floor, a chipped
driver sticking out. There were three desktop computers, for no good
reason Will could figure. A cardboard box filled with pink invoice
copies. (*Paper?* Will had thought. *Who the fuck still used paper?* But the
world was like that: never quite so high-tech as the paranoid version
of it you carried around in your head.) In the corner—

Holy Jesus.

Will's hands tightened on the wheel.

In the midst of the memory was a charge of self-congratulation:
Fuck, you're good. The Machine still works. He was smiling. (While
another disinterested part of him thought: *This is the job. You smile because you just got a stride closer to some bastard who butchers women. Should
you smile? Would the dead women want you to smile?* But if there was no
smiling, if there was no *delight* in getting the job done, would the dead
women ever have their revenge? And wasn't that what they wanted?
Wasn't that all that was left to them?)

In the corner of Dawson's office, there had been a half-life-sized
cardboard cutout of a bald guy with a very black mustache and very
blue eyes, smiling.

Wearing blue overalls with the URS logo on the pocket.

The logo they must have changed since.

The logo in the photograph.

The logo on the pocket from the dead woman's hand.

That? Dawson had said, seeing Will studying the beaming cardboard baldie. That's Frank Ransome, my predecessor. Got National
Manager of the Year back in 2010. I made a dumb-ass joke that I
wouldn't take it out of my office until *I'd* won it. Yeah. I really need
to think before opening my mouth.

The morning shift was up and running by the time Will pulled
into the URS parking lot, but Dawson wasn't in yet. The warehouse
manager, Royle, a short, wiry white guy in his fifties with a small
tough, shaved head, was.

"Jesus, yeah," Royle said when Will showed him the photograph of Valerie's Zoo Guy. "I remember him. This guy . . ." He paused. "What's the investigation?"

"Homicide."

"Shit, seriously? He's dead?"

"No, he's not dead. Just tell me what you know about him. Let's start with his name."

The reality of whom he was talking to and the dark intrigue that spiraled out from it were starting to dawn on Royle. His face was busy with wonderings.

"Jesus, you mean he's a *suspect?*"

"He's just someone we need to talk to. And that's between you and me, OK?"

Royle wet his lips with a lizardy flick of his tongue. "Sure," he said. "Sure, sure."

"Now, can you give me his name?"

"Xander," Royle said. "Xander King."

Will wrote it in his notebook. "That's quite a handle," he said.

"I know, right? But there you go. You know, you should really talk to Lester. Lester worked with him."

"I will, but can you just take me through what you know? He worked here, so you'll have his address on file. I need to see it."

Royle looked embarrassed. "Well, the thing is," he said, "he was off the books. Cash in hand. We don't do that anymore, but Ransome did. This is three years ago. I don't know if we had an address. You can get the boss to check, I guess. Or Marcy'll be in in a minute. She can look for you."

"What did Xander King do here?"

"He was a . . . Well, to be honest, he was kind of a floater. Did everything from humping boxes to cleaning the toilets. He claimed he knew the freezer business, but Ransome never bought it. Thing was, he couldn't read or write. I mean not a word. Only totally illiterate person I've ever actually met. But Ransome was a little dyslexic himself, and felt sorry for the guy. Personally, I never liked him. Matter of fact, he gave me the creeps. Even Lester didn't really know him. He was pretty quiet. I thought he was maybe a little, you know, retarded."

Royle left a pause in which was his uncertainty about whether it was OK to use the word "retarded." Will Fraser just nodded. Political correctness was one of the many luxuries being a cop meant you couldn't afford. Only the information mattered.

"Anyway," Royle continued, reassured by Will's nods, "the guy inherited some money from his stepdad or something. Came in one day and told a bunch of people he was pissed at for whatever reason that they could go fuck themselves. Then we never saw him again. Hell of a thing. *Hell* of a thing—right?"

"Yeah, that's something," Will said. Valerie's words from the last meeting returned: They could be independently solvent. "How much did he come into?" Will asked.

"No one knows," Royle said. "Enough for him to quit here, he figured."

Enough to finance a three-year killing spree, he figured.

"OK," Will said. "I need that address check. Who'd you say can do that?"

"Marcy. But she's not in yet. Shouldn't be more than ten minutes."

"What about this guy, Lester? You say he worked with King?"

Royle's face betrayed the beginnings of disappointment that his role in the excitement was most likely over now. The police spotlight was already moving away to its next actor. "Yeah," he said. "Let me see if I can find him. Damn. Xander King. Holy moly."

"Let's go," Will said.

But Lester, it turned out, had called in sick yesterday, and hadn't shown up yet today either.

Dawson's secretary, Marcy, arrived, and while she confirmed there was no address for Xander King, there was one, plus phone number, for Lester Jacobs.

Will called the number. Three times. Three times got bumped to voice mail.

49

Lousy timing. Captain Deerholt stepped out of his office into the corridor just as Valerie—with Laura Flynn and Ed Pérez—was about to pass. The door was open. Inside, Carla York was standing by the window, arms folded.

"In here, Val, please."

"Sir, we've got him," Valerie said. "We're en route right now. There's no time."

"What?" Two seconds for Deerholt to process, recalibrate, know it wasn't a ruse.

"Agent York goes with you," was all he said. "And whatever the fuck's going on between you, stow it. Warrant?"

"Halloran's gone for it. But we've got probable cause anyway. Cap, we have to go right now."

"OK, go. Agent York?"

It had taken another thirty-eight Claudia Grey minutes, but they had Leon's current address. Right here in San Francisco. A fourth-floor walk-up in the Tenderloin. DMV turned up no match for the picture, but Joy had reported back after following up on the foster parents. Lloyd Conway had sold CoolServ and retired early. But pancreatic cancer meant he got less than two years to enjoy his retirement. His death had shattered his wife, Teresa, who had been in and out of heavily medicated depression ever since. "She's not exactly crazy," Joy told Valerie, "but you wouldn't want to put her on the stand for anything." It had taken Joy more than an hour on the phone with her to piece the narrative together. Leon hadn't lived with the Conways since he was nineteen. They'd had three years of trying to make it work, but—this was Joy reading between the lines—the kid hadn't settled. He'd worked with Lloyd at CoolServ, learned a little of the business, but took off as soon as he'd stashed some money. They didn't hear from him for months, initially, then years. It had tormented the Conways. In desperation, they hired a private detective, who'd spent months tracking him down. There had been a failed reunion. But as far as Teresa Conway knew, the address was still good. Valerie had been about to go back to the databases—then, with the common sense being a cop too often buried under hypothetical complexities, she'd checked the San Francisco white pages. And there it was, the only Leon Ghast in the book: 218 Ellis Street, Apartment 4D. As far as Valerie could determine, he hadn't been in registered employment for the last five years.

The detectives and Carla York went in Valerie's Taurus. Four uniforms in two squad cars behind. Sirens until two blocks away from Ellis.

There was no rear exit from the building except via the fire escape. Three floors up, Ed Pérez took one of the blues and got badge access to it through an apartment inhabited by a pair of sleepy Hispanic retirees. Leon's apartment was on the fourth floor.

Outside the door, Valerie turned to the nearest patrol officer, Galbraith, whom she knew. "Stay here," she said. "No one gets in or out. Anyone shows up, give a shout. But keep them here."

"Got it."

"You, too," she said to his partner, whose badge said KEELY. Not a rookie, but new enough to the business not to be fully armored against horror. And manifestly readying the story for McLusky's after work. Keely nodded.

Laura Flynn was checking the clip in her Smith & Wesson.

Valerie and Carla hadn't exchanged a word. The tension between them was a subpresence in the collective adrenal mass.

There was modest-volume music coming from beyond the door. Valerie rang the doorbell.

Pause. The moments. The police moments. The moments when the universe balanced. The dead women gathered in sad silence.

The music went down. Footsteps.

The eyehole blacked.

Pause.

"Yeah?"

Valerie held up her badge. "Police, sir. Open up, please."

Incredibly—she was expecting paranoia, drama, resistance, a *dialogue*—the bolt undrew and the door opened.

Facing her was a pretty guy who couldn't have been more than twenty-five years old. Blond dreads, blue eyes. A nose ring. A white cheesecloth Indian shirt. Battered Levi's. Purple Converse high-tops. No smell of hash. Hence the opened door.

Not Leon.

"Leon Ghast?" Valerie said, for the record.

The guy was doing what people did: summoning every gram of innocence. His face was fear and good citizenship. He was racing— as everyone who was nothing more than trivially guilty did—through the mental files of sins and misdemeanors for anything he'd done years ago that could conceivably have come around to bite him in the ass. He looked like a nervous angel. His mouth was open, waiting for his brain to finish self-Googling.

"Er, no," he said. "No, I'm not."

"Is this the residence of Leon Ghast?"

The kid shifted his weight from left foot to right. "Who?"

"Leon Ghast. Does he live here?"

"No," he said, though the admission plainly didn't make him feel good.

"May we come in?"

Valerie watched him hesitate. Felt television telling him to ask for a search warrant.

"Let's step inside, sir," Carla said, flipping open the universally recognized initials: FBI. "This is an urgent matter."

There was still some calculation. But the kid was sufficiently innocent to actually be afraid of the police. It was the veterans of guilt who didn't scare so easily, who had a vested interest in Knowing Their Rights.

"Uh, OK," he said.

Valerie shot Carla a look. *I've got this. Back off.*

They followed him inside. Standard Tenderloin one-bedroom, unloved furniture, bent venetian blinds, and a TV two generations behind. But surprisingly well kept. An Inuit rug that looked recently dry-cleaned on a polished wooden floor. Steel-framed abstract oil prints hanging straight. Three or four bookcases with titles neatly aligned. Valerie noted at least a third of them were black-spined Penguin Classics. The music was something ambient and lyricless. The first thing he did was reach for the remote and turn it off.

"Sit down, please," Valerie said. He'd let them in voluntarily and was manifestly shitting himself, so, since the bedroom door was open, she took a quick look inside. The white-linened bed was made. The same minimalist neat-and-tidy story. By the time she'd finished, Laura Flynn had checked the kitchen and nodded her the all-clear. The kid was sitting on the plump, seen-better-days green vinyl couch, body tense. The apartment smelled of homemade marinara sauce.

"First things first," Valerie said. "Could I see your ID?"

"What is this?" the kid said, forcing a desperate laugh.

"Let's just see the ID," Valerie said.

The kid reached into his back pocket and pulled out his wallet. Driver's license said: *Shaun Moore. Date of birth: 04-23-1991.* Oakland address three years out of date.

"OK, Mr. Moore," Valerie said. "We're looking for Leon Ghast. He's the registered tenant at this property. Do you know him?"

"I'm just staying here temporarily."

"That wasn't the question." Valerie had perfect control of the tonal gears.

The kid looked at the other police in the room. Their eyes all gave him the relevant information: *Talk to her, kiddo. There's no help here.*

"Do you know him?" Valerie repeated.

"I've never heard of him," the kid said. "You must have the wrong address."

Valerie waited a couple of beats.

"OK," she said. "This isn't an illegal sublet inquiry. Tell us the setup. Seriously. Whatever it is, it's cool with us. It's not what we're interested in."

It didn't take long. The kid was *sub*subletting. The original sublet was to a guy named Robert Biden, who'd been living here for just over two years. Valerie pulled out the photo of Leon Ghast. "Is this Robert Biden?" she asked.

"No."

"You sure?"

"I'm positive. That's not Rob. I've known the dude for years."

"Who was Rob subletting from?"

"I don't . . . Some guy named Zan."

"Zan what?"

"I don't know. I don't even know if that's his first name."

"Look at the photo again. Is this Zan?"

"I've never seen the guy. Seriously, I wouldn't know, because I've never seen him."

"Is any of the stuff in here his?"

"What?"

"Does any of the furniture here—are there clothes or anything of his still in the apartment?"

"Rob? I don't know about the furniture. But clothes . . . All his stuff's here. But I mean . . ."

"Anything here belong to Zan?"

"I don't know. You'd have to check with Rob."

Valerie's cell phone rang. It was Halloran.

"Warrant's been issued," he said. "Deerholt called the judge."

"Where do we find Rob Biden?" she said to Shaun Moore after she'd hung up.

"He's in Europe," the kid said. "He's in France . . . no, wait. He's in Spain. They were in Spain two days ago."

"They?"

"He's with his girlfriend."

"Do you have contact details for him? A hotel?"

"I don't know where he's staying. We just text."

"How long has he been away?"

"I don't know. Like, two months?"

"You're sure he's in Europe?"

"Yeah, I'm sure. Well I can't *prove* it, but I mean . . . I got a text from him couple of days ago. That's his cat right there."

A slender black and white cat with big eyes and a small head had appeared on the window ledge outside the cracked-open window. It was regarding them with surprise and affront.

"I'm feeding the cat," Shaun Moore said. "I mean I'm staying here, taking care of the cat."

"OK," Valerie said. "A warrant's been issued for a search of this address. There'll be people coming here to go over the apartment shortly. Detective Flynn, call Forensics."

"Forensics?" Shaun Moore said. He looked unequivocally terrified now.

"You got a photo of Rob? On your phone?" Valerie asked. She wasn't expecting it to be Leon, but she had to remind herself firstly that technically there was no concrete proof that Leon was the killer, and secondly that they were looking for *two* killers. This kid (instinct was already dismissing it) could be the beta. Nor was there any reason Leon Ghast would be using his real name. Zan? *Zan* could be the beta. Maybe Zan was the alpha and Leon was the beta? Hell, maybe Shaun Moore was the alpha.

But the objects. The alphabet chart. The *signature* was Leon's. And if this kid was a murderer, then Valerie's instincts were for shit. They'd request a DNA sample anyway, and since he was innocent, he'd give them one. A formality.

"Yeah, I think . . . Hang on." He started swiping through images. "Here you go. That's Rob."

Again, not Leon. Instead, another young, good-looking guy in his early twenties, with a shaved head and mischievous black-eyelashed green eyes. He was grinning into the camera, pretending to look crazy, an off-camera girl's bare shoulder next to his. Was Valerie looking at one of the murderers? Assuming the kid was telling the truth about Biden's trip away, that would rule him out of Claudia's abduction. But maybe the alpha had given him a sabbatical?

"Could you give me Rob Biden's cell phone number, please," Valerie said.

"Holy Jesus," Shaun Moore said. "I mean . . . What is this?"

"Where were you two nights ago?"

"What?"

"Two nights ago. Where were you?"

"I was . . . Fuck. Hold on a second—"

"Calm down, Mr. Moore. It's only two nights ago. Come on. Where were you?"

"I was . . . I was at a bar with my girlfriend. And two other guys."

"Which bar?"

"Sundown," he said. "It's on Webster. We were there till, like, two A.M."

"Good," Valerie said. "No problem. I believe you. But we can call these folks and get them to verify that—right?"

"Of course they'll verify it. I was *there.*"

"I hear you. Don't worry. That's where you were, you're good. Now, could you give me Rob's number, please?"

Shaun wrote it down. His hands were shaking. Valerie did the time difference math. Should be around 9 P.M. in Spain.

Voice mail. A young-sounding male voice, the message designed to express laconic good-humored weariness with the need for leaving messages: "Hi, this is Rob. Do the thing after the beep."

Valerie left a five-second silence and hung up. Tech would be able to tell her where the call had connected.

"We'd like you to come down to the station," she said to Shaun Moore. "We're going to go over the logistics, but I promise you this isn't a tenancy issue. You've got nothing to worry about on that score. If Rob's subletting, we don't care. It's the original tenant we need to talk to. You good to go?"

"Now?"

"If you wouldn't mind."

"Fuck," Shaun Moore said. *"Fuck."*

"Detective Flynn? Can you take Mr. Moore down in one of the

squad cars? Leave me Galbraith and Moyles. We'll need to do a door-to-door here. Get Ed in, will you?"

It was unlikely, but not impossible, that someone in the building would know where to find Leon Ghast.

"You staying?" Valerie said to Carla quietly, while Shaun Moore got his shit together.

"Why wouldn't I?" Carla said. "It'll be quicker."

Valerie was midway through the apartments on the next floor down with Carla, Ed, and Galbraith (no joy so far on Leon's photo), when her vision started acting up again. She had barely two or three seconds to note the cut-glass edging on the periphery before the tunnel closed around her, and everything went black.

Her knees smacking the hall floor probably stopped her from passing out. But it was several seconds before the world came back.

"Jesus, Detective, are you all right?" Galbraith said, bending over her, reaching down. "What the hell happened?"

Valerie was aware of Carla's dark slacks and low-heeled boots just a few feet away. She'd seen. Fuck. *Fuck.*

"I'm fine," she said. But when she tried to get her legs under herself, she felt sickness surge. She put her hand against the wall. "No breakfast," she said. "I'm fine. Just give me a moment."

Carla and Galbraith weren't the only witnesses. The tenants they'd been questioning had stepped out of their apartments into the corridor to gawp. A black woman in her fifties holding a toddler in her arms. A young overweight white guy in gray sweats and slippers, smoking.

Valerie, with shuddering determination, got to her feet without taking Galbraith's hand. Carla, she noted, was observing, standing staring at her with patent excitement in her face and limbs.

"You need to take ten," she said.

"I'm fine."

"You're not fine."

"Listen—," Valerie began—but her phone rang.

It was Will Fraser.

"OK," Will said. "We're in business."

"Go," Valerie said.

Will filled her in on the trip to URS, and from there to Lester Jacobs's apartment in the Castro. Lester, a sixty-two-year-old widower with only one functioning lung, was sick with a chest infection, and hadn't bothered answering the phone. By the time Will got to his apartment, Lester's daughter had arrived to check on him, and after a few minutes' persuasion let Will in.

"Leon Ghast," Valerie said.

"What?"

"His name's Leon Ghast."

"Not the name I got. I got Xander King. ID'd from the zoo photo."

Xander.

Zan.

Valerie had imagined it beginning with a *Z*. I don't even know if that's his first name, the kid had said.

"He's using an alias," Valerie said. "Fine. Go on."

"Long story short," Will said, "it's not like him and Lester were buddies, but about six months after King quit the URS job, they ran into each other. Our guy told Lester he'd bought a place in Utah."

"Address?"

"No. But it's a *state,* at least."

"OK. That it?"

"That's not enough?"

"You're the shit, Will."

"I'll see you back at the shop."

Carla was looking at her, waiting to be filled in.

Waiting for something, at any rate.

50

The child in Claudia reached out repeatedly to the idea that some force must intervene on her behalf. God. The Spirit of Justice. A strand of benign intelligence in the universe. But the reaching out found only silence and emptiness. God did not exist. There was no Spirit of Justice. The universe had no intelligence, benign or otherwise. If she'd doubted it in the past, she knew it for certain now.

She had to give herself things to do. If she did nothing, there was nothing but fear. She'd spent a long time scanning every inch of the basement as far as the bare bulbs' light allowed. If there was anything she could use as a weapon, she had to know exactly where it was for when they next opened the cage. She had to be ready. Her eyes tried to force the recesses to yield yard tools, a rusted hatchet, a broken broom, anything. But there was nothing. There was no telling what the half dozen cardboard boxes contained, but if she got past them, she wouldn't have longer than a couple of seconds. Maybe not even that. *If she got past them.* The thought of it, the two men with their hands on her and their breath on her face brought all the horror back. The horror was like a second person in the cage with her she mustn't look at. Because when she did, she saw the woman from the video, her utter helplessness, her body straining against the ropes, the veins in her throat bulging as the gag buried her scream, Xander's rapt concentration and the knife going in, the flesh opening. The simplicity of the flesh just opening like that. The woman's pale belly a widening gory grin. The same body that had been born, and had its umbilical cord cut, and been swaddled and rocked and loved. She saw all this and it was impossible to do anything except huddle against the furnace with her arms wrapped around herself, sick and shaking and alone.

So she gave herself things to do.

Right now, she'd given herself the task of searching beneath the furnace.

There was a four- or five-inch gap. Enough to get her arm in up to just below her elbow. She lay on her belly and walked her fingers around the entire area she could reach. It was thick with dust and fluff.

And nothing else.

The effort and pointlessness exhausted her.

She pulled her arm out. Scraped a graze on the baseplate's rusted edge. A few pricks of blood welled.

Blood.

She got back onto her knees.

You're lucky. You're so lucky. He's sick. It's the flu.

Which meant that for a short time she might have one of them to deal with instead of two.

Which meant—the logic was delighted and awful—she should act sooner rather than later.

Act?

What could she do?

The logic was there again: *You have to get him to open the cage.*

How?

How do you think?

It stilled her.

It stilled her because she knew the answer.

She knew the only thing she could conceivably use.

And everything in her said she couldn't.

Except the small part of her that said: *If it's that or what happened to the woman in the video, you can.*

The logic had a coda: *And it's going to happen to you anyway.*

Brutal to have let the thought in. But since she had, there was no unthinking it. It was like having swallowed something that was now quietly alive inside her. It was part of her, yes, it had been admitted—but it was too terrifying to confront properly. She wasn't ready. She couldn't stand it. She couldn't stand the truth of it.

She turned her attention to the back of the furnace.

A similar gap, perhaps a little broader than the one beneath its base. The whole unit was bolted to the wall on four hefty metal brackets. Heavy enough so that if she smashed one against his skull, it would buy her some time. The two on the far side were out of reach. She wrapped her fingers around the lower one nearest to her and tested how firmly it held.

It was solid. Completely immovable. The notion of her budging it with her bare hands was risible. She tried the upper one. The same. It was hopeless.

Her arm dropped in defeat.

Her fingers caught on the edge of something.

It was a thin metal placard, stamped, she assumed (braille-reading, breath held) with the unit's serial number or technical specifications. It was supposed to be held by four screws, one at each corner. But only the top right and the bottom left were in. The bottom left was very slightly loose.

Claudia felt the thickness of the metal. Thicker than a tin can, but thinner than a license plate.

Bendable?

She pulled at the unscrewed bottom right. There was give. Just. She could shape it with her foot if not with her hands.

If she could get it off. If she could get it off, she could bend it—*fold* it, effectively—make a tough edge . . . something . . . Use it to prize up a floorboard?

It was a pitiful thing to clutch at, but it was all she had. It was a piece of metal. It would be something to hold. Something between her and him. Something other than her own flesh and blood.

Fingertips dreaming, she felt for the screw heads. They were rounded, with a cross groove. Phillips screws. Her dad's toolbox with its odor of grease and steel. The novelty of helping him that day he'd built the birdhouse. Right, pass me the drill bit, Claudie. She'd been six or seven years old. The awe of initiation into this paternal mystery: DIY. These birds better appreciate this, he'd said. We're giving them five-star accommodation here. We're giving them the sparrow *Ritz.* She'd loved it, the idea of the birds discovering a wonderful cozy house, moving in, taking shelter from the elements.

She extracted her arm and dug in her pocket for the change. Two quarters and a dime.

Stop shaking. Don't drop them. Do this properly.

A quarter was too big. No purchase on the cross groove. She thought: *The dime will be too small. A nickel would be (à la Goldilocks) just right. And I don't have one of those.*

The dime wasn't just right—but it was close enough.

Maneuvering was awkward. There wasn't sufficient room to turn the coin without scraping the graze on her arm. Each twist inflicted a mean, precise burn. She didn't mind. It proved she was doing something. It was a relief.

The first screw—the top right—was out. She had to be careful. The placard was now hanging by a single screw. If it dropped and slipped away from her, it might end up out of reach. She adjusted, stretched, pressed as much of her arm against it as she could without making the unscrewing action impossible.

A thirty-degree turn.

Another.

It was working. It was coming loose.

Her hand was sweaty, fingers rich with nerves. The position she had to maintain made her shoulder ache. The absurdity of her hope—a thin metal plate—was available, but she ignored it, since there was no other hope.

The screw wobbled. Rattled. Dropped.

She crept her fingers around the edge of the plate and slid it toward her—worrying too late that the metal's rasp would be heard. In spite of her efforts, the movement scored the graze on her arm. But even that was an enhancement of the feeling of small triumph.

It was perhaps ten by six inches, less than an eighth of an inch thick. Manufacturer's logo: HeatRite. Model name: XS200.5. Then a string of embossed numbers that meant nothing to her.

Don't fuck this up. Think. Maximize.

Not strong enough to lever up a floorboard. And in any case, the notion of digging herself out from under the grille was ridiculous, a feeble, long-term project that would depend on them not killing her anytime soon.

When she'd pictured the plate's potential as a weapon, she imagined bending it lengthwise—some deep grammar of defense telling her the longer the implement, the less close you'd have to get to strike. But she saw now that wouldn't work. The metal was, if anything, *too* pliable. Folded lengthways in half—and even in half again—it wouldn't be strong enough not to buckle on impact. And she'd get only one chance. The alternative (the pain this was going to cost her was there in her hands already) was to fold or roll it *widthways.* She'd end up with something only six inches long, but significantly stronger, a short, irregular cigar of metal.

A door opened and closed upstairs.

She froze.

Footsteps crossed the hall above her. Another door opened and closed.

Silence.

She wiped her hands on her jeans.

HeatRite XS200.5. Someone, probably decades ago, had started a company called HeatRite. Someone from the world she'd lost. She pictured a guy in welding goggles and denim dungarees. He'd have a life. People who loved him. Beers with friends. Anxieties about overheads and tax returns. A whole wonderful swirling mass of ordinary details he'd never appreciate unless something like this happened to him.

She began to fold-roll the metal. It wasn't easy. Her fingers protested. Two nails broke. The action reminded her of the way she and Alison used to fold the purple tinfoil wrappers from Cadbury's Dairy Milk chocolate bars when they were kids. At the memory of chocolate, a little corner of herself complained that she was hungry. She hadn't eaten in . . . how long? Nothing since the burrito at the Whole Food Feast, whenever that was. Dehydrated, too. Her head ached. You finish this, she told herself, then you drink some water.

It took what felt like a long time. She had to keep stopping and slotting her hands into her armpits to ease the pain. When she was done, there was no disguising the negligibility of the result—a stunted baton—which would do nothing unless she got it directly into his eye. If she had something to hammer it into any kind of point . . .

She put it on the floor and flattened one end with her foot. Rotated it forty-five degrees, repeated the action. A third and fourth time would have completed the job, but by now the metal was too tightly packed. An improvement, though. The cigar tapered to a usefully vicious V. She gripped it in her fist. It felt good.

And terrifying. Because now there was nothing to do but wait for an opportunity to use it.

No.

Not wait for an opportunity.

Make one.

51

Upstairs in his dull room of thrift store furniture Paulie watched the videos and tried to jerk off. No good. He gave up. Just lay there, staring at the stained ceiling, his Vaselined cock lolling like a dead fish. Outside, the silver-blue small hours sky rolled away over the empty land. The bed smelled of mold. He was simultaneously agitated and adrift. Being with Xander wasn't good these days—but being without him, losing the heat of his will, was worse. And he was losing it too often lately. The nod-outs, the fucking minizomboid vacations. Every time it happened, every time he thought Xander was going away for good, the world loomed up giant and unbalanced, filled with visions of himself alone in it—standing in sleet at a bus stop; shambling down a bright supermarket aisle; walking into a bar and seeing people hunched over their drinks—and wanting to walk straight out again.

It's like I'm carrying you on my goddamned back.

Xander had always said things like that from time to time. Used to be he'd leave a short pause and stare at you for a few seconds before grinning—so you knew he didn't really mean it—and turning away. Used to be. But recently (not so recently, if Paulie really thought about it) the grinning—the not meaning it—had stopped.

Meeting Xander five years ago had been a homecoming. Couldn't even really say how it happened. Not the certainty of it. Not the deep-down knowing. Paulie, who'd been drifting since he was fifteen, got a minimum-wage job in the refrigeration warehouse in Prescott, Oakland, and had blown off the cafeteria one lunchtime to eat his shitty pastrami on rye down by the water. He'd sat on an empty bench next to one occupied by Xander, who was Leon in those days, and after a strange forty-five minutes' conversation (he talked a lot, Xander a little) found himself full of a thrilled gravity.

Xander lived alone in a run-down apartment not far from the warehouse, and sometime after their first meeting, Paulie found himself there. The two men drank beer (again, Paulie a lot, Xander a little) and watched hour after hour of porn in rich silence. It had started with regular shit, but after a short while Xander had said: Check this cunt out—and brought from his bedroom a DVD in a plain black case. An acned Latina who looked about sixteen getting ass-fucked and cattle-branded by three guys. The production values were nonexistent. The sound was raw. There was a moist bare brick wall and a wooden floor and the girl's legs and arms were blotched with bruises. The ball gag made snot come out of her nose, and one of the guys said, Jesus Christ, that's disgusting—then wiped his dick in it, which had made Paulie laugh. Xander hadn't laughed. Just sat there in profile, not drinking his Coors.

The weeks and months that followed were a blurred addiction for Paulie. It was enough for him just to be in Xander's presence. Xander was the first person he'd met with whom he didn't feel locked inside himself. With everyone else, he was condemned to a claustrophobic privacy, as if he knew that whatever came out of his mouth would sooner or later make them look at him as if he were from another planet. It had been that way his whole life, starting with his mother and father, who could one minute be laughing at something he'd done or said, the next be beating the shit out of him. His father had left when he was small—maybe five or six. His mother had died in a car wreck a couple of years later. It had happened right outside their house in Delaware. She'd been drunk, they said afterwards, hit a stationary bulldozer in a line of road crew vehicles that had been left there overnight where they were repairing the water mains. His mother's car had ended up with its nose in the flooded, dug-out trench. Paulie, who'd been sitting just inside the screen door (she left him alone in the house for several hours every day), ran out and looked. Her head was a mess of blood and her arm was bent around the wrong way, like a doll's you could twist. Her blouse was torn and one bare breast was out.

After that he'd been shuffled around distant relations for a while, then gone to Child Protective Services.

When Xander showed him the first girl—not *Xander's* first girl, but the first one Paulie got to see—it was as if, in a moment, all Paulie's muscles and bones came into their right alignment. It was like he was recognizing something he'd seen before, something he'd *known* before, in a time before he was born. When Paulie got laid-off and was between jobs, Xander had put in for a chunk of his vacation and the two of them had taken a road trip. They'd gone all over the country, and Paulie had day by day felt Xander's aura filling with quiet energy. It vivified everything; the big skies; the wheel of a passing truck; an empty McDonald's carton.

Then one night on the edge of St. Louis, Paulie had woken in the Super 8 motel and found Xander gone. His gear was still in the room, so he hadn't *gone* gone, but still, Paulie surprised himself by feeling not panic but a kind of Christmassy excitement.

Xander returned the following afternoon with no explanation and told Paulie they had to get going. As in right now. A ripple around Xander told Paulie not to ask. They drove hundreds of miles in near silence, until, long after sundown, Xander pulled the car over. They were on a back road somewhere in Utah. Empty fields on one side, sprawling woods on the other. Xander had sat with his hands on the wheel. Then he'd said: So, you wanna know what's in the trunk?

Paulie remembered the smell of the trees and soft damp soil. His breath going up in clouds. The land had been rained on. It was heavy and fresh.

Knew as soon as I saw her, Xander said when the trunk was open.

There was a moment, just after he'd helped Xander tie her to a tree far enough from the road, when Paulie had a vision of himself turning and walking away back to the car. He saw himself in a pink-boothed diner, sitting at the counter with a cup of black coffee, a matronly waitress with a tired smile. He pictured a bright damp morning framed in the big window, the wet road glistening in the sun.

Then Xander tore her shirt open and she screamed behind the gag, and Paulie went down as on a roller-coaster drop into his own future with a sweet feeling of recognition and surrender and relief.

He'd known what to do and what not to do. His every movement was guided by invisible hands. He knew when to watch, when to move away. There was such an understanding between him and Xander. Sometimes the girl looked at Paulie as if she were trying to separate him from Xander because he, Paulie, hadn't touched her. But his eyes could always slide away when that happened. And when Xander started with the knife, she stopped looking anywhere. Just closed her eyes and screamed.

When Xander had finished, he said to Paulie: I'm going to put the stuff away. Don't touch her mouth. Just don't touch her mouth.

Paulie had seen him shove something in there, though he hadn't been able to tell what it was.

I got a spade in the car, Xander said. Don't be all night.

Don't be all night. She wasn't dead, and Xander had known it was what Paulie had been waiting for. Even Paulie hadn't truly known it was what he'd been waiting for until Xander had said it.

This was in the days before he'd started filming it all.

The days before the money came to Xander.

That money. Jesus. Why couldn't it have been him?

He tossed the iPad to one side, zipped up his fly, got up off the bed. He'd been in his room too long. He had to go and check on Xander. *Because he's sick,* he told himself. But of course, it was more than that. Always, now, when Paulie found himself quiet and alone, he'd start to get the feeling of the world coming for him. It was in the blades of grass and the colors of a 7-Eleven and someone's glance at him from a bus window. It was a creeping conspiracy that could only be held off by Xander. Or at least, being with Xander made it easier not to see it.

52

Xander was deep in a fever. Not that he knew it. As far as he was concerned, what was happening to him was just a newly gimmicked version of what had been happening for years. There were periods when he was almost convinced he was in bed at the farmhouse: there was the window with its curtains half-drawn; there was the muted TV (it annoyed him, vaguely, that an episode of *Real Housewives of Orange County* was beyond his focus); there was the wardrobe's exposed mirror, taunting him with its not-quite-accurate reflection. But every time he started to feel certain of his surroundings, the shapes would shimmy, shift away, dissolve, and other realities would take their place. The basement at Mama Jean's. No window and the shivering fluorescent light that buzzed. The front yard he was allowed into only on weekends. The crazy tree. The bedroom where they did the lessons.

Mama Jean was tall and shaped like a pear. She wore her pale jeans high up. The big curve from her belly to between her legs was soft and heavy. Leon had to force himself not to look at it. There was something about it that made him want to press his hands there. Some of the veins in her feet were fractured purple lightnings.

The alphabet chart had slipped from Xander's bed. He'd fallen asleep with his hands resting on it, but now it lay on the floor, half unfolded. He remembered the unmeasurable time after they'd found him wandering in the woods that day. How he hadn't let go of his

backpack, the feeling he'd had that if he let go of it, something terrible would happen. Then one soft-spoken woman with short blond
hair and a smiling face very gently unlocking his fingers' grip and
opening it up. Oh, I see you brought supplies. That was a smart thing
to do, wasn't it? A half-eaten apple. A banana. Potato chips. A jar of
peanut butter. His mouth had been too dry to eat, after a while. And
what's this? she'd asked, unfolding the chart carefully. She'd gone
quiet. As if she knew. But how could she? They hadn't wanted him
to keep it. But when she'd tried to take it—for safekeeping, she said—
he'd screamed and hit out at her.

He stared down at it now, while its objects and letters did their
maddening dance.

"Again," Mama Jean said. "Start again. Just do them one at a
time. You're all jittery. That's why you keep mixing them up."

This was the gentle phase. It always started like this, her voice
quiet and low. Leon's face filling with heat and an ache in his eyes
where the tears should be, but never were. The pictures on the chart
were in bright colors. The balloon was blue. The apple red. The hammer had a light brown handle and a big silver head. Leon knew it
was hopeless. The letters and their names came apart in him. The
black lines that formed them fell away from each other and swirled
slowly, formed new shapes, fell apart again.

"I know you're trying," Mama Jean said. "I can see it in your
face. I know you're scared, too. What are you so scared of?"

She always asked him this. As if she didn't know. She sounded
as if she really *didn't* know, as if this hadn't happened, in exactly this
way, all those times before. Her voice was so gentle and she was so
mystified, it made him wonder if it really *had* happened before. Had
he dreamed it? It made him look at her, which in turn made her look
somewhere else, out the window or into the smoke rippling from her
cigarette. He knew looking at her was a bad idea, but he couldn't stop
himself. It was as if it was what she'd been waiting for.

"Now you're not concentrating," she said, her face turned away,
sunlight from the window making two coins of her glasses. "Now
you're just trying to make me lose my patience."

When she said that (Leon didn't know what "patience" was, ex cept that it was some invisible thing that he somehow made go away from her, like a dog that had caught the smell of something from another room and trotted off to find it), it was the beginning of the end of the soft-voiced phase. She always seemed annoyed by having to stop being nice. She smoked her cigarette as if she were angry with it.

"I don't know why you have to do this," she said. "I really don't. Why do you keep doing this?"

Sometimes that would be all it took. The wood-framed armchair would crick with the shift of her weight and she'd be on her feet. Other times it went on longer. Like she wanted to make the nice phase last. Or not exactly the nice phase, but the one in which he was making her lose her patience.

"It's not like I'm asking you to learn Chinese," she said, and laughed a little. Leon didn't understand: Chinese was brownish noodles in cartons she sometimes had. They looked like worms to Leon. "It's just the damned alphabet. Don't you know if you don't get this, you're going to be no better than a *retard* your whole life? It's no wonder your mother dumped you."

But by this time, Leon's mouth would've locked and his face gone thick with heat. Sometimes he'd try to focus on the view through the window, the green lawn and the crazy two-legged tree and the blinding white mailbox and the woods beyond.

"You're not even *looking*," Mama Jean said. Then left a long pause. In which Leon could feel the room filling with what he knew was coming next.

53

Paulie stood by Xander's bed, watching him. He didn't like seeing him like this. Weak.

Did he?

A part of him was thrilled. In spite of the terror at what the world without Xander would be like, he found himself having the extraordinary thought that here was Xander, feeble and out of it, and that if he, Paulie, were to now go and get the gun and point it at Xander and pull the trigger and put a bullet in Xander's brain, there would be absolutely nothing Xander could do about it. Or the machete. Imagine that. Imagine the weight of the blade. Lifting it. Xander's eyes maybe fluttering open just long enough to see what was happening. Then Paulie swinging it down with all his strength. Feeling the neck go. Or the skull split.

His hands were heavy. The image made him dizzy. He thought: *Are you out of your fucking mind?*

"*C* is for elephant," Xander said with a strange clarity. It made Paulie start. He hadn't felt the solidity of the room's silence until Xander broke it.

"Jesus," Paulie said. "You don't look good. How're you feeling?"

Xander's eyes were closed and busy behind their lids. Paulie had an image of hundreds of people—police, waitresses, nurses, firemen, office commuters, and government officials in dark suits—all watching this and creeping slowly toward him.

Xander opened his eyes. His face was wet. He was shivering under the blankets.

"It's his fault," he said, looking at Paulie.

"What?"

"Fucking idiot. You break the thing. You don't do it right. Then everything goes. It should've been a kite. No, a jug. Goddammit."

"Listen," Paulie said. "Do you want me to try'n get you something? Some medicine?"

Xander slowly and awkwardly pulled his right hand out from under the blankets. It was trembling.

And holding the gun.

He pointed it at Paulie.

"It should have been a fucking *jug*," Xander said.

Paulie felt himself backpedaling. On air. It was as if only the very tips of his toes were touching the floor. Bizarrely, he was also aware of the bright image on the TV screen in the room's darkness: two incredibly beautiful bare-shouldered women having lunch at a sunny outside table with bright white napkins and the light winking off their champagne glasses and jewelry. The camera cut between close-ups of their faces. Smiles that looked as if they hated each other. Their eyes looked like dark diamonds.

The wardrobe bumped his back.

Xander fired.

Paulie went, briefly, completely blank. Except for a vague feeling of the world being upended, floor and walls and ceiling losing their connection to each other. After what felt like a long delay, the sound of wood splintering. A detail embedded in the deafening noise of the gunshot.

There was no pain. He pieced it together. It felt as if he had all the time in the world to piece it together: Xander had missed. The bullet had gone into the wardrobe.

"Fuck, fuck, fuck," Paulie heard himself saying quietly. His body was doing things, trying to move. He was on his side on the floor. His arms and legs were working to get him back onto his feet. But his limbs were wearing dozens of soft weights. Xander's hand on the gun was moist. His wrist bent for a moment, as if broken, then gradually straightened. He was leveling for a second shot.

Everything went very still. Paulie felt the room in shock from the sound of the gunshot. The smell of cordite like a scar on the odors of old wood and damp plaster. Death suddenly right there. He never thought about death. Not his own. Not the women's. There was only the fascination of their warm bodies slippery with blood that he could do anything to, and then afterwards his feeling of crazy sweet electric aliveness, and the open-ended glimmering time between then and the next time, the next one.

But now something indistinct rushed up to him in a wave of blackness. The thought of dying and going somewhere where it would be worse than the creeping conspiracy of all the people, a place where you'd be compelled forward through darkness with only a few stars, the last few stars, as if you were reaching the edge of space, toward something that knew you and saw through you, and nothing would protect you from it, you'd be totally naked and eventually you'd see it. You'd see it, and it would see you. And what happened then would last forever.

Xander's eyelids flickered and his lips moved. His sweat-soaked head made his hair look thin. Like a baby bird, Paulie thought. He moved his aim slightly, hand still shaking—then the strength went out of him and his arm dropped back onto the bedclothes. He didn't let go of the gun.

Paulie scrambled to his feet and ran from the room.

He couldn't think straight. He went downstairs and got the shotgun. Loaded it. The weight and solidity of the thing felt strange. He was breathing through his open mouth. Xander had shot at him. *It's like carrying you on my goddamned back.* Xander had *shot* at him. But Xander was sick. Crazy sick. Fever made you insane. But there was all that shit about the fucking milk jug. Like death, Paulie didn't think about the objects. They were there; they were at the edge of his thinking—but he always stopped short. He glanced out the kitchen window, expecting to see the thousands of people closing in, their faces determined. But there was nothing. Just the low outbuildings and the dead cars and the twilit empty land rolling away.

He went back upstairs, quietly, shotgun raised.

There was no sound from Xander's room.

He stood still at the edge of the open doorway.

Very slowly inched forward to get a peep inside.

Xander's eyes were closed again. His arm lay outside the blankets, relaxed, fingers loose around the automatic.

Asleep.

At a friend's house once when he was very small, a grown-up had read them *Jack and the Beanstalk*. Jack tiptoeing in to steal the harp from the sleeping giant. There was a picture in the book, the giant slumped forward on a vast wooden table. The big hands and dark curly hair. Jack the size of a monkey by comparison.

You have to get the gun away from him. He's fever-mad. He fucking shot at you. It'll be all right when he comes out of it. It'll be all right, but who knows what the fuck while he's like this?

There was another voice underneath the one saying *It'll be all right* (saying *No, it won't*) but he ignored it.

Amazed at himself, Paulie propped the shotgun against the corridor wall, bent down, unlaced and removed his boots.

It felt terrible just in his socks. It felt as if he'd taken *all* his clothes off. The women, even if you'd got them to stop screaming and wriggling, always started screaming and wriggling again when you tore their blouses and bras, when you tugged off their jeans and yanked down their panties. It was the flesh, bare. It was the exposure. For the first time, Paulie felt a weird, piercing identification with them.

But it was sucked like a spark into darkness.

Shotgun as steady as he could hold it, he crept into the room.

Three paces. Four. Five.

He was at the bed.

Every time he tried to picture Xander opening his eyes and raising the pistol—every time he tried to imagine himself squeezing the Remington's trigger and Xander's head exploding in blood—the image fizzed and heated and went into confusion. You had to not ask yourself if you'd be able to do it when the time came. Instead he told himself that all he had to do was take the automatic away for now. Then Xander would get better and everything would be all right. Xander would come out of it and everything would be all right and the little bitch in the basement was the prettiest they'd had and he could feel the gooseflesh on her tits and how sweet going into her would be, her body with the fear like a warm welcome.

He braced the shotgun, reached out. In the story, the giant's magical harp had cried out "Master! Master!" when Jack had got hold of it, and Paulie had a dreamy certainty that the handgun would do the same. But of course that didn't happen. Paulie slipped the pistol from Xander's grip and stuffed it into his back pocket.

Xander made a soft noise—a murmur—but his eyes didn't open.

Back in the hallway, Paulie rested for a long time against the cool of the wall. He was drenched in sweat, but his skin felt cold. It occurred to him that he might be getting Xander's flu.

He didn't have long to ponder what that would mean.

Because by the time he'd got his boots back on, there was a pounding coming up from the basement.

54

Claudia had thought she was resolved, but when it came down to it, she spent a long time just standing with her arms wrapped around herself, shaking. Everything she'd thought had a perverse mathematical insistence. The cold part of her brain knew it was right. But it was weak in comparison to the deep instinct. The deep instinct was to preserve being alive and more or less unharmed and alone for as long as possible. The deep instinct was to wait and hope and pray and plead. The deep instinct was not to do anything that might provoke the men who had taken her captive. Granted, she was locked in. Granted, the only thing she could hold on to was the possibility of someone coming to her rescue. But still, *right now,* for these precious moments, she was OK. The thought of doing something to change that—the thought of voluntarily doing something that would, one way or another, take her out of *right now* and into something unknown (unknown except in that it would be all or nothing, would either get her out or rush the horror of her future into her present) was all but overwhelming. She couldn't do it. She couldn't. Every time she braced herself and said inwardly: *Now*—she found herself unable to move. Every time she told herself it was her only chance, the profound habit of life gathered in her and said: *No, don't. It's madness. It won't work. You can't. You cannot do this.*

But the thinking—the reasoning—was, she knew, unimpeachable. If she did nothing and no one came to her rescue, the two men would rape and torture and murder her. She had absolutely no doubt of that. It might happen in a minute, in an hour, a day, a week—but if no help came, it would certainly happen. Which meant either waiting and hoping for help—or trying to get away. It was the part of her that made her unlike Alison that knew this. It was what made her unlikable. For Claudia, the truth had always been the truth, regardless of its ugliness. Her whole life, people had been shocked and wounded and outraged and frankly afraid of her because she had no patience with denial and white lies and looking away from things just because they were hideous. Her mother, who was quiet and intelligent and had given both her daughters lots of liberal room for their growing up, had once said to Claudia (after Claudia had sent Alison away from an argument in tears): *It's a great thing to be able to tell the truth, darling. But there is such a thing as gentleness for the people you love. Just because a thing is true doesn't mean it can't be used cruelly. Be careful with your talents.*

The truth, Claudia now realized, had never been put to the test until now. Because she knew the truth of her situation—yet remained incapable of acting on it. Fear, it turned out, was more than a match for truth.

And so for what felt like hours, she had stood with her arms wrapped around herself and the roll of metal in her pocket, the stubborn, clinical part of her mind repeatedly offering her its incontrovertible conclusions—and terror stopping her from accepting them.

But the reasoning didn't go away. If she acted now, she would, in all likelihood, have one only of them to get past. If she waited, there would be two. And she couldn't make herself believe she'd get past two of them.

She pulled the roll of metal from her jacket pocket.

And if you get past him, then what? If the house is locked? What? If you get out of the house? What? Run? Did they leave the keys in the RV? And if they did, can you drive it? She had a terrible image of herself fumbling with keys, her hands filled with madness, knowing the seconds were racing away, knowing that they were coming. Would she have what it took? If it came to running—just running on her own dreaming legs—would she be able to run far and fast enough?

But that image—of herself free and running into the good dark-ness, back in the world beyond this one—dizzied her with pure need, and her mind let go a little, and without being fully conscious of what she was doing, she lay down on the floor and began kicking the furnace and shouting as loudly as she could.

55

Nell's scream woke Angelo.

There was a pause in its wake, a shorn silence in which he had to reconstruct everything, where he was, what had happened, who she was, who *he* was.

It was dark. He had no idea how long he'd slept, but he was exhausted. It had stopped snowing. The window showed the white land and a band of fierce, starred sky. The woodstove was low, but still burning.

"Hey," he said, pushing himself up onto his elbow. "Hey, it's OK. Nell? It's OK."

She was curled up in the sleeping bag by the feet of the stove, whimpering. The residue of whatever nightmare—whatever *memory*, more like—had ravaged her. The sound she made was terrible to him, a reiteration of reality: What had happened to her had really happened—and there was no answer and no help. The world really contained such things. The world contained such things and distributed them, with random, indifferent violence.

The nerves in his leg shrieked as soon as he moved. Pain stalled him. He breathed through it. Very slowly eased himself off the couch onto his hands and knees on the floor. Since undressing her while she was unconscious, he hadn't touched her, but now without thinking he put his hand lightly on her head, brushed the sweat-damp hair from her eyes. The contact shocked her into silence—then she breathed again, let the sobs come. The smallness and heat of her skull panicked him, filled him afresh with the horror of what had been given to her. There was nothing for him to say. What could there possibly be to say? Nothing had changed. That was the news waking had brought her—again. She'd woken from a nightmare into a worse nightmare: the real world.

For a long time he stayed by her. He moved his hand to her shoulder, rested it there. The body, he thought, was there for when words failed. The dumb eloquence of human touch. It was both an admission of suffering and a defiance of surrendering to it. The humble sacrament of flesh and blood said: Even when there is nothing to say, you are not alone. You are not *alone*.

Eventually, she stopped crying. Sniffed, mightily. Her face was wet with tears and snot.

"Hold on a second," he said.

He crawled, wincing, teeth gritted, to the minimal bathroom (there was a toilet, a sink, a tub, but no hot water; he'd washed himself with water heated on the stove, though how he was going to manage that now the sciatica had returned was a mystery), took a new toilet roll from the pack he'd brought from the car, and crawled back into the living room. He tore off a length of the soft tissue and handed it to her. Keep giving her basic actions to perform. Keep her functioning.

She wiped her face then lay there, blinking, the wad of tissue still clutched in her hand. She was wide awake, staring past him, out the window.

56

"Ed, check the registers for a legal name change and see if 'Xander King' matches a Utah address," Valerie said. She, Carla, and Ed Pérez were in her Taurus en route back to the station, Ed riding shotgun, Carla in the back, getting the word out to the bureau's office in Salt Lake. They'd left the uniforms to finish the door-to-door, mainly because the likelihood of anyone in the building knowing Leon's new address was slim. They'd also searched the apartment, (gloved, pre-forensics), for documents—receipts, title deeds, utility bills—that would have given them what they needed, but found nothing. "There's no reason to suppose he's done it by the book," she continued, "especially given his illiteracy, but it's worth making sure."

". . . All Utah real estate sales for 2010," Carla said into her phone. "Could be in either name. It's not unlikely that we're looking for an auction or an outright buy, but include the financed deals anyway."

The absence of a bank account was driving Valerie crazy. If Lloyd had left Leon money or hit him with a check when he sold CoolServ, how could Leon make use of it without a bank? Short of a suitcase full of cash, there had to be a legal transaction. As soon as she got back to the station, she would find out who handled Lloyd's will.

"Must've seemed like a fucking divine green light," Ed said. "Getting the payout."

Valerie had had the same thought. It was a terrible alignment, one more testimony in the already weighty case against a benevolent God. If she thought of God these days, she imagined a being of infinite, calm schizophrenia.

"Yeah," she said. "And he wasn't short of a big idea of himself even before the money came in to confirm it. "Xander King"? He might not have heard of Alexander the Great, but he knows what a king is."

"Ghast," Carla said into the phone. "*G-h-a-s-t*. Try it without the *h*, too."

"Bank accounts," Valerie shot over her shoulder. "Both names." Carla looked at her: Don't tell me my fucking job. Valerie ignored the look. "San Francisco and Utah addresses. You can't buy a goddamned house without a bank account. And get the ball rolling for access to the Conways' financial records."

At the station, Valerie headed for her office but Carla stopped her. Her small, sharp face was flushed. Her ponytail had worked itself loose.

"Deerholt still wants to talk to us," she said.

"You're kidding me."

"No, I'm not. He was very specific about it."

"Yeah, well, I'll go when I get a second."

"I recommend we go right now. Like I said, he was very clear."

"Can I ask you something?"

"Yes?"

"What are you doing?"

"I don't know what you mean."

"You left something on Nick Blaskovitch's desk this morning."

"Who's Nick Blaskovitch?"

She was good, Valerie had to concede. The tone, the mildly perplexed face, with a dash of impatience for added realism.

"Do you think I'm not going to be able to prove it?" Valerie said.

Carla shook her head in polite bemusement, a half smile on her lips. "I really . . . Jesus, Valerie, I really don't know what you're talking about." The look switched to concern. "Are you doing OK? We all saw what happened back there at the apartment."

Valerie wanted to hit her.

"Fine," she said. "Have it your way. Let's get this over with."

Deerholt's door was closed but his silhouette was visible through the frosted glass. He was, as every cop everywhere was these days, on his cell phone. Valerie raised her hand to knock. Just before she did, Carla said simply: "Baby killer."

Then *Carla* knocked.

"Come in!" Deerholt yelled—and before Valerie could speak, the door was open and Carla was inside.

Valerie, her mouth dry, her mind tumbling, followed her. Deerholt waved the two women toward the chairs facing the desk, but both of them remained on their feet.

"OK," he said, having wrapped up the call. "Where are we, Val?"

Valerie swallowed. She was aware of her face in nude shock. Her hands felt packed with blood.

Baby killer.

Nonetheless, she gathered herself and brought Deerholt up to speed. Being a cop trimmed speech of its superfluities. The salient facts, delivered as succinctly as possible. Being a cop meant the clock was *always* ticking.

By the time she'd finished, Deerholt's face was a mixture of professional relief and personal anxiety.

"OK, good," he said. ("Good," from Deerholt, was as good as it got.) "Now, Valerie, if you could step outside for a moment, I need to speak with Agent York first."

"Sir, I—"

"I know. You'll get your chance, believe me. Just step outside for now."

Standing as close to the door as she could without being seen through the glass, Valerie tried to listen in. But their voices were lowered, and in any case, there was an open office opposite with a murmur of activity that made eavesdropping impossible. She walked down the hall to a water cooler and poured herself a conical cupful.

Baby killer.

OK, so the gloves were off.

But why didn't York just admit it the first time?

And why the *fuck* was she doing this?

They were long minutes, for Valerie, pacing up and down the twenty feet between the water cooler and Deerholt's door. She drank the water mechanically. Mechanically refilled and drank again. The drinking made her realize how dehydrated she was. Which in turn brought back her collapse in Leon's apartment building. Are you doing OK? She could just imagine what Carla was saying to Deerholt. And this time there were witnesses. The uniforms. The tenants. Jesus, even Ed had seen her crash to the floor. Did she have time, she wondered, to find him (and Galbraith, and Keely) and beg them to deny it?

The spirit of her grandfather hovered. *Should* you get them to deny it? *Aren't* you falling apart? What do you care most about? Catching these fucks before they kill again? Or running the show at all costs?

Carla exited. Didn't look at Valerie. Walked away down the corridor.

Valerie went in and closed the door behind her. Her face was cold. She was shivering. This time she did sit down.

Deerholt put his head in his hands, drew them down his face, then settled them around the iPhone on his desk. He was fifty-four, tall and bony, with dark hair on the backs of his hands. A hairdo that was perpetually on the verge of becoming a pompadour. Small black eyes in deep sockets. A face so closely shaven, it looked like the razor must have hurt.

"Jesus Christ, Val," he said.

Valerie was tight in her shoulders, her neck, her arms. The dead women were in the room with her, looking past her failure into a future without revenge. She felt, suddenly, desperate, as if the world were falling away underneath her.

"What's going on, Cap?" she forced herself to say.

Deerholt shook his head. Exhaled.

"What's going on," he said, "is that Agent York has made some pretty serious allegations against you."

"What allegations?"

"Bottom line? That you're not fit. For several reasons."

"Sir, I don't know what the fuck she's talking about. I'm fine."

"Did you collapse earlier today?"

Valerie shook *her* head, snorted, dismissed. "Collapse? Jesus, I got a *cramp,* sir. It was nothing."

"York says you blacked out. Couldn't get up off the floor. Says Ed and the blues all saw it. If I get them in here, are they going to tell me it looked like cramp to them?"

"Sir, whatever it looked like to them, I'm telling you it was cramp."

"Like this?" Deerholt said. He opened a video on the phone. Hit Play. Turned it to face Valerie.

For a moment, all she felt was the strangeness of seeing herself on film, of seeing herself as the unaware object of someone else's view. But that was hurried out by the rapid understanding of where and when this had happened.

In Reno. In the woods. After they'd found the alarm clock victim.

C is for CLOCK.

She watched the footage. Herself, walking unsteadily between the dark trees. Stopping. Dropping to her hands and knees. Obviously not from cramp. Obviously because something was seriously wrong with her.

The footage halted. Deerholt put the phone facedown on the desk.

"Well?" he said.

In the couple of seconds it took her to speak, she thought: *He's already made up his mind. How could that be?* She had an image of Claudia Grey, hands tied above her head, her face a mess of sweat and blood. The wise dark eyes drained of their wisdom by fear, by pain.

"OK," Valerie said. "That was a bad morning. I was sick and short of sleep. Come on, sir, you know how it is. Not enough rest, not enough fuel. You *know* how it is."

"I know," Deerholt said. "And I know how hard you've been pushing yourself on this."

"Don't take this away from me, Cap."

"Val, listen—"

"You know how close we are. You heard what I just told you ten minutes ago—"

"Valerie, stop," Deerholt said, raising his hand. "It's not just this."

Valerie was trembling. There were soft, invisible ambushes everywhere.

"How much are you putting away every day?" Deerholt said. "No bullshit, Val. I mean if we did a blood test right now."

Valerie felt her face go from cold to hot. It was like being caught doing something dirty when you were a kid. That time her mom had walked in on her when she'd been lying on her belly on her bed, hands down her jeans.

All she could do was shake her head. "Sir, I'm fine. I'm—"

"I drink," he said. "Christ, half the department's probably got last night's self-help sloshing around in them right now. I know how it is. But word is it's getting out of hand for you. As in, we're not just talking a marginal fail on a Breathalyzer. Plus Blaskovitch is back, and I know—"

"This has nothing to do with him."

"OK, OK, but like I said—"

There was a knock at the door.

"Come in," Deerholt said.

It was Will Fraser. Looking like he didn't know what the hell he was doing there.

Deerholt didn't ask him to sit down. Instead, the captain got to his feet.

"It's better for you if there's someone here for this," he said to Valerie. "I figured Will would be your first choice, but if there's someone else you'd rather have, now's the time to say so."

"What's going on?" Will said.

Valerie wanted to get to *her* feet, but it was as if there was an unseen mass pressing her down into the chair.

"Someone else?" she said. "What do you mean?"

"Jesus, Val, I'm sorry about this, but my hands are tied. I need to ask you if you're using."

They were police. Despite the pause of apparent incomprehension between Valerie and Will, there was only one thing "using" meant.

"Are you serious?" Valerie said.

"Sir—," Will began.

"Yes or no, Val."

"No. Of course not. This is insane."

"Would you mind emptying your pockets and your purse?"

"Sir, this is fucking idiotic," Valerie said. A tremulous part of her was actually relieved: if *this* was what it was hanging on, she was in the clear.

"I know it's fucking idiotic," Deerholt said. "When I get murdered one of these days, I want you on the case, first choice. But there are protocols. Let's just do this and get it out of the way. I know it's a formality."

With a contempt she wasn't faking, Valerie stood up and tipped the contents of her purse onto Deerholt's desk.

And saw the Baggie straightaway.

57

"What the fuck are you trying to do?" Paulie said. He was holding the shotgun.

Claudia had stopped kicking and shouting as soon as she'd seen him come down the stairs.

"I want to talk to you," she said. "I'm bored."

He gawped at her. Then he said: "Bored?"

"Yes. Bored. It's not much fun down here with no one to talk to."

His mouth was open. His face had lost its logic. "Are you . . . Are you fucking insane?"

"No," she said. "Are you?"

He just stood there, circuits jammed.

Her body was busy with tingling emptiness. Her legs wanted to buckle. She thought she was going to vomit.

"You don't . . . ," he began—then faltered. Tried to recalibrate. She could see how shocked he was by this new reality. She thought: *He's not the one in charge. It's the guy upstairs.* The thought was a frail endorsement of what she was doing. It didn't stop her shaking. She shoved her hands into her jeans pockets to conceal it. An absurd gesture of nonchalance. A deeply wrong gesture against the fear. Her own body was appalled by the dissonance. She almost took them straight out again.

"You don't get it," Paulie said. Then he laughed. The laughter had, she thought, uncertainty in it.

"Of course I get it," she said. "Do you think I'm stupid? It's not as if I think I'm here to talk about Proust."

"Talk about what? What the fuck is Proost?"

"Not 'what.' 'Who.' Valentin Louis Georges Eugène Marcel Proust. French novelist, critic, and essayist best known for his monumental novel *À la recherche du temps perdu*. Sometimes translated as *In Search of Lost Time,* sometimes as *Remembrance of Things Past.* Can you read?"

Again she watched him stall, try to unpick what was happening, try to get back to the world he knew. He was shaking his head—not in answer to her question, but in denial or disbelief. His impulse to laugh kept half-forming on his mouth—then failing.

Eventually he said: "Yeah I can read. *I* can fucking read."

She didn't understand the emphasis.

"How's your friend?" she said. "Still got the flu?"

His look of incredulity was replaced by a slight frown. She had to be careful.

"What's it to you?" he said.

"Well . . . ," she said. "I assume he's the one calling the shots. I'd like to know how long I've got."

"He don't . . . It don't make no difference. You're gonna . . ." He shook his head again. With irritation this time. She was going the wrong way. (But he hadn't contradicted her about who called the shots.) "You must be fucking crazy," he said. "You must be fucking *stupid.*"

"I think you know I'm not stupid," she said. "Plus I know something you don't."

"What?"

"I'll tell you. But don't rush me. It's embarrassing."

Better. *Better.* The novelty of being talked to in this way was infiltrating him, however slightly. He looked around the room. Checking, vaguely, to make sure the rest of reality hadn't gone similarly mad.

"You don't know nothing," he said.

"That's a double negative. It means the opposite of what you think it means."

"What?"

"Think about it," she said. "What you mean is that I know nothing—right?"

He stared at her.

"But if I *don't* know nothing, that means I know something. Do you see? It's a common mistake."

The extraordinary thing was that she could see him, awkwardly, getting it, in spite of himself, double . . . negative . . . a bud of understanding all but visibly opening in his brain. The way the truth did that. No matter what. The truth *was* the truth. It hurt her and made the fear surge again, because it was leftover currency from the world she'd lost. She thought of the woman in the video. She almost reverted, almost dropped to her knees and screamed please please please don't do this to me please please please. She lost her balance slightly, felt one foot in danger of coming off the floor. Forced herself to regain it. The woman's face with all its dignity gone. Their dense concentration. His hands holding the camera, full of excitement. It brought the reality of what she was going to have to do, and she thought again: *I can't. I can't do that.* Tears tightened her throat. She swallowed them. To do what she had to do, she had to let herself go insane. She had to leave herself behind. She had to become someone else.

"You're name's Paulie," she said. "Is that right?"

"You think I'm gonna make friends with you, cunt?" he said.

The word nicked her. With the reality of that part of her body. With the reality of what would happen to it.

Invert it. Invert everything. Insanity is the only way out.

"You think the word 'cunt' bothers me?" she said.

It threw him. Again. He was afraid and fascinated. He opened his mouth to say something, but there was nothing there. She had to be careful. Careful and insane.

"Who are you, the fucking Queen of England?" he said.

"No," she said. Pause. A genuine memory. "But I've met her."

"Get the fuck."

"It's true. In 2002, when I was fourteen. There was a parade in Cornwall for her Golden Jubilee." She saw him not understanding. "'Golden Jubilee,'" she said, "is a celebration for when a king or queen has been on the throne for fifty years. It's like wedding anniversaries. You know, twenty-five years is silver, fifty years is gold, sixty years is diamond. Anyway, I was on holiday in Cornwall with my mum and dad, and the Queen did a walkabout in the street, with bodyguards and whatnot. I was face-to-face with her for a few seconds. She said: 'Hello, dear.'"

"Get the fuck," Paulie repeated. "What did you say?"

"I told her I liked her hat."

Paulie laughed.

"Which was a lie," Claudia said. "The Queen's got shocking taste in hats. I just couldn't think of anything else to say."

It caught up with him that he was laughing. He stopped. There was fear and mistrust ready to rush back in when he caught himself. She had to watch that. Don't give him time to catch himself.

"Anyway, your name *is* Paulie, obviously," she said. "I'm Claudia, not that I imagine you're remotely interested. It's just that if I'm going to be murdered, I'd like to know by whom. Do you have a cigarette, by the way?"

"Why the fuck would I give you a cigarette?" he said.

"Well, why not?"

"You're something. I'll give you that."

"I quit smoking, actually, but if I'm going to die, what does it matter? Come on, don't be an ass. Give me a cigarette. What difference could it possibly make to you?"

He thought about it for a long time. She could see him trying to decide whether it would decrease him. He laughed, once, through his nose. His face was thin. The long coppery hair and medieval beard. He could play the lousy traitor in Robin Hood's band. He reached into his right combat jacket pocket, pulled out a pack of Marlboro reds. He set the shotgun down on one of the cardboard boxes.

He's going to come toward you and hand you the cigarette through the links and you're going to take it and you're not going to shake or flinch. Because you're insane. Because you're calm and insane. Because you're exactly what you need to be.

He came toward her, poked the filter end through the links. His jacket smelled of damp canvas. She thought soldiers must be wea-rily contemptuous of civilians wearing such gear. She felt a mo-mentary kinship with soldiers. For their passage into the extreme. For their nearness to death. For having to live with the ways it changed them.

"Obviously I don't have a light," she said.

Keep still. Keep still.

She took the cigarette, slotted it between her lips. For a split sec-ond she was getting a light from a stranger at a bus stop or in a nightclub booth.

Until she actually *got* the light. Until she had to lean close enough so that the cigarette reached the lighter's flame, her face almost touching the metal links of the grille. The Zippo's reek of fuel and the innocent magic of conjured fire were familiar, yes (in spite of her-self the mix of odors brought the cramped tents of music festivals, socks, tobacco, sweat, sex), but the nearness of his face and dirty-fingernailed hands and the greasy smell of his skin almost wrecked her. Her right hand guided the cigarette but her left was out of its pocket, too, fist clenched. The intimacy of closeness to him was an obscene dream. It took everything she had to keep her movements calm, slow, normal.

"Thanks," she said, stepping back from the grille. Just one pace. The smoking stance: left hand in right armpit, right arm bent at the elbow, wrist slightly limp, holding the cigarette. Millions of people all over the world standing in just that way on their doorsteps, mull-ing over their lives. It was a tiny help, gave her body something fa-miliar to hold on to.

He watched her. Then she saw him catching himself again. The shotgun. His lapse. He took three paces back quicker than her one, picked it up from the box.

Careful. *Careful.* So easy for him to tip into hating her for fuck-ing with him. *Don't* give him time to think.

"How many times have you done this?" she said.

"You're not fooling me," he said. Then added: "Cunt." She saw the word not coming out right for him.

"Well, don't tell me if you don't want to, but I'm curious."

"Enough times to know how to do it."

"Always the two of you?"

"I'm done talking."

"Oh come on, don't be like that."

"You think you're some hot shit?" He laughed. Not entirely forced, she thought. She was losing him. "You think you're any different?"

"Don't you want to know what I know that you don't?"

"I don't give a fuck what you think you know. You don't know shit."

"OK, but it's pretty extraordinary."

He was breathing through his nostrils, lips clamped.

She forced herself to take another drag of the cigarette. The first in six months, it was making her dizzy. The body just carried on reporting its sensations, regardless of your situation. The body didn't have any choice. The body of the woman in the video. *Oh God. I can't. I can't.*

Insanity was a trick of concentration, or rather anti-concentration, like those Magic Eye pictures you had to simultaneously focus on and blur to see the image they concealed. She mustn't give herself time to think, either.

"Why don't you show me the videos?" she said. "Show me the rest of them."

"What?"

"I'd like to see the rest of the videos. The other women."

She had him again. There had been nothing new in his life for a long time. His microclimate suffocated him, his life was a handful of repetitions. He was susceptible.

He looked at her again for a long time. It made her afraid to finish the cigarette. Finishing it would break what was in the room.

"You're full of shit," he said. "You don't want to see them."

"Don't I?"

"You freaked out."

"I know I did, but it's complicated."

"What the fuck is that supposed to mean?"

"I can't put it any other way. I told you: it's embarrassing."

"You're full of shit," he repeated.

The cigarette was almost done.

"Show me the videos," she said, very calmly. "You'll find something out. Something you never knew before."

He shook his head slowly, not quite looking at her. He was laughing to himself, but it wasn't genuine. He turned and walked to the foot of the stairs. With his back to her, he said, "You're one dumb crazy cunt. Maybe the dumbest, craziest cunt I ever saw."

But when she said, "Hey," he stopped, three steps up.

Her insanity balanced. Almost tipped her back into herself. She knew what she was going to say. She knew it could destroy her.

"What?" he said with exaggerated impatience.

The cigarette was down to the filter's cork. Her head was heavy with blood.

"He doesn't need to know about it," she said.

58

Valerie sat in the Taurus parked opposite the station lot's exit on Vallejo Street, smoking. Which was what she'd been doing for the last two hours. The Conways' attorneys were a small local firm in Fresno—closed for the holidays. Valerie had left messages on the cell phones of each of the three partners, so far with zero response. Teresa Conway had been virtually useless, too, when the woman eventually answered her landline. She'd sounded half asleep, or stoned, certainly not all there. Lloyd didn't leave any money to Leon in his will. It had all gone to Teresa. A lot of her talk had been about God was never supposed to give you more than you could bear, but she couldn't bear it. Did Lloyd give Leon money when he sold the company? She didn't know. Lloyd handled the finances. Lloyd had taken care of her. Lloyd had taken care of everyone except himself. Lloyd had *loved* that boy. They both had.

Lloyd had been too good for this world, but the world was no good without him.

It was a quarter after seven, dark, cold. The wind lifted scraps of litter, looped and arabesqued them, dropped them. The after-work traffic had thinned. A few yards away to Valerie's left, two uniforms were on the sidewalk, chatting with the owner of the Chef Bowl Inc. Chinese cash-and-carry. Every pedestrian who passed her car was talking or texting on a cell phone. She caught snippets of their lives:

". . . yeah, but Stevie says that's total ass-crap . . ."

". . . only if we can get the suede for the same price . . ."

". . . she says she's a vegetarian, but I know for a fact she ate lamb at Chrissie's . . ."

". . . that's what I'm saying. I said to him: that's what I'm saying . . ."

All the details that hung together in a secure mass until crime showed up. Break-in. Assault. Rape. Murder. Then the mass exploded. Cops entered a stranger's life in the aftermath of wreckage. All the things taken for granted now blown apart, with the victim stranded at the center like a kid in a bomb crater. You started as a cop, and at first it was a thrill. Then a learning curve. Then, if you were unlucky, an obsession. She knew police—homicide police—who'd passed through that into what she thought of as the Mature Stage: the calm, the efficiency, the ability to do the work without the work getting under your psychic skin, the manageable addiction to the drug. She'd always assumed she was headed there. Maybe the next case. Or the one after that.

But here she was. Still nowhere near it.

She, Deerholt, and Will had just stood there, staring at the Baggie (which Deerholt's eventual tip-of-the-tongue taste revealed to be cocaine) in absurd silence. Valerie had found her purse's minimal contents embarrassing: cigarettes, disposable lighter, lipstick, scrunchies, phone, gum, keys, a Milky Way that had been in there for God knows how long. It was as if the items themselves were appalled at the little bag of white powder that had been keeping them company in the dark.

Then Will had said: "Oh, come *on.*"

"Do you seriously think—?" Valerie had begun, but Deerholt had raised his hand to cut her off.

"No, I don't seriously think that if you were using, you'd be dumb enough to be carrying it around in your purse."

"This is horseshit," Will said.

"York put it there," Valerie said.

"Val—"

"Maybe at Leon's apartment. I put my purse down when we did

the search. I want a drug test right now." Which, given the booze most likely still in her bloodstream, she regretted saying as soon as she'd said it.

"OK," Deerholt had said, after the test—clear for coke, but blood alcohol way over the limit—after another meeting with Carla York, after summoning Valerie back to his office, "this is what's going to happen. As far as York knows, you're on suspension. She's going to go over my head if I don't do something, and if she does that, you're fucked."

"This is insane," Valerie had said quietly. "You know this is insane."

"Let me finish. As far as York knows, you're on suspension. As far as the paperwork goes, you're on sick leave. Make an appointment to see your doctor. Stay away from the shop. Fraser'll keep you in the loop."

"Keep me in the *loop*? We're one address away. Sir, I'm begging you not to do this."

"It's either this or an actual suspension," Deerholt said. "Gun and badge. You don't want that."

"She's going to ask to see those anyway."

"Let her try. What's she got against you?"

"I have no clue."

"Well, I don't like her any more than you do. But listen, Valerie, this is as good a deal as you're going to get right now. If it's any comfort, I got the Baggie dusted for prints, but it's clean."

As would be the envelope Carla had left on Blasko's desk.

"We were wearing gloves," Valerie said. "She's not stupid."

"You have my word you'll know whatever we do as soon as we know it."

Valerie had stood holding her elbows, staring at the floor. She had an image of herself punching Carla York in the mouth. Seeing the infuriating composure blasted.

"And listen," Deerholt said. "Go *see* a fucking doctor, will you? You're walking dead. Get some goddamned antibiotics. You need them."

•   •   •

When Carla's Jeep emerged from the lot, Valerie followed.

East on Vallejo, south on Stockholm, west on Broadway.

At Van Ness, Carla went south. Valerie had no concrete plan. Just a rage that demanded some kind of action. Deerholt's last words to her had been: Don't make this any worse than it is. Don't do anything stupid. She'd pictured herself tailing Carla all the way to wherever she lived. (Valerie visualized a spartan apartment, pictureless walls, a crisply made bed. The same plain functionality that resided in Carla's face. In her understated pantsuit and low-heeled boots. She knew nothing about her. Knowledge was power, as someone had said, and so far, Carla had it all. That had to change.) But at Golden Gate Avenue (just a few blocks west of the FBI building), Carla took a right and pulled into the lot of a mini-mart, and before she'd really thought it through, Valerie found herself out of the Taurus and hurrying to catch up.

"Hey," she said, a yard behind Carla, halfway to the store's automatic doors, in front of which a young mother was very carefully unwrapping a popsicle for her waiting toddler. Kids didn't care if the weather was cold.

Carla turned. For once, Valerie noticed, she looked bright with tiredness.

"What?"

"Why are you fucking with me?"

"Because you're no good."

The directness surprised Valerie in spite of herself. She was thrown off balance. "You're making a mistake," she said, scrambling to recover.

"No, I'm not. You're a degenerate drunk. You've lost your hold on this. You're not fit. It's time someone did something about it. Before more women die because of your incompetence."

It was appalling. Valerie remembered the heat of shame in her hands and face when the blood alcohol results had come back earlier that day. Deerholt's not quite looking her in the eye. Now, having followed Carla to attack her, she found herself shifting inwardly, into defense.

"You think you're going to get away with hacking the clinic?" she said.

"I don't care whether I get away with it. I just care about getting a degenerate drunk baby-killing slut off the case."

The consensus was that when you lost your temper, it was a blaze, a blindness, a *seeing red*. But in that moment, Valerie felt instead a deep, fleeting relaxation, as if all her muscles had exhaled and the days and months and years of tension drained, in a second, away. It was a drop of pure bliss, because for the first time in such a long time, absolutely nothing mattered.

Then she hit Carla in the face.

She was surprised, in the blur that followed, that Carla fought back so feebly. She would have been trained in hand-to-hand, but her resistance felt token. There were perhaps three or four seconds of sweet release for Valerie before her smarter self struggled back in with its dull bulletin: *She doesn't want to fight back. She wants you to beat her up. Don't make this any worse than it is. Don't do anything stupid.*

Too late.

The two women were halfway to the ground. An overweight store security guard in a brown uniform was jogging toward them, shouting, "Hey . . . *Hey!*" Peripherally, Valerie was aware of the young mother gawping, though the toddler was wholly engaged with his popsicle.

Valerie let go of Carla. Stepped back. The evening reasserted itself: the parking lot's white halogens, the ranks of cars, the cold air slightly damp at her warm throat and wrists, her blood rich and rushing. A kid pushing a train of shopping carts had stopped to watch.

"Thank you," Carla said.

59

Claudia knew the nightmare would kill her unless she accepted it. The only way to stop the nightmare from killing her was to let go of the world before the nightmare. The world before the nightmare was the world in which she was herself, free, complex, ambivalent, filled with ideas and expectations and all the nuances of consciousness. The world before the nightmare was the world in which no one was going to kill her. The longer she held on to that world, the nearer her death would come in this one. In the nightmare world, she must reduce herself to a single purpose: to get out of the nightmare world.

Which meant inverting herself.

Which meant going further into the nightmare. The nightmare was a black hole. The only way to escape its gravity was to accept its pull and pass through its heart to whatever lay beyond. Perhaps what lay beyond was a world almost exactly like the one she'd lost. Identical to it, in fact, except in one particular: that she herself would be changed forever.

But changed or not, she would be alive. And that was all that mattered now.

"Show me," she said.

She stood a couple of feet from the grille. Paulie stood up close on the other side, holding the iPad. He didn't know what was going on. His face alternated between forced sneers and grins—and long moments in which its features looked stripped of their guiding intelligence. "Show me all of them."

Her hands were in her jacket pockets, slippery with sweat.

In the right hand, the rolled-up metal plaque with its wicked V edge that she couldn't stop running her thumb over. In the last hours, it had become everything to her. A rope that could pull her out of hell. But she knew that very soon she'd have to let go of it. Very soon. Minutes. Seconds.

"You're crazy," Paulie said. His voice was thick, drugged with uncertainty. His fingernails were filthy. Claudia wondered when he'd last washed. She had an image of him sitting in a tub of grayish scummed water, hands on his skinny white knees, staring at the bathroom tiles.

She took her hands out of her pockets, thinking, with a flash of panic, what if the metal snagged, got caught on the—?

Shut it down. Don't think. Don't be yourself.

Unable to quite take his eyes off her, Paulie swiped and tapped at the screen. She saw that his face trembled a little. His odor of sweat and stale clothes pounded out of him. Her reflex was to hold her breath. But survival now depended on overriding her reflexes. She inhaled it through her nose. Let it wholly into her reality. Went a degree further into the already deep madness. At the heart of a black hole was a singularity. Where time and space collapsed. Where Einstein and Newton broke down. Where nothing made sense. Except the end of everything known—and the dark possibility of something new beyond.

Paulie laughed once, then went silent again as the screen light shivered on his face.

He turned it toward her.

Look and don't see.

Look and don't see.

They didn't speak, the two men.

The only sounds were the jostle of the iPad's mic and the woman's gagged misery. What the men were doing brought heavy silence down into them. Apart from very occasionally Paulie's unsteady snicker, when the camera shook.

Look and don't see.

But there was no not seeing.

The woman was young, maybe Claudia's age, with dark hair and light brown skin.

The same ropes. The same floor. The same room.

Claudia felt her jaws jammed together and her legs emptying. Her limbs were strands of chiffon. She couldn't do this. All her history and every tenderness and her mother's fine-featured face and her father saying, *There, there, Claudie, it's all right, shshsh, don't cry* after every bump or tumble or scrape or sting, everything she had been up to this point said she couldn't, couldn't, could *not* do this.

She felt her own misery swelling inside her. Every second said she couldn't bear this. Every second demanded the scream, pushed it farther up her throat.

Can't bear.

Unbearable.

Somewhere she'd read: *The word "unbearable" makes a liar of you unless it's followed by your death.*

The woman's body still going through the motions of denial, twisting and wrenching to find an escape, everything other than that impulse gone.

But the ropes were the ropes. The knife was the knife. The men were the men. Physics was physics. The world was the world, filled with obedient necessities. If you do *x*, then *y* follows. The world was completely innocent. Evil was solely human.

Claudia couldn't tell how long it lasted. Time was suspended. There was just what she was seeing. There was just the madness confirming itself in the heat of her face. The woman had lost everything that had made her herself. She'd lost everything except her body and the desperation to lose that as well, since it was nothing now but a vessel for her suffering. Suffering like this did away with the person, the treasures of their life, memories, jokes, ideas, hopes, dreams, everything that made them who they were, and left them only the animal cry for what was happening to them to stop.

The woman was barely moving now. Her eyes closed. She might have been restlessly asleep. The fingers of her left hand closed and opened gently. Blood from her right ankle all the way up her shin, like a torn red knee sock. Paulie's recorded voice said quietly: *Come on. She's . . . It's my turn.* Xander getting as if drunkenly to his feet. Staring down at her. Then sidling away like a dazed animal.

Paulie putting the camera down unsteadily. Two seconds of it pointing at a moldy corner of the basement's ceiling—then the footage stopped, and flicked back to the still of its opening frame.

So far, Claudia had done everything she could to keep her face blank.

But now she looked directly at Paulie—who was watching her with his small eyes gone bright and his mouth open—and did the thing so much against herself that she didn't know until the last moment whether it wouldn't betray her and release the scream that was twisted in her throat. Heat and emptiness and the threat of coming away from her body. The air around her was thick, an insistent claustrophobia.

She smiled at him.

"Show me another one," she said.

60

Valerie drove back to her apartment, fast, with the adrenaline still haywire in her limbs. She wasn't alone in the car. The dead women, crammed and murmuring. Her grandfather's ghost, filled with damning pity. Her mother's voice saying, Your temper, Valerie, your *temper*... The image of Claudia Grey, screaming, bloomed and faded on the windshield. Fuck. Fuck. *Fuck.*

Rage and exhaustion fumbled her keys at the apartment door. She dropped them. Stood for a second with her fists clenched and tears like a tourniquet at her throat. Inside she opened a bottle of Smirnoff. At the kitchen sink dropped the tumbler she was pouring it into. The glass burst with a compressed *puff* against the tiles of the countertop. With the last of her fury, she flung the bottle against the wall, where, innocently obeying the laws of physics, *it* smashed, too, and bled its clear contents down the paintwork.

She lit a Marlboro and called Will Fraser.

"Nothing so far," he said. "Utah land records are county by county. Worse is, York says there's no bank account for either Xander King or Leon Ghast here or in Utah."

"The Conways' bank?"

"York's dealing with it. A few hours."

"Keep looking," she said. "Call me as soon as."

She was about to hang up. Checked herself. "Wait," she said.

"The Zoo Guy sightings. Check the hotline tips for anything from Utah. Do it now. I'll hold."

Less than a Claudia Grey minute.

"There's one," Will said. "Came in yesterday. St. George. Anonymous female. Said she saw him in the Red Cliffs Mall a week ago."

"In a store?"

"She wouldn't give us anything more. Just that. We're still waiting on CCTV."

Valerie grabbed a pen. "Give me the address of the mall."

"Seventeen-seventy Red Cliffs Drive, St. George, Utah 84790. We called it back to the SGPD and the bureau's field office there. So far, zippo."

"Call them again."

"Val, he could be two hundred miles from there and still be in Utah."

"Just call them."

"What are you going to do?"

"I don't know."

But she did know. And laughed at herself inwardly.

She got online. The last direct flight from San Francisco to St. George left in an hour. She wouldn't make it. Everything after that had layovers, time-consuming connections in Los Angeles or Las Vegas or Denver.

Her phone rang.

"It's me," Nick Blaskovitch said.

Me. If you were lucky, you had someone in your life for whom "me" was always enough of an ID.

"I'm downstairs. Buzz me in."

The second he walked in the door, the apartment bristled with their history. You didn't realize how dead an atmosphere had been until it came back to life. Valerie thought: *Three years since he was here. Three years since the last thing he saw before he left. Me, fucking another guy.* The bedroom was an invitation and a wound.

"Will told me what happened," he said.

She was leaning against the kitchen counter with her arms wrapped around her midriff. She didn't trust herself without something solid to anchor her. "Yeah," she said. "It's been . . ." She didn't finish. He'd noticed the broken bottle, the liquor stain on the wall. She was aware of him re-creating the scene, more or less accurately. He knew her. She knew him. That was all there was to it.

"That must've felt good" was all he said.

She hadn't been, quite, meeting his eye. Now she did. Recognition. Which forced both of them to look away again.

"What are you going to do?" he said.

"I'm going to Utah. There's a lead in St. George. Pointless, probably."

He nodded.

They kept looking away from each other.

I'm still in love with you, Nick. I'm still in love with you, but I don't deserve you to be in love with me. Say it. Say it.

She didn't. He didn't speak, either. Valerie thought: *If I walk over there and kiss him, one of two things will happen. Either he'll kiss me back, or he won't. If he doesn't, I don't think I'll be able to take it. And if he does, I'm going to take him to bed and not leave this place for days.*

She knew he was going through exactly the same thought process. They might as *well* have said it. There was only the thinnest emotional veil separating them. But it was as if there were a time lock at work. A time lock neither of them could quit checking.

"You need to get out of here," he said.

"I know."

"Will you keep me posted from Utah?"

"Yes."

Yes. Single words were enough. It meant more than updates on the Case. It meant, potentially, everything.

His look said he understood.

He went to the door and opened it. Turned back.

"Be careful, Skirt," he said.

"I will. I promise."

The word "promise" hurt her heart.

When he'd gone, she stood, gathering herself. The apartment's atmosphere like a cramped fist unclenching by degrees.

In the bedroom, she threw a couple of changes of clothes

into a bag. Took a fleece from the wardrobe. Laptop, keys, purse, Advil.

Gun. Badge.

She had to get out of town anyway, before they came for those.

At the door, she paused. Took stock of herself, the shape she was in. Pictured her body's energy indicators flashing red: *Empty. Empty. Empty.* The hours of lost sleep and whatever virus she was fighting stared at her like a massed army waiting to charge. Ludicrous odds. One woman against thousands.

Well, she was going, anyway.

She didn't have a choice.

61

Paulie was in a peculiar state. Paulie was, in fact, in a state unlike any other he'd ever been in.

"I told you I knew something you didn't," Claudia said, laughing.

Claudia. She'd told him her name and now it was a weird thing nestling in his head. His cock ached in his jeans. With the others, he'd never known their names until afterwards, helping Xander burn their purses, credit cards, driver's licenses.

She had her left hand down the front of *her* jeans, working on herself. He was having trouble holding the iPad steady. Everything he thought of to say—*You're crazy, you're fucking . . . I don't believe*—died before he could get it out of his mouth. The muscles in his face were useless. But his body was wealthy with heat, his cock the throbbing center. He kept wanting to say something, but it was impossible. His mind just repeatedly dead-ended, watching the movement of her hand between her legs, the little tendons in her slender wrist tensing and relaxing, tensing and relaxing, her breathing heavy.

The last video clip had just finished.

"Fuck," she said quietly, and bit her bottom lip. "Fuck."

Paulie flipped the iPad around and ran the first clip again. He'd done it before being aware that he was going to do it. He kept finding himself doing things.

"Can't you . . ." she said. "I mean, Jesus . . ."

He watched her eyes close. Her nostrils flared. It was so fucking nuts the way something like her nostrils flaring like that made it even more . . . made it . . .

She opened her eyes. Looked at the screen. Her mouth was open, lips wet. She had small teeth. She looked like she was in a wide-awake trance. He imagined how soft and hot her face would feel against his hand. He imagined wrapping his fist in her hair, yanking her head back when he shoved his cock deep into her asshole. Then smashing her face into the floor.

Except it wasn't . . . It wasn't right. He didn't know whether it made him angry that she . . . At moments, when she'd watched the clips, her eyes had flashed at him. Then back to the screen. Then back to him. Each time she looked at him, it was terrible, pitched him further into not knowing what to . . . not knowing if . . .

"Haven't you ever thought of doing it with a girl?" she gasped.

The bizarre thing was he knew straightaway what she meant. She meant her and him instead of him and Xander. Doing it to someone. Together. It shocked him, how clearly he could see it. Her face all lit up like it was now, the smile with the little teeth. Like a kid's teeth almost. Her hand working herself while he drew the knife across some bitch's cunt. He imagined Xander knowing this was going on down here, and for a second or two the world raced away and his scalp shrank, as if a blow were about to land on the back of his skull. But then he remembered Xander as he was now, upstairs, with the room heavy around him and his big dark face pinched and sweaty. The bullet burying itself in the wardrobe right next to his face. It's like carrying you on my goddamned *back*.

"Can't you help me out here?" Claudia asked.

Her other hand came slowly out of her jacket pocket. Her fingers curled under the hem of her top. Began to push it up over her bare belly. Slowly.

62

"Where are you?" Liza Terrill said.

"Fifty miles west of St. George," Valerie said. "Utah."

Eight hours had passed since her non-fight with Carla, and she'd spent all of them on the road. Now she sat in the Taurus in a twenty-four-hour McDonald's parking lot with a cup of hot water and lemon that was too hot to drink, but the heat of which was soothing to her hands. The car's clock said 3:46 A.M. Beyond the rest area and the highway's lights, open land yawned away into darkness. The night here was ragged cloud with patches of stars. Will Fraser had called four hours ago. Carla had been to see Deerholt again. She had witness statements—the security guard, the young mother, the shopping cart kid—testifying that Valerie had attacked her. She also had the bruises to prove it. Deerholt was, in Will's words, fucking furious.

Since then, hours and miles of waking dream behind the wheel. Her body ached. Her snot when she blew her raw nose was hot. Gooseflesh came and went, no matter what she did with the Taurus's AC. Her skin whispered, shrank, went heavy and cold. The sensations brought her childhood back. Fevers that took the details of her bedroom and warped them, turned her mattress to warm molasses, made sea monsters of the carpet's scrolls, set the curtains' dark flowers free to move and morph. In childhood delirium was confirmation of the world-behind-the-world, the one imagination hinted was always there, waiting for its chance to come through. But in childhood (*her* childhood, she thought, not everyone's, not fucking *Leon's*) there were merciful intercessions: her mother's cool hand on her forehead; her father carrying her to the bathroom when she was too weak to walk. These merciful intercessions stopped you falling once and for all into the world-behind-the-world. But when you were an adult, you were on your own.

Unless you had love.

"What the hell are you doing in Utah?" Liza said.

It refreshed the absurdity of what she *was* doing: driving around in case she ran into them.

She told Liza about the sighting.

"Jesus, they could be anywhere," Liza said.

"Not if she's still alive," Valerie said. "If she's still alive, they'll have brought her to HQ."

"Valerie, all you've got is a *state*."

"I'm aware of that."

"OK, OK, don't get your pantyhose twisted. I'm calling to tell you we got the DNA from the purse sequins. It's a match. It's your boys. Or one of them."

"Great. Thanks. You'll send it over to Will?"

"No problem. How's it going with Blasko?"

They had no secrets from each other. Valerie had told her about Nick's return when she was up in Santa Cruz.

"Fearfully," Valerie said. "Both of us. I've got to get this thing . . . If we start now . . ."

"Don't mix the two things up," Liza said.

Valerie didn't need her to unpack that: Don't make you and him depend on the Case. The way you did before. The way you fucked it up.

"I know you and your crazy Catholic genes," Liza said. "You think you don't deserve it."

"I *don't* deserve it," Valerie said.

"OK, when you get back, me and you are going to go out and drink ourselves stupid. And if you don't go home and go to bed with him, *I'm* going to."

"All right," Valerie said. "That sounds fair."

"Listen, get back in one piece, will you?"

"I will."

"And watch out for those Mormon motherfuckers."

After she'd hung up, Valerie sat for a few moments blowing on her hot water and lemon. Again she pictured herself gone from all this, a woman sitting outside an adobe hut in pitiless sun, her bare feet in dust as red as chili powder. Alone. At the same time felt the promise of the warmth and peace of lying in bed with Blasko. Love. Room for each other. A future.

And between her and either vision, the whispering dead women. The child's body with its text of wounds and invisible wings of darkness. The maddening inner hiss of Claudia Grey time, boiling away to nothing.

63

The division between Claudia's hand and the metal in her pocket kept coming and going. One moment it was a thing in itself, the next it was part of her, an extension of the flesh and blood and bones in her fingers and palm. Her nerves ran ahead of her, rehearsing the second when she would lift her arm, swing it through the swarming space that separated them, trace the impossible arc that would end with the weapon buried in his eye socket. A ghost version of herself went through the movement, over and over, and each time it weakened her, as if the longer she waited, the less likely it was that she'd be able to do it. Useless thoughts and images buzzed and fluttered: her first morning at school, her face pressed to the freezing bars of the playground gate as her mother turned and walked away; wading into the Indian Ocean one evening, the warm water soft and heavy around her bare legs; sitting in her room at Magdalen with a small-hours whisky and her battered *Middlemarch,* then looking up at her dark window to see that big flakes of snow were falling; getting off the Tube at Tottenham Court Road on a Friday evening, lonely and excited and alive to the mystery of another London night. There was a superabundance of these thoughts and memories, as if her life were making an effort to gather its whole self in her before she died.

And against all that was the reality of now, these minutes, these seconds, the fact of where she was, which, regardless of where she'd been or what she'd done in her twenty-six years, was the only thing that mattered.

They hadn't spoken for a while. He'd stood there watching her, his hand massaging his cock through his jeans. His face was a fine balance of trance and mistrust. He was breathing through his mouth. She had to be careful. He was afraid of her voice. He was afraid of looking her in the eye. A degree of aversion was necessary. She was understanding the precarious nuances. If she did one thing wrong, it would be over.

She undid the top two buttons of her jeans. It was sickening to have to use both hands. To let go of the roll of metal in her jacket pocket. Just two buttons. She could still run. Nothing that would stop her being able to run. Another fine balance. Since she'd lifted her top and exposed her breasts, a fresh layer of horror had settled on her. She was contradicting instinct at the cellular level. She was forcing herself into a transformation. At times, it felt as if she were simply going to pass out. The thought of running filled her legs with weakness.

He leaned the shotgun against the wall. Fumbled in his pocket.

The keys.

This was it.

Oh God. Oh God help me please.

She opened her mouth to say something, a final word of confirming encouragement—but stopped herself. She must do nothing. Just what she was doing. What she was doing was working. One word could break the spell. He was operating beyond what he knew. He was becoming a stranger to himself with every passing second.

He bent to put the key in the padlock. The basement packed its silence around the small sounds. Claudia wanted it to stop. It was too soon. She wasn't ready. She would never be ready. She couldn't. She didn't have enough madness in her. You thought you were already maximally afraid—but it turned out, there was more fear. It turned out your room for fear was infinite.

The keys scraped the floor. Jingled. The lock clicked.

There was no going back. There was no time. She couldn't believe she'd brought this to herself. She couldn't bear it. She knew if she screamed now, she wouldn't stop screaming. It was too late. It was a mistake. She couldn't do what she had to do. She'd deceived herself.

She put her back against the wall's bare brick. To stop herself from collapsing. The mental rehearsals were chaos now. She hadn't, she saw with sickening clarity, thought through the details. He would walk up to her and smash his fist into her face. He would walk up to her and tear out a hank of her hair. He would walk up to her and rip her stomach open with the knife. In one of the optimistic (idiotic) visions, she'd seen him lying on his back, her astride him. She'd seen herself having all the time in the world to plunge the metal accurately into his eye. She'd seen him with his eyes *closed,* not seeing it coming. Now she just saw his fist hurtling toward her face. Now she saw herself winded, on the floor, him kicking her repeatedly, in her guts, her breasts, her face. Now she saw herself on her belly with her jeans and panties pulled down and his hand wrapped in her hair and the knife going leisurely into her flank.

All these permutations of her failure, her madness, her desperation, her stupidity.

The grille ascended with a violent rasp. A monster clearing its throat.

There was nothing between her and flight.

Except him.

Could she just run, *now*?

She could see in his face and shoulders, he was thinking of pulling the cage down and locking it behind him.

But he didn't. He was afraid of losing his momentum, too. He didn't know what he was doing. Only that he was moving forward into something new.

It was too late. Again. The seconds had betrayed her. He was in front of her. Less than two feet away. She could smell him. She had to stop the reflex in her right hand to go into her pocket for the metal tube.

His face was close. The blue eyes like archery targets, the absurd connection with Robin Hood again, him the sniveling traitor. The deep green of English forests. Her father saying: Do you know, Claudie, the whole of England was covered in trees once, long ago.

Very slowly, disbelieving herself, she reached out and rested her hand, lightly, against the bulge in his jeans.

It detonated him. He lunged at her.

In the blur that followed, all the images—of her family, of her past, of running—simply imploded. She'd imagined calculation. She'd imagined herself picking her moment. Instead there was just this. No time. Nothing. Everything.

But she felt his sour breath warm on her face and his fingernails digging into her breast and before she knew what she was doing her right hand was out of her pocket, the metal gripped in her wet fist.

It seemed an interminable time she held it there, raised alongside his head. The silence between them pressed on her with static urgency. The blood pounded in her skull. The open air beyond the house was a gravity, pulling her. The open air. Freedom. Life.

She drew her arm back. Her muscles said it was impossible. Everything said it was impossible.

It occurred to her—a remote, minor fact—that her right leg was between both of his. Every movie she'd ever seen in which a woman did this to a man. A boy she'd once seen in gym at school in Bournemouth; he'd been walking across the beam. Slipped. Took his full body weight on his balls. The entire class had erupted into laughter. But the boy had seemed to pause there forever, legs scissored around the wood, before comedically turning upside down and dropping to the crash mat. After a few moments, he'd vomited, which silenced everyone.

Claudia jerked her knee up as hard as she could.

She felt the breath rush out of him. Saw the extraordinary detail of his thin face with its mouth open and its roundel eyes wide. She felt his body scrambling to recover itself and failing, failing, failing. He bent forward, would have collapsed to his knees if not for her, if not for the softness of her midriff cradling his head. The intimacy of this revolted her.

Blind, deafened, thudded against by the room's crammed energy, she struck with the metal tube.

Nowhere near his eye. It smashed into the cartilage of his ear.

He made a strange, falsetto sound, as of very negligible protest.

She hit him again, vaguely aware that her grip was warm and moist with blood.

The blow felt weak, but at the same time she felt it gouge a small chunk of flesh from his skull.

In spite of which, his hands were strong. The left gripped her lapel. The right raked its nails down her breast. He was realizing. He was understanding that he was losing control. He was in disbelief. He shoved his head hard into her. He was trying not to go down on his knees. Claudia felt her body's lights blazing. A city with an overload of electricity—

His hand shot up and grabbed her throat. The front of her throat. She felt his sharp-tipped fingers already tight and tightening on her trachea, her body's oxygen warnings firing, starvation racing through her arteries. He was trying to make the dirty fingernails meet. He was trying to rip her throat out.

She drew her arm back—pictured, briefly, the tube's vicious V-edge—then screamed and struck as hard as she could at his head.

He must have seen it. He must have read, through the blur of his pain, her intention. He turned his face away to protect his eyes.

The metal went an inch deep into the side of his gullet.

Nothing seemed to happen.

The two of them froze. To Claudia it was as if he were pausing to recalculate, to get a grasp of the adjusted situation. His hand was still gripping her throat, but she could feel his weight pulling him down. She knew that if she withdrew the weapon and tried to strike again, she might miss. She was distracted by the extraordinary new sensation—of having stabbed someone, of her hand still tight around the rolled metal, of its astonishing entry into his flesh. With a curious precision of focus, she understood she had only a moment to do all the damage she could.

So instead of pulling the weapon out and trying for a second wound, she drove it with all her strength deeper into his throat.

"Fuck," he gurgled quietly, on the still indrawn breath. "Fuck."

She let go of the metal and shoved him. Two seconds of resistance, then he sank away from her, his legs buckling under him, in slow motion. His hands dropped from her and went gently—tentative, confused exploration—toward the metal buried in his neck. The blue eyes blinked delicately.

The second it took Claudia to get past him was filled with the imagined sensation of him reaching up and grabbing her ankle.

But it didn't happen.

Instead the basement's space opened to her. All her movements felt slow. She was aware of reaching up and yanking her top back down to cover her breasts. It was a minute, precious relief, a sudden integrity.

The shotgun was where he'd left it, propped against the wall. She grabbed it.

Kill him.

But the sound of the shot would bring the other one. Never held a gun of any kind in her entire life. The strange heaviness. The dark personality of the thing. The sound of the shot the sound of the shot the sound—

She felt herself raising it and turning and pointing it at him and squeezing and squeezing and squeezing the trigger.

Nothing happened. A nerve in her finger protested.

She was doing something wrong.

Safety.

There was something called a safety.

It was too much. She couldn't think. *Look for it. Time. No time. Run. Run.*

He'd found where the metal had gone into him. He was easing it out. The sight of him doing this—and of the blood that hurried out with it—snapped something in her. The bare fact of him still moving, still going about his animal business of trying to recover, his dirty fingernails and blinking eyelashes, was more than she could bear.

She turned the shotgun, gripped it by its barrels, hefted it to shoulder height—and smashed it down on his skull.

64

When Xander woke, Mama Jean was sitting in the chair from the old house, drawn up by the window, smoking. His bed was damp.

"Simplest thing in the world," she said. "Simplest thing in the world, unless you're dumb as a rock."

Xander felt his mouth locked. He knew that he ought to be able to speak. But he couldn't. The familiar heat and weight and prickling because he was making her lose her patience.

"*J* is for?"

She leaned forward in the chair. The wood cricked. She was wearing the blue check shirt and the big faded jeans. Her pale meaty feet were bare. The thick toenails she clipped on the back stoop in the sun. The smoke from her cigarette went up straight for a few inches then rippled crazily.

"*J* is for?" she repeated.

Jug. Jug. Jug.

The muscles in his face were full of soft electricity.

Mama Jean sighed heavily. Sat back in her chair. Shook her head. Smiled to herself with a sort of gentleness.

"I don't know why you do this," she said. "I really don't."

With an almighty effort, Xander forced himself to sit up. Not just the bed but the whole room seemed to tilt. His hands felt giant and useless.

Mama Jean wobbled, flickered. Started to get to her feet.

Xander closed his eyes.

When he opened them again, she was gone.

The TV was still on, sound still down. An infomercial for an exercise belt. A blond woman in a neon blue leotard and black pantyhose, walking on a treadmill. A buff guy in green sweatpants and a crisp white polo shirt, his mouth moving nonstop. The camera shifted to the studio audience. All of them looked delighted. Their teeth and eyes. Some of them were shaking their heads as if they couldn't believe how happy they were.

Xander had gotten in bed with all his clothes on, even his boots. The clothes felt as if they were knitting themselves to his skin, becoming part of him. He wanted to take them off, but he was cold.

Simplest thing in the world.

He'd waited too long. He'd let Paulie fuck up the way this needed to be done, and since then, everything had gone wrong. He'd had a dream of firing at Paulie. A dream? Where was the gun? Hadn't he got into bed with the gun?

He searched the bedclothes. Nothing. Images came back. Paulie against the wardrobe.

There was a bullet hole in the wardrobe.

He swung his heavy legs over the edge of the bed. He didn't feel right. Nothing was right. Since fucking Colorado. The snow. The kid in the bedroom. The woman.

Because he didn't have the jug. He didn't have the *J*.

The *J* was under his arm. But it glowed when he closed his eyes, too. Like kids writing in the black air with sparklers. He'd waited too long. The room now had a sound of crackling. Time burning away. Mama Jean said: *I can wait all day. I've got all the time in the world.*

He got to his feet, shivering.

There was a sound from downstairs.

Paulie.

It would be easier without Paulie. It would be, after all these years, a relief.

65

Claudia was almost at the top of the basement stairs when she thought of the keys. There had been half a dozen on the bunch in Paulie's hand.

She had an image of herself finding every exit door locked. She hadn't realized she'd been crying until this thought stopped her. For perhaps two seconds, she suffered a perfect balance between the horror of being unable to get out and the horror of going back for the keys. *Going back.* The words made going back impossible. She would throw herself through a window if she had to. There was no going back. She could not go back.

But she had to go back.

The basement door was locked.

Tears welled and fell instantly. A fracture of weakness through her whole body.

She forced herself back down the stairs. Merely putting one foot in front of the other threatened her with collapse. Each step was shakier than the one before, as if her mental schema for descending a staircase were deserting her.

Paulie was lying on his back, eyes closed, motionless, but visibly still breathing. A very gradually expanding puddle of blood where he'd pulled the metal out of his throat. Catching his smell of tobacco and damp canvas and sweat again dizzied her. She was shivering in spite of the furnace's exhaled heat. Touching him seemed inconceivable.

But she jammed her jaws together (the sounds of herself, breathing, sobbing, were loud and raw) and made herself do what she had to do.

The keys were in the right-hand pocket of the combat jacket.

She grabbed them, turned, and ran back up the stairs. At the *very* last moment remembered to pick up the shotgun. Even if she couldn't fire it, it was something to hold, it was a club, as she'd already proved.

She made too much noise on the stairs.

Not the first key. Not the second. Not the third.

Her hands were frantic birds tethered to her wrists. She dropped the bunch. Grazed her forehead on the locked door when she bent to snatch them back up.

Which keys had she already tried?

The words *start again* made her sick with rage and fear. Time. Her time. Going . . .

The second key she tried fit.

The door opened with what sounded like an amplified creak.

She was through.

The corridor she found herself in (she remembered very little of her first sight of it in the darkness) led in one direction back toward the kitchen, in the other down to another door with a pane of frosted glass in it above head height. Front door. The glass showed twilight. Dawn? Dusk? She had no clue. Opposite her two more doorways, one (to her left) with its door shut, the other (ten feet to her right) with its door ajar. Scuffed plaster and a bare wooden floor. A rotten hallway runner bunched up near the front door, weighted down with an old iron boot scraper. Chunky Bakelite light switches and two cobwebbed bare bulbs hanging from the flaking ceiling. The house was silent. The world was silent. No traffic. No birdsong. It might have been the sole building on an otherwise empty planet.

The nearness of the exits screamed at her to run. Was overridden—just—by the thought of the other guy hearing her. The other guy. Where was he?

She went on agonized tiptoe to the front door. Tried the handle. Locked.

The nightmare with the keys. Again. Her hands worse, her face trembling. The need to look at the keys and to look over her shoulder. She couldn't do both. Every time she looked down at the keys, the certainty that someone was approaching at her back. The house watching.

She tried every key.

None of them fit.

Now it was impossible to go slowly. She turned and ran back down the corridor toward the kitchen.

She was a pace past the ajar door when Xander stepped out behind her, grabbed her by her hair, and yanked her backwards, off her sandaled feet.

66

Valerie checked herself into the Best Western on East St. George Boulevard (the two women on reception were both wearing Santa hats), showered, changed, and half slept for the hour and forty minutes before the Red Cliffs Mall opened. It didn't help. When her phone alarm rang, it was like hauling herself up from an underwater realm all but impenetrably choked with weeds. She splashed cold water on her face, brushed her teeth, dropped a couple of Advil, and got back into the Taurus, shivering. It occurred to her that in her old life, she would have taken her temperature. Her old life. How long had it been since she'd lived her old life? She wasn't even sure what her old life was anymore.

She'd called Will and got him to tell the mall management office to expect her. There was, of course, the glaring fact of her having zero jurisdiction in Utah, but Will had put the requisite frighteners on them, so there was no resistance (there was deference, in fact) when she turned up a little after 7:30 A.M., cursorily flashed her badge, and was escorted to CCTV headquarters on the second floor.

"We already sent the stuff to the St. George guys," the chief security officer told her. "If it hasn't reached your people yet, that's them sitting on it, not us." His name was Marcellus Corey, a handsome black fifty-two-year-old from New Orleans with flecks of gray in his close-cropped hair and a high-cheekboned face and a smile that would politely wait out whatever bullshit you were spewing until you were ready to tell the truth.

"They've sent it through," Valerie said. "But you know, I'm here now anyway."

Marcellus smiled. The tiniest parting of his lips revealed the warm glint of a gold tooth. *He feels sorry for me,* Valerie thought. *He knows who I am.*

"I hear you," Marcellus said. "Well, we got the originals right here."

The hotline caller hadn't been sure whether it was a Wednesday or a Thursday she'd seen the suspect, which meant Valerie had, potentially, two shopping days of footage to sit through. Marcellus set her up in the control room with a coffee, but after two hours, the feeling of futility had settled on her. The caller hadn't given them anything beyond "the mall." Valerie had decided to take the general public area footage first, then go store by store. But what for? The best she could hope for was a positive ID. Where did that get her? Leon still had the whole state. So what if he was in St. George a week ago? It didn't prove he lived here. Utah had an area close to eighty-five thousand square miles. Murder HQ—and *maybe* Claudia Grey, if she was even still alive—could be anywhere from here to Logan, two hundred miles north.

Her eyes hurt. The constant strain of trying to visually compress the pixels. She paused the footage, got up, stretched. Her head was pounding, and though she'd put the fleece on under her jacket, she was still shivering. She looked in her purse for more Advil. She was out. The purse. The Baggie. The test.

Before more women die of your incompetence. Baby killer.

"Jesus," Marcellus said when he passed her on his way out of the control room. "You OK, Detective? You look . . . You don't look so good."

"Yeah," Valerie said. "I've got a cold."

"I'm not a doctor," Marcellus said. "But it looks like a little more than a cold to me."

"I'm fine. Getting a little screen-blind."

"Well, I'm going to get coffee. Can I get you anything?"

Advil, Valerie thought. *Codeine. And some fucking speed while you're at it.* But she was sick of taking painkillers. It felt like a moral failure. "Coffee would be great," she said. "A cappuccino?"

Alone in the control room (three other security officers had been in and out during the morning, but they were all downstairs now), Valerie paced, trying to reboot her concentration. There were three workstations and several monitors, live-feeding, switching angles. She wondered what it was like for Marcellus, spending his days watching people who didn't consider for a moment that they were being watched. You'd see everything from up here: flirtations; break-ups; bad parenting; happy people; sad people; lonely people; mostly people just trawling unreflectively through the inexhaustible wealth of their extraordinary ordinariness. *The work goes into you.* You'd feel like a small version of God, up here, hour after hour, day after day. Marcellus had something of that quality, a sort of patient accommodation, beyond any kind of surprise.

With a very slight sense of voyeuristic guilt, she searched for Marcellus now, wondering if he were wondering if she'd do just that. It took a little while, but she found him. He was standing outside Starbucks, the two coffees in a cardboard holder, chatting with one of the mall's cleaning staff, a small bald black guy holding a bright green cart equipped with mops and brushes.

A toddler who'd obviously slipped his mother's grasp darted out of the Starbucks entrance just behind Marcellus, face filled with delighted mischief, and ran straight into the legs of a dark-haired bearded guy in sunglasses walking past. The guy had a shopping bag in either hand, and something Valerie couldn't make out slotted into one armpit. On the kid's impact, the package slipped and fell to the floor. The toddler—a blond boy in denim dungarees, looked up at him for a moment, then took off again unsteadily, pursued a second later by his mother, a pretty young woman, hair identical blond, in a floral sundress, a short leather jacket, and bright white Nikes.

The guy bent to retrieve what he'd dropped: a yellow paper kite wrapped in cellophane, while the mother scooped up the kid. It cheered Valerie slightly that the young woman didn't seem angry, that a part of her took pleasure in her kid's wayward vitality.

The guy resettled the kite under his arm. He seemed all but oblivious of the young woman's apology as he walked away. Valerie wondered where he'd managed to buy a kite in the middle of winter. But of course, the world of retail had long since stopped paying attention to the seasons. Still, a weird present to give someone at Christmas. Kites were for summer.

She had turned away from the monitors and was heading back to her own dreaded workstation when it hit her.

K is for . . . ?

Was it "kite"?

Jesus.

She spun back to the screen, but the guy was out of frame.

The sunglasses and beard had hidden his features.

But the height and build were right.

Fuck.

There was no time.

She ran.

67

"Lock down the mall," Valerie said to Marcellus.

"What?"

"He's here. Lock it down."

How many seconds had passed? Minutes? Time. Claudia.

"I can't . . . I mean—"

"Do it. Right now. How many exits?"

"Two. But there are store exits, too. I guess—"

"Get your guys on them. White male, dark hair and beard, sunglasses, six foot, one eighty. Jeans and dark blue Windbreaker."

She took off in the direction the guy had gone. "And check the parking lot cameras," she called over her shoulder. "He might be out there. Look for an RV."

It was an agony in her wake, feeling the time eaten up by Marcellus's processing. The time it would take for him to walkie the security team, get back up to the office, get the requisite approval, throw the switches.

She scanned the stores as she went by, but the main thing was to get to the exit. One of the *two* exits. For all she knew, he could be at the other one, or out through Sears, JCPenney, Dillard's . . .

The security gates didn't come down. Human traffic flowed in and out past Valerie. As it would be flowing, she knew, through all the other ways in and out of the building.

Fifteen minutes went by. One of the uniformed security team

Valerie had seen earlier appeared. He wasn't alone. A tall, moonfaced white guy in a dark linen suit introduced himself:

"Mark Vaughn," he said, extending his hand. "I'm the mall manager. What's going on, Detective?"

What's going on is that you've probably just let a serial killer evade arrest. What's going on is that, thanks to not locking the place down, another young woman is going to die.

Before she even began the recap, Valerie could feel how long it would take. Mark Vaughn wasn't trying to be difficult. He was just scared. Shut the place down for what might be several hours on Christmas Eve. Possible crowd panic. There would be someone he was answerable to.

She decided to go in hard. Use his fear.

"You either shut this place down right now or I'll charge you with obstruction," she said. "This is a multiple murder investigation. Do you understand?"

"Look," he began. "This is . . . I mean—"

"Detective!" Marcellus was heading toward them. He looked out of breath. "He's gone," he said.

Valerie felt her face go hot.

"Sears exit camera. He must have gone out through the store right after you saw him."

Mark Vaughn's fear went up a notch.

"Parking lots," Valerie said, grabbing Marcellus by the elbow and hustling him back toward the stairs.

"I'm sorry," Marcellus said as they went up. "I had to get his clearance. I told him there was no time."

"It's not your fault," Valerie said.

She called Nick Blaskovitch.

"Skirt, how's it going?"

"Listen," she said. "Pull up the picture of the kid."

"I'm not at my desk."

"How long?"

"I'm in the evidence room."

"Get back there."

"Val, I'm in the middle of—"

"Now, Nick. Do it. I'll stay on the line. Hurry."

He didn't argue. They knew each other. They knew the tones. She couldn't stop her mind: *Catch this fucker and you can try again for love.* She knew it was madness. But what wasn't madness in her life?

"What's going on?" He was running, she could hear.

"Possible ID."

"You still in St. George?"

"Yeah."

"You saw him?"

"No," she lied. "A witness. It's only a possible. You there yet?"

"One minute."

Valerie and Marcellus entered the security office. Marcellus began rewinding through what footage there was from the parking lot.

"OK," Blasko said. "I'm pulling it up now."

"The alphabet chart," Valerie said. "Is there a kite on it? *K* for kite?"

"Enlarging."

"Apple, Balloon, Clock, Dinosaur, Elephant, Fork, Goose, Hammer—"

"Can't tell," Blasko said. "After Hammer, Icicle, then Jug. The next thing isn't in the shot. Just the edge of it. Can't say for sure it's a kite."

"What color is it?"

"Yellow. The bit I can see is yellow."

"I'll call you back."

"You got St. George PD with you?"

"Yeah." Lies, lies, lies.

"Don't lie," he said. "You get close, you call for backup."

"I'll do it," Valerie said. "I have to go."

"Val, I'm not kid—"

She hung up.

The footage didn't help. The suspect turned left out of Sears— and that was the last it had of him. There was a solitary camera angle for the parking lot exit. Flaring and subsiding sunlight on the windshields left half the drivers invisible. He was gone. He'd been *right there* and she'd missed him. She could sense Marcellus's misery joining her own in the windowless room.

"Fuck," he said quietly. "I'm sorry." Then, after a pause: "What next?"

The adrenaline was still draining. Her body assimilating the reality of the situation all over again: she had nothing.

"What next?" she said—and thought: *What next is that I drive around on psychic empty in the fucking idiotic hope that I spot him.*

"What next is I get the updated description out to your locals and every other agency," she said. "Can you print me a still from this?"

68

Red Cliffs shopper traffic was thick by the time Valerie headed back downstairs into the mall. Christmas decorations glimmered and winked from every store, though she'd hardly noticed any of it in the blur of the last few hours. Christmas. The festivals were vague things to her now, minor events that barely registered on the cop continuum. Murder was not mindful of the time of year. She thought of the Mulvaneys, the tinselled tree in the tidy living room, all the times through Katrina's childhood the family would have decked it, nothing left of the ritual's magic now, just a sparkling redundancy. They'd make an effort for the grandchildren, but the main guest at the table would always be Katrina's ghost. Always, for the rest of their lives. Meanwhile, the world—or all the world not robbed of a loved one by homicide—would carry on, wrapping gifts, roasting turkeys, downing eggnog and gobbling up chocolates, watching *It's a Wonderful Life,* spending credit. Valerie's own family had long since stopped expecting her to be an engaged participant in the festive season. Her nieces and nephews—the niece via her younger brother, the two nephews via her older sister—had been advised, quietly, that she couldn't be counted on. In fact, for several years, Valerie's mother had taken care of buying the gifts "from Aunt Valerie," which precipitated the wearying annual business of Valerie trying to find out how much her mother had spent and attempting to give her the cash, and her mother insisting that it was nothing, not worth the trouble. Valerie thought now, as she passed a Barnes & Noble window display occupied almost entirely by merchandising for the year's Superman movie, *Man of Steel,* that she probably owed her mother more than a thousand bucks. She'd lost track of the movies, too. Movie stars, big new releases. There was a whole generation of actors, it seemed, whose identities were a complete mystery to her, although on the *Man of Steel* poster a few faces came to her from the past: Kevin Costner. Laurence Fishburne. A bearded Russell Crowe in some sort of silvery sci-fi get-up. She'd never understood his appeal. To her he looked porky, sullen, and misogynistic. Like an overgrown sexist toddler was how she'd summed him up to Liza the last time the two of them had gotten together for drinks and to pretend they had a normal life. You can forgive Johnny Depp for being in love with himself, Liza had said. At least he does it with a bit of irony. But Russell Crowe—

Valerie stopped.

Crowe.

Fuck.

Joy Wallace's words came back to her: *Five years earlier, Amy (now a heroin-addicted prostitute of fluid abode) had gotten pregnant by Lewis Crowe, a bipolar Las Vegas pimp and drug peddler who'd been killed in a narcotics deal gone wrong a month before his son was born. . . .*

Amy must have given the father's name on the birth certificate. Which was probably Leon's only legitimate form of ID. With which he'd opened a bank account. Into which the money (wherever the hell it had come from) had been deposited. And out of which he'd paid for whatever property he'd bought in Utah.

Not Xander King. Not Leon Ghast.

Leon Crowe.

She called Will.

69

Claudia emerged from blackness. She didn't know whether Xander had knocked her out or whether her system—pushed beyond its limits—had simply shut down. Either way, she had no recollection of the time between then and now. "Then" was the moment she'd been jerked backwards off her feet. "Now" was—the facts were like a millstone grinding over her slowly—back in the basement, back behind the locked-down grille, back to having her hands and feet bound and her mouth straining to accommodate a plastic ball gag, the sort she'd seen in even the most cursory perusal of pornography. She could feel saliva running down her chin. Her hands were fastened to the ties that were cutting off the circulation in her ankles. *Hog-tied*. The terminology was available. You couldn't help it: the language was the language. Even if you were its wretched object.

There was nothing for her now. All the micro-hopes were gone. Her finite future filled all the space around her, so that even her slightest movement pressed her up against it. It was solid, packed, immovable. It surrounded her with certainty. She was not getting out. What was going to happen to her was going to happen to her. She felt tired. The superficial exhaustion of her body's resources, yes, but beyond it a weary contempt for the bare fact of her life having some of itself left to live. A portion of utterly pointless suffering. She was almost past fear. It sickened her that she would have to be here for the inevitable end of herself, that she would have to be (there was no arguing with this) both its subject and its witness. With not even a God to hurl her contempt at. No God, no scheme of things, nothing. Just the physical world's slavery to cause and effect. If *x,* then *y.* She'd never felt pure disgust for life before. But she felt it now. She wanted it to be over. She wanted to be done with her body, even if being done with her body was being done with herself. She imagined a state beyond death: a confused, salving darkness. A long sleep. *At Peace,* the gravestones said. She understood it now. Without your body and its suffering, you could be at peace.

Paulie was outside the cage, lying in the fetal position, covered in blood, his breathing a phlegmy rattle. His eyes were open. His thin face was wet and gray. The blood-swipe on the bare floor leading to his head said he'd been dragged there by his feet. Xander was standing over him, holding a rust-flecked machete. His limbs were heavy. His face was slack.

"You did this," Xander said very quietly.

Paulie tried to say something, but nothing came out. A bubble of dark blood formed on his lips, then burst. The sound was small and tender.

"I've been carrying you the whole time," Xander said. "Fucking Colorado." He raised his voice, as if talking to a person hard of hearing: "Fucking Ellinson, fucking *Colorado,* I said."

Paulie, bizarrely, laughed.

Xander didn't seem to notice.

"Everything was fine," he said. "Everything was fucking *fine* until you fucked it up in Colorado. Now look!" He gestured around the room with the machete. "Look at the situation! This is *all your fault.* You've never understood what I'm doing here. You've never understood that I've been *losing my patience,* for Christ's sake. Does that mean anything to you? Do you think my patience is . . . Didn't you think I'd lose my patience? I mean, why do you make me do this? Why?"

Without warning—in fact, with a curious delayed action, as if first seeing if Paulie was going to flinch—Xander raised the machete and brought it down hard on Paulie's bent hip.

Paulie screamed and jerked. The blade had gone through his jeans and into his flesh with a moist crunch. Xander had to put his foot on Paulie's leg and brace himself to yank it out. Paulie screamed several more times in an abrasive falsetto. It was as if he were trying to mimic an alarmed alien bird. But he clearly didn't have the strength to move or get to his feet. He just lay there, whimpering and shivering.

"There is a way," Xander continued. "There is a way this has to be done. Don't you get that? Do you think this is just fucking . . . *randomized*? Do you think there's no *order* to this?"

In the same hesitant, exploratory way, he hacked at Paulie six or seven times with the machete. After the first three or four blows, Paulie stopped jerking. Claudia absorbed the sounds of the blade going into the flesh. It evoked the butcher's shop she used to half-relish, half-dread going into with her mother when she was small. Cheery Mr. Donaldson whacking through lumps of fat-marbled meat, the brown fingerprints and bloodstains on his apron at surreal odds with his jolly face and bright banter. He wore a small straw hat with a blue and white striped ribbon above the brim. It intrigued and disturbed Claudia, her mother and Mr. Donaldson exchanging brisk chat over the counter's display of raw carnage. It was as if they were pretending something horrible wasn't taking place.

"She saw you," Paulie said.

There was a long pause. Xander, mouth hanging open, was returning from somewhere deep inside himself. At last he said, "What?"

Paulie coughed, struggled to get his breath. "The kid," he gasped. "The little girl in Colorado." He began to laugh again.

Xander breathed loudly through his nostrils.

Paulie was crying and laughing. Or in some elusive liminal state between crying and laughing.

"What are you saying?" Xander said quietly.

"She saw you and she . . ." Paulie's face crimped. He was silent briefly; then he released a raw animal moan through gritted teeth. "She got away. Ran all the way through the woods. You didn't even know she was there. *You* fucked up."

One of the wounds on Paulie's legs was rushing its blood out.

The blood moved over the bare floor as if desperate to map its new terrain.

Xander just stood there, bent forward slightly, hands on hips, the right holding the machete. He might have been a truncheoned cop from an old lighthearted movie listening skeptically to a kid's tall story. Then he straightened and walked a few paces away. His movements spoke of dense inner computation.

Paulie's mouth leaked blood and saliva. His hands made small, weak movements.

Xander was at the basement's far wall. He stood very still.

The machete slipped from his hand and clattered to the floor.

For what felt to Claudia like a long time he just stood there, staring at the bare brick.

Then he picked up the machete and returned to stand over Paulie.

Very carefully, he took hold of Paulie's hair and eased his head back. Paulie's breath bubbled. His eyes were closed now. One of his bootlaces, Claudia noticed, was undone. She had a brief image of him bending down to tie it. She had an imagined glimpse of his life of ordinary and extraordinary acts. All part of the same person, the same life.

Then Xander raised the machete and swung it down on Paulie's neck.

70

Claudia had shoved herself back against the wall. The ties had cut into her wrists and her hands were warm and slippery with blood. Her shoulders ached. There was no position she could adjust herself into that relieved the pain.

Xander sat leaning forward in the busted armchair, elbows on his knees, staring at the floor.

The blood pool around Paulie had stopped expanding. His head was still raggedly attached to his shoulders. Claudia had closed her eyes after the first blow, but she'd heard. Four, five, six. The sounds reported themselves, since they had no choice. She heard them, since she couldn't cover her ears, since *she* had no choice. These things had come into her life. Now there were only these things. She closed her eyes again. The cut on her throat was burning. The memory of moving freely through the house's space was still a shock in her body. Her body was still protesting at having it taken away. For the last time.

Xander approached the grille. "I've got to fix this," he said. "I've got to get your thing."

The ball gag was making Claudia's jaws ache. The piece of metal she'd used on Paulie was on the floor next to his body. It hurt her that if she'd kept it, she could have used it to slash her own wrists. Whatever he did to her then would be finite. There would be a limit. There would be an end.

But she hadn't kept it, of course.

"I've got to fix this," Xander repeated. "I won't be long."

He bent and checked the padlock, yanked it a couple of times. Pulled out the bunch of keys from his pants pocket. Looked at them. Put them back. He paused on his way out to look down at Paulie's corpse. His face had an expression of mild confusion.

Then he turned and headed toward the stairs.

It took Xander a while to get going. He kept thinking he was heading out to the vehicles, then finding that he hadn't. He found himself in the bedroom. On the landing. In the kitchen. Little bits of time between these rooms he couldn't account for.

She saw you and she got away. Ran all the way through the woods. You didn't even know she was there. You *fucked up.*

He didn't remember any little girl. He'd been through the whole house. There was no—

The little room across from the boy's. Half-painted.

In the RV he sat for a while, shivering. It was a bright, cold morning. The sunlight showed up how dirty the windshield was, all the bugs that had splatted there. He felt terrible. When he put his hand up to his face, he was shocked again at the feel of the stubble that was now a beard. He *still* hadn't shaved. It was bad that he was forgetting these things. He'd have to get batteries. The jug and the batteries.

But at the thought of the jug, a sick feeling went through him. It *wasn't* right. The jug should have been for the cunt in Ellinson. There was no escaping that. Wait. *Was* it the jug next? Didn't the kite come before the jug? The kite or the monkey?

The images shuffled and revolved and overlapped in front of him.

The monkey had a happy stupid face with round eyes and a grin. The monkey was scratching its armpit.

The lemon twinged in his throat, and the balloon always made him think of the fairground. A girl in a red and white spotted dress had had one, and she'd accidentally let go of it and it had gone snaking up into the air and within seconds become a wobbling dot in the blue sky. It had made him feel weird, that one minute it was in her hand and the next so high up and far away. She'd cried, and her mom had shouted at her. He hadn't liked it that she still seemed connected to it all the way up there. He'd felt connected to it himself. He'd felt— for a dizzy moment—that *he* was the balloon, looking down on all the people no bigger than ants.

Stop.

This was what happened. Goddammit, this was what *happened* if you didn't do it right.

The sunlit dirty windshield hurt his eyes. He grabbed Paulie's sunglasses from the cluttered dash and put them on. Slightly better, but they felt heavy on his face. Despite the shivering, there was still heat surging and receding in his skin. His teeth chattered. He clamped them shut. He imagined Paulie saying, Hey, those are *my* sunglasses, man. It would be better without Paulie. He could get on with what he needed to do. But at the same time it felt odd without him, already. Like he'd driven hundreds of miles away from a place and realized he'd left his jacket there. And he didn't know how to work the camera. He didn't like the iPad, but it was good to be able to watch the films. Seeing them again brought an unsatisfactory peace. Seeing them again brought the next one closer.

He was about to put the key in the ignition when he realized he was in the wrong vehicle. The RV for the road, the Honda was for local. There was the van, too, but the front left tire was a little low on air. The thought of getting out and switching turned up the dial on his body's troubles. He almost didn't bother.

But at the last minute (because you couldn't let these things slip, it was like the beard and Colorado, you let a couple of wrong things creep in and before you knew it the whole thing was fucked) he hauled himself out and crossed the yard to the Honda.

He would go into town and buy the jug, and the kite, and the lemon, and the monkey. He would figure it out. Even without Paulie.

71

"Gale Farmhouse," Will said to Valerie on the phone, twenty minutes later. "Garner Road, off Old Highway 91 just past the Ivins Reservoir. Cash buy two years ago, $109,000. You're looking for a wreck."

Valerie was in the Taurus in the mall's lot, with the engine running.

"Call it through to St. George," she said, entering the address on the GPS. Her hands were shaking. "No sirens when they get within earshot."

"You get there first, you sit tight. Valerie? You fucking *sit tight,* OK?"

"Yeah."

She hit her own siren and swung the Taurus toward the exit.

Man of Steel.

Russell Crowe.

Crowe.

Leon Crowe.

Christ. It was so often this way, accidents and random details aligning to illuminate what would, without them, be an impenetrable mess. A movie poster. A killer's name. An address. It was one of the things that poked the embers of her all-but-dead belief in a divine plan. Or *a* plan, at any rate, divine or not. These days when she thought about God (very rarely), the benign old man with twinkly eyes and the biblical beard had been replaced by something canny and nebulous, a faceless cosmic game designer whose parameters insisted only that there be connections between all the elements of the game, from the most mundane to the most grotesque or exalted. The parameters were there to be exploited by the evil players as much as the good. The game was absolutely amoral. It didn't matter who won which encounter, only that the designer's appetite for intrigue, for *play*, was satisfied. If there was a God, he didn't need our faith or our worship or our love. Just the entertainment we could provide. If there was a God, he was a game-addict. Trouble was, so were we. And cops were the biggest junkies on the planet.

Be calm. Just drive fast and be calm.

But she wasn't calm. Her hands were wet on the wheel. Her shoulders were tight. Excitement had burned through her symptoms, though their remains still screamed distant complaint in her system. She reached into her shoulder holster, pulled out the Glock, checked the clip. Full.

She accelerated west on St. George, hung a right on North Bluff, then left—and west again—on West Sunset Boulevard. Traffic parting like the Red Sea. What was ahead of her? They hadn't found a body with a jug in it, but that didn't mean such a body didn't already exist. It didn't mean it wasn't Claudia Grey's body, for all Valerie knew hundreds of miles from here. The cold comfort was that if he'd bought the kite just now, he wasn't any further along than K. *How many is it now? Seven. No, eight. No, nine. Maybe ten. Don't let it be ten. Please bastard game-addict God, don't let it be ten.*

IVINS RESERVOIR 2.5M

She killed the siren. Old Highway 91 was thin on traffic anyway. She pushed the Taurus up to seventy. The day was cold and brightly sunlit. The asphalt twinkled. The beating heart and the ticking clock. The dead women racing above the car with her, a fluid procession.

"In two hundred yards," the GPS said, "turn left."

She passed the Ivins Reservoir. Slowed. Took the left onto Garner, a semi-dirt road marked *access only*. The land was empty scrub here, with the exception of a small evergreen woods a little way over to the west.

Valerie slowed to a crawl. Quiet. Fifty yards. Seventy-five. Ninety. Ten miles an hour. Five.

She stopped the car.

Another hundred yards down the track, a scatter of low buildings.

Vehichles parked outside. A Honda. An old Ford on blocks. An RV.

72

Had he heard the car? Had she stopped far enough away?

You fucking sit tight.

Easy to say. Not easy to do. Not when every second might be Claudia Grey's last. Claudia Grey didn't have time for her to sit tight.

Valerie climbed over the low wooden fence. It was old, silvered by the weather. Its last coat of preserver might have been a decade ago. She could probably have pushed it over with a hard shove.

Cover.

There was no cover.

Barely any cover. A scatter of stunted gorse bushes dotting the overgrown scrub grass between her and the buildings. A farmhouse. Derelict, as predicted by Will. Two clapboard outbuildings with corrugated roofs. She had an image of Leon watching her from one of the upper windows. She had an image of him raising a rifle. Tracking her in the crosshairs. The gorse bushes looked tiny. And all that open space between.

She went low, Glock out. The wind simmered in the grass. First bush. Second. Third. The imagined cross-hairs burned like a third eye in her forehead or over her heart.

Forty yards to go. The last twenty with no more gorse.

Her death buzzed through the adrenaline. Her death was the

source of the adrenaline. Her death brought her life vivid and teeming and close. Random details assaulted her: the shadow of a high cloud on the land; a thin snail shell by her foot, its pretty nautilus whorls; the smell of the track's pale dust; the sounds of her clothes when she moved. There was no past and no future, just this expanding present. There wasn't even the decision to do what she was doing. Only the fact that she was doing it.

Last twenty yards. Completely exposed. She thought: *If I die, has my life been OK?* The answer was a blur. All the approximations and regrets. But the richness of her childhood and, later, the giant force of love. It surprised her that she found herself thinking: *It's been enough. It's been full.* But of course, that thought brought a twinge of sadness. If she died now, she would never get to say good-bye to the people she loved, the people who loved her.

Neither would Claudia Grey.

She faced the last twenty yards. She would make for the nearest of the outbuildings and work her way around it to the side of the house. In the broad light, she felt absurdly (comically, if not for what was at stake) visible, the only moving thing in the otherwise still landscape. She couldn't help thinking that even if Leon wasn't watching her, some change in the atmosphere, some tremor or jolt passing through the farmhouse walls, would alert him. She imagined him tensing, like a dog catching a thrilling scent. Lifting his head. Turning. Coming toward her.

Fine. If it got him away from Claudia Grey.

Crouched low, she raced to the outbuilding.

It felt good to get her back to the wall. It calmed her, the cold solidity between her and the inhabitants of the house. Inhabitants. Plural. (Optimistically assume Claudia Grey was one of them. Optimistically assume she was still one of the living.) Leon, yes—but the beta, too. Two guys. How many rooms? And how long for the St. George blues to get here?

The first outbuilding was nothing more than an empty shed. A bare floor of red dirt, maybe thirty feet by twenty. A sweetish smell of dry, ancient dung. Cattle once, obviously. It stood at a forty-five degree angle to the house. Behind it, parallel to the house, was a second, smaller building, one story, with two low windows of filthy glass and a padlocked wooden door on an overhead runner.

In there?

She didn't think so. A single passing glance through the window would reveal whatever was inside. He'd have her in the house. He'd go to the kitchen for a beer or a piece of cold chicken between sessions.

Sessions. Suzie Fallon had been tortured for days. The guy who'd done it would have had meals during that time, would have stood at the open refrigerator contemplating his options, deliberating over a microwaveable pizza or leftover Chinese takeout. The horror of horror was that it trundled along arm in arm with the mundane. That was what had fucked her up. That was what had made her believe she wasn't *entitled* to the mundane, to breakfasts and walks in Golden Gate Park and waking up with Nick. That was what had made her believe she wasn't entitled to love.

Hugging the wall, she made her way around the back of the outbuilding. The wind lifted her hair, slashed it across her face. She found a scrunchie in her pocket and tied it back. Switched her phone to silent. There was a clearer view of the house from here, which was, as far as she could tell, the shape of a squat T. Two stories. From where she was positioned, she could see the whole of the front face, three windows on the ground floor, four smaller ones above, and a wooden front door of flaking baby blue paint. A side entrance up two mossy little steps, probably to the kitchen. One window there. She was blind to the back and far side. Which was unacceptable. She had to get the exits in her head.

Without giving herself time to think, Valerie darted from the shed to the second outbuilding, and from there to the house's kitchen wall. Keep low. Flush to the good, solid, whitewashed stone. She thought of the house standing here for decades. She imagined a family, years back, conversations, meals, arguments, laughter, a woman in a plain sundress in the kitchen doorway, watching the sun go down, a teenaged girl bravely brushing her teeth though she was upset about something, a guy getting up early, making coffee in the kitchen before it was light outside.

All that gone. Now the house was home to this.

Inch by inch, she raised herself to peer in through the window nearest the side door.

Kitchen. Correct. Cobwebs. Antiquated plumbing and bruises of damp. A cupboard door hanging on its hinges.

Empty room.

She thought of the simple fact that she would have to go in. It was impossible and inevitable. She was in the flow now. The flow hurried you forward into the unknown. It was what you dreaded and what you lived for. If you were a cop.

It took her less than a minute, hugging the exterior, to make a full circuit of the farmhouse. She needed two more police. One for the front door (locked) and one for the door (also locked) on the opposite side of the building.

Herself for the kitchen entrance, which door she hadn't tried yet.

The breeze moved against the bare parts of her: face, wrists, throat. The land smelled clean and stony. Her hands were shaking.

73

Xander, carrying the shopping bags, opened the basement door and descended the stairs. He'd bought the kite, the jug, the lemon, the monkey, the orange, the ring, the net, the umbrella, and—fucking incredible how much these things cost—the violin and the xylophone. The xylophone had given him a goddamned headache. It took him a while to get the bitch in the music store to understand what he was asking for. Ninety fucking dollars!

The girl was, of course, as he'd left her, though she'd managed to wriggle closer to the furnace. He'd leave the ball gag in. He didn't like to hear them talk. It was always the same—*please, please, please*—but the words had been annoying him more of late. The words and the way they looked at him, those seconds or minutes before they stopped seeing anything, before they went deep inside themselves. When they looked at him like that, it was as if they were trying to see something secret, as if they were trying to search something out in him. It was as if they really believed something was in there in him, and they were trying to get him to see it. It was an irritation. It gave him a feeling of time passing emptily. Like when he was watching the carousel's painted horses going round and round, more and more time of him not being up there, and his mother and Jimmy drinking more and more beer, and the time going, going, going.

He dumped the bags by the stack of boxes and tried to clear his head. He wanted to go back upstairs and get into bed, pull the covers up to his chin. When he was Leon in Mama Jean's house, he used to tuck the bottom of the covers under his feet and the top of the covers under his chin and it felt good. He used to rub his bare feet together and that felt good, too. It was a private good thing, the pleasure of rubbing his feet together like that. He would do it for what felt like hours, in the basement darkness, until he fell asleep.

He took the jug out of one of the shopping bags. The kite, too. And the monkey and the lemon and the violin. No, that was wrong: the violin was a long way off. He should go get the chart from upstairs. The violin . . . The violin was further away, he knew, though in his head, it drifted close to the front. There had been violin music playing in the music store. The rat-faced bitch behind the counter had looked at him funny. She'd been glad the tattooed guy working in the guitar section was there. She'd been glad she wasn't in the store on her own. Xander had been able to see that in people his whole life; as soon as they were alone with him, they started hoping some-one else would show up. It was in their eyes. It was another exhaust-ing thing, year after year. He was so tired the whole time.

She saw you and she got away. Ran all the way through the woods. You didn't even know she was there. *You* fucked it up.

Mama Jean had said: A fucking *three-year-old* can do this. You ever get to school, all them little girls are going to laugh their asses off at you. Is that what you want? All them pretty little misses laughing their asses off at the big dumb baby in the corner?

The jug. He was sure it was the jug next.

But the jug should've been for the cunt in Colorado. Should he use the jug here, now? Or the kite? But wasn't that . . . You couldn't . . . The monkey . . .

It was no good. The things kept swapping places. He'd get this bitch set up here, then go upstairs and bring down the chart.

"I'll get you ready," he said. He wasn't looking at the girl in the cage. He said it to give himself something else to think about. The ropes and the knife. He liked them on their backs with their arms behind their heads and their legs spread. He liked the way they kept trying and trying no matter what to get their legs together even though they knew—they *had* to know—it was impossible once

he'd tied them down. He liked the way their whole bodies kept trying to find a way for it not to be happening. But he was completely in
control of what was happening. He was completely in control of all of
it. He *was* what was happening. There wasn't anything else. At those
times, everything else dropped away, the walls, the room, the house,
all of it. It was as if he were alone with them in endless warm soft
buoyant space where there was nothing—absolutely nothing else.
It was as if there had never *been* anything else, just him, full and rich
and perfect, with all the time in the world.

You fucked it up.

The weird thing was, he knew Paulie wasn't lying. It added to
his exhaustion that he knew Paulie wasn't lying. It was a curse, to be
able to tell. But he always could. No one had ever got away with a lie
to him in his whole life. He should have been on TV with it. A talent, like the guy who could bend spoons and stop watches with his
mind. While he got the ropes ready (there was a lead pipe running
along the base of the opposite wall where the wrist ropes went and
an iron bar he'd bolted to the floor ten feet from it for the leg ties)
he had a little fantasy of himself on a show where people had to tell
him things and he had to say whether it was a lie or not. Some of
the women from *Real Housewives* were on stage with him, and the studio audience was like the audience in the infomercial, delighted and
amazed. And he was right, every time.

The jug.

The monkey.

The lemon.

The kite.

He stood with his forehead resting against the basement wall.
It was cool and damp and soothing. His head felt big and hot again.
There was a wasps' nest in the backyard at Mama Jean's, and a heat
came off it. You could feel it if you dared to put your hand close
enough. If he used the kite now, he could go back . . . He could go
back and . . . But they'd have found her by now. Should've buried her.
Why had he just driven away like that?

Because of fucking *Paulie.* Paulie had diverted him. And then
there hadn't been a jug. He remembered getting the splinter when

he'd been running his hand over the kitchen cabinets. It was like an insult on top of everything else wrong. And why? Because Paulie had said he wanted to do one of his own, and he, Xander, in a moment of total fucking stupidity, had said OK. Surprise surprise, when it came down to it, Paulie had backed away like a cringing fucking cat, trying to grin, trying to make a joke of his failure, and Xander had had to do it himself.

The girl's breathing through her nose was annoying him. He wished he could go upstairs and lie down again, but the things in the shopping bags were a gossiping crowd in his head. It would only get louder. He had an image of the girl's bare breast and sinking his teeth into it as hard as he could, the good feel of all his weight on her and her soft throat's straining scream under his hand. She'd go deep inside herself and he'd stop and wait until she came back. Then he'd start again. It fascinated him, the way they went and came back and went and came back. It was like a dial you could turn. They never wanted to come back. It was agony for them to come back. But if you stopped what you were doing for long enough, they always did. It was one of the things you could count on.

The kite was next.

No, the jug.

You fucked it up.

He couldn't stand it anymore. His jaws hurt from his teeth clamped together. He wanted to scream. He spun away from the wall and went to the grille. The girl made an annoying noise behind the gag. The girl struggled. The ties had broken the skin on her wrists and ankles. Her hands and feet were bloody. She was trying to get into a sitting position.

Xander unlocked the grille and dragged her out.

He'd just gotten her tied down and was about to begin cutting off her clothes when he heard a sound from the floor above.

74

The house was innocently committed to giving Valerie away. Floorboards ticked and groaned. Every step detonated a new sound. Her grip around the Glock was wet. Her breathing stirred the stillness. The kitchen windows were so filthy, they cut half the light, but there was enough to show the signs of minimal habitation: canned food in the open cupboard; an overflowing garbage pail; unwashed glasses and cups; empty beer bottles; a pair of sneakers.

Beyond the kitchen, a dark corridor. Stairs going up on the right. Two doorways on the left. A closed door leading outside at the far end. Another door in the stairs' flank—surely down to the basement.

The basement.

Valerie put her left hand on the wall to steady herself. She had to keep reminding herself there were most likely two men in here. Which meant going room by room.

But the basement.

The seconds. The minutes. The time.

The basement.

She crept to the door and pressed her ear against it.

Nothing.

Very carefully, she tried the handle.

Locked.

Upstairs, a floorboard creaked.

She backed from the door. Her mouth was dry. A rogue shiver—a stubborn symptom that wouldn't quit—went through her.

Someone upstairs.

But check the downstairs rooms first.

She eased the handle on the door on her left, gun steadied and raised. The door wasn't locked. She opened it fast.

She was looking at a sitting room, heavy floral curtains, closed. A bulky fireplace with a pale ceramic surround. Dense gloom and an unused atmosphere. But for an incongruous wicker couch and a deck chair, it was empty.

She stepped back into the corridor. The next door on the left was ajar. Curtains closed. A duplicate fireplace. An elephantine dark vinyl armchair. Alcoves with empty shelves. A hole the size of a watermelon in the corner of the floor. Torn remnants of broad-striped wallpaper. Again, empty.

Kitchen and downstairs rooms clear.

Except the basement.

But the basement was locked. Which meant shooting the lock. Which meant the end of stealth. Not yet. Upstairs, first. Quickly. Or as quickly as whoever was up there would allow.

The stairs made a further farce of concealment, for all her tiptoeing. Halfway up, one of them gave out a report like a branch snapping. At the top, she turned back on herself onto a landing. A bathroom over the kitchen. Two rooms on the left. A third above what would be the front hall downstairs. The bathroom was exposed plumbing and a watermarked tub with its side panel missing, one wall bare stone, a toilet with a shit smear in its dark-watered bowl. It smelled of cramped masculinity up here, stale undershirts and sweaty socks, a meat-heavy diet, burped beer, ashtrays. Every second, the sense that they were right here—feet away—rested heavier on her. The air around her bristled. Her scalp shrank, loosened, shrank. Her heartbeat would be, she thought, *visible*.

But the bedrooms, though obviously lived-in, were empty. One of them had a television on, with the sound muted. *The Apprentice*. Donald Trump with that idiotic *croissant* of a wig. Of course they watched television. Of course they ate, drank, moved their bowels, bought cigarettes, took showers. Of course they did. They were men. They were people.

Hypotheses formed and dissolved. Leon had seen her. Had alerted the beta, and the two of them had got out the hallway door. Or only Leon *was* here. Or he was in the basement. Or they both were. Waiting for her.

She got back out onto the upstairs landing and looked up. There was a hatch in the ceiling—but it was padlocked from the outside.

They were in the basement or they were gone.

There was only one room in the house she hadn't looked in.

75

Xander cold-cocked the girl with a swipe—a flick, practically—of the shotgun's butt, then waited until he heard whoever the fuck it was going upstairs. His body was fluttery and confused. The objects were a self-repeating explosion in his head. Someone was in the house. It was impossible. Someone was . . . Who was in the house? How could someone be in the house?

The events of the last few days churned in his slipstream. He groped backwards to find the . . . To find out how . . . How the *fuck* could someone be in the house?

This was Colorado. This was still Colorado, expanding, unraveling. This was what happened when you didn't do it right.

He'd rarely thought about the police. Paulie had been the one worrying the whole time about the police. How many times hadn't Xander said to him: *Quit going on about the police. The police are idiots.* And yet, he thought now, quietly unlocking the basement door and slipping out into the hall, "the police" had always been with him. It was as if the police were with him the whole time, close enough so that he could feel them like a dumb crowd at his back, but always facing the wrong way. As if they knew something was going on behind *their* backs, but could never turn around and see it. Occasionally he'd thought about getting caught. Occasionally he'd had a vague image of the police turning up at his door. But he couldn't hold the image. The image petered out into knowing that regardless of the police, he wasn't going to stop doing what he had to do. What he had to do pulled him along with a persuasive warmth. He was in sleepy agreement with it. Even trying to imagine the time when it was finished wasn't easy. When he tried, he saw himself like someone walking out of a dark movie theater into blinding sunlight and a bleached world, dazed, vague, unsure, wanting to return to the rich colors inside. What he had to do was nothing to do with police.

He crossed the hall. Both parlor doors were open. Whoever it was had looked in the rooms. He pictured a bum, a stumbling tramp in layers of rags, lizard-skinned and with that oily reek of homelessness. He imagined this bum, with his exhausted face and matted gray dreads and one sole flapping, ignoring the sign at the end of the track and shuffling all the way down to the house. He imagined him thinking the place was abandoned. He imagined him looking for food, sellable junk, money. Somewhere to take shelter for a while.

He knew it wasn't a tramp. He was breathing shallow. Everything was happening too fast. The memory of the girl pulled at him. The swell of her little tits goosefleshed. The warmth and quickness of her struggle. Her dark head lashing from side to side. It was so good to feel all that in his hands. His hands had been betrayed. His hands were imprinted with her, and his hands had been robbed. But it would all be there when he got back. He'd throw water on her and wake her up, watch her eyes focus on him, watch her realize it hadn't been a dream, that she was really here, watch the desolation rush back into her face. At which point, he could start all over again. That was the best, being able to start all over again, seeing them seeing it wasn't over, that it wouldn't be over until he let it be. And that wouldn't be for a long, long time.

But this. Someone in the house. He didn't . . . He should . . . Everything jostled in his head: Would he have to get rid of the house? Would he have to start again? Shouldn't he just get out—now? Everything was getting away from him. First Colorado, now this.

She saw you and she got away. Ran all the way through the woods. You didn't even know she was there. *You* fucked it up.

You fucked it up, Mama Jean's voice said. *Simplest thing in the world, unless you're dumb as a rock.*

He stepped into the first parlor, set the shotgun down, and took the pistol out of the back of his jeans. The fish knife was in his back pocket. He took a little comfort in the feel of the blade pressed against him. He pushed the door half closed, just the way it had been left.

76

Valerie was in the state. She was a gathered focus flitted around by irrelevant thoughts and memories. Each step down the staircase solidified the focus, but bred new bits of mental litter that twittered and circled her: her mother looking up from the ironing and saying, Valerie, your hair looks like a Cossack's hat; riding her bike across Golden Gate Bridge years ago, the salt breeze and the colors of the cars and the sunlit dangling feet of gulls; her family's long-dead cat, Buster, who would slip in through the kitchen flap and come and look at them as if he had no clue who they were or where he was; Nick, who talked in his sleep, sitting up one night and announcing: That tube has a peanut in it. I do not want that tube. She'd woken him with her laughter.

These thoughts and dozens like them, but at the same time the monumental focus, the immersion in this expanding now, every step closer, the house like someone forced to watch and the absolute certainty that she wasn't alone. She was alive. She was thudding with life.

She felt the pain before she heard the shot.

A hot blow to the side of her head followed a split second later by the sound of a handgun's discharge, deafening in the narrow space of the corridor.

Time slowed. She had a great deal of time, apparently. Her body's fall backwards went inch by leisurely inch. She had time to see Leon step out from the first parlor doorway, gun hand still raised. His face

was moist and full of alert exhaustion. There was a dark V of per-
spiration descending from the neck of his pale blue sweatshirt.

She had time to think: *I've been shot in the head.* Already a warm
numb flower of sensation there behind her temple, an event that was
still working out its delivery of pain. The pain would come, but there
was time for Valerie to realize it hadn't begun yet, was still being unpacked by the bullet. Leon's odor came to her, the dense origin of
the smell of the bedrooms upstairs, sour and curiously sad. She had
time to feel the distant computations of her arm trying to raise the
Glock, her finger's refusal to tighten on the trigger, the walls and
ceiling pitching.

Somewhere far away, the sound of a motorcycle engine gunning
and dying.

Her head struck the door—softly, it seemed—then cracked hard
on the boot scraper. Total blackness, the tunnel vision coming, closing, and opening again like a camera snapshot. It would come again,
she knew. These were stray moments before the darkness sucked her
back in for good. She'd fallen with her gun arm trapped under her
back. Vaguely, already engaged in the dreamy articulations of attempting to *free* her arm, she wondered how you could get shot in
the head and still know what was going on. It was an immense, protracted labor to lift her hip and release her arm. The gun was heavy.
She doubted she'd be able to lift it.

Leon raised the automatic a second time just as her hand
popped free.

He said, "You fucking—"

Then Valerie pulled the trigger.

For a few long moments, Leon stood there visibly trying to as-
similate what had happened. Then he bent forward and took his right
hand in his left gently. His gun was on the floor by his feet. Blood ran
between his fingers. He opened and closed his mouth a few times.
Made a strange sound, almost a laugh.

The blackness came again for Valerie. She thought: *This is death.
This is my death.* She decided to fight it. She decided to call on every
molecule. It would be her last act, the giant, stubborn resistance to
death. She would fail, but it would give the final flicker of thoughts

a little longer to play: that she had liked being alive; that her child-hood had been filled with noticing things—skies, flowers, the per-sonalities of animals, dreams; that her family had loved her; that she and Nick had had love, such love, love so sweet.

She weathered one big pull by the blackness. Opened her clos-ing eyes. It was like fighting off the heaviest sleep, the feebleness of fluttering eyelashes against the weight of eternity. She thought: *I won't be able to do that again. The next one will take me.*

The light in the hallway changed, dimmed slightly. A walkie crackled. A man's voice said, "Freeze. Hands over your head."

Then the next wave came and Valerie went under.

77

Xander turned to see a young motorcycle cop standing in the kitchen doorway. With his gun drawn. Two-handed grip. They looked at each other. Xander felt dizzy. The woman's bullet had gone clean through his right hand. His left still cradled it. The pain was turning from ice to fire. He was confused. His life was full of changes suddenly. He felt as if everything—the walls and floor of the house, the land outside, the sky—was being shifted and rearranged. Soon, he wouldn't recognize anything. It was the clarity of this feeling of running out of time that let him know what he had to do. It occurred to him that Paulie was dead. The left-behind jacket. There was always the slight disappointment when they were dead. It was like getting the only thing you wanted and it not being enough. Just the thing that hurried you toward the next one.

"My hand is shot," he said, extending both. A little puddle of his blood had already formed between his boots. "I don't feel good."

The cop took a step forward. "Face down on the floor," he said. "Right now. Face down on the floor. I'm not going to tell you again."

Xander swayed. Pawed the air with his good hand. Crashed to his knees. Toppled slightly and came to rest in a half-sitting position, propped against the flank of the stairs. His eyes closed.

"Hey," the cop said. *"Hey."*

Xander didn't respond.

The cop came nearer. Kicked him in the hip. "Hey."

Xander's mouth was open. His head rested on his chest. He could feel a little dribble of saliva creeping over his bottom lip. The cop kicked him harder. The bike boots were steel capped. It hurt, but the pain in his hand was the big thing, a raging fire on the end of his wrist.

"Jesus fucking Christ," the cop said quietly.

Xander heard him unclipping the cuffs from his belt.

There wasn't much time. He had a very small window. He couldn't believe he'd decided to do this, back himself into a corner so that there was only one option. It surprised him that he'd made these decisions privately, without really being aware of anything beyond the agony in his hand and the parts of the world being rearranged like big cardboard scenery.

The cop had the cuffs off his belt now. Xander could sense the movements through his shut eyelids. Gun in one hand, cuffs in the other. They were designed so that you needed only one hand to work them.

Xander groaned, still with his eyes closed. Turned himself groggily. The cop set his knee against Xander's chest and reached for the bloody right wrist to snap the first cuff on.

"Ow!" Xander said, his eyes opening. "Hey, that hurts!"

Then he kicked the cop's leg out from under him and launched himself.

The gun went off (the third shot in the corridor's traumatized silence) but the bullet buried itself in the staircase. Xander had the fish knife in his left hand. The cop was slow. The situation had turned too fast for him. Xander could feel the guy trying to scramble, to react. His days were speeding tickets and iced tea, long hours on the Utah roads.

Xander drove the knife in hard and fast, more times than he could count, until the cop stopped struggling under his weight. The blood was warm between them. For the time it had taken, Xander's hand had stopped screaming. A packet of gum had fallen out of the cop's jacket pocket onto the floor. Wrigley's Extra. Peppermint. His wristwatch was big and silver with a black face.

The world was still rearranging itself. Xander struggled to his feet, slipping once in the blood and nearly going over. He was very tired. His whole body buzzed with tiredness and with how quickly everything had gone wrong. He was still catching up to how wrong everything had gone. He had to get out. He glanced over at the woman by the front door. Her jacket was open. Shoulder holster. Badge clipped to her waistband. Cop. One cop. Two cops. There would be more. How had they found him? There were so many things he had to do, but there was no time. He could feel cops like an infestation rushing toward him, hundreds, thousands, like in that horror movie where the guy had gotten swarmed over and gobbled up by cockroaches. He thought he could hear sirens. He stumbled to the kitchen. He couldn't breathe. The house was shrinking. The monkey and the kite and the violin and the lemon and Mama Jean sitting in her chair, smiling and shaking her head at what a fucking mess he was making of everything. His hand was giant and loud. He had to get out before the house started to fit him like a skin. Everything had gone wrong and there were sirens and *she saw you and she got away ran all the way through the woods you didn't even know she was there* you *fucked it up* and everything since fucking Colorado had gone wrong. *That's right,* Mama Jean said, *take your time. Hell, take all the time you like. Why don't you make a cup of coffee and put your feet up while you're at it?*

There was no *time*.

78

Valerie opened her eyes. It took her a few seconds, but she realized she was still where she'd fallen, just behind the hallway door. The boot scraper felt as if it had knitted itself to her skull. She rolled onto her side and vomited.

For the moment, all she could do was lie there, spitting out saliva. Swallowing. Spitting out more saliva. (That first time she'd got drunk, the hours in the bathroom, dragging herself up from the cold tiles to throw up into the toilet, holding on to the rim of the bowl, trying and failing to keep her hair from the mess. Her sister had said to her, standing with her arms folded: Don't bother telling yourself you're never going to do this again. You will. Hundreds of times. And she'd been right.)

She put her hand up to examine the wound on her head. The bullet had grazed her. "Grazed" was the word, but it didn't seem sufficient for the gouge the shell had taken out of the side of her head. It didn't make sense to her at first, what she was feeling—until she realized her fingers were touching bare bone. It was an appalling introduction to the fact of her skull. She thought she might vomit again. She took her hand away. Infection. She pictured herself getting stitches. Hospital. Doctors. PA system announcements. Vending machines. Magazines. The smell of coffee and antiseptic. The world she'd almost lost.

She got her hands flat to the floor and pushed herself up onto her knees. Her head felt as if it were about to rupture.

A police officer lay on his back a few feet away in a pool of blood. Outdoor air came in from the kitchen. The door was open.

Leon.

Fuck. Where was he?

Was the uniform dead? Where was her gun?

She moved slowly. The Glock was on the floor next to her left knee. She picked it up. It was a reassurance. There was no sign of Leon—but she couldn't take anything for granted. She crawled on all fours to the officer. No pulse. Multiple stab wounds, including one that had gone through the carotid. His head was haloed in blood. No pulse. His badge said, COULSON. To someone, his lover, his mom and dad (she hoped there were no kids), all his details would be precious. To someone, the news that he was dead would make them wonder if they could carry on.

"Officer Coulson, please respond," his walkie said.

Valerie unhooked it from its strap. "This is SFPD Homicide detective Valerie Hart. Officer Coulson is down. Code 10-00. No pulse, multiple stab wounds. Send medics immediately to Gale Farm, Garner Road, left after Ivins Reservoir on Old Highway 91. Proceed with caution. Suspect may still be here and is armed. Repeat, extreme caution. And where the fuck is the rest of my backup?"

"Please repeat your ID," the voice said, but Valerie was already on her feet, gun leveled at the lock on the basement door. Her head felt big and heavy and unreliable. A bull's head. It was a miracle her neck was holding it up.

She was about to fire—then realized the door was off its latch. He hadn't locked it when he came up. Before he came up. He. Them. There could still be another one down there.

She reached in and found the light switch. Almost overbalanced and went headfirst down the stairs. Steadied herself. Bare bulbs at the bottom of a staircase. Dizzy, nauseated, she went down.

The first thing she saw was the body of a white male on the basement floor with its head all but completely severed from its neck.

The eyes and mouth were open and the head was turned to face the stairs, as if keeping terrified watch.

The second thing, aged and split here and there on its folds, was an alphabet chart. It lay half open next to his feet. Apple. Balloon. Clock. Dinosaur.

The third thing she saw was the girl, ball-gagged and tied on the floor in a slew of blood. With the handle of a knife protruding from just below her ribs. Her top had been yanked up over her breasts, and her jeans and panties tugged down. A small earthenware jug had been left between her thighs. Her eyes were closed. Valerie ran to her.

It was Claudia Grey.

And she was still breathing. Just.

Valerie worked fast, though the wound in her head threatened to haul the darkness back in. She holstered the Glock, lifted Claudia's head, unfastened the gag and removed it carefully. Then the tied wrists. The ankles. The skin had been cut through by the ties, and there was a shallow wound on Claudia's neck, but the knife under her ribs was deep, buried all the way up to the hilt. The impulse to pull it out—the obscene wrongness of leaving it there—was powerful, but Valerie knew better. A blade cut on the way out as well as on the way in. Pull it out now, and you risked further hemorrhage. Right now, the knife in her might be the only thing stopping Claudia Grey from bleeding to death. Valerie took off her jacket and covered the girl's exposed genitals. *Please God, don't let her have been raped. Even if she has to die, don't let her die raped. Please.*

Claudia opened her eyes.

"You're safe," Valerie said, though the truth was, she had the Glock back in her right hand because there was no telling where Leon might be. "Claudia, listen to me: You're safe. I'm a police officer. We're going to get you out of here. Just don't try to move."

"Where is he?" Claudia said. British, the accent reminded Valerie. She'd been to London once, on vacation with her parents when she was small. The ridiculous helmets of British cops. No guns. The big leafy parks and the Houses of Parliament. They'd taken a boat trip on the Thames. She thought now how far away from all of that Claudia had traveled. She would go back, but it would never be the same. Nothing would ever be the same.

But she would be alive, however not the same it was, and that was all that mattered.

"He's not here," she said. Technically not a lie. "It's OK. Don't move. You're going to be OK. Just stay with me, OK?"

Claudia blinked. There was too much. Valerie had seen it before. The return from death. The unbelievable withdrawal of death. She'd seen it before, but not often enough. Mostly she just saw death.

"I'm . . ." Claudia faltered. "Where is he?"

"It's OK," Valerie repeated. "You're safe." She brushed Claudia's hair out of her eyes. "Stay with me, honey. They're coming."

With sirens, she could hear, despite her instructions. Right now, she loved them for it.

79

Xander's hand was on fire. Everything had gone wrong. It was in his head like an orchestra playing out of tune. It was as if for all these years, everything had been fooling him with freedom while secretly planning for this, this rearrangement of the scenery, this shift that had taken, what, minutes? Seconds? Everything had tricked him. And what had started the trick? Fucking Colorado. Fucking *Paulie.*

The kid. The little girl. She saw you and she got away.

What fucking kid? There *was* no fucking kid.

Except the half-painted room must have been hers. Being redecorated. That smell of new paint.

His mind went in circles. He wanted to go somewhere quiet and sleep.

Oh, sure, Mama Jean said. *Take a nap. Why don't you just pull over? You've got all the time in the world, right?*

He'd taken the van. The RV was . . . It outraged him, the idea of that bitch cop finding his house. It made him feel stupid.

But she was dead, so fuck her. She was dead and the cunt in the cellar was dead and he'd got the jug right.

Yeah, except the jug should have been in Colorado.

And he hadn't had time. It sent more heat through his hand, that there hadn't been time to do it properly. He'd been tempted, shoving her top up and seeing those little tits, feeling the wriggle in her hips when he pulled down her pants. It was a waste. It would have been the best so far. He would have sent her into herself and let her come back so many times.

He had to get his hand fixed. He couldn't. Gunshot wounds they had to report. The van's steering wheel was slippery from his blood. Not even a fucking Band-Aid. He'd torn the sleeve off his shirt and wrapped that around it, but that was no good. It hurt so much. He had to find a gas station, a store, a fucking pharmacy. You keep the bad hand in your pocket and pay with the good hand. He had money in his wallet. All that money and everything could still fucking . . .

Think straight, for Christ's sake. Find a gas station, wash up. A motel. Fix this. Fix it.

The shotgun was in the trunk. The machete. Pistol and a dozen clips. But the objects from the shopping bags had tipped out onto the passenger seat next to him and wouldn't leave him alone.

Paulie wasn't lying, Mama Jean said when he glanced in the rearview. *You want to fix this, you need to start with that.*

It was then that he realized he'd forgotten the most important thing of all.

He'd left the alphabet chart in the basement.

80

The world was not ideal, granted, but its randomness conferred gifts as well as curses: Angelo found the remains of a packet of Advil in his overcoat pocket. Five liqui-gel capsules still sealed in their foil backing.

"Here," he said to Nell, handing her one with the tin mug filled with water. "It's not much, but it might help the pain for a couple of hours."

She looked wary.

"It's just Advil," he said. "Here, look, you can see on the back of the wrapper. It's fine, I promise."

Her hesitation, he knew, was partly that she'd no doubt been told never to take medicines unless OK'd by her mom, and partly her weighing up if refusing it would hurt his feelings. He was planning on saving all of them for her, over the hours ahead, but to reassure her, he took one himself. "I take these for *my* pain," he said. "They do help. I wouldn't give this to you if it wasn't safe. But I understand if you don't feel you can take it. It's OK either way."

She thought about it a few moments, then popped the pill into her mouth and drank.

"Do you think someone will come today?" she said.

The question was a permanent presence in his head. Nell had been quiet all afternoon, just lying on her side and staring out the window. A numbness was insinuating itself in her, he knew. Like a submerged rock becoming visible as the last of hope drained away. He resisted the urge to say: I'm sure of it. If he said that and no one came, it would be a failure and a betrayal. In the absence of anyone else, he needed her to have faith in him.

"I hope so," he said. Then amended: "Can't be much longer."

Could it be much longer? How long could someone lie wounded or dead in their house without someone noticing they'd dropped off the radar? It was, by his reckoning, Christmas Eve. Weren't these the days when folks were in and out of each other's houses, delivering last-minute presents and borrowing crucial ingredients for the feast?

"It can't be much longer," he repeated.

That night Nell dreamed a dream of faces and voices. Sometimes she was in the cabin. Other times in her bed at home. Angelo leaned over her, saying, Drink some water. Please try. The details of his face were sharp, the pores of his skin, the cracked moist green of his eyes. His beard hair was rough silver. She tried to tell him that the bristles reminded her of the paintbrushes her mom had gotten out of the shed when the redecorating of her room had begun, but he didn't seem to understand. Her mom came and went, too, in her dressing gown. Heat lay on her like a soft, heavy body. She kept trying to get out from under it. A maddening game. Josh came in wearing his school football gear, his face flecked with mud from the field: Just get on your feet, doofus, he told her. You can walk out of here. Up the ravine to the tree. You can get across that tree easy. You can *stroll* across that tree, Nellie, Jesus. Take that crap off your ankle. What's the matter with you? In the dream, she plucked at the splints on her ankle, but Angelo's hands got in the way. His voice seemed to be coming from a great distance. His hands were enormous. Her own felt tiny. The splints were very annoying to her. The splints, she thought, were stopping her from getting up. When she looked down, she saw they were attached to the floor. Why would he do that? Nail her to the floor like that?

The golden hare from her bracelet rose up next to her, life size. It was made, she now saw, from the same yellow-orangey light that came when you scribbled in the dark air with a sparkler. I grant you safe travel, the hare said, moving liquidly around her. There is nothing to fear. *You're old enough now.* She could see herself moving across the tree, the hare weaving between her feet. Her feet barely touched the fir's bark.

Angelo hadn't meant to fall asleep, but he'd slept so little and so brokenly over the last three days that he hadn't even been aware of it taking him. When he'd lain down on the couch to rest his back the last of the day's light was waning. Now it was wholly dark outside. The oil lamp's light threw tremulous shadows.

Nell was on her feet.

Or rather, foot. She'd removed the splints and put her boots on, and was, with both hands gripped around his stick, moving in small, visibly excruciating steps, across the cabin floor, dragging the bad ankle.

"Jesus," Angelo said. "Nell? What are you doing?"

She lifted her head and looked at him. Her face was pale, drawn, wet with tears. Her eyes were raw.

"I can walk," she said. "I have to go across."

"Across?"

"I'm going to the tree."

It stunned him that she'd come to this while he'd slept. It was terrible, the thought of her lying there, gathering her resolve, removing the splints, squeezing her foot into the boot.

"Give me another pill," she said. "It doesn't hurt so much now. I can walk. I have to go."

Angelo stared at her. He could see exactly how much it hurt. The Advil might have taken the finest edge off, but it still sickened him to think of what these movements were costing her. Kids were so strong. Women. *Women and children first.* Maybe not because we thought they were weak, but because deep down, we knew they were strong. Carried the best of the species.

"Nell, you can't," he said, biting back a cry as he began to lower himself from the couch. He'd moved too quickly. Christ, there was no letup. The inexhaustible persistence of his own pain enraged him.

The single Advil hadn't touched it. He gritted his teeth. Made it to the floor. Breathed.

"I can," she said, and took another half hop, half shuffle toward him. "I can do it."

He had to think. Careful. Don't scare her. Try to stop her by force, and she'll go crazy.

She took another step. Grabbed the edge of the table. Steadied herself. It was amazing: She was training herself to withstand the pain.

"Listen to me," he said. "It's night. It's dark. You can't do it in the dark. You can't go across in the dark. You'll fall."

Nell glanced out the window as if she'd lost the awareness that it *was* dark.

"Think about it," Angelo said. (Don't tell her she can't do it. Tell her there's a better way. Buy some time.) "Think about it. There's no way you'll get across if you can't see. Wait until morning. You'll have a better chance. You'll have a *much* better chance in the morning."

He watched the sense of this forcing itself on her, against her will. She might be in delayed shock or unhinged by grief, but she wasn't stupid.

"In the morning," he said gently, "we'll figure it out properly. I'll help you. But we have to be able to see what we're doing. OK?"

She thought about it.

"You'll be stronger in the morning," Angelo said. "You can eat something. And the tablets work better on a full stomach. Get some rest now. Get some sleep. We'll wait until it's light, and then we'll try."

It took him a while, but eventually he persuaded her. To his advantage, the Advil and the exertion had taken their toll. She was asleep within minutes. In the morning, he knew, he would take the remaining pills himself and try again for the fallen tree. It wouldn't be enough. It would be impossible. But there was nothing to do but try.

He drank the cold remains of the evening's coffee and propped himself on the couch.

Stay awake, Sylvia said. *Watch her. Keep her safe.*

81

"He didn't take the RV," Will Fraser said to Valerie. "The dead guy's been ID'd as Paul Stokes, and there's a 2007 Dodge Grand Caravan registered to him, so we've got the plates out on that. We're waiting on DNA confirmation here, but it's pretty obvious he's the other half of the team."

"There was a van," Valerie said. "It was on the other side of the house."

She was in a five-bed ward at the Dixie Regional Medical Center back in St. George. The wound on the side of her head had been stitched and dressed under local anesthetic, but they were keeping her in overnight for concussion. She had a lump on the back of her skull the size of an egg. Claudia Grey was in recovery in the ICU, after four hours on the operating table. She was going to live. Will and Carla had flown in by helicopter. Carla was at Claudia's bedside, waiting for her to wake up.

"Lloyd Conway gave him a chunk when he sold the company," Will said. "A hundred and thirty grand, to be precise. Presumably because the Lord thought it would be a good idea."

"I had him," Valerie said. "I fucking had him, Will."

"There's a twenty-six-year-old girl down the hall alive right now, thanks to you," Will said. "He's fucked up. We'll get him. Love the punk look, by the way." They'd shaved the left side of Valerie's head to deal with the wound. "Not many women your age could carry it off."

"I'm going to ask them to do the other side," Valerie said. "Full mohawk. Ow. Smiling makes this itch."

"How'd you get the name?" Will asked.

"Movie poster. Russell Crowe," Valerie said. "And I still don't like him."

"Marion got a little hot for him in *Gladiator,* but she said she'd only sleep with him if she was punishing herself for something."

"I know Marion hates me," Valerie said, "but I like her."

"I'll talk to her about it. She's entered a sort of pornographic phase. I think she could go for you now that you've shaved half your head."

Valerie felt tender toward the world. It was the way of it, when you'd nearly lost the world.

Her phone rang. It was Nick.

"I'll go and get coffee," Will said. "I'll let you know when the kid wakes up."

Valerie picked up the call. "Hey," she said. "They shaved my head."

"Just your head?"

"Very funny."

"Tell me you're OK."

"I'm fine. I'm getting dressed and out of here in a minute."

"No, you're not. Will told me you've got concussion."

"What does Will know?"

"Don't make me come down there."

"I miss you."

It was out before she could stop herself. A short pause followed. She imagined him at his desk. Wondered if the guy who shared his lab was in the room. "Sorry," she said. "I shouldn't—"

"Shut up. I miss you, too."

A longer pause. Valerie swallowing tears that had ambushed her. The last time she'd been in a hospital bed was three years ago. Everything she'd been holding on to for those three years was starting to leave her. Almost. The almostness hurt her heart. For a few moments, she couldn't speak.

"How about I take you out to dinner when you get back?" Blasko said.

"Yes, please."

"Do you have any idea how good it is to hear your voice?"

"Don't be nice to me," she said. "I can't take it."

"What if I'm nice to you now but I promise to be an asshole when I see you?"

"OK."

"When are you coming back?"

"I don't know. He's out there. We're waiting for the girl to come around."

"Yeah, Will told me she made it. You did a good thing."

Valerie swallowed again. It was terrible to receive kindness when you were in this state.

"Hey," he said. "Don't cry."

"I'm trying."

"It's going to be OK."

"Is it?"

"I don't know, but let's assume that it is."

"OK."

A phone rang on his end of the line.

"Hang on," he said. "Shit. Sorry, I have to take this. You sure you're OK?"

"I'm sure."

"Stay in bed."

"OK."

"I mean it."

"OK."

"I'll call you back. Meantime, think about where you want to go for dinner."

A few minutes after they'd hung up, Will appeared in the ward doorway, pointing down the hall: Claudia was awake.

82

In a painfully bright Rite Aid on the edge of Grand Junction, Xander bought a home first aid kit in a crappy white plastic box with a red cross on it for $35.95. He bought scissors, a brand-new electric razor, batteries, water. He was thirsty all the time. The whole business took only a few minutes (he'd washed himself up as best he could in a Texaco a couple of miles back) but he was aware of the cashier, a bald guy in his sixties with steel-rimmed glasses, looking at him funny. He had to keep his right hand in his pocket throughout the transaction, and his face was wet with sweat.

"How're you doing tonight, sir?" the cashier said.

"I'm fine."

"Long drive, huh?"

"Yeah."

"I know the feeling," the cashier said. "We all do it, right?"

"Right."

"In the dark, too. I know it. Used to drive a truck myself. Those new headlamps shouldn't even be legal, if you ask me. You got far to go?"

"Not far."

"Well, if you need a rest, there's a Motel 6 just a couple miles down the road."

"What's the total?" Xander said. He realized when he'd said it that it was slightly wrong. He'd been slightly wrong with these things his whole life. The guy's smile dissolved—then recovered—but everything between them had changed.

"Your total's $127.89. And will that be cash or card, sir?"

"Cash," Xander said. He'd got four fifties ready on the counter. The cashier did his thing with the till, paused, slid one of the fifties back to Xander without a word, then handed him the rest of his change. Xander had to deal with the change before he could pick up the plastic shopping bag. He could see the guy wondering what was wrong with his right hand, and how could a one-handed guy drive?

"Thanks for the motel tip," Xander said, but he knew he couldn't put it right with the cashier. The cashier smiled when he said: "You bet," but Xander could tell that something had closed down in him.

S was for scissors. That one, he was absolutely sure of. Mama Jean had put the *S* on him with sharp scissors. Hold *still*, goddammit, this is a curvy one.

So now he had the scissors, too, though they were quite a long way off. Almost as far as the violin and the xylophone. The violin and the xylophone revolved around each other. He didn't know which came first.

Back in the van in the parking lot (there was a couple of feet of snow on the ground, and it had begun snowing hard again), he did what he could for his hand. Disinfectant that burned so bad, he sat there shuddering for a few seconds with his jaws clamped together and tears brimming. There were packs of dressings, Band-Aids, tape, rubber gloves, some black liquid in a little bottle, a roll of bandage, a thermometer, and another pair of scissors, so it was a waste of money buying the first pair. He taped a sterile dressing to each side of the wound and wrapped a length of bandage around it tight. It hurt like hell. He still couldn't use it to drive. He drank the bottle of water and set off again.

He didn't stop at the Motel 6. He wasn't going to stop anywhere—he was afraid of stopping—but after another hour, he felt dizzy and sick. He knew he was on the 70 East (the fat-faced Asian guy at the gas station had confirmed it, though he'd eyed Xander as if he were crazy), but every road sign he looked at started the objects jabbering in his head—and he couldn't stop himself from looking at them. He kept thinking how bad it had been to see that bitch cop just right there in his house—in his own fucking house!—snooping through the rooms, touching his things. It was something he'd never imagined could happen. (That was the best thing about the money, being able to have a place no one could come into, a place most people didn't even know anyone was living in.) Right at the moment he'd seen her, the world started shifting under his feet, like the moving floor in the fun house at the fair that day with his mother and Jimmy. He'd fallen on his ass, and Jimmy had picked him up roughly, laughing.

He slowed for an exit, wishing he'd shoved the jug up inside her properly, but he would've had to cut her and he'd heard sirens (hadn't he?) and all that had mattered was getting out while there was still time.

The guy on reception at the Super 8 looked about eighteen. Had some black in him, Xander thought. Long eyelashes and a girlish face with full lips and his dreads pulled back into a little ponytail.

"Cash?" he said when Xander opened his wallet.

"Yeah," Xander said. He had to hold on to the edge of the desk to stop himself from swaying. He was unbearably hot. When he got in the room, he thought, he'd take a cold shower. Having thought of this, he was desperate for it, for how soothing it would be. There was a fat plastic Santa Claus on the reception desk, beaming, standing on one leg.

"Sir, we're going to need a credit card to hold against the room anyway," the kid said.

"I can't sign," Xander said, holding up his bandaged hand.

"Oh, that's OK," the kid said. "You don't need to sign with the card, we just run it through the machine. But, hmm, you need to sign the register."

"Well, I can't."

"Can you sign with your other hand? I'm really sorry, sir. It just needs to be . . . You know, it doesn't have to be perfect or anything. That's too bad about your hand." The kid slid the registration form and a pen toward him across the desk.

Xander picked up the pen in his left hand.

Hell, this is going to be good. I can't wait to see this. Come on, genius, let's see what you can do.

The pen felt huge between his fingers. He thought he was going to throw up. The reception area smelled of damp carpet. The kid waited, smiling. His lips were constantly struggling to cover his teeth. Xander had an image of jabbing the pen into one of the kid's big, dark, liquid eyes.

He held the tip of the pen against the dotted line where the kid had made a mark. A xylophone mark. *X* is for xylophone. It always mixed him up. "Xylophone" started with the same sound as "zipper." How could that be? How could that *be*? He didn't believe in it.

"Seriously, sir, just your initials are fine. It's no biggie."

Xander knew what his initials were. He'd had to sign them for the bank, when Lloyd and Teresa got him an account. Lloyd had said: It doesn't have to be your whole name, son. It just has to be a mark on the paper that identifies you. Don't think of it as writing. Think of it as drawing a picture. I know you can draw. I've seen you do it. So look, just draw a straight leg with a straight foot pointing thataway, to the right. Then draw a big crescent moon right next to it. There you go, that's an *L* and a *C*. Now you put any squiggle you like through the middle of it—same squiggle every time, mind you, so make it one you can remember—and you've got yourself a signature.

With his left hand, Xander carved out the straight leg with the straight foot and a hopeless crescent moon. Didn't bother with the squiggle. *L* was for lemon and *C* was for clock. Yet every time he had to sign, he could only connect the marks on the paper to the straight leg and foot and the crescent moon. The lemon and the clock were something completely different. Lemon. Clock. Leon. Crowe. They had nothing to do with each other. It was why he didn't believe in it.

"Great," the kid said, big-smiling. "You're all set. Here's your room key. You're in room twenty-three, which is left out of reception, up the stairs, and all the way along to the end of the walkway. You need anything at all, just dial nine. Enjoy your stay."

In room twenty-three, Xander put the shopping bags on the

bed, undressed (avoiding the mirrors) and took his cold shower. For a few minutes afterwards, he felt better, but every time he thought of the bitch cop and the young patrolman, he got angry, and the anger turned to heat with the jabbering objects in his head. He redressed his hand, but blood still seeped a red blotch through the gauze and into the fresh bandage. He should have bought clean clothes. Should have. He hadn't done so many of the things he should have done. His head was like the wasps' nest in Mama Jean's backyard, never entirely still. And the slightest disturbance could set it swarming. His face itched. The fucking beard. Naked, he went back into the bathroom, plugged in the new shaver, found the attachment like the ones they shaved soldiers' heads with in movies, and began to remove it. The buzzing of the thing made everything worse, and it was tough to do with his left hand. But he was determined.

When he'd finished, he moved the shopping bags from the bed, pulled back the covers, and climbed in. The heat had left him. Now he was shivering.

He didn't sleep well. The pain from his hand kept waking him. Painkillers. He would buy painkillers. Why did he always think of these things afterwards?

It was just after six thirty when he went back to reception to check out. The same kid, drinking a Coke, surprised to see him. Xander observed him realizing he'd shaved off the beard.

"Everything all right, sir?"

"Yeah. Just need to get back on the road."

The kid opened his big mouth to say something—then decided not to. Smiled instead. Xander was used to people smiling when they were thinking something else. Someone smiling always meant something else. Paulie had smiled when he told him about the little girl.

You want to fix this, you need to start with that.

"Hey," Xander said (the idea had opened like a flower in his brain), "you think you could help me with the GPS?" He held up his bandaged hand again. "I can't . . . You know?"

"Sure," the kid said. "Let me get those bags for you, too."

At the van, Xander had to let the kid sit in the driver's seat to work the gadget. He smelled a little like those stores that sold incense and other Asian shit. His fingernails were weirdly perfect.

"OK," the kid said, having tapped the screen a couple of times until the destination cursor blinked. "Where you headed?"

83

Carla left the hospital immediately after the interview with Claudia Grey. During it, she hadn't said a word to Valerie, had barely looked at her. Carla had asked all the questions. She was thorough, Valerie had to concede. There wasn't anything Valerie would have asked that Carla didn't. She'd perfected the requisite calm neutrality, too: Claudia, I have to ask, though I understand this is painful for you: Was there any sexual assault? Claudia had turned her head away for a while, eyes closed. No tears. (The tears would come later, Valerie knew, in the small hours of the months and years ahead, in the quiet moments of a sunny afternoon or in the middle of washing dishes; Claudia would be ambushed by memory for the rest of her life. Claudia would be a different Claudia as long as she lived. But she *would* live. There was that.) Eventually, Claudia had said: No. But Valerie knew what an excuse for the truth that was. A letter of the law truth. In the *spirit* of the law, the whole ordeal had been a sexual assault.

"So how fucked am I right now?" Valerie asked Will in the corridor once Carla was out of sight.

"Look, Carla thinks you're suspended. I had to do a lot of sweet-talking to get her to let you sit in just now. She threatened to leak your Reno meltdown and blood test results to the press. But the truth is, Deerholt hasn't even signed off on the sick leave story yet, or he hadn't when I left the shop. So technically, it's just verbal, all of it.

And you haven't exactly made it easy for him, what with finding the killer and saving a young woman's life and all."

"Not me. Russell Crowe. And I *lost* the killer."

"Yeah, yeah, yeah. It looks like luck. It always looks like luck. But who found Zoo Guy? Who ID'd the tree in Redding? Who bothered to come down here and sit through the mall tapes?"

"OK, I'm a genius. Is Carla going back?"

"I doubt it. Not with the Colorado lead. If it is a lead. It's still a needle in a state-sack even if he's there."

"Get Leon's picture out again, with beard and without. And make sure they run the info that he's got a wounded right hand. I want it on every news channel. Ditto the van plates. Get it out right now."

"Sure, but it's Christmas Eve. Everyone'll be watching shit."

"I know. Do it."

"What are *you* going to do? Drive around Colorado with a broken head?"

"Who's on duty at home?"

"Half a dozen of the regulars. Ed and Laura tomorrow. I'm off tomorrow, but we've got my mom and Marion's parents, so feel free to call with a nonemergency."

"Any hotline calls, I need to know immediately. Anything, anywhere."

"You're staying here, then?"

"It's closer to Colorado, and Colorado's all we've got right now. Besides, Claudia might remember the name of the town."

"There's more in there she's not telling."

"I know, but whatever she did, she did to stay alive."

"Fuckin' A. Girl's a rock star."

"One last thing. My car."

"You're not driving."

"Yeah, well, since I'm still technically your boss, let me put it another way: Go get my car, fucker."

Claudia was hanging up a cell phone call when Valerie went back in to see her alone.

"Your parents?" Valerie said.

Claudia nodded. "One of the nurses lent me her phone. They're kind here."

"They coming?"

"I told them not to, but yeah. My sister, too."

"That's great."

Valerie sat by the bed. She was feeling terrible. The anesthetic was wearing off and the stitches itched. Her hands trembled. Nausea came and went. She was sweating, despite the AC. She hadn't had a drink for forty hours. The word "withdrawal" flashed, sent warm shame through her. Drunk slut baby killer. She forced herself to ask the question: Do you want a drink right now? The answer was: Yes.

"I've been trying to remember," Claudia said. "The name of the place. I'm sorry, I just can't."

"Don't worry about it," Valerie said. "Sometimes the way is to *not* think about it, then it pops right in there."

"How's your head?"

"Itchy. Should I shave the other side, do you think?"

"No, it's better like that. Asymmetry."

It was strange between the two of them. Every time their eyes met brought back their shocking introduction. An insistence on intimacy between two people who didn't know each other.

Valerie said: "I'll let you rest now."

But Claudia took her hand. "I never thanked you," she said.

Valerie felt her throat tighten. *Don't cry.*

"I'm sorry I didn't get there fast enough," she said. "I'm sorry I didn't get him."

The word "him" was an obscenity, quietly there in the room between them. Valerie thought, briefly, how such words "him," "he," would at some deep level always bring this back to Claudia. The girl looked traumatically newborn, lying there.

"You were kind to me," Claudia said. "You saved my life. Thank you."

84

Jared Hewitt, twenty-one, was doing something he'd never done before: having sex on Christmas Day. With a white girl. Not that he'd ever had sex on Christmas Day with a non-white girl. He'd never had sex on Christmas Day, period. Nor did he feel fully entitled to use the term "white girl." Not because Stacey Mallory, four years older than him, wasn't white—she was, and a natural blonde, too—but because he wasn't, strictly speaking, black. His mother was part African American, part Mexican, his father (whom he'd never met) was, allegedly, Jewish. Jared's young life had been accented by this legacy of being neither one thing nor another, of being misidentified, misdescribed, miscalculated. The upside of the legacy was that he was ridiculously good-looking. Women *looked* at him, unequivocally. Older women, especially. He had a lackadaisical relationship with the gym, but there was no denying he had the goods. Six-one and leanly muscled with eyelashes those same women envied. He wasn't vain, just willing to take on the import of empirical evidence.

"OK," Stacey said after she'd come for the third time, cowgirl style. "Your turn. What do you want for Christmas?"

Jared had already *gotten* what he wanted for Christmas, which was to be able to Do His Own Thing. It had worked out perfectly. His mom had been dating a guy for the last ten months, and the two of them had gone to Mexico for the holidays. Which meant he got the house to himself. Stacey, who was a crazy sexed-up female with such a mess of half credentials (failed actress, failed dancer, failed college student) that Jared wasn't sure which parts of her history were true, and who had come back to Grand Junction off the back of a short-lived relationship with a death metal bass player in Denver and was now crashing at her sister's, did not come from the sort of family, apparently, in which it was frowned on to not be at home for Christmas Day, even if you were in the same goddamned city.

"Turn around," Jared gasped. Their ratio of orgasms had been established a while back: Stacey had three or four to every one of his. Not because he was blessed with superhuman restraint, but because Stacey could have three or four in less than five minutes. And another three or four after he'd had his. It was the sort of wonderful thing he was scared he'd break if he thought about it too much. So he did his best not to.

"You're a bad man, you know that," Stacey said, clambering into a sixty-nine. They were in his bedroom with the curtains closed, flickered over by the muted TV's light. Last night, they'd been drinking vodka snowballs. The room smelled of sex and sugary booze.

"Uh-huh," Jared said. He was in a delicious state. He'd come straight here when his shift at the motel finished. They'd fucked twice, then slept like the dead, and now here she was again with the daylight barely up and running, wide awake and ready. Stacey had left her shoes on (she'd *slept* in her shoes), though everything else was off. Black strappy high heels with what looked like bondage cuffs around the ankles. Jesus fucking Christ, this girl knew what she was doing. She eased the condom off and took him into her heavenly mouth. Jared felt peace and goodwill to all mankind.

"Holy Mother of God," he said a little while later, when he'd more or less recovered from one of the most explosive ejaculations he'd ever had. Stacey's warm golden head rested on his thigh. His hands cradled the fabulous cheeks of her ass. "Jesus, Jesus, Jesus."

"Blasphemy on Christmas Day," she slurred. "You're going to burn in hell, my friend."

"You're an angel."

"Hardly, but I'll take it."

"A sex angel."

"A sex angel is for life," Stacey said. "Not just for Christmas. I think you should make me another snowball. Also—and this is not a minor detail—I'm starving. I'm assuming you've got food?"

"Are you kidding?" Jared said, kissing her left butt cheek, then turning his head to see what was on TV. "My mom's left enough food here to feed the—Holy fuck!"

"Again with the blasphemy. What are you, a Satanist?"

"Hey—shit—*shit*—get up a second. Holy *crap*."

"Cramp?" Stacey said, beginning to disentangle herself. "I still want something to eat, mister."

But Jared was off the bed, on the floor, fumbling for the remote. "Jesus," he said again. "I don't fucking believe it. This dude . . . This guy was . . ."

". . . a wound in his right hand," the news voiceover said. "The suspect is armed and extremely dangerous and should not, repeat *not* be approached. Anyone with information should call the number on screen now. That number is also available on the Web site at KJCT8 .com. In other news, a Denver man is suing the City for what he describes as—" Jared hit Mute and stared at the screen, mouth open.

"What?" Stacey said. "What's going on?"

85

Valerie had just gotten out of the shower back at her Best Western room when the call from Laura Flynn came through.

"How long ago?" Valerie said.

"I just got off the phone with the kid," Laura said.

"Does Carla know?"

"Ed's on the phone with her right now."

"Where is she?"

"Hold on."

Agony. Agony. Agony.

Laura came back on the line. "She's at the TownePlace Suites. There's a chopper available at the St. George PD."

"Call Ellinson," Valerie said. "Whatever eyes they've got there, tell them to open them."

"I'm on it," Laura just had time to say before Valerie hung up.

Dressed in less than twenty seconds, Valerie drove to the St. George station with the siren on. A maddening minute with the desk sergeant to establish who she was. Another maddening minute to get through to the helipad. The chopper was about to take off. Carla was on board.

"Get out," Carla said as soon as Valerie had wrenched open the door and flung herself in.

"Fuck you," Valerie said. "I'm still the lead investigator on this case, and I still have national cooperation. Deerholt hasn't suspended me, and there's nothing you can do about it. You want to put me on YouTube, go ahead. But right now, we're going to Ellinson, Colorado." She flashed her badge to the pilot. "Let's go," she said.

The pilot looked at Carla.

"Stay where you are," Carla said. "This woman is getting off the aircraft."

Valerie slipped the Glock from her shoulder holster and jabbed it against Carla's knee.

"You're going to shoot me?"

"In the knee? Sure. You'll get better. I can shoot your knee out or you can put whatever this is with me aside until we catch this bastard. Either way, me and my friend here are going to Ellinson."

"Jesus Christ," the pilot said. "What the fuck?"

Carla thought about it. "Your career's over," she said.

"No doubt," Valerie said. "But not yet. Let's go."

They hit snow an hour into the flight. Flyable, the pilot said, windspeed less than fifteen knots, but it would get worse the farther east they traveled. ATC said weather looked manageable to Denver, but he was radioing ahead to have ground transportation ready just in case. Either way, they'd have to refuel at Grand Junction.

"What've they got in Ellinson?" Valerie said to Carla.

"Less than seven hundred people. Sheriff. Three deputies, part-time. Denver's sending field agents. Aerial, too."

"Leon will be there by now, if that's where he's going. He left Grand Junction hours ago."

"He'll have been and gone before we even got the word out," Carla said.

"Yeah, well, we don't have anything else. Why don't you tell me?"

"Tell you what?"

"Why you hate me."

Carla didn't answer. Just turned and looked out the window into the slanting snow.

86

Xander drove through the dark early morning and the falling snow. It had been coming down slowly when he left the motel. Now it was hurrying to earth as if this were its last chance to show itself to the world. He still felt terrible. Hot one minute, cold the next. He'd bought five liter bottles of water. He couldn't quench his thirst. The only constant was the GPS's calm, swanky voice. That, and the burning throb of his hand. He kept off the interstate wherever he could. Every time he left it, the GPS accommodated the redirection without changing its tone, but it still made Xander feel as if he were making the thing struggle, as if the talking guy resented it and was making an annoyed effort not to sound pissed.

She saw you and she got away. Ran all the way through the woods. You didn't even know she was there. *You* fucked it up.

It filled him with rage and weakness every time he thought of it. The deep knowledge that Paulie hadn't been lying. Why couldn't he just believe that Paulie had been lying? Because he couldn't. His gift-curse for the truth. He didn't want to go back, but not going back was impossible. *You want to fix this, you need to start with that.* Half a dozen times, he stopped and sorted through the objects in the shopping bags. Something had poked through the cellophane and torn a small hole in the kite. The jug was . . . No, wait, he'd dealt with the jug. *L is for lemon.* The smell of the lemon made him feel sick every time he handled it, mixed with the smell of the disinfectant and the bloody bandage. The violin was too big. That was going to be . . . If there was a girl, they'd have found her by now. He saw the police cockroach swarm bristling in the town's main drag. But he kept driving. His mind went in circles. Mama Jean was in the passenger seat some of the time, laughing to herself. Twice when he looked over, he saw not the side of the van but the Redding bedroom spreading out behind her, her hands folded over the soft swell in her pale denims. *Any way you look at it, it was all going fine until you screwed up in that shit-hole town. If you can't fix this, you're going to have to start again from the beginning. We're going to keep doing this until you get it right. You know that. You know that.*

He lost time. He remembered pulling over in a rest area and the soft darkness edging his vision. When he came back to himself, he had no clue how much time had gone. The wind rocked the van. He took more painkillers, drank more water. There was a half-eaten Musketeers bar on the dash, but when he bit off a mouthful and began chewing, he had to spit it out. The land around him was white under the dull sky. The clouds like a too-low ceiling, pressing on his skull. It felt wrong to be so hot when it was so cold out there. He pictured himself lying down in the snow and it melting around him with a hiss.

Ellinson's streets were deserted, the handful of shops closed. Maybe it was a Sunday? He'd lost track of the days. The main drag had been salted recently, but the roads off it were snowpacked, the drifts three or four feet high. He nosed the van, headlights penciling the gloom. Light snow fell, turned to a chaos of static by the wind. Harder to steer with one hand now. He was trying to remember. The house had been well out beyond the town, couple of miles at least. The lanes and the woods and the white fields all looked the same. The snow-lined branches went on forever. There was a fascination there, if he let his mind go into it, a kind of hypnotism.

Oh, sure. Hypnotism. You got all the time in the world for that.

He dragged his sleeve over the fogging windshield and increased the speed of the wipers.

87

Fifty-two-year-old Ellinson Sheriff Tom Hurley, divorced, was not a believer in fate, nor, by extension, the *tempting* of fate, but he couldn't help blaming himself when, ten seconds after he'd thought, *Jesus, I hope no one calls,* someone called. He'd just poured himself a cup of coffee (he was driving over to the Westcotts' for Christmas lunch later, Leonard Westcott being his friend of more than thirty years and himself an honorary member of the Westcott family; they had him over every Christmas, since the divorce ten years ago) and put his feet up in front of the TV. He was channel surfing for something shiny and inane. A Christmas-morning Bond movie, maybe, those heartbreaking girls with the glossy legs and cruel faces. He almost didn't pick up the call. His son was spending Christmas in Pueblo with his mother and would still be asleep. His sister (who got the brains, and who'd been teaching Renaissance Studies at Columbia for the last twenty years) wasn't due to call until this evening. And since that was the limit of his living family, it could only be work.

"Sheriff Hurley?"

"Yes?"

"Thank God. It's Meredith Trent. Rowena Cooper's mom. Something's wrong."

Tom came work-alert instantly. Excitement and unease in equal measure. He'd met Rowena's mother several times when she'd been up from Florida to visit her daughter and the kids, but they'd never exchanged more than a couple of minutes' polite conversation.

"Hey, Mrs. Trent, what can I do for you?"

"Look, this might sound like paranoia, but I've been calling Rowena's place since yesterday evening, and there's no answer. Same with her cell phone. I called Sadie Pinker on her cell, but she's with her family in Boulder. I don't have a number for anyone else there. I'm sorry, but I'm really going crazy here. It's Christmas Day, and there's no way they wouldn't be there. Could you check on them?"

Tom grabbed the pen and the jotter he kept by the phone. The wind outside was running riot. A horror movie sound effect. "When was the last time you spoke with Rowena, Mrs. Trent?"

"Four days ago. But I mean, we don't speak every day or anything. It's just that we said we'd speak as normal on Christmas Day. Please, Sheriff, I'm very worried. She's so far from everything out there."

"OK, Mrs. Trent, don't you worry yourself. I'm going to go on over there and check on her myself, how's that sound?"

"Oh gosh, yes please. Thank you. It's just not like her to go silent like that."

"I understand, absolutely. Most likely she's lost her cell and maybe there's a problem with the landline, but I'll take a ride out there anyway. Now, do you have a pen handy? I'll give you my cell phone number."

"Are you going to go right now?"

"Right now, yes, ma'am. You ready for the number?"

Driving out to Rowena's place through the racing snow, Tom thought how small-town life simplified everything, including— unfortunately—your ability to work out when something was wrong. He imagined a New York officer getting the same call from a worried mother with a daughter living alone in the city. The number of possible explanations for why someone wasn't answering her phones. A place the size of Ellinson reduced all such explanations to unlikelihoods. He knew Rowena and the kids. She was a good woman. If he'd been ten years younger . . . Good kids, too, from what he'd seen. The boy, Josh, was quiet, protective of his mother, which

Tom liked, and the little girl, Nell, was a funny, smart little thing. Landline down *and* cell phone out of action? Optimism. An accident. These roads in this weather. He was preparing himself, en route, for rounding a bend and coming face-to-face with a car wreck. Christmas Day, a vehicle could lie overturned on one of these back roads for twenty-four hours or more, upside down, burnt out, spilling oil and smoke and shattered glass and blood. *Jesus, please don't let it be bad. Please don't let it be bad.*

88

Xander parked the Dodge a little way past the house, where trees overhung the road. It was a dull morning now, and the snow was turning blizzardy. His first thought was to cut off the road and track back through the woods, but the snow was too deep. He'd be wading up to his thighs. He'd have to use the road and hope no one came along.

It was very cold, which soothed him briefly (he wore only a Windbreaker, jeans, the poorly washed sweatshirt, shitkickers), but within twenty paces, head down, it had him shivering again. He'd lost count of how many painkillers he'd taken. His guts didn't feel right. It was a long time since he'd eaten. He couldn't remember when he'd last eaten, in fact. He felt very distant from food, as if he'd gone past the need for it. He had only thirst left to him, apparently. He wished he'd brought a bottle from the van.

Strange to see the house again. He thought he'd been expecting to see the place yellow-taped off, a crime scene. And yet when he didn't, he wasn't surprised.

The Jeep Cherokee was still where it had been, tires snow-chained. That was a good thing. When he was finished here, he could switch vehicles. The keys would be in the house somewhere. A Jeep would be better in this weather, the chained tires biting through the drifts. He could get high up. He'd be able to breathe, to think clearly with the world sprawled out beneath him.

When he'd finished here. What did that mean? He kept approaching it in his mind, but all he got was the sense that he'd know what to do when he got there. He'd planned on bringing the kite and the lemon and the monkey. But walking across the house's front yard, he found he'd brought all the bags. Their soft plastic handles cut into the palm of his good hand. There seemed to be more things in them than he remembered buying. He was afraid, now, to look at what *was* in there. He'd seen a hammer. Hadn't he already done the hammer? That was one good thing about Paulie and the iPad videos: they helped him keep track. They helped him keep the things in place. And where would he go when he *had* finished here? Every time he thought about the bitch cop and the patrolman in his house, in his rooms . . . He looked over his shoulder. No one. He wanted to get into the house now just to get out of the cold. It was soft gloom under the trees.

Ran all the way through the woods. You didn't even know she was there. You fucked it up.

He knew now how he knew Paulie hadn't been lying. Paulie had fucked his knee up. Paulie said he thought he saw someone but it was a deer. It wasn't a deer.

But if that were true, why hadn't he known Paulie was lying at the time?

Because he'd been . . . Because it had gone wrong. And he'd been searching for the jug. He'd had his mind on the jug, trying even then, even *then* (the thought made him jam his teeth together) to put it right. The whole fucking thing was Paulie's fault.

The kitchen door was unlocked. He opened it and went in. He had the fish knife in his back pocket and the automatic tucked into his jeans. It was warm inside. Heating on a timer. He set the bags down on the kitchen floor. They made a noise, but it didn't bother him much. The house didn't feel . . . The house was still. A big solid thing unmoved by the turbulence outside. And there was the smell: rich diarrhea and rotten eggs. Still, he took the gun out. He'd never tried to fire a gun with his left hand. He didn't like the feel of it, but when he transferred it to the injured right, he found he couldn't make his fingers grip.

The kitchen opened into the corridor that led to the bottom of the stairs and the front door. The bloodstains were still there. He followed them to the living room, where he'd dragged her. The memory of it twitched, the feel of his fist wrapped in her hair, a fish-flicker in his cock.

She was still there, of course. She was as he'd left her. The room stank. Flies hummed. There was a Christmas tree. Its lights winked on and off. He'd kept seeing Christmas decorations when he was shopping. It hadn't registered on him properly. He didn't remember Christmas much. He remembered the days when it was over. People's trees and gift wrap stuffed in their garbage. It was like the world was laughing at how dumb it had all been, at what a mistake all the lights and tinsel and presents had been.

He was hard, so he undid his pants and stood with his cock positioned over her blotched face and sticking-out tongue. The flies murmured, agitated.

But after a few minutes he gave up. She had nothing in her. The jug would have made her . . . The violin—no, the kite would . . . But it was too late now. His head filled up with something. His eyes felt like hardboiled eggs. He'd thought he would know what to do. The living room's objects were trying not to look at him. It was like the things in Mama Jean's house. They went tight and didn't want to look, though they had to.

Upstairs, the kid was as he'd left him, too. Still with his big headphones on. Still with the TV on mute. Funny to think of all the shows and commercials that would have run, with the kid lying there. *Extreme Makeover* was on now. A woman in a hospital bed with her face swollen and her nose taped. Looked like she'd been beaten half to death. The amplifier gave off an annoying noise, like a very quiet wasp. Xander reached out to twang the guitar strings—something he'd never done in his entire life—but couldn't bring himself to touch them. Instead, he backed out of the room.

The smell was everywhere. It was in the woman's room at the front of the house, mixed with the scent of her cosmetics and perfume and clean laundry. It was in the bathroom, with its smell of warm towels and toilet cleaner. It was in a spare room full of neatly stacked clip-tight plastic crates (Xander glimpsed a baseball glove, a tennis ball, cotton reels, CDs, magazines).

And it was in the half-painted room, across the hall from the boy's.

89

Ran all the way through the woods. You didn't even know she was there.

Xander sat down on the edge of the bed. Through the swirls and jabs and flashes of the objects and the fizzing mix of rage and panic, a part of him was working things out. If she was alive, how come they hadn't been here and found the bodies? She would have told them. Maybe she was dead? Maybe she fell and broke her leg in the woods and froze to death? Or she was hiding somewhere, too scared to come out?

It didn't help him. He was hot and confused. He got up, dizzy, and wandered back into the woman's bedroom. For a while, he poked around, opening drawers and cupboards, his mind blank, sinking in and out of the pain in his hand. The wound felt busy. He thought a fly must have crawled in. He unwrapped the bandage. He couldn't see anything, but he could feel something moving around under the ruptured skin. He thought of that story about the guy trapped in a crevasse who'd had to cut his own arm off to get out. He rewrapped the bandage. He couldn't imagine himself cutting his own arm off. But the flies. He wanted more painkillers. And water. He'd left the first aid kit in the car.

You're not fixing this, dumb-ass.

Shut up. Shut up.

He had to think.

Find her.

He had to *think,* goddammit.

The bathroom. Medicine cabinet. Painkillers. Water.

But on his way to the door, he noticed the photograph on the bedside table. A framed color print of the woman with her kids. They were standing on a snowy porch in winter clothes, quilted jackets and woolly hats. The boy had one of those dumb ones with earflaps. The woman had one in silver fur that made her look like a Russian spy. The little girl wore a blue and white one with toggles hanging down below her chin. That and a red quilted jacket. They were all smiling. Icicles hung from the porch's pitched roof. The little girl looked like her mother.

He couldn't manage the tricky metal tabs on the back, so he smashed the glass and pulled out the print. He didn't have a single photograph of himself. He didn't like the idea any more than he liked mirrors. It still did something weird to him when he saw himself on the iPad videos. He never completely believed it was him.

In the bathroom he found Advil, took some, and drank a lot of water from the tap.

Through the woods. It won't be properly fixed until you find her.

Downstairs, he took the shopping bags from the kitchen into the living room. There were more things in them than he remembered buying. Big hardware nails. A pineapple. A wristwatch. A yo-yo. A doll wearing a crown. The objects were like the flies on her, easily disturbed.

But it was the kite. He was sure the kite came after the jug.

90

Sheriff Tom Hurley parked his Explorer in the driveway and walked, shoulders hunched against the snow, up to Rowena Cooper's front door. He'd noted the Cherokee, undamaged, outside the open garage. If they had been in an accident, it wasn't in their own car. But he'd also noticed that the depth of the snow on and around the vehicle said it hadn't been driven in a while. If you weren't going anywhere, why not leave it *in* the garage? Never mind. They could have been out driving with someone else. A surprise Christmas Day visit. A relative. A friend. Hell, maybe Rowena had a boyfriend. Maybe some guy who'd met her passing through and couldn't believe his luck. Town gossip was reliable, but it wasn't omniscient.

He rang the doorbell.

No answer.

Tried a second time.

Ditto.

He drew his gun and switched on his flashlight. Sweep. Check all the downstairs windows. It wasn't a car wreck. Fuck. Don't panic. Procedure. You don't know anything.

But of course he did know.

The first window he checked was the living room's bay. The curtains were open. Christmas tree lights blinking on and off.

Illuminating the half-naked body of Rowena Cooper, twisted on the blood-darkened floor.

When did you last speak with Rowena? he'd asked Meredith Trent. *Four days ago.*

She looked at least four days dead. Christ. Shit. *Shit.* His professional machine whirred—the kids, get in and check, they could be alive, bleeding, you might have minutes, seconds—while his human self, father, ex-husband, *person,* fractured with sadness: he'd seen Rowena a couple of weeks ago in town. Hey, Sheriff. Hey, Rowena. She'd been coming out of the post office. Late Christmas cards. *Wishing you a Merry Christmas and a Happy New Year!* She'd been heading to the diner across the street where the kids were waiting for her in a booth. All that life. The rich history and the glimmering future. All the conversations she'd had. Kisses, laughs, quiet moments watching the weather, reading a book, all the thoughts and the wondering. The big events of her heart. Her husband's death. The kids. The love. The loss. A person. Gone. A sudden, obscene subtraction from the world. *Mrs. Trent, I'm sorry, I have bad news. . . .* The mother would never recover, not properly. She'd be deformed inside for the rest of her life.

All this went through his head while he made his way back to the front door, slipped the flashlight into his belt, tried the handle, found it unlocked, pushed it open quietly with his left hand, the gun held tight and not nearly steady enough in his right.

The smell hit him immediately. Like nothing else on earth. Death's unique stink. He fought back vomit. His legs drained.

He wanted both hands on the gun, but he had to see. He reached for the hall light switch—stopped. *Prints. Don't touch anything. Basic. Fuck. Calm down.* He took the flashlight in his left hand. *Call for backup. But the time. Minutes, seconds. The kids. The kids first. Jesus, let them be alive. Please God, let them be alive.*

Four downstairs rooms: living room, dining room, kitchen, utility.

Rowena had something protruding from a gash in her abdomen. It took him a few seconds to unscramble it in his head, and even then he wasn't sure. It looked like the top half of a kite. One of those crappy little things you knew wouldn't work properly. Half the cellophane wrapper was still twisted around it.

Why? Never mind why.

Dining room, kitchen, utility.

Clear.

Halfway back down the hall he saw them: wet bootprints.

Jesus Christ—was he still *here?*

It played out mentally, quick and grotesque: the killer moving in with the dead family. Making coffee. Watching TV. Revisiting the corpses. Talking to them. Fucking them. It seemed the most natural thing in the world. The world contained individuals for whom that would *be* the most natural thing in the world. Once you knew the possibilities, you couldn't but consider them. You couldn't but expect them. All the things you knew that you wished you didn't.

He went up the stairs.

Front bedroom clear.

The wind dropped. He heard the crackle of electricity when he was just outside the second bedroom. It gave him a rush of hope.

Then he looked inside.

Oh dear God.

Josh.

Oh. Dear. God.

The turgid guts sprawled. Something . . . A soft toy jammed . . . *Fuck.*

He swayed, fought off sickness a second time, managed to get his back against the doorframe. The flies on the corpse lifted, irritated, traced urgent figure eights, resettled. Even in the midst of his nausea a small part of his mind was thinking: Flies? Winter? But the heating maybe. The disgust. The Lord of the Flies was the Devil. This was why. It took him a moment.

You don't have a moment. Move. Move.

The room across the hall was in the process of being decorated. Furniture removed.

She could only be in the bathroom. He had an image of her small body, naked and bloated in the tub's long-cold dark red water, hair floating, insides bobbing at the surface.

He backed out of the room and turned.

A man with a bandaged hand was standing in the bathroom doorway, holding a gun.

91

Xander lost more time, sitting in the woman's Cherokee with the shopping bags on the passenger seat. The smell of the pineapple pincered the back of his throat. The wind made a high-pitched sound in the evergreens. He was on the trail through the woods, barely the width of the vehicle. The trees met overhead. He didn't remember stopping. When he thought back over the last hours and days, the pieces of his past came apart. They had been in a sly conspiracy to leave him like this, with nowhere to go, no knowledge of what to do, no control. Things had come at him too quickly, one after another. All the things he'd relied on had betrayed him. Paulie. Fucking *Paulie*. He needed to get far away. He was aware of that. But he was so tired. The pain from his hand had stopped being confined to his hand. It had spread through his whole body. Every breath took a little more of his draining strength.

Ran all the way through the woods.

He kept thinking he saw her, moving between the trees in the red quilted jacket.

But of course not. That was days ago. She couldn't still be here. She'd be dead of cold. It seemed to him not like days but minutes. He had to keep bringing the fact of the days back to himself. There wasn't room to turn the Cherokee around. The thought of reversing all the way back to the road made him want to close his eyes again, to sleep. It seemed so long since he'd slept, though he remembered the motel, the girlish half-black kid, the little charge of anger and sadness as he'd watched him type the letters for Ellinson into the GPS, smiling, effortless. Simplest thing in the world, unless you're dumb as a rock.

He put the car into drive and eased forward. There would be a place to turn around, somewhere. There would be a gap in the trees. The locked branches overhead had partly screened the trail from the snow. He would drive a little farther. It was better to be moving forward, though he had a vision of the trees gathering closer and closer like a crowd of people, until the way was completely blocked.

Three or four minutes crawling. The banked drifts still and white and smooth. Then the trees on either side thinned and he found himself back in the open. There was a car parked a few yards away, all but buried in the snow. It was the last thing he'd expected to see. And now whatever unexpected thing came his way stirred his fear. More shifting scenery, more betrayal.

He took the gun and got out.

There was no one in the vehicle. For no real reason he was aware of, he tried the doors. All locked. He didn't know what it meant, but he didn't like it. It was wrong, how long the car must have been sitting here for the snow to have built up so high.

He walked a few paces beyond it and saw the bridgehead. There was a sign on it he daren't do more than glance at—and even the glance set the objects buzzing. The flies agitated around her body. A ravine, stretching as far as he could see in either direction. No lights on the opposite side, just more packed evergreens climbing the white hill. He went to the edge (every step took him knee deep) and looked down. Black water twisted and winked a long ways below. The bridge hung against the rock, bent where it had struck an outcrop. Xander had never seen anything like that, a whole bridge just hanging there. Was this how it was going to be now? Everything not what he expected? Every day another shift in the scenery?

Maybe she fell in.

She fell in. She ran through the woods and fell into the ravine.

He didn't know whether that was good or not. He thought of himself down there, searching. It was impossible.

You think you've fixed this? You haven't fixed it. You haven't fixed anything.

He stood there for a long time, looking down into the icy chasm, waiting to know what to do.

But the air bit his face and his stomach hurt and the pain that had spread out from his hand through the rest of his body kept time in a steady, agonizing throb.

In the end, he turned and went back to the Cherokee. He had to get far away. He had to get far away and find somewhere quiet where he could lie down and sleep for days. But the vision of this kept dissolving, until his mind gave up trying to hold it.

92

Thirty minutes from Ellinson, Carla got a radio call from FBI Field Agent Dane Forester. They'd found the Dodge registered to Paulie Stokes near a house three miles from town.

That wasn't all they'd found.

"So?" Valerie said. The snow was falling faster now, and the windspeed was manifestly bothering the pilot. It was just after 11 A.M.

"He's been and gone," Carla said. "Three homicides at a private residence on the edge of Ellinson. Adult female, teenaged boy. And the town sheriff. The woman and the boy have been dead for days. The sheriff, a matter of hours."

"Fuck. He's switched vehicles? He can't be on foot."

"The woman's car is gone. He's got at least an hour on them, probably more."

"He went back for the girl."

"Nell Cooper. Aged ten. Her body hasn't been found."

"If Stokes's story is true, she's been missing since her mother and brother were killed. Days. If she got away, she'd have gotten help. She's either hiding or injured or dead."

They set down on the open ground between the back of the house and the tree line. The scene was busy. Five federal agents and two Ellinson deputies, both with the look of delicate trauma. A CSI team was en route from Denver. Valerie imagined the deputies' Christmas morning at home with their families, the warmth and security ripped into by the call from the bureau. One moment the tinkle of breakfast and the rich scents of the food and the ordinary wealth of domesticity, the next this: the blunt reality of three people, including their boss, dead. Murdered. They'd talk about it on Christmases to come. It would most likely be the only murder they'd ever see. Valerie wondered how many she'd seen, how many she'd forgotten.

"What's the soft toy?" Carla asked. They were in Josh's bedroom. The feds had issued nose paste and latex.

Valerie (hands visibly shaking; she couldn't still them) lifted what she guessed was the toy's head with a pair of tweezers. Sticking-out ears. A tail, barely discernible among the toughened entrails. Big, surprised eyes.

"A monkey," she said. "*M* for monkey. *K* for kite downstairs."

The sheriff's body was, as far as a cursory examination could reveal, object-free.

"*L* must be for the girl," Valerie said. Try as she might, she couldn't see how Nell Cooper could be alive. Hiding? In this weather? She'd have frozen to death. "We're going to need a full search team," she said to Carla. "Stokes said she ran into the woods. Leave a deputy here for CSI. The rest of your guys should start a sweep. There's a photo of the girl, presumably."

"Thank goodness you're here," Carla said. "I wouldn't have thought of that."

"I'm getting back in the air," Valerie said. "You can do whatever you want."

Over an hour, the weather worsened. Snow drove hard. To Valerie, it felt not as if the chopper was fighting its way through air but through a bulk of roiling water. The physics revealed the aircraft's absurdity: a tin gnat in a bad-tempered ocean. The pilot's tolerance was palpably finite. He was flying with silent determination to get to the end of it. Once he had, Valerie knew, his will would set, and short of putting the gun to *his* head, there would be nothing she could do about it. A detached part of her admired him, his willingness to take it to the limit of manageable danger—but no further. Her own hands were wet, gripping the edge of her seat. She was aware of her body, trembling, the panicked crowd of her symptoms and the web of adrenaline holding them down.

"This is pointless," Carla said. "Five minutes, and we're not going to be able to see anything at all. We're wasting time and—Jesus!"

A slab of wind hit them, and the chopper dipped and canted left. Briefly, Valerie's window view filled with a mass of snow-heaped trees. Her guts turned over.

"This is fucking crazy," the pilot said over the headset. "I'm in molasses here."

"What's the nearest town on the other side of the river?" Valerie said.

"Spring," the pilot said. "Fifteen miles northeast. But we already scoped it. They've got a better chance on the ground."

"Go over it again," Valerie said.

"Hey, you want to fly this?"

"He's long gone," Carla said.

"Please," Valerie said. "Just do it."

93

Nell had the feeling she had slept for a long time. The light said the morning was going. There was snow coming down fast, and the wind sang where it cut the cabin's edges. Angelo was deeply asleep on the couch. The empty coffee mug lay on its side by his hand. She felt sorry for him, strangely, seeing him asleep like that.

She still had on all the clothes from last night, the boots, the red quilted jacket. Angelo had begged her to let him take the boots off and put the splints back on, but she didn't want the splints anymore. They were uncomfortable. The boot actually felt better, though her ankle still throbbed with a rhythmic life of its own. It made her feel sick if she thought about it, so she forced herself not to. She felt very awake, but the effect of the pill had worn off. Her side stabbed her, meanly, every time she breathed in.

She got to her knees. The little foil packet of Advil was where Angelo had left it, on the corner of the sink. One pill had made the pain less. You could kill yourself with the wrong pills. Or too many. There was such a thing as an overdose. But an overdose would be a whole packet or something, she was sure. Whenever you saw someone taking an overdose on the TV, it was *handfuls,* and even then, most of the time, they just seemed to end up in hospital, having their stomachs pumped or throwing up. She wanted as much of the pain gone as possible. Her mother took two if she had a headache. Two for a headache. What she had hurt a lot more than a headache. Without thinking about it (or rather, thinking that even if she died, it wouldn't matter now) she popped all three remaining capsules from the foil and swallowed them with a mouthful of water from the pan still sitting by the stove.

Her hat was on the floor under the table. She would need that. *The pills work better on a full stomach,* he'd said. It hadn't sounded like a lie, and she was suddenly starving. She crawled to the cupboard. She didn't want to stand up until she had to. And in any case, surely it would take a little while for the pills to work?

Everything was cans. She found peaches, with a ring-pull opener. Surprised herself at how quickly and greedily she ate them. Angelo didn't stir. It occurred to her that this was the first time she'd seen him asleep since she got here. She wondered about him, what his life was, why he was here. He looked terrible. She imagined telling her mother and Josh about him—but as soon as she thought that, what had happened came up again like the world tilting. It made her dizzy. Her mother. All the blood all this time. Her mother was—

She had to go back. She'd waited too long. It didn't matter what happened. All she wanted was to get back to her house. She would phone 911. Medics would come. They would come with equipment, and they would know what to do. She remembered a TV show about people who had died and come back to life. One of them had floated up out of his body and looked down from just below the ceiling. He'd watched the doctors working on him. He'd watched the whole thing. Oh yeah, Josh had said when she told him about it, that's no big deal. People are technically dead all the time and then come back to life. They see a sort of white light and start drifting toward it. But then something pulls them back into their bodies, like when they get zapped with those electric gizmos that start their hearts beating again. One woman floated up and out of the hospital building and saw someone's sneaker that they'd lost ages ago sitting on a god-damned window ledge on the third floor, and she told them about it when she woke up, and they went and checked—and there it was! How cool is that?

She finished the peaches and crawled to collect her hat from under the table.

I'll help you, in the morning, Angelo had said. But what help was he going to be? He was in worse shape than she was. There was nothing he could do *to* help. At the door, clutching his stick, she felt bad, leaving him like this. He needed the stick. But if she didn't go and get help, *he'd* be stuck here forever, too. What would he do when the food ran out? It was mean, she knew, to go without saying good-bye, but he would understand. It struck her that he'd taken care of her. He'd saved her life. He looked lonely, asleep on the couch. She wondered who his family was.

She opened the door quietly, crawled out onto the porch, closed it as gently as she could, then got the stick under her and pushed herself to her feet.

The world went white, then black. She thought she was falling again. But she opened her eyes, and with a strange liquid softness, things swam back into focus. Her teeth felt numb, but with warmth instead of cold. Experimentally, she put a little weight on her damaged foot. There was pain (she pictured fine white lightnings traveling through the bones of her shin and knee and thigh), but it was oddly muted. She knew it, rather than felt it. She tried a little more weight. The lightnings brightened. Too much. Maybe the pills had only just started working? Maybe she'd be able to put more weight on it in a little while?

The wind whipped snow into her face. Her hat's toggles rattled. She wondered how long it would take her to get to the fallen tree. She knew the wind was too strong for her to go across on foot. She'd have to crawl. And find a way of keeping hold of the stick. She'd need the stick again when she made it to the other side. *If* she made it to the other side.

94

Xander wanted to stop driving but couldn't. When he thought of stopping, he saw the cockroach rivers of cops approaching from all directions. The GPS was useless to him now, since he couldn't reset it. He took roads at random, lefts, rights. For all he knew, he was going in circles. He swallowed more painkillers, but they didn't help. His throat was dry, no matter how much water he drank. There was only one of the liter bottles left. The oncoming headlights of the occasional cars needled his eyes. It was the first time in a long time he hadn't known what to do. Even Mama Jean had abandoned him. Everywhere was white open land and the dark masses of trees.

The river was part of the treacherously shifting scenery. He had thought he was driving away from it, but he found himself crossing a bigger bridge and, an indeterminate time later, entering a town. Nothing was open, apart from a solitary convenience store on the main drag, the light from which blazed, softly, green and white stripes, two men in white shirts watching a portable TV behind the counter. The blizzard had the run of the streets. He didn't want to be in a town, but the emptiness of the open spaces pressed on him with time burning away, all the time to fail to figure out what to do, where to go, how to fix things. The signs of habitation were at least a distraction, the darkened stores and the strung Christmas lights of the houses. Through the snow haze, he caught glimpses of people in the windows, laughing, eating, drinking, kids jumping around. A young girl in denim cut-offs and white knee socks and sandals, like the ones the girl on the carousel had worn, the buckle that had scratched his head, the blow that knocked him under the horses' plunging hooves.

But the sight of an empty parked squad car unhinged him. He couldn't stay here. Here he was *giving* himself to them. The squad car itself bristled when he passed it. He returned to the main drag and followed it to the edge of town. A narrower road of deeper snow wound away, hugging the slope of the hill. The river ravine on the left, the ranks of evergreens on the right. He took it. He would find a track in the woods as he had before. He would get in under the roofed avenue of trees. He would rest. He would sleep.

95

Nell hadn't gone far—maybe only thirty steps, though each one seemed to take minutes—when she began to get a little confused. The pauses to rest between each step had been getting longer. She felt sleepy. Her legs were faraway things. Not just her teeth, but her whole head felt numb. When she blinked, it was like a heavy velvet curtain very slowly descending. The snow was driving hard around her. She couldn't see more than a few feet ahead. If it weren't for the ascending slope of evergreens on her right and her own footprints behind her, she wouldn't have been sure which way *was* ahead.

She took another step but found herself easing herself down to sit in the snow. Just for a moment, she told herself. Just rest for a moment. She was thinking about the tree. Josh and Mike Wainwright had sat there that afternoon, and Nell had been terrified that if Josh tried it and fell, she would have to go and tell her mother what had happened. Her mother knew about the tree, and had strictly forbidden either of them to *ever* try to cross it. Twenty feet, Mike Wainwright had said. *Can't* be more than twenty feet. It had looked a long, *long* way across to Nell. You'd have to pick your way between the branches. You'd have to crawl. Mike Wainwright claimed he'd seen another, older boy, Francis Coolidge, do the whole thing, there and back, on foot, wearing special soft rubber shoes with what Mike called "nodular grip," but neither Josh nor Nell had believed him.

She couldn't understand why she felt so tired. She'd slept last night for what had seemed a very long time.

At which thought, the dream came back to her, and she remembered the hare.

Safe travel. You're old enough now.

She put her hand into her pocket.

It wasn't there.

Angelo woke from a dream of him and Sylvia on a boat in glittering blue water to find Nell, and the remaining Advil, gone. He knew at once what had happened, what she'd done. What *he'd* done.

And he cometh unto the disciples, and findeth them asleep, and saith unto Peter, What, could ye not watch with me one hour?

How long had he slept? How long had she been gone? The thought of going after her took stock of his energy. Pitiful, despite the sleep, which felt as though it couldn't have been more than a couple of hours. And she had taken his walking stick.

He would have to go and look for her. Dear God, if she'd tried to cross the tree . . . And in this fucking blizzard . . .

He was searching the cabin for anything that might serve as a prop when the door opened.

"My bracelet," Nell said. "I can't do it without my bracelet. Where is it?"

"Thank God," Angelo said. "I thought you'd . . . Jesus, come in, come in. Shut the door."

But Nell didn't shut the door. She just sank to her knees. Angelo's walking stick clattered to the floor next to her. "It was in my pocket," she said. "My mom gave it to me. It's for safe travel. I can go across the tree with it."

Angelo crawled to the door and closed it. The kid was different. She wasn't right. The pills? She'd taken three times the recommended dose. He would have to be careful. Right or wrong in her mind, she was more mobile than him now. Speak calmly.

"You've lost your bracelet," he said. "OK. We'll look for it. What's it look like?"

"It's a silver chain with a gold hare." She was wrestling her jacket off. "It was in my pocket," she said, going through them for what was obviously the umpteenth time. "It has to be here."

"Check in the lining," Angelo said. "That's where I found the Advil in mine. Come over by the stove in the meantime."

Nell crawled toward the warmth, dragging her jacket. "I have to have it," she said. "It's got to be here somewhere."

"How are you feeling?" Angelo said. "Any stomachache? You might have taken too many of those pills. So if you're feeling—"

"It's here!" Nell said. "I found it!"

Her speech sounded a little slurred.

The bracelet was in the first place she'd looked: under the couch. Kicked there by him, presumably, during one of his many spectacular journeys around the floor.

"Oh, good," he said. "Can I see it?"

"The chain's broken," she said. "It broke when I fell. But it stopped me going over the edge into the river."

OK, she was definitely not herself. He'd learned enough of her over the last three days to know she was too old and too smart for something like that. (*Says the man who talks to the dead.*) How long ago had she taken them? He had no idea how long she'd been gone.

"That's really very pretty," he said, examining the bracelet she held in her palm. "And it's a good luck charm for travelers?"

"My mom gave it to me," she repeated. "It's been in her family for ages."

"That's a genuine heirloom," he said. "And these days, not many—"

He stopped. They'd both heard it. The sound they'd all but given up believing they'd ever hear again.

A car. It was a ways off down the hill, but it could only be coming in one direction. There was nothing the other way except the end of the road and the wrecked bridge.

For a stretched second, they looked at each other. There were too many feelings. Nell's face had lost all its knowledge, everything. She was suspended, out of time.

"Thank God," Angelo said. He grabbed his stick, got it under himself, braced, shoved himself (one scream as S1 bellowed in protest) to his feet.

"Wait!" Nell said.

Angelo, bent double, turned. She just looked at him, trembling, willing him to understand.

He paused. He was an idiot. Had he forgotten everything already? *Who the hell was she running from?*

Still, it was very remote, he knew. The chances of the men who had attacked her mother . . .

Reason and paranoia.

Very remote. But not impossible.

"OK," he said. "I know. Christ. Let's get you . . . Quick. In there."

Not to the bathroom, but to the room next door, empty but for some old wooden crates, half of which had been broken up and used for kindling. A window looked out alongside the porch. A rickety wooden door opened into the cabin's small fenced backyard. An exit, he told himself—what for he didn't know, since even hopped-up on the Advil, she'd hardly be able to *run*.

"Don't worry," Angelo said. "It's going to be fine. It's someone from Spring maybe gone the wrong way, lucky for us."

Nell didn't answer. Neither of them had realized how much the stillness and confines of the cabin had become their world. Now that they were disturbed, it brought all the horror of her flight back to her. And the insurmountable fact of his virtual helplessness back to him.

"Anything happens," Angelo said, "you hide. Understand? You *hide*."

Outside, drenched in sweat from the effort of getting there, the cold shocked him. No coat. The wind nearly took him off his feet. Flakes rushed to his eyelashes. His jaws were tight. The pain was burning through the adrenaline, a furious inflagration. But he stayed on his feet, bent under his invisible load, shivering. The wind had blown the cabin's front door open, though he'd pulled it closed behind him.

Headlights through the snow's wild cross-hatching. The vehicle was moving slowly, a creature nosing its way. The engine sounded big and healthy. It brought all of civilization with it. Angelo's hands and face were wet. *Think. Don't assume. Think.*

Thirty feet. Twenty. Ten.

It stopped.

The driver's door opened, and a man in a Windbreaker got out, one arm up over his eyes to shield them from the snow's blur.

"Jesus," Angelo gasped, staggering forward. "Thank Christ you're here. I need help. I've got a back injury, and I've been stuck here for days. I really need to get down to Spring. Do you have a cell phone?" He'd been shouting over the noise of the wind—but it dropped, and made his last utterance sound like he was patronizing a deaf person. "I'm sorry," he said, *not* shouting, "but I've been completely stranded up here."

The two men looked at each other.

"Where does this road go?" the guy asked.

"This way's no good," Angelo said. "The road only goes as far as the bridge, and the bridge is out. Please, I really need to make a call if you have a phone. Do you have a cell phone?"

"Where does the bridge go?"

Angelo hesitated. The guy wasn't right. The guy wasn't seeing him.

"Ellinson," he said just as the wind hurled itself again, so that he had to shout the rest: "But the bridge is out. This is a *dead end.*"

Bizarrely, the guy took a few paces away, put his hands on his hips, as if that was the *last* thing he needed to hear. The depth of the snow made it look ridiculous, like an angry toddler stomping around his room.

A gust knocked Angelo to his knees. The nerves in his leg roared. He cried out. He couldn't, for the moment, get up.

The man in the Windbreaker stomped back and stood over him. He wasn't looking at Angelo. He was watching the cabin door bang open and closed, open and closed.

"This is a dead end," the man said. He still had his hands on his hips. One of them was bandaged.

Angelo didn't speak. The ground was uncertain under him. The guy standing over him looked exhausted.

"Hold on," the man said, reaching for his back pocket. "Let me see if I've got reception on my phone."

But it wasn't a phone.

It was a gun.

Which he smashed into the side of Angelo's head.

Nell, peeping through the junk room window, saw the man hit Angelo. Not the man from the house. A different man. How was that . . . They're still here, her mother had said. They. More than one. Where was the guy with the coppery hair and the thin beard? She saw Angelo fall.

Anything happens, you hide. Understand?

There was nowhere to hide. He would find her in seconds.

The door. The back porch. Under it.

There was nothing. There was nothing but the occasional blasts of pain and the certainty that this was it. It was over. It was going to happen.

She grabbed the windowsill and pushed herself up onto her good foot. No stick now. Angelo had taken it. Without it, her ribs on the left side took her breath away with the first step. She went down.

Hurry. *Hurry, Nellie.*

It was her mother's voice. Her mother's face with the blood on her lips. *I'm going to be all right, but you have to run. Now!*

But she couldn't run.

Your mother is dead.

She crawled. The smell of the floor was intimate, old wood and the freezing soil beneath it. She wondered how long the cabin had stood here. She wondered, too (vaguely, as if she had all the time in the world), why Angelo had come here. She had never asked him. Now she would never know. It came to her in spite of everything that he had been kind to her. She wished she'd thanked him. The image of the other man hitting him with the gun replayed in her head. It snapped a small stem in her heart. The water he'd warmed for her, and the clean smell of the soap and the towel. She'd felt better afterwards. He had done so many small things for her.

Hurry!

At the back door, she had to push herself up again to reach the latch. She had no thought. She was just moving. She would move as long as she could, and when she couldn't move anymore, whatever was going to happen would happen. It was a blankness ahead of her. Except the feeling that she would see her mother on the other side of it. It comforted her. It would happen; then it would be over and she would be through.

As soon as she got the door open the blizzard rushed her face. The snow was a soft, urgent suffocation. The pain in her ankle felt like it had layers upon layers of warmth wrapped around it. It would make her sick if she thought about it. On her knees, she pulled the door closed behind her. The porch had a dusting of snow, but the area beyond it was deep. Deeper than her, if she crawled. If she tried to crawl under the porch. If there was even a space under the porch. It was impossible. He would open the door and see her immediately, half buried in the snow, going nowhere, a helpless animal still moving, long past the point at which it should have given up.

The porch roof was low, a handrail, uprights supporting the pitch at either side.

I'm not worried you'll fall. I'm worried you've got monkey genes.

She looked at it. There was a rusted hanging basket bracket halfway up the upright. Good leg first. Knee on the handrail. Hands on the upright, then she could reach the edge of the roof. Pull herself up. Left foot on the bracket.

And then what? It was impossible. She couldn't put that kind of weight on her right leg. The thought of it made her dizzy. She hadn't realized she was crying.

But there was nothing else to do. The alternative was to go back inside, in which case, he'd find her. Or wait here on the porch, in which case, he'd find her. Since all she wanted now was to go through and see her mother again, shouldn't she just *let* him find her? What difference did it make where?

The prospect of this tempted her sweetly, with a quiet voice in the midst of her dinning blood.

The girl's red jacket was on the floor next to a sleeping bag. Xander had seen it when the door blew open. The door had kept opening and closing, showing it to him every time. The door was determined he should see what he needed to see. The door was on his side.

He stood over the old man in the snow. The old man's head was bleeding, but he wasn't unconscious. His eyes and his mouth were open. Xander kicked him in the stomach, once, twice, three times. He felt relief flooding him, warming him from the inside despite the icy air on his face and hands. The cold even numbed his hand a little. He stood in the deafening wind, enjoying the sensation. All the hours and days, all the gathered weather and miles were leaving him, a swarm that had covered him and made every movement slow was tearing quickly from his body to be carried away on the racing snow. He could feel the weight lifting. Mama Jean laughed quietly, right next to him. It was going to be all right. He was going to fix it. He was going to fix everything.

He aimed a final kick at the old man's head (felt, through his boot, the strange little detail of a bone cracking), watched his eyes close, then turned and mounted the porch steps to the cabin's front door.

There was no one in the living room. The stove fire was going and the oil lamps were lit. The big shadows wobbled. There was a smell of fried food. The red North Face jacket that had been waiting for the door to show it to him. He tightened his grip on the pistol. He was getting used to using his left hand.

The two other rooms—one with only broken crates in it and the other a cramped bathroom—were empty.

He went back into the living room. Looked in the cupboards, behind the couch. Nothing. He returned to the empty room. A wooden door at the far end. She was out back. There was no other explanation. He could feel the seconds catching fire as they passed, the heat of time burning away. The relief he'd felt only moments ago was already starting to back up in his veins.

The door opened onto a short, roofed wooden porch and small wire-fenced yard beyond it, knee-deep in untouched snow. A solitary bare tree a few feet away, a rotten birdhouse nailed to its trunk. Untouched snow. *No footprints.* But there was nowhere else she could be. For a crazy moment, he convinced himself that she was hiding *in* the snow. He had a brief vision of himself digging in it with his hands. But she would have left tracks. How the fuck could there be no tracks? He started to get hot again. Fuck. *Fuck.*

The old man must've hidden her somewhere. Maybe there was a place he'd missed, a trapdoor in the floor, a crawl space under the goddamned porch . . .

He ran back through the cabin to the front, grabbed the old man with his good hand, and dragged him inside.

Nell almost stopped. There was a point—the point she'd known would come—when she didn't believe she could do what needed to be done. She'd gotten her knees onto the handrail, holding the upright for balance. She'd gotten her hands in the pitched roof's gutter. But in order to get her good foot onto the hanging basket bracket, she had—for a moment, at least—to let her bad one take some of her weight. That was what she didn't believe she could do. She kept hearing Angelo saying, I'm pretty sure your ankle's broken. . . . The words "ankle's broken" had a feel of breakage themselves. She tried to imagine how bad the pain would be. There was a TV ad for Tylenol that featured a transparent CGI athlete, running, his skeleton and nerves visible, blue lightnings shooting up them to represent pain. She could feel preparatory lightnings in her teeth already. Advil was like Tylenol, she supposed. And though the strange, sleepy numbness had spread from her teeth through the rest of her, it was as if her ankle were telling her that wouldn't be enough. Nowhere near enough.

Don't think about it.

She pulled as hard as she could with her arms, and lifted her left leg.

Her mouth closed over the scream. She felt it in the bones of her skull. Her eyes closed. For a second or two, she thought this was death. Everything disappeared except the pain. Total blackness. There was nothing but the pain.

Her left foot found the bracket. Slipped from it. Found it again.

Even with her weight transferred, her ankle kept sending the lightnings. It kept sending the lightnings because it wanted her to know that she must never, ever do that again. It was a transgression for which the punishment had to be so extreme as to prevent her ever repeating the offense. She felt weight*less*, as if she were going to faint.

A long time seemed to pass in which there was nothing she could do but keep still, receiving the pain. Her right leg hung useless. Her ankle was heavy. She thought its own weight would tear it from her leg.

But she had her head and shoulders above the edge of the roof now. The snow in front of her was three or four feet deep. She would freeze to death. Josh had told her that the last thing you felt if you froze to death, your last sensation, was that you were blissfully warm. She could believe it. Her head was warm now. That wouldn't be so bad.

The next maneuver was the same as when you had to haul yourself over the edge of a swimming pool.

Not the ankle, this time. The ribs.

She would do this one final thing, she thought, this one final horror to herself, and if the pain didn't kill her, she would lie down in the snow and wait to feel warm for the last time.

Cold water crashed on Angelo's face. He woke up, gasping. He was lying on his back by the stove, hands and feet bound with snap plastic restraints. The guy in the Windbreaker stood over him, holding the saucepan he'd used to drench him. He set it down on the stove and took a white-handled fish knife from the back of his jeans. The cabin door was closed and bolted now. Inexplicably, there were three or four shopping bags on the table. A pineapple was visible poking out of one of them. More bizarrely, the neck of a violin. In spite of himself, Angelo thought of Christmas shopping, gifts waiting their wrapping.

"Where is she?" the guy said.

"Who?"

Without warning and with astonishing precision, the guy bent, yanked up Angelo's left pant leg, and drew the knife quickly over the exposed calf. Angelo screamed.

"I can do that for hours." With his bandaged hand, he picked up Nell's red jacket. "Where is she?"

"She's gone," Angelo said. "She was here, but she's gone."

The guy dropped the jacket and cut Angelo's calf a second time. Deeper.

Angelo screamed again. "Fuck, stop, please stop! I'm not lying. Listen to me. For God's sake, listen to me. She was here, three days ago, but she—No, don't! Wait!"

He lifted Angelo's sweater, knife poised.

"Stop! Listen! She was—"

A sound froze both of them.

Unidentifiable. Some giant groan from above.

The two of them in shared suspense. Children interrupted in the middle of something they shouldn't be doing.

Snow. Shifting. On the roof.

A chunk that sounded the *size* of the roof sheared off, slid, crashed behind the cabin.

A second absurd pause in which they shared the decoding.

Then the guy in the Windbreaker looked down at Angelo. It was a moment of purity. Of knowledge. Sylvia was very close. Not speaking. Just radiating love like heat from a blast furnace. *It's out of my hands,* Angelo thought, as the knife caught the light. *Wherever you are, my love, I'll find you.*

A slab of snow shifted beneath Nell, fell, crashed below. She knew she had to move. There was only one place to go. Up.

She could barely feel the pain. The pain was like a sound coming from a room many locked doors away. The wind raced over her face. A strand of her wet hair was in her mouth. She felt sleep like a weight on her. She pulled herself forward up the roof's incline on her elbows. Her body was very far away from her. She drifted free of it, watched herself from above. The sight looked familiar, as if she'd dreamed it long ago, or lived it in a life before this one. As if the sole purpose of this life were to lead her back to this scene, to bring her home to her beginning. The golden hare morphed next to her, then vanished.

"Where are you going?" the man's voice said.

She turned her head. He was standing where she had stood, on the handrail, his forearms resting comfortably on the back porch roof, though the blizzard swirled around him. He looked like someone waiting patiently at a hotel reception desk.

She kept going. Her sweater had ridden up. Her bare belly was pressed against the snow. It didn't seem odd that she couldn't feel the cold. It seemed, in fact, like the most natural thing in the world. The apex of the roof was three feet away. But she knew when she reached it, that would be the last of her strength gone. When she reached it, she thought, she would close her eyes and never open them again.

"There's nowhere for you to go," he called out to her. He sounded friendly, as if he were good-naturedly indulging her in what he knew was an amusing waste of time.

"Well, I guess I'll have to come up there," he said.

She couldn't reach the apex. Her arms were finished. It irritated her vaguely, that it was so close but still beyond her. It was like a minor job left annoyingly unfinished. In a last, halfhearted attempt, she bent her left leg under her and tried to push herself up onto her knee. It would be good at least to see over the top, to look out over the ravine and across into the woods, toward home.

She did get one glimpse over the summit, though in the chaos of snow there was nothing to see. She felt her hair streaming out behind her and her mother close by her side. She turned her head to smile at her, to tell her that she loved her.

Then something went out from under her. She fell.

She almost got past him. She came slithering down on her belly in a soft-roaring mass of sliding snow. If he'd missed, she'd have had enough momentum to carry her off the edge of the porch and into the yard's smooth white drift below.

But he didn't miss.

The moment his fingers closed around her wrist was a perfection to him. He'd been waiting for it for such a long time.

You're dying, Angelo thought. *Here it is. Je vais chercher un grand peut-être,* as Rabelais had said. *I go in search of a big perhaps.* It comforted him, that his life contained such memories, so much of the best and loveliest that had been said, though now that it had come to it, he knew that it didn't count for much, that we knew nothing, even via our grandest intimations. Sylvia was gone. There was nothing of her with him now except an intuition. The kind of intuition you might have on entering a still, quiet room in which someone had left you their last words, in a note. It seemed right to him, that you were obliged to make the last part of the journey, the *very* last part, alone. He felt peaceful. He smiled.

But there was the child. It was a terrible counterforce, that she was still alive, that *her* life was about to end. It was a wretched connection, as yet unsevered, to the world he knew he must leave. The great physical temptation, a seduction in his veins, was to yield. He would be dead soon—minutes, seconds—so why not just let go, let be? His contract with the world was being—moment by racing moment—unwritten. What difference did it make whether the child lived or died? What difference did it make if the entire universe ceased when he drew his last breath? Why was it still his responsibility?

He smiled again. There was a new equation: All fear was, in the end, fear of death. Once you knew you were dying, there was nothing left to fear. It gave you the last great gift: infinite courage.

He sat up. It was the simplest thing in the world: He would use what little allowance he had left. It was hopeless. It was—he imagined God chuckling—ridiculous, but he would make it his last project to go on until he could go on no longer. He was fascinated by it himself. How much longer *could* he go on? It was a surreally titillating question.

His hands were tied. That would have to change. He laughed. His inner tone now was of a new no-nonsense but benign headmaster entering a hopeless school. *This won't do, not having the use of your hands.*

He opened the stove door. There was the fire. There were the flames. Here were his tied hands. How long would it take? What was the melting temperature for tough plastic? At what point did first-degree burns become second-degree, then third?

He knew he couldn't do it. And that he had to.

It was impossible. So he would do it, because there was nothing else, and because he had the strength to do it.

He would fail. The failure was already there. It filled his whole being. He wouldn't be able to stand it. He had no time. He knew he couldn't do it.

So he would do it.

He raised his hands. The flames shivered. The heat was already close to unbearable. The thought defeated his imagination.

It took the certainty of death, perhaps, to bring out the brain's full talents. Because without the licking flames and the heat and the defeated imagination and the pain and the guarantee of failure and the levity and the infinite courage that was all but indifference, without any and all of these things, perhaps, he would never have remembered the axe.

He'd thought it would alarm Nell to see it when she woke up.

So he'd slid it under the stove.

It was going to be all right, Xander thought. He was exhausted. Carrying the girl in (she was unconscious by the time he'd grabbed her at the roof's edge) had set his hand off again. His shoulders ached and his skin was heavy and damp. But it was going to be all right. He had her and he had the things he needed. He was fixing what needed to be fixed. After this, he would be back on track. He would go somewhere far away for a little while (he had a very clear vision of himself sitting alone on a warm beach in the evening sun) and get it clear in his head what he had to do next. He would recover his strength and find someone to fix his hand. Things had almost got away from him, but he'd gathered them back. He would deal with this, and then he would go to the warm beach and sleep for a long, peaceful time on the sand.

He entered the living room and stopped. The door was open and snow was blowing in.

He didn't understand it. He couldn't have been more than five minutes.

But the old man was gone.

It took an extraordinary effort of will for Angelo not to cut the ties on his hands first. But in the micro-time of these moments his brain had become a scrupulous high-speed realist: *You only have seconds. You can move without the use of your hands, but not without the use of your legs.* So he'd cut through the plastic binding his ankles, then dragged himself and the axe to the door and out onto the front porch. The sciatica, seeing no reason why imminent death should stop it going about its business, didn't let up. The same agony with every movement, with competition now from the fiery wounds and the swelling pain of his broken jaw. His mouth tasted strange to him, until he realized it was his own blood in there, welling repeatedly from where a tooth had been kicked out. (Where was the tooth? Had he swallowed it? Imagine if he wasn't dying. He would have to go to Speigel, his dentist, who would be quietly amazed if not outright disbelieving of how he'd lost it.) Now he hunkered in the doorway of the freezing woodshed that adjoined the cabin with the blade wedged between his ankles and his bound wrists poised. The cold was astonishing. As was the warmth of the wound in his guts. It was a little pleasant satisfaction to him to have gotten this far. It tickled him, that the guy in the Windbreaker would be exasperated to find him gone.

Xander dumped the girl on the living room floor and ran to the open door. He was thick with gathered anger. The objects buzzed and clamored as he passed the shopping bags on the table. Every time he thought he was on top of things . . . every fucking *time*. All he wanted was to deal with this and then sleep. He couldn't take much more. It was very hard to think, but with a great haul of himself he paused, forced his brain to do the work. First, find the old man. That would be the lemon. No, the monkey. Goddammit, he'd already finished with the monkey. The video images shuffled. That bitch he'd had to get the goose into. He'd broken one of its feet wedging it in. It had snapped off in his hand. Paulie, filming, had said: "Ooops," and laughed. He'd nearly killed him then. Paulie had spent their time together with no fucking clue how often Xander had nearly killed him. It was a miracle he lasted as long as he had. But the memory of Paulie brought back the last girl in the basement. Why hadn't he done it properly? The fucking jug should have been *inside* her. He'd made so many mistakes. But the bitch cop had ruined everything. The uniformed asshole, too, with his fucking wristwatch the size of his head and his stupid peppermint gum.

W is for Watch.

Did he have the watch? The watch was for later, wasn't it?

You made a mistake, Mama Jean said. He had a strange, vivid memory of seeing Mama Jean's underwear lying on the bathroom floor. He'd been sitting on the toilet taking a shit, his skin still on fire from the mark she'd put on him that morning. Her big white bra and panties had been lying by the wicker laundry hamper. He'd finished his business and flushed it away, though the stink still lingered. He remembered getting down on his hands and knees and smelling her panties, like a dog sniffing its food. A feeling like excitement and complete emptiness he hadn't understood. It had done something weird to him in his guts and his cock.

He shook himself. Christ, what was wrong with him? The old man. The old *man,* goddammit. He trudged across to the Cherokee and opened the trunk. The shotgun. Why the fuck hadn't he brought the shotgun to start with? The wind buffeted him. He slammed the trunk shut and turned back to the cabin.

Which was when he heard something coming up from the ravine.

96

Valerie and Carla saw the collapsed bridge at the same time, and had exactly the same thought. Valerie put her hand on the pilot's shoulder. "We need to check down there," she said.

The pilot's resistance—this was crazy; he was already beyond safe flight protocols—came off him like electricity. She could feel it in his shoulder. He shook his head. "Listen," he began, but Valerie leaned forward. "She's ten years old," she said. "You got kids?" The resistance was still there. He shook his head. The chopper pitched right. "She's *ten years old,*" Valerie repeated. "You want that on your conscience?"

"No," he said. "And I don't want to kill the three of us either."

But he dropped down into the ravine anyway, adding, "Fuck. This is . . . Goddammit."

Valerie pressed her face up against the window and cupped her hands around it. The maddening contrast between the searchlight's wobbling radius and the impenetrable gloom beyond. Black rock veined with snow. White water where stones broke the river's edges. *She's ten years old.* Yes, and if this was where she was, she was dead. It was two hundred feet from the bridge to the bottom, and even in the extreme unlikelihood that she'd survived a fall, what then? Cold water carried heat away from the body twenty-five times faster than air of the same temperature. Hypothermia would kill her in minutes.

A gust swung the chopper. The ravine's west wall loomed, terrible with innocent detail. The pilot climbed, dipped, climbed again. "Enough," he said. "This is suicide. We're heading back."

"You can't," Valerie said.

"I can and I am. As far as this bird goes, I'm in charge. Christ, we might not even *make* it back. That's it."

Climbing felt to Valerie like tearing an umbilical. She imagined the little girl, concealed in a recess or under an overhang, hearing the helicopter, seeing them, waving her arms, calling for help as her last hope of it drifted up and away into the darkness.

"We'll get a team down here," Carla said.

"It'll be too late," Valerie said. "It's already too late."

The chopper cleared the eastern wall of the ravine.

"Jesus," the pilot said.

Then the windshield exploded and his head snapped back.

Half his face had been blown off.

The chopper swung one complete revolution, pivoted on its nose as if it had been pinned. But a second later, it tilted left, losing altitude. As clearly as if it were the scene in a snow globe, Valerie saw below her the Cherokee and the cabin and the lone figure with the shotgun still raised. The sound of the chopper's blades seemed to change pitch. She could hear Carla next to her shouting something. The drop was too big. She couldn't believe what she was doing. There was no time for belief. There was no time for anything. She opened the door. One image of the bones in her shins slivering; Carla's hands on her—then she jumped.

It took her a few moments to lift her head. The snow had received her with shocking cold. She was winded. A pain in her ankles and forearms, but she didn't think anything was broken. She was less than twenty feet from the parked Cherokee. Carla lay a few feet to her right, facedown, not moving. The wind dropped. In the quiet (it was as if the weather had hushed itself for this), the sound of the chopper's blades receding, dropping back into the ravine. Then what felt like a long, complete silence—before an explosion and a swell of dull orange light as the chopper struck the western wall. She heard metal grinding and crashing as the aircraft dropped to the river. The wind, having stilled itself not to miss the spectacle, lifted again. Flying snow drove into Valerie's face.

The Cherokee was between her and Leon.

He was trudging through the snow toward her.

She pushed herself to her feet and reached into her shoulder holster.

Just in time to see Leon raise the shotgun.

The impact knocked Valerie off her feet. She felt herself falling backwards before she felt the pain.

Then the pain.

The snow's embrace a second time, with an odd little noise, a crunch-gasp, as if she'd knocked the wind out of the ground rather than vice versa. She remembered it from making snow angels as a child. Wet jeans and your face looking up at the low sky.

Her left shoulder. Her lungs emptying. The exhalation slid away from her, a breath that had gone all the way to the bottom of a long, long slope. It was inconceivable that she would ever be able to drag it back up again. She would never breathe in again.

Leon stood over her. Snow clung to his hair. Snow swirled around him. The bandaged hand cradled the shotgun's barrel. His face was wet, fraught, vivid.

"You?" he said. *"You?"*

Then he turned the weapon, raised it, brought it down.

She saw the rubber treads on the shotgun's butt, a curious design to stamp and endorse the end of her life.

Then darkness took her.

Nell opened her eyes to the cabin's now familiar floor, sweeping away from her. She was lying on her side. One of the oil lamps had been blown out by the wind. The door was open. It had stopped snowing, though the wind still tore through the ravine. The doorway framed her mother's Jeep. Warmth flooded her. It was impossible. Her mother was here. But propped against its flank, like Raggedy Ann dolls, two women she'd never seen before. One of them, slumped lower than the other, bleeding into the snow. The man in the Windbreaker was standing over them with—Nell thought her mind had gone wrong—shopping bags at his feet.

Valerie swam back through the folding weight of dark water to consciousness to see Leon reach into Carla's shoulder holster, remove the sidearm, and stuff it into the back of his jeans. Her own weapon was gone. Carla stirred. Her eyes opened. Her breathing was shallow. The two of them were slumped against the Cherokee. The wheel housing cut into Valerie's back. A strange little thing to be aware of past the pain in her shattered shoulder. Beyond Leon she could see the open doorway of the cabin filled with yellowy flickering light. A girl's body lying on the floor. Dead, presumably. The one that got away. Except didn't, in the end. The snow had stopped falling. It comforted her, for no reason she could fathom. Maybe just because she could see. She could see the world before she said goodbye to it. That was something. Carla looked at her. Opened her mouth to speak, but her eyes closed again.

Leon was going through the shopping bags, lifting items out and setting them in the snow. A pineapple. A doll wearing a crown. A yo-yo. A xylophone. A bag of nails. He had a lemon in his bandaged hand.

"You were in my house," he said, turning on Valerie. "You were in my fucking *house*."

Carla opened her eyes again. "He was never the same," she said.

"Shut the fuck up, cunt," Leon said.

Carla shook her head, as in mild refusal. She slurred a few quiet words, but Valerie couldn't make them out. Other cops she knew carried a second gun. In a side holster. In a boot. She wasn't one of them. When she'd driven to the farmhouse, she'd forgotten to put on the bulletproof vest. It had been in the Taurus's trunk. There had been no time. It hadn't even occurred to her. And she wasn't wearing one now. She was a terrible cop. She had a very clear image of herself lying in bed with Nick Blaskovitch, her head on his chest (summer sunlight making softly glowing ingots of the apartment's window blinds) saying to him: I'm a terrible cop, you know. She had said this to him, once, long ago. He had remained silent for a long time. Their bodies had been warm and sleepy. They'd had so much sex, merely summoning the energy to get out of bed seemed implausible. Then he'd said: Not only are you not a terrible cop, but you've got the prettiest ass in the Western world. Everyone hates you. Even me. Now, look: What about breakfast? The memory was so clear and disinterested—her soul sorting out its hierarchy of things to pack before death—that she smiled. It wasn't a bad thing to die, so long as you'd had a life full of life. And she had had that. It turned out all you needed to be OK with dying was knowing you'd lived.

Leon, manifestly, was not happy. His face was pouchy. He was a man being hurried against his will. He was a man being forced to compromise the quality of his work just to get the job off his desk. As she watched him, he turned and barked: "I'm doing it. For Christ's sake, I'm *doing* it!" as if to a guardian angel only he could see. Scowling, he unbuttoned Carla's pants, pulled them and her underwear down around her ankles, then straightened up to look at her. It hurt Valerie to see Carla's tibia poking through the skin of her shin. Bone. We were skin and blood and nerves and bone. It was a knowledge so terrible that God concealed most of it from view.

"Bit cold for that sort of thing, isn't it?" Valerie said. She'd lost all feeling in her left shoulder. A part of her was indulging vague doctorish speculations about how the damage to her clavicle and scapula might be painstakingly repaired. She pictured a surgeon, who would be an arrogant asshole in the consultation room but who, once he was in theater, would devote every atom of his ego to fixing the thing that shouldn't, by rights, be fixable. He would wear gold-rimmed spectacles and have Mahler playing in the background. You'd hate him, but you wouldn't want anyone else on the case.

"Shut the fuck up," Leon said, pointing the fish knife at her. "Shut. The fuck. Up."

He grabbed Carla's blouse and tore it open. Seeing the prettily laced black bra, Valerie felt sad. It occurred to her that she'd thought of Carla as a sexless being.

Carla opened her eyes and tried to turn away. Leon slapped her. Yanked her back into a sitting position by her hair.

It was a great relief, Valerie discovered, to realize you were ready to die. It gave you liberty for all sorts of academic exercises. One of them was to make this as annoying as possible for Leon. She raced back through everything that had happened (while other parts of her speed-read her own life of densely packed childhood and anguished adolescence and fraught adult lust and professional approximation and love and love and love [and loss]) convinced, though she conceded again the academic nature of the exercise, that there was, even now, even *now* . . .

Who was never the same?

The rogue question distracted her for a moment.

Carla opened her eyes again. She was back, this time, properly. Just in time for the bad news. The worst news. The only news that mattered.

Leon, still holding the lemon in his right hand, got down on his knees and pressed the fish knife's point against the bare flesh of Carla's midriff. A bead of blood sprang up and trickled down the blade. Carla lifted her hand as if it were the slowest, heaviest thing in the world. Leon swatted it away.

"You dumb fuck," Valerie said.

Leon paused. The blade quivered. Went in a little deeper. Carla cried out.

"Hey," Valerie said. "Leon. Yes, you. I'm talking to you, you dumb shit."

He looked at her. He appeared sweetly surprised.

"You fucked it up," Valerie said. "You know that, right? I mean, you do know that even now after all these years, you still can't get the simplest thing in the world right? Christ, you're stupid." She laughed, holding her shoulder. "Stupid, stupid, stupid. You think you've got this? You haven't got this. Want me to spell it out for you? Want me to *spell* it out for you, genius?"

Leon withdrew the knife and got to his feet.

"It's the lemon after the kite. It's the *lemon* after the kite. *K* is for Kite, *L* is for Lemon. Jesus Christ, how fucking slow are you? *J, K, L.* Jug, kite, lemon. Whereas what did you do? Come on, tell me: What did you do?"

Leon frowned, breathing through his nose. His hand was tight around the knife's white handle.

"Cat got your tongue?" Valerie said. "I'm not surprised. I'm not surprised you're embarrassed. You should be. You went jug, kite, monkey. *J, K, M. Monkey.* It's an insult to monkeys, Einstein. And now you're standing there like a fucking lemon, *holding* . . . what? A lemon! It's priceless, Leon, priceless. Leon the lemon. Can you spell 'incompetent'? Can you spell 'fuckup'?"

Leon took a pace to his left to stand directly in front of Valerie.

Behind him, she saw a figure crawling toward them from the cabin.

Angelo was at the end of his strength. His chest ached. L5 and S1 had, if anything, entered a new, intense relationship, a passionate affair to maximize his pain. His head was reduced to the thud of his broken jaw. Memory, liberated and lawless, now that its life work was done, told him that Muhammad Ali fought Ken Norton for two rounds with a broken jaw, getting hit in the head repeatedly. This forced an amusing concession: He was not, at least, getting hit in the head at the moment, so how bad could it really be? He would crawl.

He pushed the axe ahead of him through the snow. He wanted to look back to see Nell one last time, but he was afraid the movement would paralyze him. The wind roiled and sang, as if delighted with all this human madness.

Nell had inched forward on her elbows and collapsed in the cabin's open doorway. Everything seemed invaded and broken now, the stove's warmth and the lamps' soft light. The wind going through the place like a burglar, completely free to handle whatever it wanted. It seemed a year ago that she had crossed the ravine. The days since her mother told her to run had been longer than all her life before. She felt ancient, as if the old lady she would one day have been were visiting her now, like a ghost from the lost future.

"And that's not all," Valerie said to Leon. "The girl in your basement? She's alive. You couldn't even get that right. I got into your shit-hole house and you thought I was dead. But look: Here I am. You thought *she* was dead, didn't you? She's not. I saved her. She's very much alive. She's laughing right now at the mess you've made. Her and every cop in the country. Your picture's all over the news. The dumbest killer in history. Your grandmother must be so proud. Your grandmother must be laughing her dead, fat ass off."

Leon had gone very still. The wind had dropped again. Valerie was aware of Carla, sobbing softly.

Leon raised the knife.

And screamed.

The sound silenced even Carla.

A long time seemed to pass. The snow globe was at rest.

Leon dropped the knife. Very slowly reached behind himself and pulled out the axe Angelo had buried in the back of his thigh. He looked at it, puzzled, then turned.

The old man was lying on his side in the snow, eyes closed, wheezing.

Valerie got her legs under her. Her shoulder was dead and her hands were numb but her face was alive with seductive heat. Leon's jacket had ridden up where he'd stuffed Carla's Beretta in his jeans.

Nell saw Angelo collapse onto his side. The man in the Windbreaker stood over him, both hands wrapped around the axe. The bandage had unraveled. It hung from his wrist like a party streamer. The wind had died, as if a switch controlling it had been turned off. The snow brought every sound close to her. She could hear Angelo struggling for breath. One of the women was on her feet now.

Angelo drifted gently toward a soft-edged darkness, like an ocean at night. His body seemed a faraway thing, negligible, of no more consequence than the clothes he might have left on the beach before swimming out from a shore to which he knew he would never return. He thought of Sylvia saying: *It made leaving bearable, knowing I'd had that kind of love in my life. Knowing I'd had the best thing.* There was no one to see, but he was smiling.

• • •

Reaching for the Beretta, Valerie thought: *I need two hands for this.*

You don't have two hands. So you do it with one.

She bent forward. Extended her arm.

Felt the cut-glass rainbow edging her vision.

Not now.

Oh God. Not now.

She jammed her teeth together. Force of will. Force of *will*.

Darkness encroached. The aperture starting to close. No time. No time.

Her hand shook. Her hand had an infinite number of ways to get it wrong.

One chance.

Pickpocket.

Very gently wrapped her fingers around the Beretta's grip.

The aperture shuddered, narrowed a little more.

She yanked the weapon out of Leon's jeans. Clicked the safety off.

"Drop it, Leon," she said, holding the barrel to the back of his head. "Drop it now or you're dead."

The darkness shivered. The circle of light narrowed, expanded, narrowed. *Kill him now. While you still can. Kill him. End it.*

That's not what you do. You arrest him. You take him in. Justice. Not execution. Murdering a murderer is still murder.

The camera eye opened fractionally. Her jaws ached. The rainbows flickered. Flirted with giving up.

Cuffs. Call. Court. Lawyers. The law. The families. Words. Katrina Mulvaney, smiling by the double-trunked tree. The sprawling hopelessness of Leon's history. And before that, Jean Ghast's history, the as-yet-unknown antecedents, an infinite regress, nesting dolls with no end. Causes.

Make this easy for me, Leon.

He did.

He raised the axe. And turned.

He got one word out. "Cunt."

Then Valerie pulled the trigger.

97

At the Sterling Regional MedCenter, Colorado, Valerie made a new friend. Morphine. The buckshot had gone through her deltoid, clipped the humerus, missed the subclavian artery. But there had still been a lot of damage to repair. She was, in the surgeon's words, a godawful mess. And he wouldn't give her a straight answer about the nerves. Her arm was dressed and in a sling. She had no idea if she'd ever be able to use it again. She tried to imagine that: the Disabled Detective. Couldn't. Got an image instead of herself at the apartment's kitchen sink, failing to peel a potato.

She wasn't supposed to be out of bed, but she'd sweet-talked Carla's colleague, Field Agent Dane Forester (who'd come with them in the ambulance, and who appeared not to be in on Carla's hatred) into scoring a wheelchair and taking her to see Nell.

The girl was barely awake. Her foot was stirruped in a cast. She was mildly sedated, and would be kept that way until her grandmother arrived from Florida. She was expected imminently.

For a while, Valerie just sat by her bed, enjoying the sight of her wrapped in the arms of high-tech care. The monitors, the IV, the crisp white linen. The little plastic ID bracelet around her wrist said NELL LOUISE COOPER. Her fingernails were filthy. Snow-reflected sunlight came in slats through the venetian blinds. The world was a wonderful place. Full of nightmares.

She was about to call Forester back in to wheel her away when

Nell stirred and opened her eyes. It took a moment for her to focus. Valerie didn't know how much they'd told her, but her face said she already knew. Your mother and brother are dead. Maybe she'd known ever since she ran.

"Hey," Valerie said. "Remember me? How's your ankle?"

They were practically the first words she'd spoken to her. Back at the cabin, she'd managed to call in their location and tell Nell that she was a police officer before passing out. By the time the cavalry arrived, Nell was the only person on the scene still actually conscious.

"I can't feel it," Nell said.

She was visibly exhausted. Childhood force-fed adult horror, adult loss. The look of absorbed suffering you saw in the eyes of starving children, as if they were compelled to stare at all the universe's cruelty and meaninglessness while you spent your entire life distracting yourself from it with pleasures you took for granted and more than enough to eat. The eyes of starving children were an accusation—and the eyes of this little girl would always have something of that in them. In whatever new place she ended up (with her grandmother in Florida, for now), at whatever new school she joined, people would sense it, the something different in her, the something unnatural, the something wrong. Her life ahead would be a terrible accommodation. She would grow, she would live (assuming she didn't break down or kill herself), but everything she did and everything she became would have its roots in what had happened to her.

"I can't feel my shoulder, either," Valerie said. The discrepancy between what life needed and what words could do. This girl would have been reared on stories with happy endings and miraculous justice. And denied the chance to grow out of the fantasy naturally. Valerie felt the moribund reflex, that there ought to be something you could do to stop it. But there wasn't, not for her. All she could do was try to stop the ruiners before they did it again. It wasn't enough. If she did it for the rest of her life, it would never be enough.

The door opened. Forester entered with a woman in her early sixties. Meredith Trent, Valerie understood, Nell's grandmother. She was a tall, handsome woman with well-cut dyed auburn hair that fell in two thick waves down to her shoulders. A long green woolen over-coat and black corduroys. She was clutching a soft, dark leather shoulder bag, and her eyes were raw. At a glance, Valerie could see the effort she'd put in to lock down her grief. She'd lost her daughter and her grandson, but she was forcing herself to be strong for her granddaughter. Forcing herself. She would have spent the whole flight in tears, had *been* crying, Valerie knew, right until she got outside the door to Nell's room a moment ago. All the trauma was there in her face, barely held back from unraveling her features. It was as if the air immediately around her trembled with what the composure was costing her. And the second she saw Nell lying in the hospital bed, the tears came again, though she didn't make a sound.

Nell said: "Grandma."

In a moment, she was on her knees by Nell's bed, her arms around the little girl. "Nellie, Nellie, sweetheart, I'm here. I'm here," though she could hardly get the words past the tears.

Valerie nodded to Forester, who wheeled her out quickly.

"I'll come back in a little while," Forester said, depositing Valerie at the side of Carla's bed.

"Thanks," Valerie said. "Can you make sure there's someone there for Mrs. Trent?"

"Done," Forester said.

Carla's leg was in an incomprehensible contraption.

For a while, the two women didn't speak.

Then Carla said, "You still don't know, do you?"

"What?"

Carla blinked slowly. "Carter," she said.

Valerie waited. Let the pieces come together. *Agent* Mike Carter. Three years ago. The other candidate for fatherhood of the lost child. Along with Nick Blaskovitch.

Carla smiled without amusement. "He was nothing to you," she said. "He was a lot more than nothing to me."

There wasn't anything to say.

"He was never the same," Carla said, studying Valerie now with a sort of empty fascination. "I don't know what you did to him, but, you know, congratulations."

After several moments, Valerie said, "I'm sorry. I didn't know. I didn't know there was anyone."

"Would it have made any difference if you had?"

She thought about it. The way she'd been then. The will to indiscriminate wreckage. She didn't have it in herself to lie.

"No," she said. "I guess it wouldn't."

Carla reached for the glass of water on the bedside table. Took a few sips through the straw. "And now you've saved my life," she said. Then after a pause: "Which obviously doesn't help."

There was still nothing to say. Valerie didn't know if Carla hated her or felt grateful to her. Then she realized that Carla didn't know either. They were both stalled by the simple incompatibility of the facts.

"What are you doing here?" Valerie's nurse said, appearing in the doorway. "You're supposed to be in bed. Back. Now. Immediately."

Ten minutes after Valerie was returned to her bed, her room phone rang.

"Skirt, do me a favor," Nick Blaskovitch said. "Don't get shot anymore, will you?"

"OK."

"Because there's a limit to how much of this I can take. It's bad enough you've shaved your head."

"Everyone else likes it."

"Everyone else is irrelevant. Have you given any thought to where we're having dinner?"

It was terrible how badly she wanted to see him right then. For a few seconds, she couldn't speak. "Well," she said, swallowing. "At the moment, anywhere I can get away with only using a fork."

"One armed and half bald. Terrific. I suppose you're going to need help getting undressed, too?"

"It looks that way. I'm sorry. If you want to bail, I'll understand."

If you want to bail. Please don't. Please don't.

Pause.

"Are you all right?" he said. Not banter anymore. His voice. The familiarity. The quiet allegiance. The love. Everything she didn't deserve. She was very close to letting herself feel . . . Not happy, but ready to try to have what they could have. Very close and very afraid. There was nothing more dangerous than love.

"I'm all right," she said. "I'm fine."

"OK, well, do me another favor."

"Yes?"

"Look in your doorway."

Three seconds. Four. Five.

Then he walked in, smiling, still holding the cell phone.

"Sorry," he said. "I got impatient."